GENA
SHOWALTER

The Darkest
TOUCH

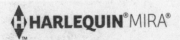

Published in Great Britain 2014
Harlequin MIRA, an imprint of Harlequin (UK) Limited,
Eton House, 18-24 Paradise Road,
Richmond, Surrey, TW9 1SR

© 2014 Gena Showalter

ISBN 978-1-848-45319-7

59-1214

Harlequin (UK) Limited's policy is to use papers that are natural,
renewable and recyclable products and made from wood grown in
sustainable forests. The logging and manufacturing processes conform
to the legal environmental regulations of the country of origin.

Printed and bound by
CPI Group (UK) Ltd, Croydon, CR0 4YY

Gena Showalter is the *New York Times* and *USA TODAY* bestselling author of the *Lords of the Underworld* series, *Angels of the Dark* and *White Rabbit Chronicles*. She has written over forty novels and novellas. Her books have appeared in *Cosmopolitan* and *Seventeen* magazines, and have been translated into multiple languages.

To learn more about Gena and her books, please visit www.genashowalter.com and www.genashowalterblogspot.com.

Over the years I have been unbelievably blessed. I have met some amazing people and made incredible, lifelong friendships. I'm looking at you, Kresley Cole. You are gorgeous, brilliant, witty and talented, and you inspire me in so many ways. THANK YOU!

I'm also looking at you, Jill Monroe. You've been around for all the highs and lows, cheering me on, offering comfort. You never hesitated to say yes when I called and said, 'Let's get away for a few days.' Even better—you never hesitated when I somehow managed to book us a honeymoon suite. Twice.

To my amazing editor Emily Ohanjanians. You aren't afraid to tell me when something doesn't work and then guide me toward something better, and I'm so grateful! Remember my first attempt at writing this book? Well, I'm super glad no one else will have the chance. LOL

And to Naomi Lahn, my contest winner. You are a delight and your support is beyond appreciated!

"What's my sign? Cancer."

—Torin, Lord of the Underworld

CHAPTER ONE

"DON'T DIE. Don't you dare die." Frantic, Torin dug through a backpack crammed with clothing, weapons and medical supplies. He'd packed it days ago, blindly filling it with everything he'd thought he might need. There was no mouth guard. Fine. He'd proceed without one.

He hurried to his companion's motionless form, straddled her waist. Her precious life slipped away with every second that passed. CPR was a last resort, but suddenly her only hope, and because they were locked inside a dungeon, no one else inside their cell, the responsibility belonged to him alone. The guy who'd rarely ever come this close to another person.

Just call me Wonder Doc.

He flattened his gloved hands over Mari's delicate chest—*still, too still*. But rather than proceed as he should have, he found himself pausing to savor the rare and extraordinary connection with the opposite sex. *So soft. So luscious.*

What the hell am I doing? Jaw clenched, he pushed.
Crack.

Too hard. He'd just broken her sternum and probably several of her ribs.

Guilt pierced straight through his heart, and if the organ hadn't already been shredded beyond repair, it might have hurt. Sweat trickled down his temples as he pressed against Mari's chest more gently. Nothing else broke. Good. Okay. He pressed again and again, gradually increasing his speed. But how fast was too fast? What helped? What damaged?

"Come on, Mari." She was human, but strong. Fragile, but resilient. "Stay with me. You can survive this, I know you can."

Her head lolled to the side, her glassy eyes staring out at nothing.

"No. No!" He checked her for a pulse, waited…but never felt even the weakest of beats.

As he returned his hands to her chest to start over, his gaze locked on her blood-splattered lips; his mind willed them to part, a cough to escape. It would mean the sickness still plagued her, but sick was better than dead any day of the week.

"Mari, please." He heard the desperation in his voice, didn't care. *I can't be the one to kill someone so sweet.*

Torin pushed harder, heard another crack.

Hell. He wasn't some pansy crier, but damn if tears didn't scald the backs of his eyes.

He'd come to think of this girl as a friend, and despite the numerous centuries he'd lived, he didn't have many of those. He always protected the ones he had.

Until her.

If not for him, she never would have sickened in the first place.

Again he felt for a pulse. Still no beat.

Cursing, he set back to work. Five minutes…ten… twenty. He was Mari's life support, the only thing standing between her and death; he would do this however long proved necessary.

Pull through, Mari. You have to pull through.

"Fight this!" But as another eternity elapsed without any change in her, he finally admitted his efforts weren't doing any good. She was already gone.

Already dead.

And there was nothing he could do to bring her back.

With a roar, Torin wrenched away and paced the cell like the caged animal he was. His arms shook. His back and thighs ached. But what was physical pain compared to mental? Emotional? This was his fault. He'd known what would happen if ever he touched the girl, and he'd lured her closer anyway.

Monster! With another roar, he punched the wall, enjoying the unrelenting throb of pain as skin split and bones fractured. He punched again and again, cracks appearing in the stone, dust pluming around him.

If he had just stopped to question why a girl like Mari would be so starved for companionship she would agree to be with *him* she would still be alive.

He pressed his forehead against the battered wall. *I'm keeper of the demon of Disease. When will I accept the fact that I'm meant to fly solo?*

To be forever denied what I crave most.

"Mari, darling," a slightly accented voice rang out. Female...*delicious*—even soaked in panic and pain as it was. "The bond is broken. Why is it broken?"

The blood in Torin's veins turned into fuel, igniting as if a blazing match had just been thrown inside him. He became increasingly aware of his own heartbeat, speeding up, the need to stalk to the cell's door and rip away every metal bar consuming him; anything to erase the distance between him and the speaker.

An extreme reaction. He knew that. Just as he knew

such excruciating awareness of another person was unusual for him. It was also uncontrollable and unstoppable, his entire world centering around this one woman.

And this wasn't the first time it had happened. Anytime she'd spoken, no matter the words she'd uttered, the huskiness of her tone had always carried a promise of absolute pleasure. As if there were nothing she wanted more than to kiss, lick and suck on him.

Masculine instincts he'd spent countless years denying shouted, *Come, little moth. Come closer to my flame. Or I'll come to you....*

He strode to the bars and, like a thousand times before, willed the shadows between their cells to part. But it did no good. Her appearance remained a mystery.

Somehow his sick obsession with her only intensified...and he thought that, for just five minutes of that kissing, licking and sucking, he would have happily risked a worldwide plague.

Hate myself. Someone should string him up by the collarbone and cane him. Again.

"Mari!" his obsession said. "Please."

Disease whipped into a frenzy, banging against Torin's skull, suddenly desperate to escape.

Escape *her?* Another unusual reaction. Usually the demon adored such close proximity with a potential victim.

How the fiend had laughed at Mari....

Hate him, too.

"Mari can't talk right now," Torin said. *Or ever.*

The admission...like pouring salt over my wounds.

Bars rattled. "What did you do to her?"

Nothing...everything.

"Tell me!" the female shouted.

"I shook her hand." The words exploded from him, bitter and cutting. "That's it." But he'd done far more than that, hadn't he.

He'd put a lot of time and effort into charming her. Feeding her. Talking and laughing with her. Eventually she'd felt comfortable enough to remove one of his gloves and intertwine their fingers. On purpose.

Nothing bad will happen, she had said. Or maybe her gaze had said it. The details were hazed by the fog of his eagerness. *You'll see.*

He'd believed her. Because he'd wanted to believe her more than he'd wanted to take his next breath. He'd held on to her so tightly, a thirsty man who'd just discovered the last glass of water in a world burning to ash, nearly brought to his knees by the force of his physical response. Sensation after sensation had overwhelmed him. Feminine softness so near his masculine hardness. A floral scent in his nose. The ends of her silky hair tickling his wrist. Her warmth blending with his own. Her breath intersecting with his.

I experienced an instant connection, immediate bliss, and very nearly creamed my damn jeans. From a handshake.

She'd died from it.

With him, it never mattered if the touch was accidental or intentional, or if the victim was human or animal, young or old, male or female…good or evil; any living creature sickened soon after contact with him. Even immortals like himself. Difference was, immortals sometimes survived, becoming carriers of whatever illness they'd contracted from him, capable of spreading it to others. As a human, Mari had never even stood a chance.

"Tell me the truth," his obsession demanded. "Every detail."

He didn't know her name or if she was human or immortal. He only knew Mari had made a deal with the devil to save her.

The two women had been imprisoned here for centuries—wherever "here" was—for no real crime Torin could perceive. Cronus, the prison's owner, had never really needed a reason to ruin someone's life.

He'd certainly helped ruin Torin's.

He had owed Torin a favor, and Torin, being Torin, had chosen to overlook the male's shady reputation and ask for a woman who wouldn't sicken at his touch. Cronus, being Cronus, hadn't bothered to search for a suitable candidate and had simply recruited one of his prisoners—sweet, innocent Mari.

"Cronus made a deal with the girl," Torin said.

"I know that." His obsession huffed and puffed, a veritable big, bad wolf. "Mari was cursed to flash to your bedroom one hour a day for nearly a month, all in the hopes of convincing you to touch her."

"Yes," he croaked. And in return, Cronus had promised to set her dearest friend free—the woman currently grilling Torin for answers.

No big surprise Cronus had lied.

At least he got his in the end.

Torin had wanted to haul ass to a hospital the moment he'd realized Mari was sick, but that stupid curse had bound her to this prison with invisible chains. She'd *had* to return. Left with no other option, Torin had held on to her as she'd moved from one location to another in a blink, traveling with her. He'd tended her to the best of his ability.

But his best hadn't been good enough. Would *never* be good enough.

"I don't care about the whys," the female said. "Only the outcome. What is Mari doing *right now?*"

Decomposing.

Can't say it, just...can't. Silent, he removed his gloves and used his hands as a shovel, throwing scoop after scoop of dirt over his shoulder. *Not the first makeshift grave I've dug, but I hereby vow it will be my last.* No more impromptu friendships. No more hopes and dreams for what could never be. *I'm done.*

"Ignoring me?" she asked. "Do you have any idea the being you provoke?"

Torin never paused in his task. He would bury Mari. He would find a way out of this hellhole. He would continue the job he'd abandoned when he'd chosen to come with the girl. The search and rescue of Cameo and Viola, who'd gone missing several weeks ago—friends who comprehended his need for distance.

"I am Keeleycael, the Red Queen, and I will be more than happy to take a coat hanger and fish out all of your internal organs...through your mouth."

Disease went still and quiet.

That, too, was a first.

The Red Queen. The title was somehow familiar to Torin. From a children's storybook, yes, but there was more to it than that. He'd heard it...where? An image flashed through his mind. A dilapidated bar in the skies. Yes, of course. While working for Zeus, the king of the Greeks, he'd tracked many fugitive immortals there. The words *the Red Queen* had been whispered behind the trembling hands of fearful men and women, right along with *insane* and *cruel*.

He'd always enjoyed pitting his skills against the strongest and vilest of predators, and such a visceral reaction to the supposed Red Queen had intrigued him. But when he'd asked the whisperers who she was and what she could do, they had gone quiet.

Maybe this prisoner was the one they'd spoken of, maybe she wasn't. Hardly mattered anymore. He wouldn't be fighting her.

"Keeleycael," he said. "That's quite a mouthful. How about I call you Keeley instead?"

"An honor reserved solely for my friends. Do so at your own peril."

"Thanks. I will."

A soft snarl from her. "You may call me Your Majesty. I'll call you My Next Victim."

"I usually prefer Torin, Hotness or The Awesome." Nicknames to help smile through the pain. *Should probably have gone with Proctalgia Fugax—meaning a literal pain in the ass.*

"Why has Mari gone silent, Torin?" Keeley asked as if they were discussing nothing more important than tomorrow's dinner menu. (Rat casserole.)

She knew Mari was dead, didn't she? Making him admit it was some sort of punishment.

"Before you reply," she added, "you should know I would rather save the enemy who tells me the truth than the friend who tells me lies."

Not a bad motto. *Lie and die* happened to be his.

And, really, if the situation were reversed, he would have wanted the same thing: answers. But again, if the situation were reversed and *she* had led to the demise of one of *his* friends, he would have moved heaven and earth to administer justice. But trapped as they were in these cells created for the strongest of immortals, there was nothing she could do but stew in her rage, helpless as the emotion grew darker and darker, perhaps even driving her mad. It was a cruel fate.

It was also an excuse.

Time to put on my big-boy panties. "Mari is… Dead. She's dead."

Silence.

Such oppressive silence and, with it, darkness, as if they'd somehow fallen into a sensory-deprivation tank.

He spoke in a desperate bid to dull his mounting sorrow, explaining, "Since you know about Cronus's deal with Mari, you must know I'm a Lord of the Underworld. One of the fourteen warriors responsible for stealing and opening Pandora's box, unleashing the demons from within. As punishment, we were each cursed to house one of those demons inside our own bodies. I was given Disease, the world's worst SSTD. Skin-to-skin-transmitted disease. I make people sick. That's what I do, and there's no stopping it. She touched me, like I said. We touched each other. But that's all it took. She died. She's dead," he repeated hollowly.

Again silence.

He locked his jaw to prevent himself from admitting the other Lords hosted baddies like Violence, Death and Pain. That thousands of innocents had died at their hands, and thousands more had lamented the vileness of their deeds. That, despite everything, none of his friends were as wretched as Disease. They chose their victims. Torin did not.

What a freaking prize I am.

Who would ever want him? *Single immortal male looking for someone to love—and murder.*

He couldn't even comfort himself with memories of past lovers. When he'd lived in the skies, he'd concerned himself with his war duties and very little else, women nothing more than an afterthought...until his body demanded attention. But every time he'd chosen a lover, his warrior instincts to dominate and subdue had overtaken him, and his unintentional roughness had made the females cry before their clothes had ever come off. Which meant their clothes had *never* come off.

Perhaps he could have coaxed the females to continue, but his disgust with himself had been too great. He excelled on the battlefield but couldn't master the mechanics of sex?

Humiliating.

Now he would trade what little remained of his integrity for skin-to-skin *anything,* desperate to have what he'd once disdained, unable to fight his enemies in the down-and-dirty way he'd once—still—loved.

"Torin," Keeley said, and despite the strain he heard, he still reacted with the same raw hunger as before. "You realize you killed an innocent girl, yes?"

He settled in the hole he'd dug, pulled on his gloves and rested his head against his upraised palms. "Yes." His gaze flicked to Mari. She might have known about his condition, but some part of her must have trusted him to keep her safe.

Now look at her.

"Torin," Keeley said again. "Have you also realized I will punish you for your crime?"

"You can't hurt me any more than I'm hurting right now."

"Not true. I have heard of you and your friends, you know."

What did that have to do with anything? "Explain where you're going with this, and I might decide to invest in the rest of the conversation." Otherwise, it was time to find his way free.

"You may have the world's worst SSTD," she said, "but I throw the world's worst temper tantrum."

Interesting, but not applicable. "Are you chastising me or applying to be my sidekick?"

"Silence!"

Disease recoiled like the coward he was.

"I'm sure you've heard of Atlantis," she continued easily. "What you probably do not know is that I ensured the island was swallowed by the sea simply because I was a wee bit annoyed with its ruler."

Truth? Or exaggeration?

Either way…it excited him with the same fervency as her voice. *At last. The opponent of my dreams.*

"You have garnered more than my annoyance, warrior. I had one friend here. Only one. She is—was—my family." A pause as Keeley sniffled. "Not by blood, but something far greater. I was once a creature of hate, but she taught me to love. And you took her away from me."

Her pain sliced at him.

"Torin," she said, and he knew instinctively this was the final calm before a great and terrible storm.

"Yes, Keeley." If she asked for his heart—a life for a life—he would give it to her.

The storm broke, revealing the temper she'd lauded.

"I'm going to kill you," she screamed. "Kill you so dead." The bars of her cage rattled with increasing fervor. "You'll experience agony in ways you've never dreamed possible, for I will do to you what I've done to so many others. I will skin you with a cheese grater and stuff your organs into a blender to make a smoothie. I will donkey punch your skull so hard your brain will ooze out of your eye sockets."

"I...don't know how to respond to that."

"Don't worry. Soon I'll cut out your tongue and use it as a cleaning rag—you'll never have to respond to anyone ever again!" A rock skidded into his cell...the first of an avalanche, rage and grief giving her the strength that centuries of imprisonment had surely stolen.

I'm wrecked. He'd robbed this woman of her best and only friend, leaving her with nothing but pain and misery.

Story of my life.

He wished his next deed would kill him but knew it would only make him *wish* he'd died. Any wound he received damaged his resistance to the demon and thereby his own immunity, allowing Disease to rise up and infect *him*. At least for a little while. Still. Torin did as he'd imagined. He clawed his way into his chest, scooped out his heart...and rolled it into Keeley's cell.

CHAPTER TWO

KEELEY WASN'T SURE how many days or weeks had passed since the warrior had offered his still-beating heart as a macabre gift the darkest parts of her had actually appreciated. All she knew was that he'd spent the next *however long* moaning in agony and, if she had to guess, coughing up pieces of his lungs.

Sickened by his own demon? *Deserved.*

And while his suffering had dulled the sharpest edges of her rage, she still planned to kill him. *I won't forget. I won't, I won't, I won't.*

"It's the right thing to do. Don't you agree, Wilson?" she asked the rock that liked to watch her every move.

He remained silent, always silent. Cold-shoulder treatment was his specialty.

She wasn't upset by his attitude. They'd never really gotten along.

"I had plans to free Mari, you know. I only needed time. Just another few weeks, in fact." Or months. Maybe years. Time had ceased to exist. But Mari hadn't cared about herself—she'd cared only about Keeley.

The girl had known what Keeley was doing to herself day after day. Well, maybe *known* wasn't the right word. She'd suspected. And she had hated the thought of Keeley in any kind of pain. So Mari, sweet Mari, had decided to act, to take Cronus up on his suicidal offer and procure Keeley's release the only way she could. *Despite* Keeley's protests.

"Cronus didn't even keep up his end of the bargain," she explained to Wilson. Mari had died upholding hers, and yet Keeley had not been freed.

Hatred burrowed deep inside her, taking root in the darkness of her soul and feeding on the rich soil of her bitterness. *So much to do.* First she would take care of Torin. Then she would do to the king of the Titans what she'd once done to Prometheus, who wasn't the good guy everyone thought. He hadn't blessed the world with fire. How laughable. But he *had* tried to engulf every inch of it in flames.

"But I punished him, didn't I?" She laughed with maniacal glee. "I cut out his liver every time it regenerated and fed it to a flock of birds." Day after day... year after year.

Zeus, of course, had taken credit for the deed. *But not this time.*

I am the Red Queen. The entire world will learn of me at long last—and fear.

"Soon," she said.

Wilson might have snorted.

"You'll see." Keeley huddled in the corner of her cell, stabbing the lower part of her arm with the rock she'd sharpened into a shiv. Blood poured from the throbbing wound, and spiderwebs of black drifted through her vision. Still she pressed on, cutting harder, going deeper.

Experienced far worse than this.

Like losing Mari...the only ray of sunshine in a life as black as pitch.

"Mari always offered comfort rather than censure. Not once did she say a cruel word to me." Keeley pointed the bloody shiv at Wilson, adding, "But you…oh, you. Don't even think about denying the fact that the only thing you've ever given me is grief."

The bastard smirked at her.

"You have always mocked me, but she constantly fed me. I can't count the number of rodents she tossed to me." How many people shared so selflessly, giving away the only meal they were likely to find, knowing they would eventually starve? None!

Was it any wonder a literal bond had formed between them, tying them together?

But then, such bonds were the lifeblood of Keeley's people, the Curators. Or, as other races liked to call them, the Parasites. The bonds were imperceptible to the naked eye and, like mystical tentacles, latched on to others with or without approval to syphon strength…and whatever else the person on the other end had to offer.

The more bonds Keeley procured, the more power she wielded and the more control she had over that power. But she had to be careful. Bonds worked both ways. She took, but she also gave.

It was never fun to have her own strength used against her.

"But the bond failed to help Mari, didn't it." And now it couldn't.

Keeley's rage returned and redoubled. She screeched, dropping the shiv. Captivity had long since whittled away her humanity, and she suspected that had never been more apparent as she stood and ripped hunks of rock from the walls, until nothing remained of her fingernails. Hot tears streamed down her cheeks.

Royalty doesn't cry.

Royalty. Doesn't. Cry.

That's right. Tears were a weakness she could not afford. She wiped at her eyes, her arms shaking. Her newest wound protested, bleeding more profusely. Inhale…exhale.

Currently Keeley had only one remaining bond. To the land around her. It would have to be enough for everything she had planned.

She sank next to Wilson, saying, "I'll strengthen. I'll succeed."

Will you? he seemed to ask.

She raised her chin. "No one steals from me and lives to tell the tale."

She'd had so few things worth treasuring. A kingdom—eventually everyone in it had rejected her. A gorgeous fiancé—until he lied to her and betrayed her. And then Mari, who'd *never* hurt her…

Now gone. Forever.

A sob burst free.

Royalty doesn't cry. Royalty endures.

"I'm just a girl." The words razed her throat, making her feel like she'd swallowed acid. "A girl without her friend."

Torin gave an agonized groan. "Sorry. So sorry."

Healed already? Too soon! "Your apologies will never be good enough." She swiped out her hand, sending more debris into his cell. Wilson, too, rolled out of her cage.

Screaming, "Wilson!" she frantically chased after him. He made it into the hallway—where he stayed put, once again staring at her, forever out of reach.

"Fine," she told him, her chin quivering. "Be that way. You're nothing without me. I never really liked you anyway."

"Keeley?" Torin asked.

Rejected by a rock. "Stay out of this, warrior. It's between Wilson and me." Too agitated to sit, she paced in the center of her cell. *Out of sight, out of mind.*

At least in theory. *I'm alone. Again.*

"Been here centuries," she muttered to herself. "Wilson stayed with me through it all. Even when I was shackled to the wall." With no weapon, she'd had to gnaw through her wrists to free her arms, and then, after her hands had grown back, she'd had to sharpen rocks and bone into blades and hack off her feet to free her legs. "And he abandons me now? He's as much a bastard as Cronus."

Well, he would miss the big finale. She would finish the painstaking process of cutting the brimstone scars out of her skin...and everything would go *boom.*

The scars had a name...a name...wards! Yes. That's what her people called them.

The wards! Though it took several tries, her fingers nearly too swollen to close around the shiv's handle, she managed to pick up the weapon.

"Stupid wards and stupid brimstone," she grumbled. Somehow they were the Kryptonite of her entire race. Basically, Keeley's worst nightmare.

Running the sulfuric rocks over spirit or flesh would scar even an immortal, but on her, those scars were accompanied by weakness. If she had enough of them, they would totally negate her power. Even as immense as it was.

Brought so low by so little.

She couldn't punish Torin and Cronus properly until every single one of her wards had been removed. And they had to be punished.

Considering her flesh sometimes wove back together—with the scars still intact—it was meticulous, frustrating work. Everything always depended on the condition of her body. Well-fed, she could create brand-new cells. Starved, she merely regenerated the old ones.

Exactly why I saved every bug to pass through my cell these past few weeks. Dead beetles crawling. *Had a big breakfast just this morning.*

Once, the wards had covered every inch of her. To remove them from her back, she'd had to treat the walls like scratch pads from hell and rub, rub, rub. Her face, torso and legs had been easier, though no less excruciating. All she had left were a few tiny scars on her arm… and one that had regenerated again and again.

Not this time.

"I truly am sorry," Torin said.

She would have found the throaty, masculine tenor of his voice thrilling if she hadn't hated him so much. Was his remorse even genuine?

"At least you still have Wilson," he added. "Whoever he is."

"My pet rock. We recently parted ways."

"Oh. I'm…uh, sorry about that, too."

"Don't be. It was a mutual decision."

A pause. Then, "I'm still sorry."

"Just…save your breath, as it will soon be your last." Her hand tightened on the shiv. What was done was done and could never be undone. Never, never, never. "I made the mistake of pardoning someone who wronged me once before." The man she'd loved and had planned to marry. "I've had to live with the consequences ever since."

Although…she should probably be grateful to Hades.

Before she'd met him, she'd had very little control of her abilities. With a single burst of power, she'd slaughtered more than half of her people—in less than a second.

The rest of her people had sought revenge.

Hades swooped to the rescue, carrying her to the underworld, his home. He'd taught her everything she needed to know to not only survive but thrive. He'd even praised her when she'd leveled his palace and he'd had to build a new one. *That's my good, fearsome girl.*

Keeley rammed the shiv so deep she hit bone.

"I know you crave vengeance," Torin said, his voice a life raft of calm in the sea of her mounting anger, "but even if we get out of here, you won't be able to claim it. You can't touch me or *you* will sicken."

He sounded remorseful about that, too.

A lie, surely.

"Killing you isn't the only way to achieve vengeance, warrior."

A pause crackling with tension. "What are you saying?"

"I told you I had heard of you, yes?" Galen, the keeper of Jealousy and False Hope, was one of the greatest enemies of the Lords of the Underworld…and he was a prisoner here. Had been for months. They'd spent the first few weeks of their association exchanging information and would have continued to do so if he hadn't deteriorated from illness and hunger and gone radio silent.

Which was unfortunate. Knowledge was more precious than gold, and she always craved more. *The very reason I once set up a network of spies stretching from one corner of the world to another.* She knew things even the Titans and Greeks didn't know. She just had to remember them.

"You love your friends," she said. "Provide for them. Protect them."

"What does that have to do with anything?"

As a former royal soldier for the Greeks, who made Roman gladiators look like marshmallows, he had to know where she was going with this. "Stop me if you've heard this one, but...I can kill *them*."

The bars of his cage rattled.

Direct hit.

"You won't go near them," he bellowed. Either he'd returned to full strength, or his mounting rage now drove him. "They've done nothing to you."

"Like Mari had done nothing to you?"

"You weren't there. You don't know how things went down. You're blaming me for an accident."

"We both know you blame *yourself*. Why shouldn't I?"

A moment passed, and when next he spoke, he was cool and collected once more, his tone actually languid. "Don't you go getting all psychoanalytical on me, princess. I blame myself, yes. You can blame me, too. But take it out on me, not anyone else."

Though he couldn't see her, she raised her chin. "I am a queen. Call me 'princess' again and I will castrate you before I kill you." For many years, castration had been her preferred method of punishment. The secret was in the turn of the wrist.

He muttered, "You should be grateful *princess* is all I'm calling you."

"And you should know I will do whatever I deem fitting to whomever I deem deserving."

"Your attitude makes me think you're still unclear about the huge mistake you're making." He'd moved from calm to charm, but not even that dulled the sharp-edged steel accompanying his every word. "You may or may not be the Red Queen immortals fear, but I am a warrior with whom one does not screw. On the field of battle, I *enjoy* the feel of a blade slicing through my opponent. I *like* the scent of blood. It invigorates me. I even think screams of pain make a beautiful soundtrack while I'm working out."

In their world, strength mattered. And the way he'd just described himself...

Sexy.

No, not sexy!

"Yawn," was all she allowed herself to say.

"Yawn?" The bars rattled much harder. "Did you just *yawn* me?"

"Just so you know, I've eaten warriors like you for breakfast."

He didn't miss a beat. "Well, did you spit or swallow? Never mind. Don't answer. Your sexual kinkiness has no bearing on this situation. I'd appreciate it if you'd focus."

Heat flamed her cheeks. "I wasn't talking about *that!*"

"Hey, I'm not here to judge. I'm here because I'd hoped to—" He stopped, a palpable sense of amazement thickening air that never quite lost the stench of unwashed bodies and filth.

What was going on? "You hoped to...what? Help Mari? Well, too late. You didn't. She's gone, and—" Keeley's chin quaked so violently she had trouble getting out her next words. "And someone has to pay. Several someones."

"Trust me. I'm—" c*lick*... "—paying." The groan of rusty hinges accompanied the last word. Then... pounding footsteps sounded?

She frowned, confused. Had he just—

Escaped!

Keeley jumped to her feet, the shiv falling from her hand. Torin stood in front of her cell, a backpack hanging from his shoulder. *Oh...my.* He was everything a girl could want—and more. Mercenary-tall and cold-blooded-killer honed. *My favorite. My weakness.*

She'd gone centuries without seeing another person... without touching one. Why did Torin have to be so magnificent? His hair was snow-white, but his brows and lashes were night-dark, and the contrast was a sensuous delight. But, oh, his eyes...they were his most startling feature. They were the rarest of emeralds, intertwined with different shades of green, all without a single flaw.

Nerve endings she'd thought long deadened stirred to life and tingled. Moisture flooded her mouth. The blood in her veins turned molten.

Close the distance...touch him...

Definitely not...well, maybe. There was a rip in the collar of his shirt, causing the material to gape over a massive, muscular chest completely healed from his impromptu self-surgery. *Taste...*

"How did you escape an inescapable prison?" she demanded. *I'm deprived. That's all.* An aardvark would have had this effect on her.

"A secret I forgot," he replied.

"That's not an answer."

"Wasn't meant to be." His gaze raked over her, the intensity of it staggering—aggression in its purest form. His pupils dilated, black quickly overshadowing green. The most exquisite eclipse. One caused by...lust? Did this bad boy find her attractive despite her oddities?

The blood in her veins utterly *boiled* with desire.

What about his crime?

The boil tapered to a simmer. "You had best run while you can, warrior."

"Or what, princess?"

"I'll hurt you worse."

He flicked his tongue over an incisor. Struggling for the tranquility he'd seemed to display so easily before? "I will warn you once. Only once. Never again threaten my friends. You do and I'll end you. I won't want to, and I'll even hate myself afterward, but I will do it. Do you understand?"

Oh, yes. She understood. "You're even more of a protector than I'd realized."

For a moment, she experienced a keen jealousy directed at his friends. They were loved by this man wholeheartedly, nothing held back. With Mari gone—*razors in my chest, slashing at me*—there was no one in the world who would defend Keeley. Not that she needed defending. *I am, and will forever be, a powder keg without equal.* But the gesture would have been welcome.

He rattled the bars. "I said, do you understand me?"
So fierce...

She breathed in deeply; the leather and musk of his scent should have been a welcome reprieve from aeons of rank, but the goose bumps breaking out over her arms aggravated her. If he'd been any other man, she would have called the reaction *animal attraction.* But he wasn't. And if she'd possessed a weaker will, she would have given in to her craving and moved closer. She would have remembered how it felt to be a woman rather than a prisoner.

But she was the Red Queen and she *didn't* possess a weaker will.

She planted her feet and remained in place. The male disturbed her. Noted. There was no reason to make the situation worse by flirting with temptation.

Such beautiful temptation.

Nothing would stop her from avenging Mari.

"Keeley," he prompted. "Pay attention to me."

Orders? "Tell me what to do again and I will rip out your spine through your mouth."

He didn't even blink. "That's harder to do than you probably realize."

"Oh, I know. It takes experience—which I have. In spades."

Again, not a blink. "Hubris is never a good look."

"I'm not wearing hubris. I'm wearing truth." *Calm.* "Here is what I understand, warrior. Once I vowed to hurt anyone who hurt me, and I never lie. Especially to myself." She raised her chin, knowing she was the picture of stubborn female. "You, Torin, have hurt me."

He sighed with dejection, and yet excitement glowed in his eyes. The juxtaposition confused her. "So we are to war?" he asked.

She offered him a cold smile. "We're *already* warring, warrior."

"In that case, I would be wise to kill you now."

"Please. Try it." He'd have to open her door the same way he'd opened his own…something she'd attempted a thousand times. *How did he do what I could not?*

He frowned at her. "You actually think a woman like you can defeat me?"

A woman like her? What did that mean?

Beads of anger rolled through her. "I've taken down bigger and better than you."

"Bigger maybe, but better? Doubtful, considering there is *no one* better."

Hubris certainly looked good on *him*. "Have you heard of Typhon, the supposed father of all monstrosities? Half dragon, half snake. All attitude. Zeus likes to brag about defeating him, but *I* am the one who ripped him into a thousand pieces and stuffed him under a mountain. And do you know why? Because he frowned when I walked past him."

"Yawn," Torin said.

Her spine went rigid. "You have underestimated your opponent. A fatal mistake many before you have made. You could ask them about the experience…but they are dead."

His gaze shifted between the lock on the door and the wound on her arm. Finally he said, "You're mourning the loss of your friend. I'm going to give you a pass. This time. I won't give you another."

Aw, did the big bad warrior think he was being nice? "You have a choice. Stay in this realm or leave. One day soonish I will topple this entire prison. The moment I do, I will come for you. If you have stayed, we will conclude our business here in this realm. You have my word. If not, I will hunt your friends and start with them."

He punched one of the bars.

Temper, temper.

A shiver stole through her.

"You can't win against me, Keys. Why put yourself through a battle?"

She disregarded his familiarity, saying, "I suggest you use your remaining time alive setting traps for me." No matter what he did, he would lose. But the effort might make him feel better about the defeat to come. Or not. Probably not.

His eyes narrowed. "Very well. Until we meet again… *your majesty*." With a final glare that, shockingly, rendered her breathless, he left the dungeon.

KEELEY WORKED AT a fiendish pace, cutting and carving at the final brimstone scar. *This is for you, Mari.*

She would have finished already, but her mind had constantly drifted to Torin.…

Hate him!

And yet she couldn't stop wondering if his white-blond locks were as soft as they appeared. Or if his wicked lips would be firm against hers or soft. Or if his bronzed skin would burn oh, so good, and the hard muscles beneath clench every time she touched him.

A full-body shiver overtook her. Bad Keeley. Bad! But after everything she'd suffered, she *deserved* pleasure. And really, Torin owed her a little—

No way. Not going there.

Torin was forever off-limits, no matter how desperate she happened to be. He was pretty, there was no denying that, but she had to keep things in perspective. Look at Hades. A few inches taller than Torin, with a strength she'd never seen on another. His black hair was never not sexily mussed, and his midnight eyes always promised a wild carnal indulgence he was perfectly equipped to deliver. And yet Hades was just as likely to peel the skin from his bed partner as her clothing.

Keeley, the queen who had never known affection, had been helpless against his appeal. She'd fallen for him. Hard. A sizzling romance had bloomed, spanning centuries.

"You are so powerful, pet," he'd announced one day. "But that power is unstable. You could accidentally hurt me…unless we ward you and mute the worst of your abilities. Only then will I be safe from you. And I want to be safe. I want to spend my eternity with you. Don't you want that, too?"

She had loved him, and she'd also agreed with him. Her powers *had* been unstable. Bad things happened every time her emotions had gotten the better of her—whatever the season, the weather had responded in kind. Tsunamis. Hurricanes. Polar vortexes. Tornados. Wildfires. If ever she'd harmed the male she was to wed, she would have wanted to die.

When she'd pointed out he could be safe from her power by scarring *himself* with brimstone, negating her power over him specifically, he'd pointed out that his *people* would never be safe, and she couldn't expect everyone under his command to go to such lengths, now could she?

So reasonable.

Such a manipulator.

Hades, the fiercest warrior in existence, the male with hundreds of demon armies at his command and quite literally the ex from hell, had feared her power had become greater than his own, nothing more and nothing less. He simply hadn't been able to bear it.

But the scars weren't even the worst of his crimes. After he'd weakened her, he'd sold her to Cronus—for a barrel of whiskey.

There are two things I'll never forget. The crimes committed against me—and my power. And Hades is going to pay so *hard.* She planned to cut off his head and scoop out his brain. *I'm thinking pumpkin innards at Halloween.* She would set up a booth in the lowest level of the skies and allow everyone he'd ever wronged to come and use his skull as a toilet.

In a word: *magical.*

Keeley hissed as the shiv came out the other side of her arm. Unsteady, she set the weapon aside and lifted the newly shaved hunk of branded skin. As blood leaked to the floor, she studied her arm in the light. Would this last scar return?

She waited, one minute ticking into another. Her skin wove back together—without scarring! She'd…done it? Succeeded?

It couldn't be….

She pressed a hand to her chest where her heart hammered erratically. *I'm* me *again?* Centuries of work, finally finished? She lumbered to her feet, expecting a sudden surge of power to hit her any…second….but there was nothing.

Miss it so much.

She also expected an overwhelming sense of triumph but…she didn't feel that, either. Resolve filled her up, leaving no room for anything else. There was so much more for her to do. Kill Torin. Kill Cronus. Kill Hades.

Mourn Mari.

She stuffed the hunk of skin she'd just removed into the pocket of what remained of her gown. *My trophy.* She would have to be careful not to touch it since the brimstone would weaken her upon contact. But she also couldn't discard it and allow just anyone to find it and perhaps use it against her.

She walked to the bars of her cell, each step more confident than the last, her mind clearer. She attempted to push out the barest stream of power—the metal widened instantly.

I really am me again. Giddy anticipation replaced her resolve, and without pausing in her steps, she picked up Wilson.

"If you had stayed with me," she told him, "I would have protected you. Now? Forget about it." With a squeeze, she turned him to dust and focused on Mari's cell. Another stream of power caused those bars to widen, as well.

The enclosure was the same size as Keeley's, the walls smoother and unmarked by blood. In the center was a coffin-sized mound of dirt.

Anger shot through her—and as it did, bolts of lightning exploded from her pores, crackling all around her. Yes! This! A second later, she was yanked off her feet by a gust of wind, her skin sizzling deliciously and her blood fizzing as she hovered in the air.

The entire dungeon began to shake, dust and debris raining from the ceiling. All too soon, the havoc was too much for the aged walls to bear. They crumbled, one by one, the bars of the door bending, then crumpling, the ceiling cracking, then falling.

Not a single piece of rock or concrete dared brush against her.

Calm...steady...don't want to destroy the entire realm. Not yet anyway.

Deep breath in...out.... The shaking slowly faded, then stopped, the dust gradually clearing. Keeley floated down, down, the dungeon nothing but a heap around her. She landed on a boulder, wind whipping at her hair.

Closing her eyes, she basked in her first taste of freedom in forever. The sun peeked out from behind a wall of clouds, stroking her face despite the winter chill. *Glorious.*

The snap of a twig echoed, and she stiffened, scanning the forest surrounding her. Blackened trees, scorched ground. Wafts of smoke and ash.

Welcome to the Realm of Wailing Tears, where happiness comes to die.

When it rained without the aid of Keeley's emotions, it *rained,* waterlogging the entire realm. She'd lost track of the number of times she'd nearly drowned inside her cell.

Once the home of Cronus, currently the home of the Unspoken Ones, a race of creatures so bloodthirsty and vile hardly anyone dared speak their name.

And yet the Unspoken Ones fear speaking my *name.*

She grinned, and knew anyone looking on would think she was pure evil. They would be correct.

Poor Torin.

She'd made sure he would do anything to remain behind, if only to end her to save his friends from her crazy. Which meant he was out there somewhere, waiting.

Anticipation...

Can't get excited. This was business.

Bloody, bloody business.

An idea formed. Soon, Hades would send his minions after her. Every few weeks, they arrived to check on her and ensure she remained a prisoner. Watching them munch on Torin could be fun. He would experience writhing agony, and they would sicken. Then she could remove each of their heads.

The ideal end to so many of her enemies. *It's decided.*

Okay. There was no help for it. *I'm excited.*

CHAPTER THREE

DUDE. THE *RED QUEEN,* Torin thought, incredulous. No wonder the immortals in the skies had merely whispered about her. Insane? Cruel? Hell, yeah. They'd probably assumed saying her name aloud would have a Beetlejuice effect and actually summon her.

Now, at least, he understood the title. With such power, she could kill entire armies in a snap and then some. *And this is the female who threatened my friends. My only family.*

Seriously. Duuude.

The demon shuddered.

Hidden by gnarled tree limbs that were covered with thorns and brittle leaves that snapped at him with actual teeth, Torin watched Keeley from a distance, like a creeper, completely dumbfounded by her. She'd stood in place as hunks of the dungeon rained around her, and not a single injury had she sustained. Well, that wasn't exactly true. Her arm was a wreck. But still. She'd brought the prison tumbling down, just as she'd claimed, and she hadn't seemed to lift a finger to do it.

What else could she do?

Something stirred within him. The same fierceness he used to feel on the battlefield. The very sensation he'd once lived for—and had never thought to have again.

He smiled.

Idiot! This was one battle he may not be able to win.

Could anyone? Had he not freed the other prisoners on his way out, every single one of them would have died today. Would she have cared?

Definitely not.

Speaking of the prisoners…one of the males had been familiar to him. Emaciated, but familiar, rousing a sense of anger inside him. Torin had been unable to place him—or later, to find him.

Not that it mattered anymore. He had a bigger threat on his plate. In more ways than one.

He'd lost track of the number of times he'd almost gone back for Keeley. Not to hurt her or yell at her as he should have wanted, but simply to see her again, to tease her. To beg for her forgiveness. To prove she wasn't as heart-stoppingly gorgeous as he remembered. To end the stupid tugging, an invisible cord constantly urging him closer. To just…be with her.

How stupid was that?

I have to kill her.

A pang of remorse ripped through his chest as he pictured the powerful, courageous beauty dead in a grave.

Damn it! He shouldn't feel conflicted about her fate. And he shouldn't have to remind himself of her threat against his family.

Time for a little negative reinforcement. Torin circled his fingers around the thick tree branch at his side, granting the foliage permission to feast on him.

Razor-sharp teeth grazed his skin, and blood dripped from his hand. The leaves erupted into a feeding frenzy like piranha, leaving nothing but bone. Hurt like hell as he pulled his arm away. He didn't have to worry about the plant spreading the illness—it would die within the hour.

As he healed, he studied Keeley more intently. Two things became uncomfortably clear. The negative reinforcement hadn't helped, the desire to slay her remaining curiously absent. And a desire to throw her down in a test of strength grew. A test of strength—that was all.

Her eyes were wide and sensuously uptilted as if forever beckoning the men around her to bed. *Strip me*, they said. *Do anything you want to me*.

Though her hair was caked with dirt and tangled, the strands glinted brilliant cobalt-blue in the muted sunlight. Her lips were red, erotically plump, the kind women were willing to pay a fortune to have…and men were willing to pay a fortune to have *all over them*. Her skin was flawless, as pure as ice, and also tinted blue.

Extraordinary. A living, breathing Sugar Plum Fairy, Dungeon Edition.

Cue the porno soundtrack.

He groaned. *Not this. Anything but this.*

Centuries ago, Torin had spent the bulk of his time screwing every woman he met—in his mind. And he'd been good. A god among men. Nothing like the too-rough soldier who'd been unable to seal the deal. He'd taken his lovers against walls, bent over coffee tables and on the ground as wild as an animal, and they'd loved it.

My gateway drug, opening doors I will never be able to enter, taunting me with what I can never have.

Keeley lifted her arm and stretched out her index finger. Lightning split the sky, striking the tip. She wasn't felled and never even wavered on her feet. But she did smile.

What the hell *was* she?

Disease banged against Torin's head, reckless in a bid to get away from the girl.

For once, Torin agreed with the demon. Warring with Keeley would not be a quick grab and stab as he'd expected. It would take time. Time he didn't have. Cameo and Viola weren't going to find themselves. And let's not forget the need to hunt and destroy Pandora's box. It was the only thing in this world or any other capable of killing him and all his friends in a single swoop.

Or so he'd thought.

Though he'd made no noise, Keeley's head snapped in his direction. Her ice-blue gaze locked on him and narrowed. Despite the distance between them—roughly a hundred yards—he felt as if he'd been punched in the stomach.

And he liked it.

Just kill her and go.

"Hiding?" she asked. "I'm disappointed in you."

Damn. In their time apart, he hadn't built an immunity to her I-just-want-to-suck-you voice. Though it probably wouldn't have mattered if he had. She wore a dirty, tattered dress, the sleeves torn off, the thigh-length hem frayed, and it was totally Tarzan's-Jane sexy.

He stepped into a beam of light. "Well, I'm curious. How did you topple an entire building? And why did you wait so long to do it?"

"Torin, Torin, Torin." She tsked. Despite her seeming composure, her eyes blazed with hatred. "You are demon-possessed. You murder people with a touch. I doubt using my secrets against me is too far outside your wheelhouse. You'll understand if I refuse to answer?"

"Of course. But with your skills, I'm surprised more people don't know about you."

"I rarely leave survivors. There's less gossip that way." She looked him over once…twice…going more slowly the second time. She licked her lips, making him think—

No. Don't think. He was already hard as steel.

Not even Cameo, the gorgeous keeper of Misery, had affected him this strongly—and with so little—and they'd dated for months.

"Feel like doing a girl a favor?" Keeley asked. "Tell me how you opened the door to your cell. The prison was designed to respond to Cronus, and you, Lord of the Underworld, are not him."

It had taken Torin only a second to unlock the door, and he'd wanted to kick himself for not escaping days ago. How could he have forgotten Cronus had sealed the All-key inside his chest? That it could open any lock, anytime, anywhere.

"No favors," he said. "Not today." *Attack her. Now!*

"Of course." She smiled and, though it was nothing more than a malevolent display of teeth, it was like she'd found a hidden, magic button connected directly to his reproductive system.

For intense, sizzling arousal, press here.

He backed up a step. *Isn't her. Can't be her.* His hobbies usually distracted him from unwanted desire, but he didn't currently have access to a computer or video games, or a kitchen, or a camera, or a pool table, or a chessboard, or a pack of cards, or a thousand other things. And, okay, wow. Apparently not thinking about sex, not trying to get sex, and not actually having sex equaled lots of free time for Tor Tor.

But even though it wasn't her—*really, really can't be her*—he couldn't stop himself from imagining her dressed as a concubine. Glittery bra. Blue, of course, paired with sheer pantalets. No panties.

In his mind, he pushed her to her knees and demanded she swallow every throbbing inch of him.

She had that penchant for swallowing, after all.

She obeyed him eagerly—couldn't live another moment without knowing the taste of him—opening her mouth, taking him deep. All the way, until she reached the base. A moan of rapture left her, the sound vibrating along his length, intensifying his pleasure.

Yes. That. That's what he wanted.

He had to grit his teeth against the magnificence of the sensations coursing through him. The longing for what he could never have—and shouldn't want. The heat. The race of his heartbeat.

Enough. Stop!

Had Mari taught him nothing?

Had Cameo? She'd never flat-out stated her dissatisfaction with their arrangement, but he'd felt the emotion like another entity in the room. She'd had needs. To be handled by her lover. Petted and caressed. Massaged. Comforted. Squeezed, kneaded…filled. Needs he couldn't meet.

Destined to disappoint. Always.

Besides, this female meant to kill him. And if not him, his friends. For a crime he *had* committed. This was no silly misunderstanding they could work out with a simple heart-to-heart convo.

Keeley splayed her hands, all *look how awesome I am.* "I'm going to do you a favor and let you pick how this goes down. Would you rather I remove both of your arms or force you to dig out each of your organs with your own hands?" Somehow she appeared even calmer and the flames of her hatred even hotter.

"How do you plan to do either of those things if you can't touch me?"

"Why tell you," she said, "when I can show you? Spoiler alert: my next trick is going to nut-kick the last one."

"Nut-kick?" If not for her murderous rage, she might have been the perfect woman. "Real queens don't talk that way."

"This queen does."

A second later, the foundation dropped out from under his feet. No, not true. It hadn't dropped; he had been catapulted into the air where he hovered, his limbs pulled taut…and tauter…until both of his shoulders were jerked from their sockets. His skin began to tear. Sharp pains, everywhere. Any moment, he would lose each of his limbs.

The perverse thing about the experience? He liked the pressure, savored it.

"How are you doing this?" he asked through panting breaths.

She blew him a kiss.

Hardcore. Like foreplay for warriors.

I'm a sick man. Har har.

"Right now," she said, "you are experiencing an extreme bout of helplessness. The same helplessness Mari must have felt as your fever pillaged and plundered her immune system."

Forget the pressure. Guilt choked him.

Keeley's chin trembled. "You made her cry, warrior. Sometimes I swear I can still hear her sobbing."

He squeezed his eyes tightly shut. "Do it, then. End me." He deserved it. And she would be satisfied, his friends safe from her wrath.

"So quickly?" she asked. "No. We're just getting started."

Some of the pressure eased.

"Come on!" he shouted as his wounds healed. "What are you waiting for? You won't get another chance like this."

"Actually, I'll get as many chances as I like."

"That confident in your ability?"

"Perhaps I'm that confident in your *lack* of ability."

The taunt burned so badly he could have used a little aloe vera on his soul. *Always on the bench, never in the game.* Forcing an easy tone, he said, "I've been nice to you on account of your loss and everything—"

"Which was your fault!" she spat, the pressure increasing all over again.

"—but my goodwill has officially run out."

An animalistic roar suddenly echoed through the forest, interrupting the beginning of a long, rambling speech that would have had no point but that of postponement, giving him a chance to think of a way out of this.

Torin dropped, crashing into the ground. Even as he lost his breath, he jumped to his feet. Behind him, twigs snapped. Limbs slapped together. Another roar sounded, this one louder, closer.

Something was headed this way—and fast.

He'd been in these woods for days, and there'd been no sign of life. Well, other than the carnivorous plants. Now *this?*

He looked to Keeley. She put her hands on her hips, every bit the annoyed female. Funny thing. Even that was sexy.

He punched the side of his skull in an effort to clear his thoughts, and it actually helped. He palmed a dagger he'd brought from home, ready to face this newest challenge.

The creature arrived, surrounded by a cloud of dust. Realization hit—*this is an Unspoken One*. Half man, half beast. Rather than hair, snakes danced and hissed from his scalp. And rather than skin, he had what looked to be the charred remains of fur. Two long fangs protruded over his bottom lip like sabers, reaching his chin. Though he had human hands, his feet were razor-sharp hooves.

His black gaze roved over Torin, cataloging every detail, and his forked tongue stroked over his lips. "Mine."

KEELEY STUDIED HER newest opponent. Such an ugly thing. The Unspoken One must have heard the prison fall and come running, determined to find out what had happened.

Now he appeared eager to have a nice Torin dinner.

Get in line. She might not be a carnivore like the Unspoken One, but she would have liked a nibble—or ten.

Stop flirting with the idea of seduction and fight! She thought of all the times this creature and his siblings had invaded the prison, frantic to break through the bars and feast on the prisoners. Though they'd never gotten past the bars, they *had* reached through and managed to grab hold of those who'd stepped too close; she'd heard the horrendous fruits of their labors. The screams. The pleas for mercy that were never granted. The victorious cackles of glee.

Payback was going to hurt.

As she prepared to render her first strike, Torin flew through the dust and sliced the tip of a dagger across the creature's throat...only to disappear. Where had he gone? He had to be nearby. According to Galen, Torin was not an immortal capable of flashing.

The Unspoken One remained on his feet, healing quickly and growing angrier.

Torin reappeared and struck—again and again and again—inflicting more damage every time. The Unspoken One tried to latch on to him. *Tried* being the key word. Torin displayed excitement rather than fear, always ducking at the perfect moment.

As much as she hated to admit it, the warrior's masterful skill impressed her.

The problem was he wouldn't make actual contact with the beast or throw a punch. Wouldn't even kick out his legs. Determined to prevent a plague? Even among the vile Unspoken Ones?

Maybe he truly *did* feel bad about what he'd done to Mari—Keeley flattened her hand against her stomach to slow the sudden churn of sickness—but that wouldn't change his fate. It couldn't. She had one redeeming quality: her integrity. She'd promised to end him, and she would.

The Unspoken One swiped a claw at Torin, and this time Keeley took it personally.

Torin was *hers* to kill. No one else's. Anyone who so much as *thought* about harming him automatically signed their own death warrant.

"I'll give you a five-second head start," she shouted to the Unspoken One. "I suggest you run—fast."

At the sound of her voice, the creature froze. His black gaze swung to her and narrowed. "You."

"Four." Keeley fluffed her hair. "I'm sure you've heard the rumors about my fondness for viscera and my distaste for showing mercy. Well, I assure you, they're both true. Just ask your brother. Oh, wait. You can't. He approached my cell and I gutted him. Three."

Torin dove through the air, slicing through the Unspoken One's eye. A bellow of pain echoed. The beast at last got his paws on Torin, batting him in the chest. Torin soared over what remained of the drawbridge into the murky moat below.

Death warrant signed, sealed and about to be delivered. "Two. One."

"Always thought you'd be the tastiest," the beast crowed, returning his attention to her. He took a step toward her, and though a hundred yards separated them one moment, he was in front of her the next. He towered over her, his fetid breath fanning her face, burning her skin. "Finally get to find out if I was right."

"No one taught you the value of a good toothbrush, I see." She waved her hand under her nose.

"Don't worry. I'll clean my teeth…with your bones." He swung at her—Unspoken Ones so enjoyed tenderizing their meals.

She sent a bolt of power slamming into his chest, causing his entire body to seize. She was about to send another bolt when something hard slammed into her side, knocking her out of the way. That something maintained a tight, intractable hold, traveling with her, twisting midair, taking the brunt of impact when they landed.

She caught her breath and regained her equilibrium— only to realize a panting, scowling Torin loomed above her, a muscle flexing in his jaw.

Fool! "Why did you do that?" she demanded.

"What kind of idiot female just stands there while a beast triple her size prepares to knock her brains right out of her ear hole?"

He is...helping me?

But why?

Thoughts...derailing...

Wet hair clung to Torin's face, droplets of water trickling down, down, washing away streaks of dirt. Spiky lashes framed emerald eyes glittering with a sensual blend of menace and lust.

He was raw sexuality, his masculinity proving savage enough to batter through every feminine defense she'd ever erected, drawing a hot, carnal response from her. Tremors, breathlessness.

Unending hunger.

Knowing the Unspoken One was out for the count, at least for a few minutes more, she reached up to trace the outline of Torin's beautiful lips. He stayed put, perhaps trapped by the same desperate need she felt—definitely daring her to do it, to take what she wanted—but at the last second, he reeled backward, as if she'd planned to strike him rather than caress him.

"Don't," he snapped. "As long as there are clothes between us, you'll be fine, but skin-to-skin will destroy even you."

Anger. With him—and herself. How could she have forgotten his taint?

Relief. Weakness of any kind was not allowed.

Anger again. He was Mari's killer! The enemy. Desire for Torin could not be stronger than desire for revenge.

Her bones began to vibrate, the ground to shake. The wind whipped into a dangerous frenzy. Thunder boomed as the sky darkened to an oppressive black.

Torin searched for the source of the tumult, not realizing it came from her.

The Unspoken One recovered sooner than expected

and flashed to them, swatting the distracted Torin out of the way and grabbing Keeley by the neck. She didn't struggle as she was lifted off her feet. There was no need.

"Not so haughty now, are you, female?"

"Someone has a toilet-paper word of the day, doesn't he?"

A sharp lance of pain in her neck. He'd just broken her spine. Oh, well.

"I want you to know the great pleasure I will derive from squeezing you so forcefully your head pops off." His voice was like razors, slicing at her, his grin slow and triumphant…and all the more evil for it. "I'll use the wound like a straw and drain you dry."

Creative. "It'll take…more than you…to end me." The vibrations around them intensified, soon spilling into him.

Confusion furrowed his brow just before the ground opened up, threatening to swallow him whole. He released her in a bid to jump to safety, though she didn't fall so much as an inch. No, she remained in the air, the wind coming harder, lashing the ends of her hair and the hem of her ruined gown.

The night-dark clouds undulated, screaming as they travailed…and finally gave birth to a violent storm. Daggers of ice pelted the land…the Unspoken One. *Slash. Slash. Slash.* The cuts went deeper than those Torin had given him, his skin tearing, blood leaking.

Grinning, she crooked her finger at him. The Unspoken One tried to plant his heels and remain in place, but he wasn't strong enough to oppose the lasso of her power, and all too soon he stood only a few inches away from her, at the edge of the rupture. He'd hoped to harm her. Had hoped to harm Torin.

Now he died.

Torin swooped in low, running his dagger across the Unspoken One's ankles. With a bellow, the beast dropped to his knees. But just before he landed, he twisted and once again swiped a beefy arm at the warrior. He missed. Torin rolled to a crouch several yards away, and even though the ice pelted him, too, causing the same slashing damage, he kept his narrowed gaze on the Unspoken One, preparing to launch another attack.

Can't let him. My emotions…almost too strong to control…

If she wasn't careful, Torin would be killed in a moment of chaos.

Where was the justice in that?

Deep breath in…out…but "almost" had already crashed and burned. She'd felt too much for too long, without any kind of outlet. She attempted to flash Torin out of range. Maybe she succeeded. Maybe she didn't. The rage kicked down the walls of her defenses and burst from her; she lost track of her surroundings. Her spine realigned, healed and arched, causing her body to bow.

Howls of agony erupted—and they did not come from her.

The *riiiip* of skin.

The *crrrack* of breaking bones.

The *pop* of a body bursting. The *whoosh* of rushing blood. The splatter. The downpour of shredded organs.

Warm liquid splashed over her. Shrapnel beat against her.

But as quickly as the storm had come, it quieted. Keeley floated to the ground. She wiped her eyes to clear her field of vision. The Unspoken One had been reduced to debris—and none of it was identifiable. He would not be able to recover from this. He would never regenerate. This was it for him, the end.

Good riddance.

But…there was no sign of Torin.

Either she'd flashed him away as hoped, or he'd died, his guts mixed in the carnage. Remorse speared her straight through the heart. Because she might not get to exact the kind of revenge she'd hoped. *Not* because of— *no, impossible*—an underlying sense of loss.

I can't miss him.

Or could she? Torin was Mari's killer, yes, but he was also the only link Keeley had to the girl. Her only link to the land of the living.

She attempted to flash to him. When she stayed put, panic snuck in, an assassin to her calm. She could lock on anyone…except the dead.

Well, he wasn't dead. He was a fearsome Lord of the Underworld, and he could simply be moving too quickly for her to pinpoint.

Yes, that had to be it.

She marched forward. He was out there, and she would find him. No matter where he hid. They would finish their war, and she would find *another* link to the land of the living.

Life, meet perfection.

CHAPTER FOUR

TORIN RACED THROUGH the forest, careful to avoid the traps he'd set—traps he would have set even without Keeley's suggestion, thanks. Limbs slapped at his face and leaves tried to bite his cheeks, but he hardly noticed. One second he'd been preparing to launch a final attack against the Unspoken One, the next he'd been a good distance from the action. Keeley must have flashed him.

Why would she do such a thing? She wanted him dead, right?

Does the answer really matter? He needed his backpack, like, yesterday. He couldn't let Keeley near his friends—his only family—and if that meant he had to put a bullet in her brain, so be it.

And the Worst Enemy in the History of Ever award goes to...the Red Queen.

Not because she was powerful enough to topple a building—though that certainly put her in the top tier— but because she could make a beast burst apart at the seams, raining blood and guts.

Seriously. She'd beaten that Unspoken One like morning wood with the same end result: an explosion.

Torin could imagine Keeley's acceptance speech. *I'd like to thank my victim. Without him and his internal organs, I wouldn't be here.*

In all the centuries of his life, he'd thought he'd seen the worst of the worst when it came to gruesome.

He'd been wrong.

He smashed through a wall of snapping foliage he'd spent hours erecting yesterday morning. A pitiful defense, but a guy had to work with what he had. Three of the prisoners he'd freed waited in camp despite his threats to kill first and ask questions later if anyone neared him. They expected him to find a way out of the realm.

So far he'd had no luck. Never mind Keeley's threat.

Torin knew there were hundreds of different realms, some beside each other, some stacked on top of each other, and some even wrapped around the others. He just wasn't sure how to get from one to another without the ability to flash.

"Hallo, mate," Cameron said. "So nice of you to join us."

The trio consisted of two males and one female. Cameron, the keeper of Obsession. Irish, the keeper of Indifference. And Winter, the keeper of Selfishness.

They were cursed with demons even though they hadn't been among the immortals who'd opened Pandora's box. But. When it came to evil, there was always a "but." At the time, they were prisoners of the underground realm of Tartarus. And since there'd been more demons than Lords, a good chunk of the inmates were given the leftovers.

"Time to abandon ship," he said. Keeley would be coming after him, and if the trio was anywhere near him, they would be nailed in the cross fire.

No one seemed to catch his urgency.

Whatever. He hadn't signed on as their custodian. If they wouldn't listen, they deserved what they got.

Cameron eased beside Winter, offering her a bowl of forage stew. The two were siblings, maybe even twins. Both had the same lavender eyes rimmed with silver, the same bronzed skin and hair.

"This little clearing has the best cold spring in the entire forest," Cameron said, "and daddy needs his happy bath times." He picked up the tattoo gun he'd created with metal parts he'd found lying on the ground and continued inking a currently indistinguishable picture on his wrist. Apparently he had a compulsion—obsession—to chronicle each of his imprisonments in his flesh. "We're not leaving."

"Then you'll soon experience the joys of self-combustion." It was as simple as that.

Irish perched on a horizontal tree stump, busy carving a branch into an arrow. He wasn't as civilized in appearance as his friends. Two horns stretched from the crown of his head. Dark, straight-as-a-board hair hung to his waist, multiple razors woven into the strands. He had sharp cheekbones. Black, mysterious eyes. Hands permanently clawed. And while—for the most part—he had the top half of a man, he had the bottom half of a goat. Fur and hooves.

He was part satyr, part something else, and sensing Torin's scrutiny, he glanced up. "Fack aff," he said in his Isle-rich brogue. Hence the nickname. Real name— Puck something. Or maybe Puke something. Hard to tell when you couldn't care less.

Torin shrugged. "Like I said, it's your funeral. Enjoy it. Or not." He dropped to his knees in front of his backpack and emptied his pockets. When he'd thrown Keeley to the ground, he'd frisked her and stolen—he frowned as he looked over the only item she'd carried—a hunk of bloody, scarred skin.

Well, why not? Hotpants McCuddlesworth was just the type to carry a souvenir of someone's torture. Except, as Torin's mind returned to the topple of the dungeon, the dust clearing, he remembered the wound on Keeley's arm, a mess of crimson-soaked muscle. As if a hunk of skin had just been cut away.

He considered the scars more closely. Thousands of tiny orange flecks sparkled inside the tissue.

He frowned as he ran his thumb over the flesh. It was overwarm, the heat unnatural. From…flames? Maybe. Probably. But why wasn't the flesh melting? Only bits of brimstone could burn bodily tissue without actually—

Brimstone. Of course. Sulfuric rocks with veins of lava running throughout, found deep in the earth, and—hell. The bottom dropped out of his stomach. This was meant to be a ward. The kind used to defeat the Curators.

Was Keeley a Curator? A parasite? Or had she hoped to *protect* herself from one?

If she *was* a Curator, she was one of the last of her kind—if not *the* last—and even more dangerous than he'd realized. Curators created invisible bonds with those around them, and like vampires, sucked them dry.

The bond is broken, she'd shouted.

Oh…damn. She was. She was a Curator.

Disease shuddered.

"Ever heard of the Curators?" he asked his unwanted guests.

A sharp inhalation from each.

"No," Irish finally said, his tone dry. "We're morons without a clue."

Will take that as a yes. "One of them just escaped from the prison, and while that's bad enough, she's determined to kill me." Would have done so already if not for the Unspoken One.

"Then you're as good as dead, my friend." Cameron never glanced up from his task. "Because I'm guessing Keeley is the Curator, and check it, that chick is loco in the noco. You get what I'm saying, my man? Her elevator only goes to floors F and U."

"Got it. Thanks." *Jackass.* Torin could talk smack about her all he wanted. But apparently if anyone else did it he wanted to hollow out their liver and fill it with rocks.

He busied himself, withdrawing the semiautomatic he'd packed, then the pieces of a long-range rifle.

"I tangled with a Curator once." Cameron finished off a…rain shower? Ocean of tears? "She was out to destroy my entire family, but she was a real wildcat in the sack. The crazy ones always are. That's probably why they're my favorite." A pause. "Although, I once slept with a centaur who liked to—"

"Don't start with one of your stories." Irish threw a stick at him. "Besides, they're never yours. You collect them from other people."

Scowling, Cameron said, "And how do you know?"

"Because the one you're telling is mine, idiot."

"Who are you calling an idiot, half-wit?"

"I'm not a half-wit, you fool."

Children.

What else did Torin know about his new enemy?

Curators were created before humans. Once spirits of light, they were tasked with the safekeeping of the earth, bound to it and its seasons. But everything changed when they betrayed their leader, the Most High, and mated with the fallen angels who'd attempted to usurp him as supreme ruler of the highest heavens. What the Curators hadn't understood until too late? The fallen were cursed with eternal darkness of the soul, and that curse would soon spread among their race.

Their offspring—like that of humans and fallen angels—were known as Nephilim…and even demons.

Backtrack. Curators were spirits—without bodies. How Keeley had gotten one, he couldn't fathom. But she *had* done it. Otherwise she couldn't have been imprisoned or thrown those rocks at him. Or ended up underneath him when he'd pushed her out of harm's way…

Not going there. He'd harden—again.

He needed brimstone. But as scorching hot as the rocks were, there was no way he could carry one to Keeley, hold her down and rub it against her. And, anyway, he didn't like the thought of scarring all that flawless skin. The simpler solution was to scar *himself.* Wards worked both ways, after all.

He sheathed the handgun at his waist and swiped the tattoo equipment from Cameron. "Gonna borrow this. Hope you don't mind."

The warrior gave a spot-on impersonation of Chuck Norris. *He once made a Happy Meal cry. He strangled an enemy with a cordless phone. He destroyed the periodic table because he only recognizes the element of surprise.*

But I'm worse.

Torin's smile was a cold invitation to hell as he removed his gloves. "You're welcome to try to reclaim your stuff, but you'll walk away with a hacking cough and an inability to ever touch another living creature without starting a plague. Totally up to you."

Silence.

That's what I thought.

He carefully unhooked the motor, then tinkered with it to give it more juice. He found a thick steel pipe, and with a few more parts, created a makeshift jackhammer to crack through layer after layer of hard earth. Sweat poured from him, but it was a good sweat. From honest labor. *Missed this.*

When the motor died, he used his hands. His companions never issued even a token offer to help, just continued eating their stew. Fine. They wouldn't share in the reward. And rewarded he was.

Two feet down...four...six...eight, making sure to leave grooves along the wall so that he could climb out, he discovered a small patch of brimstone. The quarter-sized rocks were exactly as he remembered, black with gold cracks throughout, and hot, close proximity causing him to blister.

He climbed out of the hole and stuffed his gloves in his back pocket, then worked a little more magic with the steel pipe, using it and a branch to create a pair of tongs. Back inside, he managed to scoop up one of the rocks. The branch caught fire on the way up, but he made it to level ground before the end turned to ash and the rock dropped.

Victorious, he sat down beside it.

The Terrible Trio gaped at him.

"Here," Winter said, speaking up for the first time.

She strolled to him with a feminine swagger he'd seen many try to emulate but only a rare few ever perfect, and eased between his legs.

He should have responded to *that,* but there was zip, zilch, nada happening down below, and tendrils of annoyance wafted through him. Why Keeley and not her?

Winter reached for him, saying, "Let me help you."

Torin scooted away from her, snapping, "This is your final warning. Come this close again, and you'll lose a hand. Make a play for the rock, and you'll lose even more."

Cameron snorted. "Something you should know about my sister. She always wants what other people have."

Her eyes glittered with determination and, granted, even that was a lovely sight. *She* was lovely.

Zip. Zilch. Nada.

He didn't like the thought of Keeley, and only Keeley, being able to affect him.

His reaction to her would make a great porn title, though. *The Lonesome Chub.*

Dude. *Enough!*

"Save yourself a battle," she said, waving her fingers at him. "Give me the brimstone."

"Do it," Irish said. "I don't want to have to take sides."

Like he hadn't already. He might be the keeper of Indifference, but some part of him valued the girl. The longing gazes he cast her hadn't gone unnoticed.

"You should have helped me dig," Torin said.

"And dirty these nails?" She shook her head. "Never."

"Tell you what," Torin said. "I won't give you the brimstone, and in return for your understanding, I won't kill you. How's that?"

Slowly, as if every step was agony, she walked away from him. "Fair enough."

Pretty words. But she was already planning that battle she'd promised him, guaranteed.

Oddly enough, he wasn't excited by the prospect of another worthy opponent.

Done with distractions, Torin rubbed his arm against the rock. Once on the front, once on the back. That's all it took. There was an immediate burn, his flesh and muscle cooking. He almost bellowed. Fine. No almost about it. He bellowed and he cursed, then fell to his back panting. The scent in the air…enough to gag. Bits of brimstone bonded to tissue, scarring him, never allowing total regeneration.

Winter dove for the rock.

Uh, uh, uh. He kicked it down the hole before she could snatch it and hurried to cover it with dirt.

"Like I said," he announced when he finished. "You didn't help me dig."

"Like *I* said," Winter echoed. "Battle."

"Mistake, my man." Irish tsked.

"Sharing is caring," Cameron said. "Greediness gets you killed."

"I'm your only ally out here," Torin reminded them. "Dial down the threats or leave my camp."

Winter scowled. The other two shrugged. They might not like him, but they needed him.

And I need to find my Curator. Where are you, Keeley?

He'd engaged in countless blood feuds throughout his long life, but this just might be the first one he'd ever actually considered…fun. He didn't deserve to have fun, and it was certainly wrong of him, given the nature and gravity of the situation—*but it's too late to turn back.*

This time he would be ready for whatever Keeley dished.

A ROPE SNAGGED around Keeley's ankle. In a single heartbeat, she was whisked into the air and hung upside down.

Seriously? This again? She flashed to the ground.

One more mark on the ledger of Torin's crimes.

Only forty-six hours into her hunt, and she was already on edge. He was alive, yes, but he'd evaded her. His traps had annoyed her.

Thunder boomed overhead. The sound bothered her, reminding her that another rain was due any day. One that would have nothing to do with her emotions. *Have to be gone by then.*

And where were Hades's minions? She'd abandoned her plan to feed them bits and pieces of Torin. She just wanted them dead so she could concentrate fully on the warrior.

She stalked forward, pushing out streams of power to fell the trees in her path. *I will find him.*

How many times had she tracked an enemy with Hades? Countless. She was good. The best. A little rusty, perhaps, but she'd take determination over skill any day.

Whoosh!

An array of arrows flew at her. She easily dodged, spotting the manticore leaping from the branches of a still-standing tree. He had the head of a man, the body of a lion and a crossbow for a tail. She caught him with a stream of power, holding him in place. Then, with only a thought, she ripped off his skin, leaving it in one piece, and stuffed his bloody carcass back inside it—inside out. When he hit the ground, he stayed there, writhing.

Word of the Unspoken One's death had spread, and creatures were out in droves, apparently ready for a five star dine and dash.

They must not have realized she was the infamous Red Queen.

A loud *click clack* captured her attention, her ears twitching. A laelap appeared around the corner, gunning for her. A metal dog that would never give up once it had spotted prey. It could be blinded, its legs cut off, blood pouring from the wounds, but still it would try to find a way to reach its intended victim.

Don't have the patience for this.

Sighing, Keeley released another stream of power, crushed the creature into a ball and flattened him like a pancake. Tiny metals parts flew in every direction.

Torin's masculine scent drifted by on a tendril of wind, claiming her attention. He was close!

Come out, come out wherever you are.

As she sniffed, she picked up the scent of three other prisoners, as well. Two males, one female. Keeley bit the side of her tongue until she tasted blood. Who was the female to Torin? His latest girlfriend?

Probably. He was too pretty to spend his nights alone.

The thought annoyed her, but she couldn't fathom why. Unless… Yes, of course. Mari had been forever denied a chance at a happily-ever-after, so Torin should be, as well. It had nothing to do with Keeley's sizzling attraction to him.

An attraction that hadn't lessened with the passage of time, but grown.

I'm too smart to go through another bad-boy phase. Yes? Please?

But it was becoming harder and harder to convince herself that Torin's appeal centered around her desperation, that any male would have affected her just as strongly. Only one male had emerald eyes twined with different shades of green, each brighter than the last. Only one male had those sensuous lips... What would they feel like against her skin?

Did he prefer a soft press...or a hard demand?

No! No pleasure. Not from him. Only revenge. She—

Tripped on a strategically placed vine and stumbled. As she regained her footing, she heard another *whoosh*. About fifty feet away a crossbow was anchored to a branch that was connected to the vine. She caught the arrow by the shaft before the metal tip could sink into her hammering heart.

Well, well. Another mark against Torin.

Flickers of anger. Thunder booming.

Perhaps she needed to expand her Kill Torin plan. *Find him, torture him for being so irresistible, and then slay the girlfriend in front of him.*

In a word—*perfect!* Mari would have been proud.

Keeley's shoulder drooped, her chest aching all over again. Actually, Mari would have scolded her for such a plot. The girl would have said, her tone gentle, "Keeley, love, you yourself have killed many people, and every victim had a best friend left behind. You know this. Do not hate someone else for committing the same sin. And do not wallow in the past. It's like quicksand and will keep you trapped. Forgive and move on."

So wise, her Mari.

But…could Keeley allow Torin to walk away from the travesty he'd caused?

Can't do it. Just can't.

Her heart was broken. Only vengeance would spackle the pieces together again.

As she motored along, lost in thought, she stepped onto a dilapidated board. The center snapped and she fell, crashing into the bottom of a pit before she even realized what had happened. Her ankle twisted, and her knees buckled. Sharp pains exploded through her, but they were nothing she couldn't handle.

Gold star, Torin. He'd done his job well.

A shadow fell over her. "It didn't have to be this way, you know."

Skin prickling with an insane amount of heat, she glanced up. The diabolical warrior stood at the top edge of the pit, the barrel of a rifle aimed at her head. Breath caught in her throat—but not because of the weapon.

He's even more beautiful than I remember.

He's also a thief. He stole Mari. My sunshine. My happiness.

"Really, Torin? *Really?*" she asked, as though disappointed, hoping to mask her humiliating reaction to him. Blood, heating right along with her skin. Every cell singing, begging for a rush of sensation only the press of male hardness against female softness could give. *Hands, itching.* To touch him. No, no. To kill him. Of course. For Mari. Sweet Mari. "Bringing a gun to a power fight? Not wise."

"You don't want to know everything I brought, princess."

"You're right—because none of it will help you." She flashed to the top of the pit and smacked the weapon out of his hand before he had a chance to fire. The fragrance of sandalwood and spice drifted from him, and her mouth watered. *One taste, just one.* And then…

I'll want more.

How was he doing this? How was he sweeping her up in a maddening storm of unstoppable chemistry, causing anticipation to build inside her until she shivered? Just by nearing her!

He stroked his white-hot gaze over her. His breaths began to come shallowly, and he licked his lips.

He lusts for me?

He might as well have touched her, so strongly did she react to the darkly intoxicating thought. The ache… too much, too intense. Overwhelming.

No! Just no.

"Gotta say, Miss Keys. You're looking very fine."

Reveal nothing. Hide everything. "Obviously," she said, then ruined the bold statement by self-consciously combing her fingers through her hair.

Since last they'd faced off, she'd scrubbed from head to toe with enough force to skin herself—again. Even though the dirt was gone, she had been unable to find new clothes and still wore the same tattered rag.

Keeley would rather start every conversation she ever had with "Do you want to see my big fat lady balls?" than not look her best. Her own people had found her lacking in every way, and Hades's minions used to delight in teasing her about her odd coloring; she'd never quite shaken the heart-crushing sense of not being good enough, not fitting in.

"But what does that have to do with anything?" she finished.

"I'll tell you…after you tell me how good *I* look," he said, and he appeared to be fighting a grin.

Entrapment! Do not respond. Exploring him with her gaze, on the other hand…

He wore a long-sleeved black T-shirt that read "One Of These Things Doesn't Belong: William. Panties. Women." His leather pants were ripped. Black gloves covered his hands. A metal chain hung from around his waist. The typical bad-boy uniform hadn't changed, it seemed…and still revved her motor.

Forgive me, Mari.

She found herself saying, "You look like…dinner." She'd meant the words as an insult. A reminder that carnivorous beasts were out there, just waiting to devour him, but every sensation already coursing through her poor, neglected body suddenly heightened, nearly dragging a moan from her.

His voice reminded her of smoke dusting over gravel, soft but gritty, as he said, "You want to eat me, huh?"

I do. I really do. I want my mouth all over him. "I will not stoop to your level by answering." *Or mortify myself with the truth.*

"Well, then, do you have any interest in a bargain?" he asked, surprising her.

"What do you mean?"

"Rather than trying to kill me, you can get your pound of flesh another way. Like, say, a spanking? No? How about a good whipping? Twenty lashes? Thirty?" When she remained silent, he added, "All right, forty. But that's my final offer."

It was…tempting. A way to satisfy her need for bloodshed while ending the strife between them. Except, he would recover from a whipping, while Mari hadn't recovered from her illness. *Has to be like for like.*

"I must respectfully decline," she said.

"Fine. Fifty lashes."

Why was he— Understanding peeked its head above her confusion. "Oh, I get it. You saw my power in action. You're afraid of me."

His nostrils flared, and he actually recoiled from her. "Afraid? Princess, I was trying to do you a favor, save you a little embarrassment over the major defeat you're about to suffer. For some reason, I'm no longer feeling quite so magnanimous." He squared his shoulders. "Let's do this. Take a swing at something covered by clothing."

She balled her fist, only to hesitate. "*You* take a swing. You're wearing gloves. Which strikes me as odd now that I think about it. Shouldn't you *want* to make me sick? That would solve all your problems."

"No, it would add to them. I hate knowing I'm responsible for Mari's death. Adding yours to the mix isn't my idea of a good time."

The words unnerved her. But maybe that was his plan. Throw her for a loop and then strike at her while she was too dizzy to notice. Well, she would show him!

Keeley stretched both of her arms toward him, saying, "I'm going to do it. I'm going to hit you with a blast of power, and you're going to writhe in the worst pain of your life. Nothing will ease you."

"Great." Then, when she hesitated, he had the gall to add, "I'm waiting…."

"You should be running."

"Why? Do you want to stare at my ass?"

How was she supposed to react to his total lack of fear? "Any last words?"

"Sure." His gaze raked over her slowly, so wonderfully slow, and when next he spoke, his voice dripped with melted honey. "If I had one last wish, I'd use it to put my hands all over you, zero consequences. Hell, my mouth, too. I'd like to touch you and taste you and make *you* explode."

Suddenly breathless, she said, "Don't talk like that."

He smiled at her, but it only made the breathlessness worse. "Do whatever you've got to do, Keys. I'm ready."

"Fine. I will." This was it, then. The first strike in their war. A bit of vengeance for Mari. One item checked off Keeley's to-do list.

So why did remorse hold her immobile? "Nothing will stop me," she said.

"Didn't think it would."

I can do this. She rolled her shoulders, shook out her hands. *All right, okay. I won't make him suffer. For you, Mari, I'll make it quick and painless and simply finish him here.*

She stretched out her arms, lightning shooting from her palms. Torin stumbled back, but rather than frying to a crisp as she'd planned, he seemed to absorb the heat and energy.

His mouth opened and closed for several seconds before he snapped, "I can't believe you actually did it."

"I told you I would." Confused, Keeley shot out another bolt of lightning. Again, he stumbled back without frying. "I don't understand what's happening."

He gripped the collar of his shirt and yanked the material over his head to look himself over. The lightning should have left gaping holes of black, but there weren't even streaks of pink to indicate he'd been struck. But there were muscles. Lots and lots of muscles. A lump

filled her throat. She'd thought him beautiful before…
but *this* was beautiful. No one had a physique like his.
Cut with rope after rope of strength, skin pale and flawless, a black butterfly tattooed on his stomach.

"You're staring," he said.

And probably drooling. "So?"

"So it's time for me to share with the rest of the class."
He peeled back one of his gloves, revealing thick scars
running up one side of his arm and down the other. Scars
with flecks of yellow-orange peppered throughout. "This
is why you were unable to kill me."

The lump dissolved and she inhaled sharply. He knew
she was a Curator, and he'd taken precautions against
her.

And she'd thought to make his death quick and painless. A mistake she wouldn't repeat.

"You think you're so smart," she spat. "Well, I've
got news for—"

"Shut it, Keys," he snapped, speaking over her.

Baffled by him, she actually pressed her lips together.
Very few people had ever spoken to her like that, too
afraid of her reaction. *So domineering…*

Won't shiver. Would rather die.

"You once gave me a choice." His eyes became twin
infernos, burning everything they touched. And they
seemed to touch her everywhere. "Now I'm giving you
one. Walk away from me and your vengeance—or suffer."

CHAPTER FIVE

TURNED ON—CHECK.

Yeah, I put the "fun" in dysfunctional.

Torin should probably call a doctor. Not even Cialis was supposed to cause such an intense reaction.

What has one hundred and thirty-two teeth and holds back the Incredible Hulk? My zipper.

For a moment, he found amusement in the fact that his penis had decided to act like a third wheel on a date and pop in to complicate things, butt in to private conversations and demand attention at the most inappropriate times. But the amusement didn't last long.

Keeley had tried to murder him with her earth-shattering power—twice!—and she totally would have succeeded if he hadn't circumvented her with the brimstone. So the fact that he had an erection the size of a battering ram, all because she'd peered at him with those icy eyes, daring him to take a swing at her, was messed up. Even for him.

But the kicker? He was trying to Jedi mind-trick her into choosing option B. To suffer. Because it was the only way he'd get to spend more time with her.

I'm worse than a monster.

No, no. He had this all wrong. His reasons for wanting to spend more time with her were completely altruistic.

If she was occupied with Torin, she wouldn't switch her focus to his friends.

And that, ladies and gentlemen, is how you work any situation to your favor.

The blue-tinted beauty raised her chin, the perfect study of feminine stubbornness. "I choose…suffer," she said, moving into a battle stance. "I may be weakened by what you've done, but I'm still the most powerful being you've ever encountered. I've killed kings, toppled kingdoms."

Shouldn't grin.

The demon banged against his skull, impatient to get away from the girl.

Not happening.

"You're more than weakened, princess. You're severely limited." The brimstone actually *stopped* her from harming him, because her power was an extension of her. "Are you sure you don't want to take a moment and reconsider this? Maybe make a pros-and-cons list?"

"Is this to be a debate or a physical battle? I've considered."

Well, all right, then. "Don't forget. If you touch my skin, you'll sicken. And if, miracles of miracles, you survive the raging fever and bloody cough, you'll become a carrier and infect others."

"Talk, talk, talk, blah, blah, blah," she said—and struck. She must have flashed a branch into her hand because one second her fist swung at his face, the next the jagged branch slammed into his jaw.

Blood in his mouth. A lance of pain. He stumbled, straightened and wiped his already-swelling lips. He should have been annoyed. Or angry. Yeah, anger was probably the proper response. Instead, he was—

shocker!—invigorated. He'd handicapped the chick, but she'd found a way to strike anyway.

Maybe aliens had taken over his brain.

"If you want a chance to win this," he said, "you'll have to hit me harder."

"Oh. Okay." *Whack!*

Stars behind his eyes, and yet he kind of wanted to laugh. She'd merely given him what he'd asked for, and he couldn't fault her for it.

Definitely aliens.

When she swung a third time, he was ready, catching the stick and jerking it from her grip. She yelped, startled by the disarming. Hadn't expected him to be a worthy opponent, had she? He released the pimp-slapper, but it vanished before it hit the ground.

He didn't have to wonder what had happened. She'd flashed it somewhere else.

"You can't defeat me," she said, circling him. A predator with a meal in sight.

Adrenaline spilled into his blood, riding the waves in his veins. "I can...but I'd be willing to accept your surrender."

A shrill cry suddenly echoed. He and Keeley looked up in unison as a sphinx flew in circles overhead, dodging clouds with expert precision. The bare-chested creature had the haunches of a lion, the wings of a great bird, and the torso of a woman. A fresh-off-the-pole, looking-to-give-you-the-lap-dance-of-a-lifetime woman.

Come on Little T. You gotta be interested in getting a little of that.

Nada.

The sphinx bared a mouthful of fangs, spread her claws wide and angled face-first, swooping down, clearly intending to grab a little takeout. Keeley waved a hand through the air and both of the creature's wings crumpled like a tin can under a stomping foot. Down the sphinx spiraled, crashing into the tops of trees a good distance away.

Well, hell. Keeley could use vast amounts of power to turn anything or anyone into a weapon despite the nearness of the brimstone scars. Good to know.

End this. He kicked out his leg, tripping her while she was distracted. She fell backward and would have tumbled into the pit if he hadn't grabbed her by the center of her dress and spun her. He quickly released her. She stumbled over a tree root, falling to her ass.

"Still think I'll lose?" he asked, at last allowing his grin to make an appearance.

When her head snapped up, her eyes—those eyes as cold as ice—narrowed to tiny slits. There was a moment of startling connection, man and woman…a moment of visceral desire before her anger took over. He reeled, even as the thunder started up again and the ground beneath him shook. It was what he'd felt just before the prison had come tumbling down. What he'd felt before the Unspoken One had exploded.

"I warned you about my temper, Torin."

"Aw. Is the little princess mad because she's getting spanked?"

The shaking intensified. It came from…her?

Because Princess *was* getting mad?

"I told you. I'm not some lowly princess!" As Keeley pushed to her feet, wind whipped up around her. One branch after another appeared, slapping at him.

What am I waiting for? Act! He could have fought through the attack and punched her in the head. Unconscious, she would be unable to defend herself, and he could do whatever he wanted with her. Like, say, tie her up and—

Not going there.

But he couldn't bring himself to hurt her physically. Which was freaking inconceivable! When he'd worked for Zeus, he'd been an equal-opportunity torturer and killer. *Nothing* had stopped him. Now *this?*

"This all you got?" he said.

The branches vanished as he and Keeley circled *each other.*

"Oh, don't worry." She scowled at him. "I've got more."

Footsteps sounded from the left *and* from the right. He didn't have to look to know the cavalry had arrived, and there was no longer any need to stall.

Keeley turned.

Cameron broke through a line of foliage at one side, and Irish and Winter through a line of foliage at the other. Keeley had focused on the duo, allowing Cameron to do what Torin had not and punch her in the side of the head. She slumped to the ground, her eyes closing. The thunder and shaking ceased.

From zero to max in a single second. That's how quickly unholy rage boiled inside Torin.

"That wasn't the plan!" Using all of his considerable strength, he slammed his gloved fist into Cameron's nose. Cartilage didn't just snap, it shattered. Blood spurted as the warrior stumbled backward. "You don't hurt her *ever.*"

Winter and Irish fronted on Torin, not daring to touch him but glaring daggers.

"What are you complaining about, Sickness?" Winter cracked her knuckles. "We're the proud new owners of a Curator. It's what we all wanted."

"That's right. What we *all* wanted. You pussed out, and I swooped in to the rescue," Cameron snarled back at Torin. "The girl was seconds away from leveling the forest, which is our only source of protection. I did what was necessary."

Reasonable—but it wasn't going to save him from Torin's wrath. As long as Keeley remained on her feet, pain-free and focused on him, the forest and everything in it could fall. And it had nothing to do with his hard-on for her. Or his need to touch her, all of her. Hard at first. Then soft. To pinch and to knead. To discover whether her skin was as cold as it appeared—or if it was white-hot. But because she deserved the right to punish Mari's killer. Or at least to try.

Torin balled his fist, his rage redoubling.

"Strike my brother again," Winter said, her quiet tone laced with menace. "See what happens."

Irish crossed his arms over his massive chest, claws glinting in the light. A silent but deadly challenge.

Anticipation. Eagerness. *Can't engage. Must protect the Red Queen.*

"The Curator is off-limits to you," he said. "To each of you."

The trio might as well have run their feet through the grass. They were *that* ready to charge him.

He spread his arms. By now they should know the drill. "What are you going to do about it, huh? Come on. Try something. Please."

He wouldn't have to worry about these three becoming carriers. He would touch them, yes, and they would sicken. But afterward, before they could ever come into contact with an innocent, he would kill them.

"You don't want me as your enemy," Cameron said, spitting at his feet.

"I see you haven't gotten the memo." Torin pegged him with a hard stare. "We're *already* enemies." After what the guy had done to Keeley, that wasn't going to change. Ever.

Crackling silence.

"She's a parasite," Winter said. "She'll destroy you and everything you love."

"A chance I'm willing to take," he said, surprising even himself. *What's happening to me?*

"Mistake," Cameron said. "Big mistake."

"Won't be my first."

"Come on. Let's go." Winter pulled her brother away. "He'll see the truth soon enough."

Because she planned to *make* him see?

Irish stood there for a moment longer, rubbing his thumb across his jaw as he considered his options. Then he, too, backed away.

The three disappeared in the foliage.

They would be back, certainly. But they would just receive more of the same.

Torin crouched beside Keeley and carefully eased her to her back. A cut on her temple had left a crimson slash across her brow. The shadows cast by her lashes couldn't mask the bruise on the sweet rise of her cheek.

Should have killed Cameron while I had the chance. Torin reached out but fisted his fingers before they could brush against Keeley's delicate skin.

Wearing gloves, remember? Won't hurt her.

He snorted. The voice of temptation was always oh,

so sweet. And this time, it just happened to be right. He *could* touch her, and he could learn the contours of her exquisite face. He wouldn't hurt her. Not like this.

An ache flourished in his chest, so strong he couldn't stop his groan.

But he *shouldn't* touch her. He would only want to do it again…and again…until his already-frayed resistance unraveled the rest of the way and like an addict, he went for skin-to-skin contact.

He scanned the area. Trees all around. No real clearing to allow him to see the enemy coming. He would have to—

Keeley kicked out her leg, swiping his feet out from under him. He fell, landing with a hard thump as she rolled with her momentum and ended up in a crouch of her own, right knee and left foot on the ground. One hand braced to hold her weight while the other aimed the crossbow Irish had cut from the tail of a manticore—she must have stolen it—an arrow cocked and ready.

"WELL, WELL," KEELEY said. *I'm gloating. I shouldn't gloat.* "Our audience is gone, and any potential alliance you had with the three douchketeers has been severed. I believe I have you in what's known as a pickle."

A vein bulged in his forehead, a testament to his rising anger. "Feel free to eat my pickle, princess. Anytime."

Was that anger directed at her? Or himself?

"Was that a penis joke? And I told you. I'm *not* a lowly princess." She'd earned her title the hard way, thank you.

Suddenly, memories she'd locked inside a Time Out box fought for freedom. No! No, no, no. Not here, not now. She needed to concentrate on Torin, on their battle. But…it was too late, the tide too powerful. The past spilled forth and consumed her.

During her sixteenth summer, she attended a royal gala. Like every other girl in attendance, she spent the majority of her time drooling over the prince of the Curators. He flirted with her, even asked her to dance—which was when his father, the king, took notice of her.

Because she was an innocent of the upper class, the king was unable to have her without wedding her. Rules were rules, even for royalty. So he did it. He killed his current spouse and wed Keeley. *Despite* the fact that she refused his proposal.

But then the choice had never really been hers. What King Mandriael wanted, he received. Always. Might equaled right, and he'd been the strongest among them. Not by fate, but by force. All Curators were given a small ward at birth—except the king. That way the citizens were never stronger than their ruler.

Forcing her to say her vows had been so easy for him. A simple bolt of his power, paining her, and she'd blurted out a desperate "Yes!"

For years he'd controlled her every action, punishing her whenever she displeased him. She would have given anything to leave him, to sneak away and never return, but on the day of their wedding, a bond had formed between them. She'd hated him, but still she'd needed him.

And for all my suffering, I was not crowned queen during his rule. He'd refused. He'd also killed his heirs, including the handsome prince, so that no one would have any claim to his throne.

Against Mandriael's knowledge, Keeley had taken

measures to prevent pregnancy—her one rebellion; none of the slain children had been hers.

No, her title had come after the king stripped her nude and whipped her. In public. For daring to look him in the eye while speaking to him. Agonized and bloody, desperate, she'd cut away her ward—*just wanted a taste of power*. But an ocean of energy had filled her up and exploded from her—exploding *the king*.

Got what he deserved.

Mere hours after her coronation, however, the people she'd planned to liberate had revolted.

Queen for less than a day.

They'd ambushed her, swarming into the throne room to surround her on the royal dais. No one had carried a weapon. But then, they hadn't needed swords and daggers, not anymore. They, too, had removed their wards and their power had battered against her, a maelstrom. But hers had still been greater, so much greater, and she'd catapulted them into the air, all at once, without any real effort.

There had been whispers among the Curators, claims the king had quashed. Some were supposedly born with the ability to not only wield the energy around them but to connect with it, manipulate it, even control it and stop others from using it. Those claims—prophecies—were written in a book that had vanished decades before, either stolen or destroyed.

She'd wondered if *she* could do those things…even as her people had hurtled hate-filled obscenities and threats.

You're nothing but a whore!

You can't keep us here forever. The moment we're down, you're dead.

I will dance in your blood!

Rage had brewed inside her, at last seeping out. A violent storm had risen outside, crushing everything in its path, even the palace. The Curators remained in the air, battered by ice, water and debris. But not Keeley. She'd remained untouched, unharmed. Villagers had stopped racing for cover to stare in horror as, one by one, the entire upper class burst into grisly pieces.

She'd feared hurting others, innocents, and decided there was no other recourse but to run. The villagers followed her, determined to end her and save themselves from a similar fate.

She'd spent weeks in the jungle, hiding, on her own for the first time in her miserable existence, scavenging with no real results, doing her best to survive—failing. That's when Hades found her.

A life could change in a single heartbeat.

The entire world could change in a single heartbeat.

Hades was the dark prince she'd considered too handsome to resist, realizing too late he'd drugged her at every meal in an effort to keep her mind fogged so that her every decision could be easily manipulated. He hadn't known the drugs were unnecessary, that she'd been as starved for affection as she'd been for food.

Oh, how that galled! What easy pickings she'd been. Desperate to hold on to him and make him happy. Only to be betrayed. Blindly believing everything he said. Willing to do anything he asked.

Never again! She'd learned her lesson. Decisions should never be based on emotion. Only logic. Otherwise mistakes were made.

And I've made a huge mistake with Torin, she realized. She'd hesitated to render the deathblow simply because he had a pretty face and made her insides sing with pleasure.

"Keeley," he said, snapping his fingers in front of her face.

She blinked into focus, barking, "What?"

He smiled at her, his emerald eyes twinkling. He picked up the conversation as if it had never lagged. "Think of my pickle comment as an invitation. And you don't want to hurt my feelings by refusing, do you? I think I read somewhere that royalty is bound by stricter forms of etiquette than us regular folks."

How did he make her want to smile back at him rather than attack him? And why hadn't he disarmed her and killed her while she'd been lost in her head? "This queen *is* going to refuse, etiquette be damned. She would prefer *not* to eat a pickle that comes with a side of typhoid."

The sparkle faded, and she actually mourned its loss.

"Or does it come with a little black plague?" she forced herself to continue. "No? How about botulism? Lassa fever? Am I getting close?"

"Oh, you're getting close all right," he said. "To a smackdown you'll never forget."

"We both know the only one getting a smackdown today is you."

"Talk, talk, talk." He batted her arm out of the way, then grabbed her by the neck at the same time he hooked his leg behind her ankles, tripping her.

As she fell, she twisted to catch herself. But the next thing she knew, she was face-first in the dirt, gasping for breath, her arms locked behind her back.

A beat of stunned silence as she regained her bearings…and realized his hard body was pressed against her. She fought the decadence of the new position. No. The *humiliation* of the position.

"Would you call *this* a pickle?" he asked casually.

"I'd probably go with Mexican standoff," she managed just as casually.

"Standoff implies both parties have the other in a precarious situation. With our current position, I'm not exactly feeling threatened."

Heat radiated from him, enveloping her. And his scent…all that sandalwood and spice. All male. Her cells did that singing thing, her blood beginning to boil with desire.

I'm so sorry, Mari.

Must gain control.

"Let's see if I can do something to alter your perspective." She flashed behind him—nope. She remained in place. Why—realization crystalized suddenly. The brimstone! As long as it was embedded in his skin and he maintained a grip on her, she would be powerless against him…against everything.

Powerless…helpless. Flickers of panic, burning her chest.

Can't be helpless. Not again.

She kicked her leg, her heel slamming into his backside.

"Be still," he commanded.

Helpless…so helpless…soon imprisoned. Left in the dark, forced to eat the scourge of the earth, rotting in my own filth, dirty so dirty, hungry so hungry. Forgotten. No, no, no!

She bucked and she kicked and she flailed. Snowflakes poured from the sky, piling around them.

He tightened his hold. "Keeley. Stop."

Have to get free. Ignoring the pain in her shoulder as he further tightened his hold, she fought her way to her back. Then he released her—yes!—but only long enough to grab both of her wrists and pin them over her head.

Snowflakes in his lashes, on his skin…on hers. Cold, so very cold. Helpless.

"I don't want to hurt you." He bared his teeth, his scowl menacing…almost desperate. "Want to do things to you… Trying not to think about them… Not succeeding. Be still. Please, be still."

"Let me go." A plea formed, but she swallowed it back. She'd once begged Hades for her freedom, and he'd laughed at her. She wouldn't give Torin the same opportunity. "Let me go!"

"Not until we've come to some sort of arrangement."

She continued to struggle, gained no new ground. *So helpless!*

She couldn't breathe, had to breathe. She wiggled her hips, bucked some more. When she attempted to wedge one of her legs between them and place her bare foot against his bare chest, he wrenched away just before contact.

Finally free.

She lay on the hard ground, sucking in precious air. "Th-thank you."

He moved over her again, but this time he didn't hold her down. Didn't touch her in any way, so she didn't fight him. He simply shielded her from the onslaught of snow, his features dark with concern.

"Are you okay?" he asked.

Strange question, coming from him.

Her heartbeat slowed, though her limbs grew heavier

with every second that passed. "I don't know," she answered honestly.

Torin looked up at the sky, then down at her. The sky, her. He nodded, as if he'd just unraveled a mystery, and made to move away from her.

"Don't," she said, surprising herself. *I want him closer?* "I...need your warmth." Truth. In part. She craved the connection to another living creature...to him. It had been so long.

He remained in place. His gaze locked with hers, and it was both torturous and rapturous. Without the panic, her desire for him—for sensation—had no filter, becoming a driving force she couldn't deny.

Don't do this.

Must. "Is the woman you've been staying with your lover?" she asked.

He blinked down at her. "Woman? Oh. You mean Winter. No."

I am...relieved?

Maybe. His condition was a hard sell for any female, true, but Keeley wasn't any female. She could have him.

But why would I want him? I hate him. Even still the urge to reach up and trace her fingertips along the ridges of his chest bombarded her...so she did it, she reached. *I'm far too strong to sicken.*

She paused midway to gauge his reaction.

His jaw clenched tightly. "Don't," he croaked, but he remained in place, as if he wanted her to do it—*needed* her to. "I mean it. Don't."

"You'll thank me." Truly, his demon would be no match for her. Who would? *In a class by myself.*

She reached the rest of the way and flattened her palm just over his heart. Skin-to-skin. He flinched but didn't pull away. Hissed, but also moaned. As if the sudden connection between them was equal parts pain and bliss. Hell and heaven.

"Keeley." A rasp of demand…and necessity.

Asking me for more. Has to be.

He was hot enough to burn, soft as silk yet hard as steel, and *nothing* had ever felt this good. *A simple touch has felled me.*

"You are…" *Everything I've ever wanted or needed or hoped would be possible.* She traced her fingertips along his collarbone, up his neck…to his lips. They parted and she took advantage, pressing in to feel the moist heat inside his mouth.

He sucked, hard, and she moaned. The sound jolted him out of whatever magical haze had been woven. He reared back, horror radiating from him. The same kind of horror the villagers had once cast at her.

"Torin?" *Give me more.*

"Keeley." He shook his head, rubbed his chest, as if he could still feel her. "You shouldn't have touched me. I shouldn't have let you. Even if you live through the infection, which you probably won't, you'll be immune to it but still able to spread it. The very reason I'll have to kill you, despite your recovery."

CHAPTER SIX

MY FAULT.

The words echoed in Torin's mind as he built a fire, and it was like taking fists to the chest. Keeley sat on the ground, watching his every move. He knew, because he could feel the hot ping of her gaze drilling holes in his back. Since "the Incident," she hadn't attempted to fight him. She'd gone still, quiet.

Soon she would sicken. Just like all the others. And he would curse his very existence.

He sought a sense of numbness as he dug through the pack he'd hidden behind a tree, withdrawing every bit of leftover medicine. A few antibiotics, fewer antivirals. Cough suppressant, antihistamines, decongestants. Painkillers. Even vitamin strips that would dissolve on the tongue.

He tossed the antibiotics and strips at her, plus a canteen of water. "Take two of the pills. Suck on one of the strips. They'll help stave off the infection."

In a perfect world, that would be good enough. But their world wasn't even close to perfect.

No response from her.

If he had to force her to—

He heard a rustle of clothing, a gulp of water being swallowed.

Good girl. He wasn't sure how he would have reacted

to forcing her…to putting his hands on her again. *There is no woman softer.*

Guilt pricked at him, as determined to ruin him as Disease. It was never far from the surface, always looking for a moment to spew its poison. Next would come sorrow…rage. At Keeley. At himself. Mostly himself. He'd wanted her touch more than he'd ever wanted anything.

While Disaster had screamed at him to get as far away from her as possible, he'd pretty much raced to the razor's edge of temptation, telling himself Keeley was so powerful she would be immune. That he could finally have everything he'd ever secretly craved.

But it was a lie. It was always a lie.

Why had he encouraged a battle with her? Why had he sought to comfort her after her panic? The only possible outcome had happened. What a shocker.

Now Keeley would pay the ultimate price for his weakness, and he would be responsible for either killing one of the only remaining Curators or creating another carrier. And while in that perfect world he wished he lived in a female carrier would mean he'd finally have someone to touch and to hold and to kiss and to please, without any further consequences, that wasn't how it worked. If Torin touched her a second time, he would pass on a *different* illness.

The demon didn't just specialize in one ailment, but countless.

Disease often changed strains with the times. The black death of the thirteen hundreds had given way to the cholera pandemic of the eighteen hundreds. Made it harder for the world to combat the evil, he supposed. For *Torin* to combat it.

"Has anyone ever *not* gotten sick after tangling with you?" Keeley asked.

The hope in her voice…he crumbled, utterly agonized. "No."

"But I'm, like, super powerful."

She wasn't just super powerful; she was the most powerful person he'd ever come across. "Sickness feeds on certain types of power. How else do you think it grows?"

She nibbled on her bottom lip, fiddled with the bottle of pills. "I feel fine."

"That won't last."

Shoulders wilting, she said, "How long do your victims usually survive?"

"About a week. Rarely any longer." He settled on the other side of the fire. *Not sure I can hold myself together.* "How did you get an actual human body without a human in it?" he asked, hoping for a distraction. "Curators were—are—spirits."

A flare of ire in her expression, the world around them trembling. "Someone gave it to me. Why?"

He ignored her question. "Who gave it? And how?"

"Doesn't matter." Wistful, she added, "I used to be able to commune with animals, you know."

Not actually surprising. So had every other fairy-tale princess. "I'm sure you and your animal friends had some real stimulating conversations."

"Yes." She sighed. "The body changed everything."

"You can't leave it behind?" Something that might have saved her.

"Hardly. I'm fused to it." Her gaze sharpened on him. "Why are you still here? Why aren't you abandoning me to my hideous fate?"

He chose levity over brevity. "There's no way I'd abandon you when we're about to play my favorite game. Incompetent Doctor and Uncooperative Patient." But he failed to achieve the desired results.

She frowned at him. "So…you're going to help me? Again?"

"I'm going to try." But would it be enough? It hadn't been with Mari.

He gnashed his molars. Human versus supervillain. Big difference. This was a whole new ball game.

Look at me. Hoping for the best-case scenario even though I know better.

"Why?" she asked. "I'll only repay you with pain and agony, and eventually death."

She'd stated the words so simply, as if they were merely discussing her toenails—which glinted like diamonds. He almost smiled. Almost.

"I understand your reasons for wanting to harm me. Your beef against me is legit, and you'll do whatever is necessary to make things right. Well, as right as they can be, considering the depth of my crimes. But I'm not going to leave you out here to suffer—" to die "—alone."

He experienced a keen sense of loss he didn't quite understand. At the thought of her death? Why? He barely knew her. She wasn't a friend. He should feel the guilt, yes, but nothing more.

"But why?" she insisted. "You warned me. I even chose to suffer this way. Remember?"

She claimed to value truth, so that's what he gave her: the truth as he knew it. "I'm sorry Mari's dead. I'm sorry I touched her. Sorry she sickened and died such a terrible death. I'm sorry you lost a dear friend. Sorry I wasn't strong enough to walk away from her…or you."

The sting in his chest proved far more lethal than a blade or claws. "Especially when I knew nothing good would ever come of it. I'm so sorry for everything, and yet there's nothing I can do to change anything. The past is the past. Over, done. Like you, I can only plow ahead and do my best to make things right."

She turned her head away. To hide tears?

The sting inside him sharpened. But he welcomed the pain, deserved it. "Don't cry. Please, don't cry."

"Never!" she snarled, her hackles raised.

Better.

She inhaled with great force, then exhaled with greater force. "Perhaps I need to walk away from you and go after Cronus. I'll have time to think." She dragged her finger through the dirt, creating a symbol he didn't recognize. "I heard him bargain with Mari. *After* he attempted to bargain with me. He knew she would die, and despite my protests and willingness to change places with her, he let her go to you anyway. He must be punished."

"Cronus is dead." And the world was far better for it. "He was decapitated."

"Who would dare deny me my vengeance?" she gritted, her shock surprisingly adorable.

"It wasn't intentional. My friend took him out on the field of battle. She's now leading the Titans."

Blink, blink. "A woman?"

He nodded. "The mate of a Lord of the Underworld."

"And the Titans haven't refused to serve her?"

"No. Why would they?"

Awe in her eyes. Envy. "Because...just because!"

There was a story there. Hell, there were probably a lot of stories, and he would have liked to hear each one. "What of your people?" he asked. "Any others out there?"

"As far as I know, I'm the only pure breed left, the remaining Curators having mated with fallen angels, thinking it would make them stronger. But all they managed to do was dilute their bloodline and die out."

An honest answer, though it was offered with zero hint about her emotions. Did she miss the others? Mourn their loss?

And another question: Why did he wish he could hug her?

Dude. Hugging could lead to kissing and kissing to sex. Wasn't like it was rocket science.

He wouldn't be the oldest virgin in history anymore. Finally he would know the feel of a woman's inner walls. The hot clench. The wet clasp he doubted his own hand had ever quite been able to replicate.

He gripped the tree root at his side in a bid to hold himself away from her—*can't do it, can't take her*. Even though he still tingled where she'd touched him…

Would giving in to his attraction to Keeley really be so terrible? Especially now? The worst of the damage was already done. She would die anyway, and—

Stop!

He couldn't risk giving her two diseases at once. There'd be zero chance of survival. If there was any chance at all.

"Why didn't *you* mate with a fallen angel?" he asked.

"I already had a fiancé, and by the time we split, the truth had been realized. The fallen angels were poison to the Curators, spreading their curse of darkness. Oh, and I was locked away."

Something hot and dark shot through him. "You were engaged?"

That's *what I focus on?*

"Yes," she said. "Why?" She threw a twig at him. "Is it some big surprise that someone once found me so appealing he wanted to keep me forever?"

"Sheath the claws, wildcat. I meant no offense." He couldn't call that hot and dark thing burning inside him jealousy. There was no reason for him to be jealous. He'd call it…indigestion. Because that's what it was.

What kind of man had won her heart? The kind who had fawned over her, surely. As soft and delicate as she appeared, Torin could well imagine her as some whipped sap's favorite sexual trinket, to be taken out and played with whenever the mood struck. And it had probably struck often.

His indigestion grew teeth and gnawed at his organs. "Where's the guy now?"

"Don't know. Probably somewhere he can behead puppies and gut kittens without anyone complaining."

The relationship had ended poorly. Got it.

"Look," she said, and sighed. "I appreciate the conversation. I really do. I'm not ever going to be your biggest fan, but I'm willing to admit you're not the hellhound I thought you were. Which is why I still think it'll be better if we part ways and resume our war at a later date."

"Stay. Let me take care of you."

"I'm not sick."

"We've covered this. You will be."

"No. I'm telling you, I'm too powerful. You've never met anyone like me, so you can't know how I'll react to—" A gut-wrenching cough interrupted her denial.

She hunched over, the force of it too great for her body, and covered her mouth.

Minutes passed before she quieted. She held out her trembling hands. Spots of crimson were smeared over her palms.

Snow began to fall once again, and this time, bright flashes of lightning accompanied it, streaking the sky. He'd realized the weather responded to her moods and figured this must be a sign of fear and pain.

She met his gaze, shook her head. "No. No."

Yes. "You're infected."

In less than an hour, she was hacking up rivers of blood.

In less than two, she was ravaged by fever.

She tried to tell him something, saying things like "rain," "drown" and "minions," but the meaning was lost on Torin. The only thing he understood was "don't… kill."

He'd told her he would kill her if she became a carrier. And he should; it would be best. For her, for the world.

Then why try to save her?

Because he couldn't shake the urge to hug her. Because he owed her.

Because he couldn't have her, ever, if she died.

He punched the ground, flinging dirt. They would deal with the carrier thing if and when it became necessary.

As gently as possible, he plied her with medicine. He used some of the canteen water to keep her brow cool and poured the rest down her throat. But by the middle of the next day, the water was gone and she needed more. Her cough worsened, and her fever intensified, growing dangerously high. The woman who'd been powerful enough to topple a prison for immortals weakened until she could no longer even writhe in pain, her chest barely rising and falling, her breaths wheezing…sometimes even rattling.

The death rattle. He knew it well.

But the most telling sign of impending doom? About twenty feet around her, the grass had withered. Nearby trees had slumped over and dried up, leaving nothing but brittle leaves and blackened bark.

At least the snow had stopped. Small consolation.

"Just hold on, princess," he said, knowing she couldn't hear him but compelled to speak anyway. He picked her up, careful to ensure their clothes remained a constant barrier.

But even without skin-to-skin contact, she managed to deluge him with endorphins, wave after wave of the most intense bliss he'd ever known saturating him. He hardened. He throbbed.

Need her hands on me again.

Enough! He carried her through the forest, heading for the clearing he'd shared with the Terrible Trio. They would fight him. They wouldn't understand why he was helping a woman so determined to kill him. He barely understood it himself. But they weren't there, and it looked as if they'd been gone for a while, saving him the hassle of combat.

Torin eased Keeley onto the ledge of the spring. He dipped a rag into the frigid water before draping the material over her sweat-beaded brow. Her teeth chattered, and every few seconds she convulsed, but the fever never abated.

He picked her up and eased her into the center of the pool, dress and all. The liquid rippled and lapped all the way to her chin…but the heat she projected actually warmed the water. Frustration and fear ate at him.

"Hades," she mumbled, her voice little more than a broken rasp. "Mine…"

A terrible stillness came over him. Hades, the former ruler of the underworld? A male Torin wouldn't trust with a stick of gum, much less a life? Pure evil? The father of William the Ever Randy and Lucifer, king of the demons?

Although, to be fair, Hades wasn't William and Lucifer's natural father. He'd claimed them through some sort of shady, supernatural adoption. But to be even fairer, that kind of made him worse.

Keeley called for *that* guy? Seriously?

"Don't," she begged. "Please, don't do this."

Hades had hurt her? No big surprise, and yet Torin cracked his knuckles. *Whatever was done to her will be revisited on the male a hundredfold.*

"Shh." In an effort to calm her, Torin smoothed a gloved hand along the curve of her jaw. *This isn't for me—it's for her.*

Lying to myself now?

He marveled at the delicacy of her bones and had to fight against a thousand more waves of bliss, each headier than the last. "I'm here. Torin's here. Nothing bad is going to happen to you, princess. I won't let it."

"I love you. You love me. Our wedding…please."

He stiffened, several facts becoming crystal clear. Hades was the fiancé she'd mentioned. She'd actually planned a *future* with the guy. Had *begged* for it.

Jealousy. Yes, he felt it. Jealousy, and not indigestion. He could deny the truth no longer. However, he would not tolerate such an emotion. Keeley wasn't his. She didn't belong to him, and never would. Because even if they worked out their problems—not likely—he would never be able to satisfy her. What he had to offer would never be enough.

He'd learned that the hard way.

To watch discontent settle in her eyes? He would rather die.

Experienced enough humiliation on that front.

"Helpless," she whispered. "So helpless. Trapped."

"Shh," he said again. "I've got you. I'm not going anywhere."

"Torin?" Her head tipped toward him. Her arms floated along the surface of the water, brushing against the curling ends of her hair. Wet, the strands appeared honey-brown rather than blue.

Will look so pretty wrapped around my fist. I'll angle her just right, take her mouth with a skill she's never before encountered and—

Nothing.

He pushed out a ragged breath, only then realizing the water had cooled significantly.

Had her fever broken at last?

He lifted her out of the spring and eased her onto a patch of grass, tense with dread as he waited for the blades to wither. When one minute ticked into another and they remained lush and green, he relaxed.

His gaze slid over her. The color of her skin had vastly improved, the fever flush of red gone. But her dress was plastered to her skin, outlining every magnificent curve.

Tensing all over again...have to look away. But no matter how diligently he tried, his gaze remained glued to her. Her breasts were luscious, in need of kneading. Her nipples were beaded, practically begging to be sucked. Her stomach was concave, allowing water to settle inside her navel.

Water he could lick away.

Stop this. Wrong on every level.

Her legs were long and lithe, the perfect length to wrap around his waist. Or his shoulders. She had no scars or tattoos, her skin like mile after mile of cobalt silk.

The promise of sex *seethed* from her.

His already frayed control threatened to snap.

No! He scrubbed a hand down his face, at last breaking the spell she'd somehow woven. *Yeah. Blame her. Idiot!* What the hell was wrong with him? She was sick, possibly dying, and he was scheming on her?

I suck.

Get her well. Then get rid of her. Afterward he could continue his search to find Cameo and Viola with a clear conscience.

Like the Terrible Trio, Viola had been incarcerated in Tartarus at the wrong time and had received one of the leftover demons. He shuddered. She'd gotten Narcissism. The worst of the worst. Viola was a flat-out nightmare to be around, but she was also part of his family.

A man protected his family.

Mari had been Keeley's only family, he thought. *And I took her away.*

He owed the Curator more than vengeance. He owed her another family. But there was no way he could introduce a carrier to innocents. It would be like shooting fish in a barrel with a rocket-propelled grenade.

His friends, on the other hand... They knew how to deal with carriers. They'd been dealing with Torin for centuries, and not one of them had ever gotten sick.

They were experts at evading him. Maybe *they* could be Keeley's family—he wouldn't have to kill her.

The idea…did not repel him.

She threatened their safety.

Yes, but Torin knew she wouldn't hurt them. He'd seen the core of honor underneath her rage.

She might even find a measure of happiness with the group. Two of his friends were dating Harpies, a race of females known for causing massive bloodshed…and for making grown men pee their pants in fear. That had to be dream best-friend material for Keys. And, not that it mattered, none of the males would make a play for her; everyone was taken.

Well, except for William the Ever Randy, who lived with them, but the guy had been watching his ward, Gilly, a lot more intently lately. Girl was a human and due to turn eighteen very, very soon.

Torin wasn't sure what would happen between the two the day of her birthday—he just knew something *would* happen.

Not important. Keeley would probably protest the move to Budapest. Probably? Ha! But he would have to find a way to convince her to do it. Because there was no better solution…and no other way he could keep her.

CHAPTER SEVEN

CAMEO, THE KEEPER of Misery, jimmied the lock on the back of an old ice cream truck. Rusty hinges creaked as the door swung open. She jumped inside the vehicle and dug through the freezer on each side until all of her fingers were numb from cold. Surely she would find what she was looking for— Curses!

Unleashing the snarl her male friends had once dubbed "Blue—she must be PMSing—Steel," Cameo punched her fist through the back of the driver's seat. If she didn't find chocolate soon, she was going to commit cold-blooded murder. Any kind of chocolate. Fudge pop. Ice cream sandwich. Neapolitan.

And she already had a target in mind.

"Are you going to cry?" the target in question asked. "I bet you're going to cry."

He stood in the open doorway, peering inside the truck, watching her with his patented smirk. His name was Lazarus, and they'd been partners for... She wasn't sure how long. Time had ceased to exist.

In a bid to retrieve her...friend? Ugh. No. Acquaintance? Better. In a bid to retrieve her acquaintance Viola, Cameo had touched the Paring Rod, an ancient artifact created by the Titans; it was some kind of bridge between worlds, supposed to lead the way to Pandora's box.

Can't wait to smash that box into a thousand pieces! It was simply too dangerous.

One second she'd had her hand on the Rod, the next she'd been in another dimension...realm...whatever!

Lazarus had touched the Rod, too, only he'd done it months before. He'd found a way to glom on to her at just the right moment and come out the other side with her. She wasn't sure how or why he'd done it. She'd asked him, but he wasn't one to hand out answers. Or understanding. Or compassion.

What she did know? They'd found a doorway to another realm and they'd walked through it. From there, they'd found yet *another* doorway, another realm. None of which she'd been familiar with. Some areas were primitive. Some were well populated and modern. All were dangerous.

"Have you considered Zoloft?" Lazarus asked. "It's supposed to help with bouts of crying. Or so I've heard. It might help with your voice, too. Have I mentioned your voice is tragic?"

About a thousand times.

She closed the distance between them. He was a beautiful man. One of the most beautiful ever created; just ask him. But he was intense. And savage, and when he killed, he *killed*. After he played a bit. Not even her demon-possessed friends fought as brutally or played so violently, and they had been known to reach into an enemy's mouth and rip out the spinal cord.

Standing inside the vehicle as she was—while his feet were planted firmly on the ground—she should have been the taller of the two. She wasn't. And it irritated her. She was five seven, not short by any means, but she was a tiny fluff of nothing when compared to Lazarus.

"Have you considered the fact that I have daggers and I'm not afraid to use them?" she asked.

He cringed, inky hair falling over his forehead. "Why use daggers? Your voice is weapon enough."

She *knew* every word she spoke was layered with sorrow, dipped in regret and rolled in sadness, thank you. "If my voice makes you want to kill yourself and saves me the trouble of rendering the final blow...well, why don't I spend the next few hours telling you all about my life?"

His lips quirked at the corners. He took her by the waist and swung her around, setting her on the ground. His hands stayed put, remaining on her, and his dark eyes gleamed. "Why would I kill myself? Being around you is torture, yes, but it's also highly entertaining."

Most men were intimidated by her. Her friends were protective of her and did everything in their power to spare her feelings. This guy provoked her at every turn, unafraid of the consequences.

She slapped his hands away, but he held on to her for several seconds more, just to annoy her, she would bet.

But...this. This was the reason she would not allow herself to be attracted to him—no matter how handsome he was. Personality mattered, and his sucked.

So does mine. Doesn't that mean we're perfect for each other?

No!

"Let me go," she demanded.

"Not yet."

A minute passed. Two. She could have fought him, but why waste the strength...especially since she kind of enjoyed where she was?

He released her only when he decided he was good and ready.

She stalked away from him. Today she found herself in a land very much like the world she was used to. Only, there were no people. Cars were crashed and abandoned. Roads were deserted. Trees and foliage were overgrown. Buildings were crumbled.

The bones of the dead were *everywhere.* But power lines still worked and batteries hadn't run down. It was weird.

"Have you ever had a boyfriend?" Lazarus asked, keeping pace behind her.

"I'm thousands of years old. What do you think?"

"I think you're a spinster virgin starving for a little man-meat."

She took a deep breath...held it...held it...slowly released it. *I'm a calm, rational woman.* "I've had several boyfriends, and I'm no virgin. And if you call me a slut, I will cut out your tongue."

"No, you won't. You want my tongue where it is. Trust me. But I'm curious. How many boyfriends?"

"None of your business."

"Too many to count. Noted. What are you like in bed?"

"You will never know."

"Please. I can guess. Every time a guy has gotten inside you, you've moaned, but not in pleasure. You were faking it, because you were miserable. He immediately lost his erection and took off, spouting some nonsense about having somewhere else to be. You were left unsatisfied, and he never spoke to you again."

She would have been infuriated...if he hadn't been right. For the most part.

She'd tried relationships, but only once out of love. With a deaf human her enemies had later killed. Twice, out of mutual respect and admiration. With possessed immortal warriors just like her. Countless times, out of desperation. With anyone who showed her the slightest bit of interest and seemed capable of disregarding her flaws.

"I've been satisfied in bed," she said, "and so has my man."

"Man, singular. Interesting."

How is he running so many circles around me? "I've been with others."

"Yes, but you mentioned nothing about achieving satisfaction with them."

And she couldn't, without lying.

"Shut up," she snapped.

"Did I hit a nerve, sunshine?"

Only the rawest one she possessed.

She missed Alexander, her human, every day of her life. *Despite* what he'd done to her at the end of their relationship.

He'd been cast out of his home at the age of eight, when he'd gotten sick and lost his hearing. Somehow, though, he'd survived the slums of ancient Greece to become a well-respected blacksmith, growing into a handsome, strong and honorable man.

He'd been her one shot at happiness.

Can't think about him. It would only make her demon stronger, feeding his need for misery.

"Just…shut up," she said. But she knew Lazarus wouldn't. He never did. He would press and prod until she erupted, and then he would sit back and laugh as she struggled to get control of her emotions. He loved to laugh. And she wanted so badly to join him. It looked fun. But she was in no mood to be his entertainment. "What of you and your wife, huh? Did you pleasure her?"

He sucked in a breath. "Don't call her that."

Finally. She'd hit a nerve, too. "Why not? That's what Juliette is, right?"

"She's an enemy. You'll learn the difference when next I find her."

Juliette was a Harpy, and Harpies mated for life. The girl had taken one look at Lazarus and decided he was the one for her. Her consort; she had gone to great lengths to keep him at her side, somehow enslaving the powerful warrior. To escape, Lazarus had allowed Cameo's friend Strider, the keeper of Defeat, to behead him, and the Paring Rod to suck his spirit and body inside... where the two parts had somehow been able to reunite and heal.

She didn't understand it, but there it was.

Why did I have to stumble upon him and not Viola? Stupid Rod.

"My friends will find me, you know." Torin had watched her vanish. He was looking for her, she knew he was, and he would never give up. He loved her.

As a friend. Maybe...as a girlfriend.

Torin was one of the only two immortals Cameo had messed around with. Working around the no-touching thing had been difficult, but they'd done it, pleasuring themselves in front of each other. It had been fun, exciting...at first. But they'd both held a part of themselves back, preventing them from moving to another, deeper level. At the time, she hadn't known why. Looking back, she could clearly see fear was the culprit.

He'd expected her to grow tired of their arrangement, desire something better and leave him.

She'd expected him to develop a distaste for her voice, desire something better and leave her.

"At this point in our journey, *I'm* your only friend," Lazarus said, a bead of anger in his voice. "You won't survive without me."

"Actually, I might know true happiness for the first time in my life without you."

He flattened his hands over his heart. "Ouch. It's like you've stabbed me with one of those daggers you're always bragging about."

I wish.

"But just to be clear," he added, "you're telling me you've never known true happiness, even when your man was giving you all that amazing pleasure?"

Could she hide nothing from him? "Why are you so interested in my sex life?"

"Don't get your hopes up, sunshine. I haven't reached a firm conclusion yet, but I'm considering giving you a go."

Incredulous, she stopped to stare up at him. "Giving me a go?"

His dark eyes sparkled with merriment. "Yes, and you're welcome. But like I said, don't get your hopes up. I'm currently leaning toward the no box."

She pressed her tongue into the roof of her mouth. "Let me save you the trouble of taxing your poor abused brain with the pros and cons. You are, apparently, the last man on earth and I still don't want you. I would rather mate with a porcupine."

"So you're into pain? Got it."

Gah! She left him in the dust.

He hurried after her, calling, "Any other delightful surprises I should know about? Because this little revelation has put you closer to the yes box."

She flipped him off without looking at him.

"An affinity for pain *and* she likes to give the cold-shoulder treatment. It's like I've won the lottery," he said. "I won't ever have to worry about a clinger situation. All I'll have to do is prick your temper and you'll leave on your own."

Anger filled her and—

She stopped, utterly shocked. That's right. Anger filled her. *Filled her.* Leaving no room for sadness.

It was the law of displacement in action. If you were full of one thing, there was no room for anything else. Had that been his plan all along?

No, no. Of course not. He would have had to care about her feelings.

But it was the first time in a very long time she'd felt no hint of depression or anguish or distress or a thousand other variations of Misery. She closed her eyes and savored, breathing in air that suddenly smelled fresher and basking in the warmth of a sun that no longer seemed to burn too hot.

But all too soon, a plug was pulled and the anger drained. The sadness returned. Always, it returned.

Never had she been able to feel any sort of enjoyment…or amusement…or happiness for more than a few seconds. Mostly she was bombarded with little irritants throughout any given day. A sound that was too loud, too constant. A temperature that wasn't quite right. An ache in her chest that wouldn't go away. Each worked together to build into something truly terrible: a misery that couldn't be fought.

It was a truly awful existence.

Why don't you just give up?

The demon's words, not her own. *Screw you.*

She wouldn't give the bastard the pleasure.

Lazarus didn't say a word as she pushed back into gear, and that saved his life.

They came to an abandoned grocery store that hadn't yet toppled. Dust covered the cracked glass door. She palmed one of her weapons and brushed away the dust to peer inside. No lights. Only darkness. But no shadows were moving, and she made her way inside.

"I wonder if the pharmacy is stocked," Lazarus said.

"Going to get high?"

"Going to grab you some of that Zoloft we talked about."

Hate him.

She grabbed one of the carts and stalked down the aisles, forgoing the cans of fruit and bottles of water even though she hadn't eaten in days and her stomach was grumbling with hunger. She went right to the refrigerator section, and after draining two cans of beer, threw a couple of six-packs in the cart. Then she went to the candy aisle.

Gummy bears. Red Hots. SweetTarts. Cartons of sour gumballs. But no chocolate.

Why me?

Lazarus threw in a jar of peanuts, a plastic gun and a pair of fake handcuffs.

"Seriously?" she said.

"What? I like to play cops and robbers."

"I am *not* playing cops and robbers with you."

"Like it's really a game I'd play with you."

I'm a calm, rational woman—her new mantra. "I don't see anyone else around. Do you?"

"Of course I do."

She stiffened. "What's that supposed to mean?"

He sighed as though dejected. "I thought you were freakishly brave, unconcerned by what was happening around us, but it turns out you're just blind. It's almost heartbreaking." He placed a hand over his heart. "I hate to break it to you, sunshine, but your cool points just took a nosedive."

"Tell me!" she insisted. The last time he'd told her she wasn't really looking at what was taking place around them, there'd been a bona fide behemoth in their vicinity.

"I'll do you one better. I'll show you." Suddenly serious, Lazarus bent down, putting them nose-to-nose, and peered into her eyes. "I can see spirits and I can share the ability for a short time by linking my mind to yours. You're welcome."

She tried to look away—he was too intense, too mesmerizing, and every instinct she possessed screamed that if she wasn't careful, she would completely lose herself and never be found. But he gripped her by the chin and held her in place, forcing the connection to remain.

Little flames leaped to life in those black, bottomless orbs of his. Crackling, smoking. Literally smoking. Tendrils wafted from him and saturated the air between them. Every time she breathed, she caught the scent of peat and ash. Her mind fogged, and her thoughts derailed. He became all that she saw, all that she knew.

All that she wanted.

"What are you…doing… Stop," she said, and thought she might be swaying on her feet.

He released her, breaking the spell. She blinked rapidly, and shook her head. The fog cleared. The intoxicating scent faded.

"Look," he said, his tone grim.

"Don't ever do—" What the hell? What were those things?

They. Were. *Everywhere.* Alligator bodies, human heads—human *zombie* heads. They were climbing the shelves, inching across the floor, and each one was staring at her as if she'd make a delicious all-you-can-eat buffet.

"Did you know that nearly two hundred thousand people die a day?" she said, voice strangely devoid of emotion. "In our world, I mean. Our other world."

"And since there are only the two of us left in this one, we're definitely next. Is that what you're trying to say?"

She palmed both of her daggers. "No. I'm saying I'm going to meet today's quota by killing those things."

BADEN, THE FORMER keeper of Distrust, stood in the center of a circle of boulders. A jacked-up version of Stonehenge. Between each of the boulders was a wall of fog, and playing over the different areas of fog were movie-like scenes. Scenes from the lives of his friends.

Cameo needed his help. She couldn't see past her companion's rugged exterior, didn't know he was more of a monster than the ones surrounding her. And Baden couldn't tell her. He was trapped here.

Life pretty much sucked because he wasn't just trapped, he was trapped with Cronus, the former keeper of Greed, and Rhea, the former keeper of Strife, both displaced royalty on the lookout for a humble servant. *Not gonna find one here.* And then there was Pandora.

She'd never been a demon-keeper, lucky girl, but she'd always been a pain.

All four of them had been beheaded in their natural life, and all four of their spirits had left their mutilated bodies and floated here, unable to stop the journey—now, unable to leave…whatever this was.

"Why do you torture yourself this way?"

The soft, sweet voice came from behind him. The cadence was a deception. One he knew well. He turned and watched as Pandora stepped through the fog. She was six feet of bad attitude with a shoulder-length crop of hair so black it gleamed blue. Her features were sharp yet pretty, the rest of her almost as muscled as him. Altogether she was a nice package—if you liked your women with hearts of ice.

He preferred a little heat in his bed, thanks.

Since moment one of his arrival, they'd been at war, striking at each other in every way imaginable. But the moment Cronus and Rhea had arrived, they'd united, striking at the royals.

"Torin is with the Red Queen," he said. "And she has—"

"What! The Red Queen? Let me see." Pandora moved to the section of fog displaying Torin's interactions with the legendary female whose immense power had somehow created the mystery of the Bermuda Triangle, whose temper had ushered in the Ice Age. A woman who had set up a network of spies throughout almost every realm in existence, inside every royal house, within every race of immortals and humans alike. There was very little she didn't know.

Very little she couldn't do.

If two clans were fighting and she picked a side, the opposers immediately raised the white flag of surrender.

For a dead man like Baden, she was a pot of gold.

She and Torin were in the Realm of Wailing Tears where they were playing Dr. Ken and Homicidal Maniac Barbie. Baden had never seen Torin so determined to heal anyone.

Trying to get laid despite the consequences?

Can't blame him. Though, if Baden had his pick of beauties, he'd go with someone a little less...murderous. He'd been stuck with a dark-haired viper for thousands of years. "Sweet" would be a nice change.

Anyway. Baden knew how badly Torin wanted to retrieve Cameo and Viola and return to his friends.

"Do you think the Red Queen can save us?" Pandora asked, all but rubbing her hands together.

"If she survives the disease...and if Torin learns the magnitude of her particular skill set... Yes. He will ensure she launches a successful search and rescue."

First and foremost, Keeley would be able to procure a pair of serpentine wreaths from Hades, who had wheeled, dealed and killed to acquire every set ever forged. The mystical relics could be worn by humans or immortals and would make every spirit tangible to them. But more important, the relics could be worn by a spirit like Baden, making *him* tangible to everyone and everything.

I can reclaim everything I've lost.

"But, Pandy," he added with a smile. "We both know she'll come for me and me alone. You'll be left behind— unless I decide to take you with me. Think about that the next time you want to strike at me."

CHAPTER EIGHT

I HAVE ANOTHER choice to make, don't I?

For three days Torin had taken better care of Keeley than her neglectful parents, sadistic husband and deceitful lover ever had. Combined! He'd catered to her every need, provided her with food and water, protected her from scavenging animals, and cleaned her brow when perspiration dared bead atop it. He'd even carved an entire zoo of miniature animals out of planks of wood, each a treasure trove of exquisite detail.

He'd thrust the pieces at her with a grumbled "Here," as if he was unsure how she would receive the gifts.

Mine! I'll never share!

Now she owed him death *and* she owed him life. And she had no idea what to do about it.

Had he taken such great care with Mari, too?

Keeley remembered the way he'd cried, "Don't die. Don't you dare die." And, "Come on, Mari. Stay with me."

He *had* taken care of Mari, she realized. In her grief she had completely overlooked his pain.

Back in prison he must have removed his heart as a means of survival because it was broken and he was no longer able to deal.

Stomach cramp.

Again, she heard Mari's counsel in her mind. *Forgive him. Clear his ledger. It's the right thing to do.*

She tried to think up a protest, but her worldview was too busy shifting. Torin had made a mistake. One he regretted. He was hurting—would probably hurt for the rest of his life. She didn't need to do anything more, did she?

"Torin," she said.

He was busy preparing her next meal, his back to her. His shoulders expanded, as if the muscles had just knotted with tension. "Yes, Keys?"

"Am I completely out of the danger zone?" Never having experienced so much as a case of the sniffles, she'd been ill prepared for round one with Torin's demon. The sensation of ingesting acid repeatedly? Check. The feeling of being burned alive? Check. The surety that every bone in her body had been broken and the cracks had leaked ice…more fire…ice again? Check, check, and mate.

But at least I'm alive.

Were all sicknesses so vile?

"You might wish otherwise," he said. "You're a carrier, but yes. You'll survive."

"Good." Was it, though? Being a carrier meant *she* could now make people sick.

She would have to abandon her secret desires and greatest dreams: conquering a small kingdom of immortals, ruling as their benevolent queen and then marrying a nice man who would never prick her temper, finally creating a family of her own.

For the first time, Keeley would have been adored and pampered.

She swallowed the lump in her throat. "I don't feel like a carrier."

"What you feel doesn't matter. Remember? You can't afford to slip up."

"Like you did?"

"Exactly," he croaked.

She offered a trembling, "Just wait. I'll prove you wrong."

"Please don't. People will die."

"They won't."

He ignored her, saying, "The first thing we need to do is find you a pair of gloves."

No. No! The ground gave a little shake. "I have enough handicaps. I won't tolerate another one."

"I'm sorry, princess, but we can't undo what's been done."

But they *could* find a cure. Surely. *I wasn't given so much power simply to fall prey to a measly disease.* "You said you'd kill me if I ended up being a carrier. Why haven't you tried?"

"Changed my mind."

"Why?"

The ensuing silence dripped with stubbornness.

Fine. She switched directions. "Can I make *you* sick?" Could she touch him without consequences?

Did she *want* to touch him again?

She remembered the way he'd shielded her during the fight with the Unspoken One, how his hardness had pressed against her softness. How luscious it had felt to be desired by the fiercest of warriors.

How his touch had been more wonderful than his sickness had been horrible.

How she couldn't breathe anymore without picking up hints of sandalwood and spice. Couldn't close her eyes without seeing those bright emerald eyes, glinting naughtily, or that cascade of snow-white hair falling over his forehead, playing peekaboo with his black brows. Or those lips, so red and soft.

A blistering current of need swept through every inch of her. *I do. I want to touch him.* And she wanted him to touch her…everywhere.

"No," he said. "I'm already a carrier. But I can make *you* sicker."

Disappointment cooled her desire. She drew her arms around herself, asking, "What are your plans now that I'm better?"

"Get out of this realm. Get home." He paused. "Take you with me."

He wanted to stay together? "But, Torin," she said, surprised by her sudden breathlessness.

"Yes, Keys."

The huskiness of his voice was a silky, intimate caress, somehow kicking open a mental door, allowing her yearning to return. She meant to say "That isn't wise." Instead, she said, "Have you ever had a girlfriend? And if so, did you sleep together?" *Dangerous topic. Proceed with caution.*

And she'd thought him tense before. "Yes…and no."

"How did she—or they—take care of your needs? How did you take care of theirs?"

"We're not having this conversation, Keeley."

"Because you're embarrassed?"

"Because it's none of your business."

"Wrong. The world belongs to me—I'm bonded to it—which means everything about everyone is my business."

He waved a hand through the air, an unmistakable dismissal. "Speaking of bonds, don't create one with me."

Eight words. One rejection. A hurt stronger than she would have thought possible. She snapped, "Don't worry. A permanent tie with the bubonic plague isn't high on my list of priorities."

"Good," he snapped.

A light mist began to shower them. "Did the females leave you because you couldn't meet their physical needs?" she asked. *Must hurt him the way he hurt me.*

He twisted and locked his gaze with hers. Water droplets caught in his lashes. Fury radiated from him, and yet his skin paled rather than flushed. "Yes," he admitted softly. "They did. Happy now?"

Not even close. Which bewildered her. She'd just given tit for tat, and yet she longed to apologize. *What's wrong with me?* "So you never touched them? Even with your gloves on?"

"Very rarely." He frowned. "What about you and Hades?"

"What about us?" she asked, the mist vanishing as quickly as it had appeared.

"You slept together, right?"

Had he heard of their tumultuous courtship? "We did. We also broke up."

"Why?"

"Because, like you and your previous girlfriends, he couldn't meet my needs." Namely, the ones to avoid brimstone scars and dungeons.

Torin ran his tongue over his teeth. "Are you difficult to please, then?"

"Hardly. I'm the easiest."

"Hardly," he mocked. "I've been taking care of you for days, princess. If you could have rung a bell to get my attention every time you decided you wanted something, you'd never have stopped ringing it. Even though I've only been a few feet away."

He said that like it was a bad thing. "I'm a queen. That's what we do."

"Well, then, it's no wonder royalty has such a bad rap."

Oh, no, he didn't. He couldn't insult her without suffering the consequences. "You're honored to be in my presence, warrior. Say it."

"Or what? You'll explode me? Sorry, princess, but that threat had a shelf life and it's already expired."

Streams of anger, a crash of thunder. "Are you implying I can't harm you because of the brimstone? Because we've discussed this. I can find a way, I promise you."

Tone low, almost sad, he said, "I'm saying I'm not afraid of the possibility. Death happens to all of us sometime or other."

Well. How was she supposed to deal with this man? She'd never had trouble intimidating an opponent before.

Another clap of thunder, even louder than the first.

With a sigh, Torin moved in front of her and framed her face between his gloved hands. "Look at me, princess. Please."

He's touching me. And it's good, so good. I need more. Have to have more. She couldn't *not* focus on him.

"I've got something to tell you," he said. "Something that's going to change your life."

Don't ever let me go. "O-okay."

"Knowledge is knowing a tomato is a fruit—wisdom is not putting it in a fruit salad."

She blinked, her mind unable to compute his meaning. "I...don't know how to reply to that."

His thumbs traced the seam of her lips. He glanced up at the sky, nodded and released her, the corners of his mouth twitching. "I think our storm decided to go away."

"That's nice." *Touch me again.*

He returned to the fire pit.

Tempt him...anything to prompt another physical connection.

Self-perseveration spoke up. *Have we not learned our lesson? Must we be taught twice? Bad boys do bad things.*

Don't care.

She wanted Torin. And so she would have him.

Yesterday we longed to kill him. Today we long to seduce him?

So what? I'm a girl. I'm allowed to change my mind.

They would be a couple, she decided. Touch—pleasure—had been denied her for far too long. A fact his presence had never allowed her to forget. He'd had other girlfriends so he knew how to handle a romantic relationship. They could do this, could make this work. And they would be vigilant, cautious, never courting danger.

All she had to do was get him to agree.

There was no better time to try. "I'm dirty," she announced. "Absolutely filthy, and I'm going to take a bath."

"Good for you."

So mocking.

So unaware of his coming fall.

"Be a dear and help me remove my dress," she said.

A strangled sound left him. "It has no ties, no zipper. You tug it on and off."

"Well, good news, then. As strong as you are, you shouldn't have any problems."

His gaze swept over her and heated. He licked his lips, as if he could already taste her. "What game are you playing, princess?"

"Does it matter?"

"Yes. And why the hell are you looking at me like that?"

"Like what?"

"Like I'm a hero. I'm not a hero. I'm a villain."

Did he not realize that only made her want him more? "Well, be a good little villain and *help me out of my dress.*"

"No." His tone dovetailed into guttural as he added, "I'm not going near you."

He's definitely tempted. How thin was his control?

"Very well. *I'll* near *you.*" Hips swaying, she closed the distance between them. She reached out.

He jerked away only to return—closer.

She wrapped her fingers around his wrists and guided his hands to her hips.

He resisted. At first.

"Relax, warrior. We're protected by our clothes."

His fingers clenched around her and held on tight. Did he think she would float away like a forgotten balloon?

"What's…next?" he gritted.

Not exactly surrender, but close enough.

She leaned forward, careful as her breath fanned over his ear. "All you need to do is feel good."

"I can do that." He tugged her against him. Suddenly they were flush, the softest parts of her cradling the hardest parts of him. A growl rose from low in his chest as if, in this stolen moment, he'd regressed into little more than an animal. "I'm doing it right now."

The pleasure…thoughts of being careful evaporated like mist. "Would you like to do more?"

"More. Yes." His lips parted as he fought for breath. Eyes glazing with a wildness she'd never seen from anyone other than condemned prisoners, he squeezed her hard enough to bruise. "I'm going to take more, and you're going to like it."

Any other day, she would have loved such unrelenting pressure. But the fever had left her fragile and sore and there was a good chance that, this close to the brimstone, she was weakened more with every second that passed.

"Be careful with me," she whispered.

It was like she'd punched him. He cursed and stepped back, severing contact.

Unacceptable. She followed him, and when he could go no farther, she wrapped her arms around his shoulders. "I didn't tell you to stop, warrior."

"You should have." His lids slowly dipped, hooding his eyes. "What about your vow to hurt me?"

What about it? Her blood heated as she rubbed, rubbed against him. The delicious friction heightened her need for him, tension coiling deep in her belly. What would happen if she nipped at his lips…thrust her tongue in his mouth?

Must resist the urge!

"Keeley."

"Don't talk," she said. "Just move against me."

A moment of inaction. Then he undulated his hips, his erection pressing against her core. As she gasped, he retreated. He circled back and another gasp left her. He jerked her even closer, rubbed her even harder.

Yes. Yes! This was exactly what she'd needed. But his

hands squeezed her harder, too, and it hurt just a little, and she groaned. A second later it was—

Over?

He pushed her away, clenched and unclenched his fists as he fought for breath. "I'll say this once, and only once. Nothing is going to happen between us, princess. If you try something like that again, you'll see a side of me even monsters fear."

Her knees trembled, threatening to buckle. "Fine. Have it your way." For now. Not one to give up, she smiled what she hoped was a siren's smile and removed her dress—while he watched. "I'll take care of myself."

His nostrils flared, and he once again stumbled away from her. But his gaze...his gaze remained locked on her, heating...eating her up one tasty bite at a time.

"Get in the water," he said. "Now."

"Why? Do you find me repulsive?" Slowly she turned and strutted to the spring. But she didn't climb into the water. She braced a foot against the rocks and looked back at him, praying there was something about her that he found appealing. Running a hand along her side, she said, "Or do you find me irresistible?"

FOR THE ETERNITY it took Keeley to submerge under the cover of the water, Torin had to fight his most basic warrior instincts. Touch. Take. *Own.* Then never let her go. She would be his, only his.

The woman was so gorgeous his insides were ripped to shreds every time he looked at her. But the attraction went deeper than her appearance. She was open and honest, such a rarity. She was also fearless, the first potential lover to mention the giant demon in the room—*did your girlfriends leave you because you couldn't meet their physical needs*—as casually as if they were discussing the weather.

Everyone else had always tiptoed around the issue as if the truth would somehow break him, never realizing he was *already* broken. But this girl…she didn't seem to understand he would never be enough for her. That she would soon need more than he could give her.

Hell, why didn't *he* understand? His hands still itched for her. Those breasts…that tuft of cobalt between her legs…he could play with her…sink his fingers in nice and deep. He wouldn't be too aggressive for her, not again. He wouldn't squeeze her too tightly or thrust too forcefully. He wouldn't let himself. She would like what he did.

Or not.

Disappointment was his specialty. As he'd just proven.

Keeley leaned over the spring's edge and dug through his backpack. The tips of her exquisite breasts peeked up over the line of water, her nipples like ripe little blueberries.

Dude. Look away.

She withdrew a bar of soap and held it up like the prize it was, grinning seductively. But then everything about her was seductive, stealing bits and pieces of his sanity.

"I'm about to become the queen of clean, what what," she sang. Then, voice dipping huskily, gaze sweeping over him, she added, "But I could certainly be convinced to get dirty all over again."

Had a man ever died from too much desire or would Torin be the first?

What did she want from him?

How had Hades pleased her?

Stupid question. One Torin despised. The guy was at the top of his must-kill list. Enemy one.

Need distance. Now! "I'll hunt us some dinner and return."

Keeley jolted, gasping out, "But—"

"You gonna complain about missing me, princess?" He put just the right amount of sneer in his tone, guaranteed to irritate her. "How sweet."

Her eyes narrowed to tiny slits. "If I'm a princess, then you're Prince Charming. So you go ahead and take all the time you need, Charming. Right now I'm pretty sure I'll have more fun on my own anyway."

Direct hit.

He turned to go.

"Torin," she called, her sex-me voice no longer giving anything away.

"What?" he snapped.

"It's due to rain soon. Trust me, we want to be long gone from the realm before that happens."

"Why?"

"Do you like drowning?"

"Does anyone?"

"That's why."

What did a little rainfall have to do with drowning? "I'll be back when I'm back." He took off as if his feet were on fire. The rest of him certainly was.

Why was she doing this to him? Acting as if all was forgiven? As if she cared about his well-being…and would die if she didn't get him in her bed? Or on the ground. Or in the tub.

Punishment? Maybe. But he didn't think so. The way

she'd looked at him before stepping into that bath…as if she could already feel him thrusting inside her…

He had to readjust his pants before his erection burst free.

Was she truly attracted to him? He wasn't irresistible like his friend Paris, the keeper of Promiscuity, or determined like Strider, the keeper of Defeat, but okay, yeah, he rocked warrior fierce. Since his possession, many women had tried to get a little some-some of his goods and services.

But I can't even toe the line of dangerous with Keeley. Gloved touches here…there. Can't live with the consequences if I mess up.

He stalked through the forest for over an hour before finally picking up the trail of…something. A group of four-legged beasts, their origins indeterminate. He tracked the combination of hoof and paw prints until he caught sight of his prey. Ginormous deer-things, facing away from him, clueless that they had just become the main course of his dinner buffet.

He'd left camp without the handgun or the rifle, he realized. He'd have to use his dagger. Fine. Whatever. A battle would do him some good. He scaled one of the trees, positioned himself for attack, and whistled.

All of the creatures stiffened. The biggest one turned and bounded over to search for the culprit—and that's when Torin computed the truth. He wasn't dealing with any kind of deer; he was dealing with something else entirely. An amalgamation of a lion, demon, gorilla and honey badger don't care.

Torin went quiet. *Maybe I can escape notice.*

Of course, that's when the creature looked up and met his gaze. Neon-red against otherworldly green.

Too late.

Here goes nothing, he thought—and jumped.

SNAPPING TWIGS ALERTED Keeley to an impending visitor. Hades's minions at last?

Angry muttering let her know exactly who that visitor was, and it wasn't a horde of demons. Perhaps a little too excitedly considering his parting words, she pushed to her feet and smoothed the tank and camo pants she'd found inside the backpack, ready to face Torin.

He broke through a wall of foliage and spotted her. He stopped abruptly, his gaze raking over her, narrowing— and erupting with heat.

She waited for the praise to begin.

"There was a storm while I was gone," he said.

Okay. Not the opener she'd hoped for, but not a total loss, either. "Yes." As long as she'd been alive, she'd learned to work *any* conversation in the direction she wanted. "The rain caused flowers to bloom, much like—"

"Even though it didn't last," he interjected.

"Correct." Because it hadn't sprung from the realm, but from her. "Much like my bath caused—"

"You didn't drown."

Argh! "No." She traced a hand down her side and rushed out, "Me to bloom" before he could interrupt her again. "Wouldn't you agree?"

He looked her over a second time and shrugged. "I guess."

He *guessed?*

Disappointment struck.

She returned the once-over, thinking she needed to insult him. Like for like. But she became snagged by the scowl darkening his features and found she wanted only to calm him. "Are you okay?" she asked. He had scratches all over his neck and arms, and in his hand was the leg of the Nephilim he'd been dragging.

"I'm fine. Here's dinner," he said, throwing the creature at the fire she'd built. "You don't have to worry about getting sick because I've touched him. The disease died with him."

"Backtrack just a bit. You don't have to worry...as in *me?*" She thumped her chest for emphasis. "*I* don't have to worry?"

"Yes, you. You cook. We eat."

Because of Hades and his poison, she only ever ate what *she* found.

"Meanwhile," Torin added, "I need to bathe."

Bathe? "No!" she shouted. "Don't go near the spring." Not yet. It would kill the hello-how-are-you vibe they had going.

He frowned and, like the stubborn, obstinate warrior he was proving to be, stalked to the spring. "Seriously?" he bellowed.

"Well." She shifted from one foot to the other. "Two of the prisoners you released showed up, and even though I was a perfectly mediocre hostess, they thought they'd evict me—*after* they finished ravishing me." The reason for the storm. "*They* found me irresistible," she grumbled.

He scanned the campsite, and she wished she possessed the ability to alter a person's perception. A mess of blood and guts surrounded him. Thankfully the spring had some kind of filtering system and was no longer... chunky.

"You killed them before they touched you?" he asked.

"I'm the undefeatable Red Queen. What do you think?" The awful look in their eyes as they'd approached her, coupled with the disgusting words coming out of their mouths, had angered her to the point of no return.

"Good." Torin bent down to pinch what looked to be a piece of a small intestine between his gloved fingers. He flung the thing into the farthest tangle of trees. "I think they got what they deserved."

He wasn't afraid of her power, wasn't running from her—but then, when had he ever?

Want him more than ever.

"Now," she said to distract herself. "About dinner. I've already prepared you a feast. Sorry, but there are no roasted entrails."

She'd heard the way to a man's heart was through his stomach. Which was an odd saying, because she'd punched her way through many a male torso, and she knew for a fact that the way to a heart was through the fourth and fifth ribs, but she understood the spirit of the phrase. If she could soften Torin's emotions toward her, maybe she could more easily tempt him to pleasure her.

He owes me, after all. Hadn't he made her sad? Wasn't he obligated to make her happy? *Only way to completely clear his ledger.*

"I know I'm not overselling this when I say you're about to have the best dining experience of your life." Approaching Torin, she held up a stone plate piled high with goodies. "You're welcome."

He grimaced as he looked over her offering. "Twigs. Leaves. Mushrooms. Bugs? Pass."

"I'll take that as a yes, please, and thank you."

"Take it as a no."

"A soft no? Like absomaybe?"

"A hard no. Like absolutely not."

"So…I should save some for later?"

"Save some for never."

"But…" *I foraged for you.* "Never mind." She shrugged to mask her upset, and popped a mushroom into her mouth. "Your loss."

"My win."

"Someone's clearly in the mood to argue," she said.

"What can I say? You bring out the worst in me."

A sudden, light mist began to fall over them. "Are you proud of yourself?" she asked softly. "I'm five seconds away from killing myself and then killing you."

Torin looked around, sighed. "Did you know that fifty-one percent of all statistics are useless?"

"Uh…no?"

"Yep, and seven-fifths of people do not understand fractions."

"That's…bad?"

The mist stopped, and Torin said, "I'm taking that bath." He grabbed his shirt by the collar and yanked.

A protest died before it ever left her lips. Looking away proved impossible. Drugging warmth swirled in her mind, making her light-headed before racing through the rest of her.

He stilled with his hands on the waist of his pants. He met her gaze and arched a brow. "Turn around."

"Why? Are you shy?"

"Maybe I think there's no reason to tempt a starving woman with what she'll never have."

A stinging reminder of his resistance, meant to discourage her. Well, she would let him think he'd succeeded. For now. Every victory came with a kickass plan. It was time she created one.

"I'm going to pass on your offer to cook," she said, turning away.

The rustle of clothing pricked her ears. "I don't recommend you do that. I'm starved, and as you've probably noticed," he added darkly, "I get cranky when I'm starved."

"Do you really want to feed on the offspring of a fallen angel?"

"Excuse me?"

As water splashed, she swung back around. He was submerged to his shoulders. "How old are you?" An older immortal would have recognized the beast he'd slain.

"Old enough to know better. Old enough that I can only use one pickup line appropriately—hey baby, you better call life alert because I just fell for you and can't get up."

Pickup line…pickup line…she racked her brain until she found an explanation and brightened. "Mine would be—roses are red, violets are blue, if you don't do what I say I will kill you."

He blinked over at her for a long while, looking ready to burst into laughter—or curse.

"Seriously," she said. "How old?"

"I'll say at least three thousand and leave it at that."

"So…basically you're a fetus." No wonder he was too embarrassed to tell her.

When he merely picked up the bar of soap, she pushed him from her mind, spending the next half hour disposing of the Nephilim, not wanting the stink of his rotting corpse to draw the notice of his friends. And he had friends. They always ran in packs. Evil was a parasite, dependent on others for survival.

Which was exactly how the world saw Curators, she thought with a sigh. Was that how Torin saw *her*?

Yeah. Probably. His attitude about the bond…

Bonding to him *was* possible. It was always possible. She'd have to be more careful than ever, especially with the new direction of their relationship.

"How do we get out of this realm?" Torin asked.

"Wouldn't you like to know," she snapped, irritated with him.

"Um, yes. That's kind of why I asked."

Calm. Steady. He's done nothing wrong—at the moment.

She couldn't resist another peek at him. He'd already pulled on a clean pair of pants, but they hung low on his waist, revealing a dark goody trail, a match to his eyebrows. *So beautiful.*

"It's simple," she said. "We find the key and unlock the door."

"What if I already have a key? Where's the door?"

A key, he'd said. Not *the* key. Interesting choice. What was his game? "It's at the edge of the realm. About three days from here. Or I can flash you there. Won't take but a second. All you need to do is cut out your brimstone scars."

He smiled at her, irritating her all over again. "Thanks, but I'd rather walk."

She shrugged as if it were no big deal. Meanwhile, it was a big freaking deal! "More time for us to spend together, then."

He pulled on a shirt, saying dryly, "Yay me."

A flash of anger, a boom of thunder. "I'm sensing you don't realize how lucky you are. How privileged. People have paid me fortunes to stay by their side during war."

"Except that I'm your opponent."

"I thought not, but I could certainly be convinced to change my mind again."

As he opened his mouth to reply, the three prisoners he'd worked with to subdue her suddenly charged the campsite. Instinctively she summoned a great gust of wind to knock them backward, but they must have given themselves brimstone scars to block her powers, because they stepped right on through it, closing in on her and Torin—who had swiped up a dagger and stepped in front of her, prepared to guard her.

Some of her anger with him drained.

Before the trio could reach him, she flashed hundreds of branches into their path as she'd once done to Torin, but this time, she added trees. So many the warriors couldn't find their way through. But they tried, diligently, violently, more determined to reach her than she'd realized.

"How would you like this to end?" she asked Torin. "I'm open to suggestions."

"Let's make our way to the door."

"I can hold them off with trees even when I leave the camp, but the immortals are sure to break free soon enough and follow us."

"If all goes the way I'd like, we'll be in the next realm before they catch up."

"We'll have to hurry. The scars—"

"Are staying."

"Very well." *But when I finally get you into my bed, Charming, those scars will be the first thing to go, whether you agree or not....*

CHAPTER NINE

THE NEXT FEW days proved to be the hardest of Torin's life. Literally.

Keeley was temptation wrapped in desire, dipped in ecstasy and rolled in satisfaction, and there was no doubt in his mind she'd been designed simply to torture him.

The way she walked and talked—living sex. The way she smelled—edible. The things she radiated—pheromones and crack, surely. Her incomparable strength. Her sense of humor, a little warped. A perfect match to his. The way she thought. He wasn't ever sure what went on inside that beautiful head of hers, and the mystery intrigued him. The things she said sometimes baffled him, sometimes amused him, sometimes even angered him, but never ever bored him.

Her loyalty to her friend might just surpass his. The little sounds she made when she enjoyed what she was eating—an audible caress. Not that she ever ate much, which he didn't understand, but she'd shut him down any time he'd asked her about it.

She was nothing like he'd first assumed. Not cruel, not insane...not really. Well, not to him. She was...perfect.

He was consumed by a need to protect her, even from herself. He wanted to be near her, just in case she needed him, to soothe the worst of her emotions before the world

around them had time to react. The storms when she became angry. The snow when she grew sad. The glow of
the sun when she was happy. A very rare occurrence.

He alone seemed capable of rousing each of her emotions, as if he held her heart in the palm of his hand and
turned it however he willed. And that, right there, was
another reason he craved her. Because he affected her—
and he liked it.

As they'd traipsed through the realm, he tried focusing on his hobbies. Anything to get his mind off desires
he had no business entertaining. He carved an entire set
of gnome-shaped chess pieces. He folded a thousand
leaves into flowers.

Keeley stole them.

Something else he liked about her. She took what
she wanted.

"It's raining," she said from behind him.

"I noticed." The pounding storm had nothing to do
with her emotions. It had started yesterday morning and
hadn't let up even once. The puddles of water—lakes,
really—now reached his ankles.

But even the constant cold shower failed to help his
situation. He ached. He craved. And he wasn't sure he
could go another hour let alone another minute without
putting his hands on Keeley. He'd wear gloves, wouldn't
let his skin brush against hers. He would cup her breasts
lightly, and play between her legs gently, and that would
be enough.

It would have to be enough.

But it wouldn't be, would it?

Icy water trickled between his shoulder blades as he
hacked through a thick wall of foliage with more force

than necessary, clearing a path. He glanced over his shoulder to make sure she hadn't lagged—again.

She had stopped to check her cuticles—again.

He should have been annoyed. She needed a good toweling, not a manicure. He was just glad she hadn't taken off on her own. With the Terrible Trio scarred with brimstone and on the loose, she needed a strong, strapping warrior to guard her.

It was an excuse. He knew that. Keeley had more than proved she could defend herself against anyone, anytime. But the hard truth of the matter was this: she couldn't actually *take care of* herself. She never ate unless prompted. She only slept when she was sick. She often slipped inside her own head, the rest of the world forgotten.

What did she think about in those moments?

Hades?

Want to rip off his balls and stuff them down his throat.

"Keeley," Torin snapped. "Walk."

She pursed her lips as she flounced past him. "Grumpy much?"

Damn. The sway of her hips… Was his tongue hanging out?

Gotta be a man, not a besotted puppy.

He'd never acted this way before and decided there could be only one reason he would do so now. Gritting his teeth, he demanded, "Did you bond with me?"

She flicked an irritated glance over her shoulder, water falling down her cheeks like tears. "As one of the smartest people on the planet, I can happily say *no*."

"Good," he replied as he took the lead. That was *not* disappointment he was feeling.

Snowflakes began to descend, blending into the rain, floating around him.

He'd hurt her feelings, he realized.

Great! He had to deal with guilt on top of everything else. Time to distract them both. "Have you noticed the forest creatures have stayed away from us?"

"Word of my exploits has clearly spread."

As good an explanation as any. "Do you think they wonder why we kill people who kill people for killing people?"

"Probably not. I mean, if the creatures here have only half a brain, they're actually *gifted*."

He snorted, and then she chuckled, and then they were both laughing outright. The snow stopped, proving he'd done what he'd intended.

He hacked a new wall of foliage to shreds, the tree limbs stretching toward him, ravenous leaves snapping. "After you."

"My hero-villain," Keeley said, moving past him. "Does your mother know you're such a gentleman half of the time?"

An ache in his chest. "I don't have a mother."

"What?" She rounded on him. There was no pity in her eyes, only curiosity. "You've never had anyone tuck you in at night, either?"

Either? "I came into this world fully formed. What of you?"

"The old-fashioned way, though I don't enjoy thinking of my emotionless mother and greedy father getting frisky"

Emotionless and greedy. *He* didn't enjoy the thought of little Kee Kee subjected to such things. The Sugar Plum Fairy should have been pampered.

He reached up to smooth away the wet hair clinging to her cheek but ended up fisting his hand and dropping his arm. *Can't forget. Not for a moment.* But it was becoming harder and harder to catch himself.

"They were cruel to you?" he asked, walking around her and taking the lead.

"During the best times, yes." She stepped up to his side, keeping pace. "During the worst, they paid me no heed at all. Which is probably why I ensured there were as many 'best' times as possible."

Breaking my heart. A daughter so neglected she would rather be punished than ignored. "I'm sorry."

A faux-casual shrug as she said, "The past shaped me into who I am. How can I regret it?"

Not one for pity. Got it. But he wanted to know more about her. Wanted to know *everything* about her.

Because…*shouldn't admit it…can't help myself*…he was in total like with her. Stupidly, foolishly, but there it was. There was no question he liked her looks—his constant erection was proof of that. But more important, he liked *her.* Who she was, even what she was.

Never had a relationship been more doomed.

"I've heard Curators were created before humans," he said. "True or false?"

"True. The earth was ours. But as you know, the fallen angels challenged the Most High, lost and came here. The Curators who bonded to them lost their light and it wasn't long before most of the earth was infected."

Most of, she'd said. "Not all?"

"There was a walled-off section, a garden, where the humans were created. But the leader of the fallen angels later found a way in there, too."

Lucifer? "These lights," he said. "I've heard talk of them, but I'm not sure I understand them."

"Imagine Curators are lightbulbs. We literally glow. It's an outward sign of the conscience we possess within."

"And without the light?"

"Absolute darkness. No conscience."

"How have you kept *your* light all these centuries?"

"What makes you think I haven't lost it? I mean, you can't see it. It's hidden inside my body."

"I thought you had. At first. Now?" Simplest explanation? "I'm still alive."

Minutes ticked by without a response from her. "The truth is," she finally said, "I did almost lose it. For a while, bitterness was my best friend and suffocating dark closed in. Then Mari showed up and chased it away. I could breathe again, could think clearly, and realized I would have endured a thousand imprisonments simply to meet her."

And I took her away.

He thought he'd come to grips with that. But could anyone ever really come to grips after destroying someone's only source of joy?

"Where will this doorway lead us?" he croaked.

"To the next realm."

"Which is?"

"Someplace different than this one."

Such a fount of information. "I want to go home."

"No problem." She blinked at him, all innocence. "Cut out the scars and I'll flash you there."

He was tempted. Extracting a pound of flesh no longer seemed to be her objective. But if she were to turn on him, the scars would be his only weapon against her. A warrior never surrendered his weapons.

"I want to go home *without* cutting out the scars."

She expelled a breath. "Well, then, I've got good news and bad news."

"Start with the good news."

"Bad news," she said, and he rolled his eyes. "Flashing is the only way to skip through realms. Well, that, and opening portals. But I can't flash you, and I can't open a portal without the necessary tools. That means we'll have to travel from realm to realm until we reach your home, and it could take *years*." She marched in front of him and held out her hand, stopping him. "But the good news is, we've finally reached the doorway."

No way in hell. They stood at the edge of a cliff, a sea of nothingness stretching for miles ahead.

"Let me guess," he said dryly. "We're supposed to jump, and you'd like me to go first."

She rolled her eyes. "Always thinking the worst of people is a disease, you know. Courtesy of your demon?"

"Courtesy of me."

"Well, I suppose it'll take someone nicer than me to cure you of it."

"You're nice."

Please. "Flattery is just another form of lying and will get you a dagger in the gut." How nice was *that?*

"A mean person wouldn't have warned me. A mean person would have simply struck."

Clearly fighting a smile, she pivoted and stretched out her hand. Crackles of electricity shot from the tips of her fingers and hovered in the air, growing wider, longer, creating cracks in the atmosphere, each pulsing with a vibrant array of colors.

A single burst of bright light expanded through the colors like a bullet, causing them to widen...before being sucked back inside, leaving—

A doorway!

While he could still see the black nothingness around its edges and the accompanying rain, he could see a new world in the door's center. One without rain.

"Your key," Keeley said, motioning to the doorway.

Though he didn't like the idea of using the All-key in front of another person, considering the number of people who had tried to kill Cronus to possess it, he strode forward. Seeing no knob and not knowing what else to do, he flattened his palm against the center of the door. It was solid to the touch...at first. Soon the grain beneath his hand began to shimmer, waves rippling from top to bottom. Then, as easily as that, the block vanished and there was only air between him and the next realm.

"So. You have the All-key," she said. "Taken from Cronus just before he died, I'm guessing. No wonder you were able to escape the prison."

No comment. No reason to promote a conversation that would invariably lead to Mari. "What's next?"

"This might seem a little wild, but...walk through."

Smart-ass. He entered the dry land and nearly howled with relief.

Keeley remained close to his heels. Too close for comfort.

He looked around, seeing another forest, this one straight out of a nightmare. The trees were black from trunk to tip, with twisted vines slithering along the branches like snakes. Small fire pits blazed in every direction. Smoke billowed, thickening the air.

"Welcome to the Realm of Lost and Found," Keeley

said, holding out her arms to encompass the ruined landscape.

As she moved, she…changed. Sapphire hair darkened to a deep, rich red, several thick locks of chocolate woven throughout. Iced skin took on a peaches-and-cream glow, and her eyes…those darkened to a luscious amber-gold.

He'd thought her beautiful before. But this was…

Breathtaking.

"What the hell just happened to you?" he demanded, furious. How was he supposed to resist her now?

She blanched, and he didn't need a change in the weather to tell him that he once again had the distinct honor of hurting her feelings.

"Must be fall here," she said coolly.

He sighed. "I'm sorry I was rude."

She hmphed and started forward. "Come on. There's a cabin just over the anthill."

The ends of her red hair reached her waist and curled, and he wondered if they would tickle his stomach when she straddled and rode him, hard and fast, and—

Torin moaned.

Disease protested. Loudly.

Shut up! Torin still found it odd that the demon wanted to escape the girl, and yet the fiend hadn't hesitated to strike her with illness when the opportunity arose. Or maybe not so odd. Like a rabid dog backed into a corner, Disease had attacked.

Rabid dogs need to be put down.

A welcome thought. "If this is an anthill," Torin muttered, "I don't want to see the ants."

"Wise."

After a few minutes of silence, he said, "How'd you change colors like that? You never told me."

"Actually, I did. The change happens naturally. I am the season around me."

Okay. That made sense. He wondered what she would look like in the spring and summer—and hardened.

A vine stretched out, stopping to hover near her as if sniffing her, preparing to strike. Torin reached for it. Without turning her head, Keeley grabbed it before he could make contact. A high-pitched shriek echoed as the vine withered to ash.

"Impressive," he said.

"Obviously."

Don't smile. It would only encourage her. "You once asked my age. It's my turn to ask yours. How old are you?"

"Far older than you. I've been growing old disgracefully since the beginning of time. Which means I'm far wiser than you, too. I know things your small mind could not even begin to understand."

Probably true. "Insulting the beauty of my brain when you haven't even seen it naked? Bad form, princess. Bad form."

She stiffened, then sighed. "You speak true. My apologies."

His little stick of dynamite had gotten better at controlling her temper. Before, his statement would have sent her into a tirade about queens never being wrong.

His mind seized on a thought. As smart as she was, as much as she seemed to know and as long as she'd been around, she might be able to find Cameo and Viola... and Pandora's box.

Been searching so long. Had almost given up.

But could he trust this woman with such critical tasks?

Actually...yes. If she said she'd do something, she'd do it. Her sense of honor would allow nothing less.

In war, he'd never had any real honor of his own. He'd always fought dirty. Filthy, even. He'd had no qualms about striking a target from behind. No qualms about kicking someone while they were down.

With her, everything had been flipped upside down and inside out.

At the top of the mountain, he got his first look at the "cabin," a ginormous log structure capable of housing an entire football team plus the field. Smoke rose from the chimney, and the scent of roasted *something delicious* fragranced the air, making his mouth water. Torin had been living off twigs, leaves and mushrooms—bugs would never be on the menu—and that just wasn't good enough anymore.

Did a friend or foe wait inside? "Do you know the owner?"

"Probably not."

"Probably? You don't know?"

"Warrior, my mind is like a corkboard. I have millions of memories pinned to it. Pictures, conversations, plans, battles, hopes, dreams, pains, sorrows, and sometimes information gets lost. Sometimes, there's too much and I have to store certain years in a Time Out box."

How...adorable.

Hell. "Whatever. Let me handle this," he said, moving ahead.

"Are you sure that's wise? This particular realm is filled with a race of giants."

"Strengths? Weaknesses?"

"Yes. They have them."

He rolled his eyes. "What are they?"

"I just told you. Giants."

"And you're the smart one of our little duo? Princess, I meant what are the strengths and weaknesses *of the giants.*"

"Oh. Well, you should have made that more clear. But you didn't, so the mistake is yours. *Anyway.* Their strength is, of course, in their size. Their weakness is in their joints. They carry so much weight their joints deteriorate quickly."

Well, all right, then. He knocked on the door. He tightened his hold on his dagger, ready to go for the giant's knees. There was no reason to use his guns and draw unwanted attention from anyone who happened to be nearby.

Hammering footsteps. Screaming hinges as the door opened. Torin had to look up, up, up. A Mack Truck of a man stood in front of him—a giant to other giants.

"You must not have gotten the memo, human. I enjoy hunting my food." Mack Truck's voice boomed like thunder. "I don't like my meals to show up on my doorstep. Takes all the fun out of it."

"I don't know about my companion," Keeley said, toying with a lock of her hair, "but I'm so sweet I'm just certain I'd make a great dessert."

Mack Truck looked at her and squealed like a frightened little girl. "You!"

"I'd say he knows you," Torin muttered.

"Probable victim of the Time Out box," she allowed.

"I refused to spy for you, so you ripped out one of my kidneys and made me eat it," Mack Truck said through chattering teeth.

"And I'm sure you loved it. As for today, I'm here to—"

"Make me eat the other one, just like you vowed," he blurted. "I know!" He didn't wait for her reply, but barreled outside and ran. Just ran.

Torin pinched the bridge of his nose. "I have a feeling this is going to be a common occurrence with you."

"Thank you."

"Yes, because I totally meant it as a compliment. Wait here while I check for any other occupants."

"Wait here? You do know I'm the creature the boogeyman hides from, right?"

"And you know the boogeyman is a douche, right?" Dude liked to ring doorbells and hide in bushes.

"Right. But nevertheless."

Oh, this girl. "I do know you are one scary-ass female, but your particular skill set will be a last resort." If she had to fight, she would destroy the house and everything in it, and he was looking forward to three things: a decent meal, a soft bed and, in his fantasies, a willing woman. "Just pretend I'm your humble servant and seeing to your every comfort."

"Ha! It's not like we entered Impossible is Finally Possible Realm."

Dude. He wasn't that bad.

Torin stalked through the massive living room, even more massive kitchen, and are-you-kidding-me-with-this bedroom. Animal heads hung from the walls, their beady eyes surveying his every move. Most were creatures he'd never before seen—and never wanted to see again. At least no one living waited in the shadows.

On his way back to the foyer, he discovered Keeley had not only entered the house but had also made herself at home in the kitchen, the backpack resting at her feet.

"Did you misunderstand the meaning of *wait here?*" he asked, filling two bowls with the soup simmering on the stove. A clear broth with what looked to be a variety of vegetables. No meat had been added—yet. Next to the pot rested a giant slab of *something;* it was as black as tar and must have come from a diseased animal.

Or the humans Mack Truck liked to hunt.

Torin threw it out the window and washed his gloves before stalking to the table. He caught the scent of autumn leaves and cinnamon, and tensed. The sweet fragrance came from Keeley, as if she'd just sprayed herself with Obsession by Mother Nature; it was as different and tantalizing as her new appearance, filling his head and his lungs, bringing with it a fog of dizzying arousal.

Have to get my hands on her. Soon.

Never.

He set her bowl in front of her, then plopped into his seat with a hard thud.

Disease banged against his skull.

"I didn't misunderstand," Keeley finally said. "You, however, are under the laughable misconception that you can give me orders." She played with the food, never actually taking a bite. "By the way, I'll let you…but only in bed. A girl has to draw a line somewhere."

He gripped the arms of his chair with deadly force, the effort to remain in place, away from her, gut-wrenching. Sweat trickled down his temples. His heart nearly burst free of his chest. "Eat. And we will never end up in bed, Keys. That's a promise. Trust me, it's for your own good."

"I know," she grumbled, swirling her spoon around the broth, "but that doesn't make abstinence any easier."

Pouting because she couldn't sleep with him? Every. Man's. Dream.

My dream.

Deep breath in…out. *Have to change the subject.* "Do you ever hire out your services?"

"My superb sexual skills?"

"No!" The arms of the chair broke off in his hands.

She scowled at him. "You act as though I had no reason to go there, and yet it was a logical conclusion considering what you said before you asked."

"You're right." *Killing me.* He dropped the splintered wood pieces to the floor. "I meant your superior Curator abilities."

"Why? Do you have an enemy you'd like me to whack?"

"I need help finding my missing friends. I love them the way you loved Mari."

"Well, well. Look at you. Proving demons are expert manipulators. Good job."

"I'm just stating a fact. I will do anything to find them."

She arched a brow, suddenly intrigued. "Anything?"

The low tone of her voice…now husky with arousal… shot a lance of pleasure straight to his groin.

How many of those lances would he feel before this conversation ended?

"Anything except put your life at risk," he said.

CARING FOR HER. Protecting her again. How was a girl supposed to maintain any kind of emotional distance with him?

Better question: how was a girl supposed to maintain any kind of *physical* distance?

Keeley had just watched him hack through a forest, his muscles straining and rippling, and all she'd wanted to do was throw herself at him. Then she'd had to watch him prowl through this house, determined to ferret out an enemy and, what? Protect her. Was she just supposed to overlook her wildest fantasies coming to life right before her eyes?

Need him so badly. Every delicious inch of him.

The consequences were beginning to matter less and less. Sick shmick. It was the deprivation that would kill her.

And, really, he could be wrong. What if they could be together, and she wouldn't sicken a second time? She'd fought the effects of his demon and won, hadn't she? That had to mean something.

Have to shatter his resistance the way he shattered mine.

Besides, he owes me.

Actually, no. He didn't. At the moment, he didn't owe her anything at all.

The truth will set you free.

What she'd blamed him for? She shouldn't have. Mari would have found a way to touch Torin even if he'd told her no—even if he'd taken measures to stop her. Mari, for all her goodness, had been stubborn and hardheaded.

Keeley finally accepted her friend's culpability for what had happened. The girl had agreed to Cronus's terms.

Any lingering resentment she'd harbored toward Torin completely withered, his ledger wiped as white as snow. Problem was she'd just lost her only defense against his appeal. There would be no stopping a bond from forming.

He would flip out—hate her.

Can't let that happen.

Her head tilted to the side as she considered her next move. "I don't understand you," she admitted.

His gaze dropped to her lips, lingered and heated. "That's good, because I don't understand you, either." He pushed the bowl of soup he'd given her closer. "Eat. Please."

The "please" almost convinced her.

Enjoy the moment. Seize the day. Take what I can, while I can.

"You want to know what it'll take to get me to help you find your friends?" she asked. "Fine. For each one I find, you'll touch me. *Pleasure* me. When I say, how I say." He *hadn't* owed her—but he would.

He was determined to resist her, and that, at least, was something she understood...but wouldn't stand for. He needed a push, and she was going to give it to him.

PUT MY HANDS on Keeley? Yes, please.

Pleasure her? A thousand times yes.

Torin would have gladly paid for the privilege, yet here she was willing to pay *him*. Did life get any better? Or worse?

Proceed with caution—or else. "You want me?"

A slow nod from her.

"Why me?" he asked. He had to know.

"Why not?"

Why not, indeed. He worked his jaw. "Do you want the top ten reasons—most of which we've already rehashed—or will one or two suffice?"

She leaned back, drummed her fingers against the

arms of her chair. He could practically hear the wheels turning in her head as she pondered the proper response.

"Are you irritating and even defective?" she said. "Yes. But you're also hot. And yes, I'm just a little shallow. I'm also desperate."

The word *defective* was a poison in his mind, infecting everything it encountered. "You're desperate, are you?" *Knew that already. Why so upset by it?* "Wow. I'm flattered."

Looking like a little kid who'd just turned in an art project, unsure whether she'd created trash or a masterpiece, she said, "Should I not have admitted that?"

"No! A guy likes to think he's special." Torin scrubbed a hand down his face. Had those words seriously just come out of his mouth?

"You misunderstood me. You *are* special," she said, earnest. "Did I mention I like to look at you?"

He scoffed. "Is physical appearance all you think about?"

"Did I mention I'm shallow?" she said. A teasing note had entered her voice, cooling the worst of his anger.

"But what I was *trying* to tell you," she added, every word measured as if she didn't want to reveal too much, "is that, while you are all of those things, you are also strong and fierce, even bloodthirsty. And while you are as tough as nails, you're also sweet. You are a walking contradiction, and I find myself fascinated. Sometimes I'm certain you're attracted to me, sometimes I'm not so sure, but because of your demon, I'm certain you'll never do anything about it even if you are. That places the responsibility in my hands. I want pleasure. You're here. You can give it to me."

The first part of her speech heated him. The second

part chilled him. He was a convenience, nothing more. "Tell me," he gritted. "Why would I want to give plea-sure to a woman who is aggravating and also defective?"

She gasped and said, "I'm not defective."

"Princess, your temper tantrums make you as defec-tive as an open-ended condom." He couldn't help but add, "But you are fun and witty, fragile and yet amaz-ingly stalwart. You are dangerous to every rule I've ever set for myself. And you are also smoking hot. I like look-ing at you, too."

Her jaw dropped.

"What? If you tell me no one's ever waxed poetic about how beautiful you are, I will personally hunt down everyone you've ever met and call them an idiot."

"Smoking hot?" Her hand fluttered to the pulse now hammering in her neck. "Really?"

Get this runaway train back on the track. "But I have to refuse your oh, so generous offer. Make-out sessions, no matter how tame, will put your life at risk." As if he could be tame with her. "I shouldn't have to remind you that you barely recovered from the first sickness."

"But—"

"No buts. I hated watching you writhe in pain. Hated hearing you cry out for mercy you'd never receive. You're better now, but who knows if you'd recover a second time."

She shifted in her chair, her gaze locked on him and chilling. "Are you trying to politely tell me you didn't enjoy touching me?"

The demon banged against his skull, shouting ob-scenities, still determined to leave her.

"No. I'm not politely trying to tell you anything. I don't do polite. Haven't you noticed?" The situation would have been a hell of a lot easier if he could have stripped away his conscience and lied to her, but nooo. To anyone else, sure. But not to her.

A ray of sunlight filtered in through the window.

"Do you ever *think* about touching me?" she asked, hesitant.

All. The. Damned. Time. "Princess, I *burn* for you." Let there be no misunderstanding between them on that score.

She inched down her chair until her knees brushed against his, and he had to swallow a nearly animalistic roar. Had to grip the table to keep from reaching for her...but the edge of it snapped off, too.

Another gasp left her...one of surprise, maybe even of arousal.

"But you need to think about the ramifications before we travel this route." Damn it! From a definite no to this? "Accidents could happen, even if my gloves are in place and we both remain fully dressed. Also, your expectations might be too high."

She frowned. "What do you mean? Too high?"

He wasn't going to explain, had too much pride, and waved his hand through the air. "Yes or no. Are you willing to take a chance?"

What the hell am I doing?

There wasn't a single beat of hesitation from her. "Yes," she said with a nod. "I am."

He subdued the urge to yank her into his lap. He needed to plan the best way to proceed...to see to her needs without harming her.

"Now that the payment plan has been established..." She straightened, suddenly all business, and asked, "How many friends are missing?"

"Two. Three if you know how to track spirits of the dead." Torin had been searching for the former keeper of Distrust ever since he'd learned Baden's spirit was still out there, trapped in another realm. "He was killed several centuries ago."

"I track spirits the same way I track everyone else. Easily." She hooked a lock of hair behind her ear, so inherently feminine Torin's deepest masculine instincts responded. As usual. "I will expect the same payment."

He would pay her. He would pay her so hard.

No, gently. Have to proceed gently with her. He would rather die than scare her, hurt her, or make her regret her desire for him. "You'll get it."

Gaze intent, she said, "That's it? Only three tasks?"

Hoping for more payment? *In too deep already.* But still he replied, "One other, if possible. Locate and destroy Pandora's box."

"DimOuniak, you mean."

The "official" name. He nodded.

She thought for a moment. "I can do that, too. Which task would you like me to start with?"

"Cameo and Viola."

The drumming of her nails started up again. "Are they your girlfriends?"

Jealous?

The idea turned him on.

Oh, what a shocker. It wasn't like *everything* about her turned him on or anything.

"No," he said.

"Good. What happened to them?"

"They touched something they shouldn't have and vanished."

"I need more details."

"Do you know what the Paring Rod is?" he asked.

"Doesn't everyone?"

Okay, then. "Do you know what it does?"

"Most assuredly."

Well, no one else did. "Tell me."

"It works in conjunction with three other artifacts. The Cage of Compulsion, the Cloak of Invisibility and the All-seeing Eye. I'll need all four to do the things you've asked, but that's not a problem because I know where they are. I stole them and hid them long ago and—"

"Actually, you don't know where they are. My friends and I found them."

"Wait. I want to make sure I heard you correctly." She leaned forward, flattening her hands on his thighs. "You *already* have them?"

The heat of her skin seeped through the leather of his pants, and he hissed. Too much…not enough.

Need more. I need more. Must have more.

"Correct." Somehow he found the strength to set her hands away from him. He would pay her when the time came—*pay her so hard…damn it, gently*—but he could allow nothing else to happen between them. No spontaneous handling. Not ever again. It would be his downfall.

But what a way to go.

"You don't need me," she said with a pout. "You can find the females, the deceased and the box without me."

He rubbed his chest, saying, "We don't know how to make the artifacts work."

"You're telling me you have the means to locate anyone or thing in the world, including the most desired object in existence, as well as open a portal anywhere in this world or another, and yet you don't know how to proceed?"

"Explain. Please," he added. "What is the most desired object?" *The box?*

For a moment, clouds rolled through her eyes. "How could I have forgotten it? Even for a moment," she said, reverence in her tone. "He's part of a war he doesn't even understand, which means, thanks to my spies, I have answers to questions he doesn't even know to ask."

Please don't retreat mentally.

Thankfully the clouds cleared a second later and she added, "You'll have to give the artifacts to me. All four. I must own them. I can't find and free your girlfriends without them."

"They aren't my—" He sighed. Why argue? "Fine. They're with the other demon-possessed warriors. All of whom you must vow not to kill. Or harm in any way. Or let anyone else kill or harm."

A pause. Then, voice devoid of emotion, she said, "What if they attack me?"

Outside, a light rain pattered.

Well, hell. *What'd I do this time?* "They won't."

"How can you be sure?"

"I won't allow it."

The rain stopped as suddenly as it had begun. Had she thought he would stand back and watch his friends attempt to fell her?

Never.

"Very well," she said with a nod. "I vow it."

He released a breath he hadn't known he'd been holding. So much had hinged on her response. "Tell me about this war I don't understand."

A gleam of calculation in her eyes. "That information wasn't part of our bargain, warrior. It'll cost you."

That would make five payments in total. But this one...this one she would insist he pay *today*. He knew it.

Just like that, his resistance crumbled. Was there really a reason to delay?

His hand shot out and gripped her by the hair, yanking her toward him. "Keeley."

Her warm breath caressed his face. "Yes, Torin."

His mind shouted, "What are you doing?" even as the desire to thrust his tongue deep inside her mouth plagued him far worse than any disease ever had. "I want—"

You safe, he thought.

But a single moment of weakness could cost them both.

A swift return of his resistance. He helped her settle in her chair.

"Agreed," he managed.

Tremors rocked her, and he wondered whether she feared what had almost happened—or wished he'd followed through.

"The Titans and Greeks want the box," she said. "Not because they hope to end the terror-filled reign of you and your friends—that was just going to be a bonus—but because they want what is still hidden inside it."

Still? "There's never been anything inside it but demons, and I assure you, no one wanted those."

"You're wrong."

"I'm right," he insisted.

"No, you're very, very wrong."

"Right."

"Listen to me!" she said as a sudden burst of wind tousled her hair. "Zeus didn't command Pandora to guard dimOuniak because of the demons trapped inside. Does that really sound like him? He is selfish. Power-hungry. He doesn't care about the fate of the humans or even the Greeks. He cares about his own and nothing more."

Inarguable. "So why have someone guard the box?"

"Because of what is still inside it."

Frustrated, he said, "And now we've come full circle. Demons were inside it. They were released and placed inside my friends and me. The box is now empty."

"There's a huge gap in your reasoning, warrior." She rubbed her temple, her own frustration clearly just as keen. "Demons are a dime a dozen. Why care about the ones in the box and not the others still running rampant?"

"Because ours are more powerful."

"An attempt to flatter yourself?" She shook her head, clearly unimpressed. "Think about it. The demons weren't put inside the box to save the world from evil. Evil was already here. The demons were put inside the box to keep people from obtaining the treasure."

The word *treasure* was like a hook in his mouth, drawing him deeper into her story. "What treasure?"

Her entire countenance softened, and she said worshipfully, "The Morning Star."

He racked his brain, came up empty. "And that is?"

"Something the Most High made, an extension of his power…a power far stronger than what even I wield. With it, nothing is impossible. The dead can be revived. Any disease can be cured. Demons can be removed with no adverse consequences."

What she described…it was his every dream come to startling life. He could be freed from Disease and returned to his former glory. He could have the life he'd always desired…could have *everything* he'd ever desired.

He could bring Mari back to life.

He could have Keeley in his bed. Naked. His to do with as he pleased. No consequences.

He would put his hands all over her. He would trace her every curve and bask in the warmth and softness of her skin. He would make her moan and writhe, louder and harder than before. He would put his fingers inside her, take her that way first. Then he would lick up the honey she offered him. Then…oh, *then* he would fill her up with all that he was.

Torin's entire life plan shifted. His end goal— changed. Hope—ignited.

Will stop at nothing to have the Morning Star.

"Knew you'd like that one," Keeley said with a grin. "Humans originally owned the Morning Star, but Lucifer stole it and had it placed inside the box right along with the demons, most likely to frighten thieves away. Somehow Zeus got hold of it."

"But if this Morning Star is so important, why give it to Pandora? She's just one warrior. And an incompetent one, at that."

"Think about it," Keeley said again. "She wasn't given the box for what she could do, but for what she couldn't do—resist its allure. I have heard of her insatiable curiosity."

"But…if *that's* true, why didn't Zeus open the box himself? And why punish my friends and me for doing so?"

"Silly warrior. He wanted the Morning Star, not the wrath of the demons. And you weren't punished for opening the box…you were punished for *losing* it."

Torin absorbed the inundation of new information, shocked to his soul. "If Zeus had been waiting for it to be opened, why not grab it while we were busy fighting the demons?"

"Someone beat him to it."

"Who?"

"It doesn't matter." She stiffened, her attention whipping to the side. Her ears twitched, reminding him of a dog that had just heard a strange noise—and he would never, ever admit that aloud. Even though it was cute as hell. She scowled.

He barely stifled a moan, thinking she was about to retreat again.

But she said, "Hades's minions have found me," and jumped to her feet, swiping a blade from the kitchen counter.

CHAPTER TEN

EMOTIONS GOT THE best of me one too many times. Keeley tightened her grip on the knife. The minions had tracked her to this other realm. They wouldn't settle for taunting her, as they'd been forced to do inside the prison.

Shall I bow to you, Your Filthiness?

Here doggy, doggy. A rat was thrown through the bars. *Have a delicious snack.*

Cackle, cackle. Oh, how she'd hated the cackles.

No, today they'd come to fight her.

Who—or what—had Hades sent this time? There were so many different kinds of minions to choose from. Animal-like. Humanoid. Nephilim. Spirits. And everything in between.

"Do you have any true battle experience?" Torin asked, swiping a blade from the kitchen counter.

Did he not remember being smacked in the face with a branch? "Some." However, most fights with her ended in seconds, and she never even had to throw a punch. But she couldn't go that route; she'd topple the house. Torin would be hurt—because of his stupid brimstone scars, she wouldn't be able to flash him to safety.

"If you leave," she said, "I can—"

He raised his hand, speaking over her. "I'm not going anywhere."

"But—"

"No, princess. If you're here, I'm here. End of." A tone as hard as iron.

She stomped her foot. "Not end of!" The house began to shake. "I've got crazy-mad skills and I'm going to use them. Your presence hinders me. So you're going to walk away, or I'm going to…going to…"

"Now, princess," he said, and traced the line of her jaw with a gloved finger. "You concentrating on me?"

He's calming me….

Knows me too well…knows he's my weakness.

"I realize you're Super Powerful Wonder Woman and all," he continued, all seduction and heat, "but I've been itching for combat. I *need* it. So do me a solid and let me field this. Please?"

Must disregard the little flutter in my heart.

The shaking faded…ceased altogether. "Terrible plan," she muttered. "I won't be able to control my re-action if you're harmed. Maybe it'll be best if there's not a fight at all." Yes. Excellent idea. She pulled away from him—surely the toughest thing she'd ever done—and raced to the doorway, cutting her wrist along the way.

"What are you doing?"

Fat crimson droplets pooled in front of the door. But by the time she reached the first window, the wound had sealed and she had to cut again. "I'm blocking the demons from entry."

"Well, you just stop that right this second. If the enemy isn't able to get to us here, they'll just pursue us elsewhere."

She ignored him, saying, "Evil cannot enter a home marked with the blood of the pure. And as I still have the light of a Curator inside me, I'm still considered pure." As she raced to the final window, eight minions burst through the glass. Shards sprayed the room, several biting into her flesh.

She drew up short.

The creatures were of the animal variety. Her least favorite. Spiderlike, with ten legs each, crawling along the walls. But the ends of those legs weren't soft and sticky; they were metal hooks and *scrrraped* everything they touched.

All of the minions peered at her, their hairy lips lifted in sneering grins, revealing long, sharp fangs.

Something prevented her from flashing each one to another realm...and there was only one viable answer. They were warded. Hades's doing, surely.

"Our king heard of your escape and would like a word with you, Keeleycael. Don't expect to enjoy it."

Hades could flash anyone anywhere—except her. He'd always hated that. "Oh, don't you worry. I'll be having a chat with your king soon enough." Calm on the outside while she trembled on the inside. *Not ready to face him. Not yet. But soon.*

Before her conversation with Torin, she had forgotten about the Morning Star. If—when—she possessed it, she would be able to kill Hades, free Torin and all of his friends of their demons and bring Mari back to life. All in one swoop.

Then Keeley could create the kingdom of her dreams. Vast, impenetrable and diversified. A home for immortals who'd been rejected by their own people.

She would rethink her decision to marry a kind, sweet male, however. She was beginning to think she would do better with someone...volatile.

"Going to give you boys five seconds to leave." Torin claimed a position in front of her, his stance one of challenge, aggression and excitement. He'd grabbed another blade and gripped the two in his gloved hands. "Stay, and I will reroute your intestines—through your mouth."

The threat didn't sit well with the minions. They hissed at him.

"One." Torin's voice rang out, eager. "Five." He gave no other warning, just launched forward.

The spiders dropped from the ceiling and walls and headed straight for him, Keeley momentarily forgotten. Concern took root…unfamiliar to her. If a single hair on her warrior's head was—

Wow. Okay.

Needn't have worried.

Torin dove to his knees and slid the rest of the distance, going *under* one of the minions and running the tip of his blade through the creature's torso. Guts splashed onto the floor; organs thudded.

One down. And so spectacularly.

She jumped up and down, clapping—and seven sets of beady eyes suddenly focused on her.

Grinning coldly, she said, "Can't fault the keeper of Disease for his actions. He *did* warn you."

Different degrees of rage met her words. Each of the minions kicked into high gear, closing in on her. Scratch that. Not "each." Torin had grabbed two by the legs and jerked them behind him. As the creatures flailed, trying to find purchase, he released them—only to stab each one through the skull.

Three down.

Stop watching adoringly. Engage!

Right. Five minions, almost within reach. Keeley sprang into action, cutting off a claw aimed for her neck as well as a claw aimed for her heart. A third claw slammed into her arm, but she flowed with the momentum, going to her knees and spinning outside the fight circle.

Jab. Jab. She stabbed a minion from behind, shredding both of his kidneys.

Four down.

This was almost fun.

A claw swiped at her. With one hand, Torin yanked her out of the way. With the other, he slashed at the culprit. Another thud rang out.

Music to my ears.

"Stay," Torin barked.

Barked...at her? Not music. "I was doing so well."

"But it's my turn." As Torin danced through the minions, his arms moving swiftly, crisscrossing then straightening, always removing a body part belonging to one of the spiders, he flicked her a hard glance. To make sure she watched him?

Trying to impress me?

Warm tingles in her chest. No one had ever done such a thing for her. King Mandriael had been so impressed with himself, he'd just assumed everyone else was, too. Hades simply hadn't cared enough. His motto: *take me or leave me—hell, just go ahead and leave me already.*

Wait. Warm tingles...the beginning of a bond? She gulped, shook her head. No! Not here, not now. Not ever. Not with him. But the warmth grew more intense, the tingles stronger.

Have to stop this.

A still-beating heart rolled in her direction.

It was a gift.

The warmth inside her kicked up another notch until perspiration created a sheen on her skin.

If I bond to him, he'll kick me out of his life.

Another claw joined the ever-growing pile of goodies, then a spinal cord…a pancreas. An-n-nd, here came a sloshing stomach.

Warmer…no, hotter. So hot. Burning her up, the tingles more like slashing daggers. *Going to happen any moment…whether I like it or not…*

Maybe Torin would change his mind about the bond. He'd carved her chess pieces, after all. He'd held branches out of her way and foraged for treats, never realizing she'd secretly tossed every morsel, unwilling to risk poisoning. Still. He'd done it. For her.

He'd also ensured she had a soft pallet every night. Had asked if she was cold and stoked the fire when she said she was.

"You weren't even watching?" he demanded.

His voice—loud and filled with incredulity—yanked her from the dread and hope of her musings. He stood in front of her, covered in the blood of the enemy. Hair soaked red was plastered to his scalp. His shirt had several rips, revealing deep wounds in his chest.

Never looked more beautiful…

"The demons—" she began.

"Are dead. They can't become carriers." He scowled. "You didn't watch."

"I did," she assured him, trying not to betray the fact that her knees had gone weak. "Truly impressive wet work, Charming. Some of the best I've ever seen."

His expression neutralized even as his chest puffed with pride, a reaction she'd seen from him once before. *Liked it then, really like it now.* "I can be fearsome," he said.

Had someone told him otherwise? *I'll force the cul-*

prit to kneel before him and beg for mercy that will never come! "You can be—and you were."

He nodded, satisfied with that. "Will more demons hunt you?"

"Probably not today. But soon." When the spiders failed to return to Hades, he would know they'd been slain. He would seek revenge.

He wasn't one to let even the mildest of offenses pass.

"Why did they attack you?" Torin asked.

"They are tasked with reporting my condition to Hades."

He planted his feet wide apart, as if preparing for another battle. "Why? Does he still want you?"

"Maybe. But not because he loves me, if that's what you're thinking. He didn't even love me while we were together or he wouldn't have sold me to Cronus for a barrel of whiskey." *Bitterness showing.* "I'm a threat to him, and he does not like threats."

Rage detonated in Torin's eyes. "A barrel of whiskey? You, who are priceless?"

And just like that, the bond clicked into place.

A cry of pain parted her lips, an inferno raging inside her. Her power buoyed, crackled, and need for Torin suddenly intensified to a nearly unbearable level.

"What's wrong?" Torin demanded. "What happened?"

How could I have allowed this?

Can't tell him. Shouldn't even think of it.

Must never rely on it.

"I'm…fine," she gasped out, all systems go. "Just fine." *Never experienced anything so delicious.*

Must touch him.

No, no.

A sharp hiss of breath from him. "Your eyes are glowing. That's bad enough, but paired with the way you're looking at me…"

She licked her lips. *Must kiss him.* "How am I looking at you?"

"Like I'm not just a hero…like I'm something special." He spat the words as if he couldn't quite believe them even as he spoke them.

"That shouldn't be a surprise. I told you that you were."

"But I'm not!" he burst out. "Not yet."

Yet? Not until…what?

Must have him.

"I'm a bad bet right now," he said and backed away from her. "You know this, but you're allowing desire to influence your thinking. I thought you were smarter than that."

Blaming her?

Or fighting his own emotions?

That. His desire pulsed through the bond, feeding hers.

Have to pretend I can't feel it.

Can't pretend. Too desperate. "And I thought *you* were smarter," she said. "You don't get to decide what happens between us. Not anymore." She approached him slowly, purposefully. She could have brushed against him but didn't, not yet. She stopped a whisper away. "You're not the predator in this situation. I am. I take what I want."

He continued trying to distance himself even as a passion-fever flushed his cheeks.

She trailed him, determined. "I won't be denied my prize."

His gaze dipped to her mouth, his pupils spreading like spilled ink over his irises. The heat that radiated from him was a magnificent stroke. "Prize…for information?"

"Use whatever excuse you'd like." For the first time in a very long time, she didn't care about tomorrow, only today. This moment. Being with this man. "But this *is* happening." At last Keeley brushed her chest against his.

He didn't back away, not this time. He remained in place, teeth grinding as he struggled for control.

I will help him lose it. She traced her fingertip from the collar of his shirt to the waist of his pants, careful to avoid his wounds. He cursed her, but still he did not move away from her.

"More?" she asked, flattening both palms on his chest. His heart thudded fast, erratic. Slowly she moved her hands up…up…until her arms were wrapped around his nape.

"Keeley," he said on a groan. Then he shook his head. "We should wait. The Morning Star."

"I don't want to wait. Not anymore." She rose to her tiptoes, their lips coming closer and closer with every second that passed. Closer and closer to the point of no return. "I want what I want when I want it."

He stopped breathing. *She* stopped breathing. They hovered there, lost in a suspended moment of utter agony. Agony and pleasure. Mmm, the pleasure. They weren't actually doing anything, and yet the promise of more was an irresistible temptation…driving her closer and closer still…until she couldn't stand the tight coil of tension a moment longer and pressed her lips to his.

He jolted. She licked. His lips remained closed to her,

but they did soften. *Still thinks to resist me?* She dissolved against him, fusing their bodies, and gave another lick; this time his tongue peeked out to meet hers.

That's all it took. With a moan, he opened the rest of the way for her. Their tongues thrust together, a tide of ecstasy completely overtaking her...drowning her and making her like it...even making her crave the end.

His kiss was rough and raw, desperate as he backed her into a wall. He gripped her by the waist and lifted her, his mouth never leaving hers. Suddenly their bodies were in perfect alignment. Two puzzle pieces fitted together. As she wrapped her legs around him, his hands moved into her hair, fisting the strands. But they didn't stay there for long. They roamed over her, squeezing her shoulders, cupping her breasts.

The lower part of him rubbed against the lower part of her. "You're so wonderfully hard," she gasped.

"You're so amazingly soft." He kneaded with the most decadent force.

She moaned his name with all the need pent up inside her, and he—

—roared with agony and scrambled away from her. She fell to the floor.

He was trembling.

She was trembling harder, and panting. She straightened.

He stood there for a long while, peering at her through narrowed eyes, fighting for air. "You shouldn't have done that. I shouldn't have let you."

"The damage is done—if there's any damage at all."

"Prolonged contact—"

"I don't care," she said, "I want more."

His hands fisted and unfisted as he weighed her

words. Finally, he said, "You want more, princess? Very well. Against my better judgment, you'll get it. I just hope you're ready."

TORIN GRABBED KEELEY by the back of the neck the way he liked, the way *she* liked, and hauled her against him. Hunger had been clawing at his insides since he'd finished the fight with the spiders—hell, long before.

He should be well acquainted with it. He'd always known hunger. Since his possession, there hadn't been anything else for him. He'd never really learned to go slowly, to just take a little bit at a time. To make a meal last. As he'd proven. And now all he wanted to do was gorge and gorge and gorge until there was nothing left. When she had dared close the gap between them, the scent of cinnamon wafting from her, filling his nose, fogging his brain, his mouth had watered and his hands had itched and resisting had been futile.

Then she'd kissed him, and he'd felt like a man who'd just jumped out of a plane—without a parachute. He'd loved the ride down, the free-fall, but hated the landing. Or would have, if he'd survived. The old Torin had burned away, flames bathing him. But a new Torin had risen, stronger, weaker, everything in between, and Keeley had become his only source of water. A man needed water to survive.

He thrust his tongue into her mouth. Their teeth banged together, causing a sharp lance of pain. He fought for control and eased off. His tongue rolled against hers, giving rather than taking. She met him stroke for luscious stroke, giving back. Her hands fluttered around his waist, holding on to him as if she feared he would float away at any moment.

He savored her, this fine wine he didn't deserve, and worked her just right; he forced himself to be gentle with her. Good, good. Like that. Taking his time, allowing him to memorize every exquisite detail. The silk of her hair brushing against his face. The softness of her lips. The velvet caress of her skin. The honey of her scent. The sugar of her taste.

"Torin," she panted, then lifted her head and took all that goodness with her. "I want—"

"No," he said, knowing the worst had happened. She had decided to end things. "I'll do better." He would. Because he wasn't done. Didn't think he would ever be done. She had become every fantasy he'd ever had. No, she was *greater* than every fantasy he'd ever had.

"Impossible," she said with a soft, sweet smile.

He relaxed and tugged her back against him. "I want more."

"Yes," she said against his lips. "You promised. I crave. I just wish…"

Everything but his raging heartbeat stilled. "What? What do you wish? Tell me, and I'll give it to you."

"Let me show you." She pushed him to the floor and straddled him. "Keep your hands at your sides."

Not touch her? The idea alone proved worse than any of the threats she'd once issued—he would rather have his skin removed with a cheese grater, his organs turned into a smoothie.

"Why?" he croaked. "Am I too rough with you?"

"Too rough?" She rubbed her nose against his. "Warrior, there's no such thing as too rough with me. But this is the first time I've gotten my hands on you…probably the first time *you've* had this. I intend to relish every second and make sure you love it, too."

Relish...yes. "I can't not touch you." He cupped the fullness of her breasts, luxuriated in the feel of her plump softness, the heavy weight. The tips distended under his palm—he *felt* the transformation. *Magnificent.*

She grabbed the collar of his shirt and ripped the material down the center. Then her hands were on him, her nails in his freshly healed flesh. "Touch me, then, but whatever you do, do not stop kissing me, Charming."

"Nothing will stop me." He fisted her hair and yanked her back for another taste. *Careful.*

But she moaned her approval and after a while, the warnings inside his head ceased to matter. No such thing as too rough, she'd said, and she never lied. Her tongue eagerly met his, thrusting hard, eliciting a wild, carnal pleasure inside him. The more she demanded from him...the more she responded to him, the more he devoured her—feasted.

Have been starving, and she's a banquet.

"More," he commanded.

She tangled her fingers in his hair and tugged the strands. To make him stop? "I'll give you more if you stop holding back," she said. "I won't break."

Well, he might. He was already panting. *But my woman is panting harder.* Her mouth was red, moist and swollen. Claimed.

"You don't know what you're asking for," he told her.

"Asking? No, Charming. I'm demanding. Give me harder," she said and pressed her mouth against his, firm and determined as she licked inside.

The leash on my control is fraying....

His tongue rolled against hers with more force, and though he hated himself, knew the pressure was too much; even though she'd demanded he take, take, take, he couldn't stop. Because he ached. Terribly. His muscles were clenched on bone. The fiercest desire he'd ever experienced raged through his veins, an unquenchable fire. He didn't just want to touch Keeley. He wanted to own her and force her to feel as violently as he was.

Leash...broken.

Screw gentle. He would bring her to climax and then he would chase his own.

He took her harder, and faster, but she didn't seem to mind. Moaning, she squirmed against him. Her nails scraped his back, and if not for what remained of his shirt, the material barely hanging on, she would have drawn blood.

He loved it.

He palmed her breasts again, those full, heavy breasts, and scored his thumbs over her nipples. The gloves annoyed him, and he stopped kissing her only long enough to rip one off with his teeth. That hand returned to her immediately, his thumb once again stroking over that sweet little bud. Still a barrier. He yanked her shirt over her head, cupped her and shuddered. She was as soft as satin. Warm. Perhaps the sweetest thing he'd ever touched.

He lowered his head. She gave another moan, arching into him, and his shaft jerked against his fly. Damn. He was close to tossing her to her back, tearing her panties off and plunging inside her, the pressure inside him building to an almost unbearable degree.

She had been made for him. He was sure of it.

He cupped her ass and forced her into a hard, punishing grind against him, but she didn't seem to mind that, either. Her nipples abraded his chest, and she seemed to love the friction as much as he did, gasping his name again and again.

Slow down! Any moment, he would blow. This need…

It was too much. Too intense, he thought again. Rushing through him, firing up his blood—she was kindling, making him burn all the hotter. Addicting him.

Can't ever give her up. The demon didn't matter—wouldn't matter until later.

A shower of ice inside him.

The demon. Later.

The words echoed in his mind, the ice drizzling through the rest of him. Keeley was going to sicken. Again. With their actions, they'd made sure of it. For all he knew, the longer he kissed and touched her, the sicker she would become.

He'd only ever touched someone briefly. Never had this kind of prolonged contact. This was new territory for him, and he couldn't be sure of what would happen next.

What if she died this time?

With a roar, he wrenched away from her. She plopped to the floor as he stood. Damn it! What had he done? "I'm sorry. So sorry, princess. I should have forced you to wait."

She lumbered to trembling legs. "I'm only sorry you stopped." Eyes dazed, she reached for him.

He dodged her. *Killing me!* But better his death than hers. "Don't. We can't."

"We can." Again, she reached.

Again, he dodged. "No, Keys, we can't." He took another step away from her. *At my breaking point.* If she came at him again, he might just let her catch him. "We should prepare ourselves. You're going to sicken."

She stopped, the reminder changing her entire demeanor. From pliant and willing to tense and guarded.

"I'm sorry," he repeated, but the words would never be good enough.

CHAPTER ELEVEN

KEELEY DUG TWO T-shirts out of the backpack. One proclaimed "Strider Can Beat Me Anytime," and the other "I Left My Heart In Paris." She couldn't mask her trembling. After she and Torin dressed, she rummaged through the house for a pair of scissors, a needle and some thread.

"Your shirts have the weirdest sayings," she muttered.

"My friends make them for me."

No wonder he loved the men so deeply.

She sat in front of the crackling fireplace and got to work, cutting and sewing bits and pieces of their old shirts, though her mind wasn't on her task. *What have I done?* How had she managed to convince herself that she wouldn't sicken…and that, if she did, enduring another illness would be okay? Sick equaled weak and weak equaled vulnerable.

Outside, snow blustered, her emotions turning the autumn season to winter.

"How do you feel?" Torin asked, breaking the silence as he paced in front of her.

"Fine." And it was true. She did. But she'd felt fine the last time, too.

"Good. That's good."

But how long would it last?

She held the shirt to the light. Great! She'd done everything wrong. She undid her stitches and, doing her best to remain calm, started again.

"Distract me," she said.

"Okay. Who stole Pandora's box after it was opened?" he asked. "You never told me."

"And I won't." She'd heard the rumors, knew Torin was friends with the man. He might not believe her, might even take sides against her. "I don't want to talk about the box."

"Fine. We'll play the question game. I'll ask you ten easy ones or a single hard one. You pick."

"Hard." Of course.

"If seeing is believing, then how are looks deceiving?"

"Seeing *isn't* believing. I thought you said this would be hard."

"Yes, but how do you *know* seeing isn't believing?"

"Sorry, Torin, but you said you'd only ask *one* difficult question. I've already answered."

He laughed, shrugged. "I'm out of ideas."

"Tell me what you were like before your possession."

"Fierce. Bloodthirsty."

"In other words," she said, "nothing's changed."

"Don't be ridiculous. I'm *nice* now."

"What kind of crazy person told you *that?* You're as nice as I am."

"Since I think you're made of sugar and spice, I'll take that as a compliment." He ran his hand through his hair. "But this isn't the time to tease me, Keys. I'm close to shaking you so hard your brain knocks against your skull. Maybe that will finally knock some sense into you."

"So nice," she quipped.

He glared at her.

"Have you ever forgiven an enemy, wondered if their actions were an accident, like yours often are?" she asked.

"No."

"And that doesn't strike you as *mean?*"

"Fine! I'm mean. What does it matter?"

"Self-actualization is just one of the many services I offer."

"I prefer my women silent."

I'm his woman?

Stupid heart, skipping a beat.

"Maybe a bond with you would prevent another sickness," she said softly. *Don't do this. Don't go there.*

Too late.

What if the bond *helped* her?

He stopped pacing to stare at her and curse. "Or maybe it would make you even sicker. A direct line to the demon? No."

Hope, quickly dashed. Was he right? Would she suffer more this time around?

She finished her project and threw it at him. "I know, I know. I'm super talented and beyond thoughtful. You don't know what you'd do without me. You're welcome."

He held the material up to the light. "What is this?"

"Only the best thing ever for a man with your particular ailment. A shirt with a retractable hood. That way you can cover your face during fights and not have to worry about your opponents accidentally brushing against your skin."

"I don't worry about that anyway. If my opponents aren't killed by Disease, they're killed by me."

Yes, she'd seen his dagger work. "Well, I was your opponent and I'm still here."

He offered her a half smile. "You're right."

"Always."

"I don't know what to say."

Had no one given him gifts before? "Say thank you, and put it on."

"Thank you." Motions swift, he removed his shirt and pulled the new one over his head, then anchored the hood in place.

"Well?" she prompted. "What do you think?"

"Don't take this the wrong way, princess, but I kind of feel like Batman."

"Well, *are* you Batman? Has anyone ever seen the two of you in a room together to prove this—" she waved a hand over him "—isn't your secret identity?"

He lifted the hood to glare at her, and she laughed. A ray of sunlight shot through the window as if purposely seeking her.

His expression softened with an emotion she wasn't sure she'd ever seen from him. Tenderness, perhaps.

"Your eyes are glowing again," he said.

"They are?" The laughter faded into breathless giggles.

"They are. And it's lovely."

Losing her amusement, she flattened her hand on her stomach, which was now roiling as if World War III were taking place inside it. "I...hurt," she gasped out—and gagged. She placed a hand over her mouth, but there was no help for it. She hunched over and vomited.

TORIN RACED THROUGH the forest, his boots leaving deep impressions in the dirt. Anyone with a modicum of skill would be able to track him. *Find me and die*. Even the most powerful person in the world—if that was indeed what Keeley was—fell prey to Disease.

How could he have let this happen?

Again!

She wouldn't last much longer. She needed a doctor, medicine.

Torin knew which plants would help her. Yarrow, elderberry flowers and peppermint would help with the fever. Ginger, chamomile, slippery elm, raspberry leaf, papaya and licorice root. All used to stop vomiting. So many options—and yet he could use none of them.

He'd studied the plants in *his* realm, not the ones in *this* realm. Were they the same? Different? Perhaps poison?

He had to find help.

He tracked multiple sets of ginormous footprints to a town with multiple buildings made of mud and straw, each a height and width that made the cabin look like a toddler's punishment pen. There was a bar, a grocery, another bar, a— He wasn't sure what that was. A pelt shop? The "fine leathers" looked to have come from humans.

A male with piercings all over his face entered the farthest building on the right. The sign outside it read Heeling Tonacs & Xotic Elicksirs. There. That's where he needed to be. The misspellings instilled zero confidence, but what other choice did he have?

Torin fit his new hood in place—his chest constricting as he remembered how diligently Keeley had worked on it—and launched into motion, urgency driving him. He remained in the shadows as a horde of giants strode down the street. He managed to get to the proper porch without being noticed. Or giving himself a hernia when he opened the massive front door.

"—get the warts off," Piercings was saying. "I'll pay twenty pounds of diamonds." He dropped a black velvet bag on the counter in front of him. "And you'll get twenty more if you never speak a word of this."

"I have just the thing," replied a man—surely the pharmacist—who was covered in tattoos. "But it'll cost you *forty* pounds of diamonds."

Um, that's what the guy had offered.

"Thirty," Piercings said.

"Done!" Tattoos replied.

Seriously? This *is where I'm to find help?*

Torin wasn't in the mood to waste time or negotiate. As quietly as possible, he turned the lock on the front door and switched the sign to *Closed*. He knew his own limitations, knew he couldn't fight two giants at once without severe consequences, and considering the pelt store down the road, there was a good chance this pair of fine fellows would want to skin him; he was going to have to take one of them out.

He moved forward, stopping just behind Piercings. The top of his head came to the middle of the giant's back. He palmed the blade he'd taken from the cabin, bent down and sliced through the male's Achilles tendons.

A howl of pain echoed from the walls. Piercings dropped to his knees, and the entire building shook. Torin reached around and slit his throat.

The lifeless, bleeding corpse slumped to the floor.

Torin stared up at Tattoos. "I hated to do that, and I apologize if he was your friend, but as you can see, I'm willing to do anything to get what I want."

Tattoos narrowed his eyes. "And what is it that you want, human?"

"I'm not human. And I want a concoction for a friend who's feverish and won't stop vomiting blood." He plowed ahead as if the guy would do what he demanded—because he totally would. "If you give me something poisonous to punish me for what I did to the other guy and my friend suffers or dies, I'll come back for you. I won't kill you right away. I'll play with you first…until you beg me for the sweet kiss of death."

Far from impressed, Tattoos leaned forward and gripped the edge of the counter separating them. "You assume you'll leave this shop alive."

Grinning coldly, Torin sheathed the weapon at his side. Then, he began to tug at the fingers of his gloves. "I want you to know, you chose this path. I didn't. So. Here's what is going to happen next. I'm going to touch you, and you're going to be infected with the same disease that's killing her. Did I forget to mention I'm Torin, the keeper of the demon of Disease? Once you develop symptoms, and you will, you'll mix yourself a concoction, hoping to save yourself. You'll be too weak to stop me when I take it from you."

Tattoos paled beneath his ink and took a step backward. The shelf walls stopped him from retreating farther. "You're lying."

"You'll find out, won't you?" Torin stuffed the glove into his pocket and pulled at the other one. "Once I have what I want, I'll leave and shout that you're in need of help. Your friends will rush inside. They'll touch you, and they, too, will become infected. A plague will sweep through your world, and thousands will die. All this because you refused to help the Red Queen."

That male's eyes nearly bugged out of his head. "You're an emissary of the Red Queen?" Suddenly he had trouble catching his breath. "I heard a rumor she had returned... Didn't want to believe... Yes, yes, of course I'll do anything to help her most exalted majesty. Please tell her how eager I was to offer my services." He raced around the shop, gathering vials.

What, exactly, had Hurricane Keeley done in this realm?

Five minutes later, Tattoos offered Torin a large canteen filled with a dark pungent liquid. "This will soothe her."

"I wasn't kidding. If it harms her, I will be back. If you run, I will find you."

"No harm. I swear! Have her swallow a single mouthful three times a day. It's not a magical cure," Tattoos rushed to add, "but it really will help. If she dies, it won't be my fault. Make sure she knows I did everything I could."

If she dies...

Those words haunted Torin as he retraced his steps through the forest. If she died, it wouldn't exactly be the giant's fault.

Well, she couldn't die. She just couldn't. Not because he'd once again fallen prey to a friendship he should have avoided. And not because she amused and delighted him and revved him up in a way no other woman ever had. But because the world would be a dark, dark place without her.

She truly was a light.

I won't be the one to snuff her out.

His hands fisted, and the canteen he held nearly popped. *Careful.*

In the cabin, the scent of blood had yet to dissipate. He wasn't sure whether it came from the spiders or from Keeley, who remained sprawled on the couch. Sweat poured from her, causing strands of hair to stick to her face. Her cheeks were flushed with fever, her lips chapped from being chewed.

I did this. Me.

Leaving her in this condition, alone, unable to fend for herself, had agonized him. The tonic had better be worth it.

Her eyes were closed, her head thrashing from side to side. "Daddy, please. I don't want to stay with the king." A procession of dry heaves. "You gave me to him—now help me leave him. Please! I can't… Just can't take any more…."

Her own father had given her to a male she despised? A male who'd clearly hurt her. Bastard!

Torin paused as guilt, rage and sorrow tangled up inside him, a special cocktail he drank daily. What a hypocrite he was. He had hurt her more than anyone else ever could.

He double-checked to make sure he'd returned the gloves to his hands before smoothing the hair from Keeley's face. "I'm back, princess," he said. "I'll protect you with my life, even from your memories."

Her chest rose and fell in quick succession as she writhed against the cushions. "I spoke to no one today, I swear. Please, don't kill her, Majesty. Please. She has a family. She— Noooo!" Sobs. More dry heaves.

"Shh, princess. Save your strength." Torin draped a cold rag across her brow before stroking the corners of her blood-splattered mouth with his thumbs. "Everything's going to be okay."

Her lips parted, just the way he'd wanted, and he poured a mouthful of the tonic down her throat. A gagging fit would have caused the liquid to spill out, so Torin forced her to swallow by applying pressure to her jaw and massaging her throat. Cruel to be kind. One of the most difficult things he'd ever done.

She beat at his hands, but her efforts were wasted. As weak as she was, she couldn't have shooed a fly.

So much power inside her, he thought, and yet still she was so fragile.

He waited for any sign of improvement. Instead, she worsened. Blood gurgled from her mouth, choking her, which led to another spell of vomiting. He wasn't sure how much medicine she kept down.

Damn it!

The demon laughed, gleeful over the turn of events. Helplessness…hatred. *Wish you were dead.*

The laughter only grew louder.

"Hades," Keeley suddenly shouted. "Help me."

Torin pressed his tongue to the roof of his mouth. "Torin's here, princess."

"Torin…" At last Keeley calmed and slipped into what seemed to be a peaceful sleep. Torin dragged the dead spiders outside the cabin. The snow had stopped falling, and the sun had stopped shining. The sky was just…gray.

A sign of impending doom?

No!

When he had all eight bodies and their various severed parts in a pile, he lit a match and threw it in the center of the carnage. It wasn't long before the flames spread, and dark smoke curled through the air, carrying the pungent scent of charred flesh. The creatures had slashed through his skin, and even though they were already dead, he didn't want Keeley coming into contact with them when she awoke.

And she would. He had to believe it. Because the thought of going a single day without her was suddenly intolerable.

BETRAYED BY HADES, the only man to ever claim he loved her? No. Impossible.

"Torin's here, princess."

Torin…her new man.

But…he can't be here. I'm trapped. Alone.

Keeley struggled between memory and reality… wasn't sure which won…only knew it was impossible to create order from chaos and if she failed to clear her thoughts…

…She was pacing the confines of a chamber, her heart utterly shattered. Hades's men had come for her an hour ago, locking her inside the smallest, sparsest bedroom usually reserved for the lowliest of servants. Her betrothed couldn't know she was here. Even though his soldiers did nothing without his express permission.

She should have been able to fight her way free of their hold, but her new wards prevented her from doing *anything*.

How had this happened?

She remembered how Hades had given her a special wine to put her to sleep so that she wouldn't experience any pain when the brimstone touched her. How one of his minions had stood by, ready to give Keeley a single ward, one to temper the worst of her power, so that Hades and his people would be safe around her.

But Keeley had woken up alone, with hundreds of wards, weakened, unable to do much more than breathe.

Hades would kill the minion when he found out what had been done to her. Surely he wouldn't have ordered this. He loved her and would never purposely hurt her.

"Hades," she screamed for the thousandth time. If she kept this up, she would lose her voice. "I need you!"

Finally he appeared, flashing into the center of the room.

He was a beautiful man with dark hair and eyes— eyes that pulsed with red any time he considered making a kill. He was six foot seven and lofty. But he wore it well. He had the strength to back up the attitude. Women everywhere desired him. *But he chose me.*

"I trust your new accommodations are comfortable," he said.

He was so casual….

He knew.

A deep wound cut through all the scattered pieces of her heart. "Why? Why did you do this?"

"You were too powerful. If ever you turned on me—"

"I would *never* have turned on you!"

He plowed ahead, saying, "—I could lose everything I'm trying to build."

"Keeley."

She frowned. The newest voice belonged to a male, but not to Hades.

"It's time for more medicine, princess."

Torin's image filled her mind, overshadowing the confines of the hated chamber…the hated memory. She saw his shoulder-length white hair. His catlike green eyes. The smoldering sexiness that always made her mouth water. Like now. Ugh! That was a lot of water. An embarrassing amount. Choking her… *Can't breathe, have to breathe…*

"Swallow."

Cool liquid washed down her raw, shredded throat and into her equally raw stomach.

"Good girl," he said.

Something warm smoothed across her overheated brow, offering comfort. Not his hand. Surely not. He refused to touch her.

Touch her. The words resonated in her mind, prodding her. He hadn't touched her, not at first, but *she* had touched *him.* Then he had grabbed her and given her the hottest kiss of her life. She'd become sick. Horribly sick. All because of his demon.

That's right. The demon.

Hate that demon.

Anger burned through her, hot, so hot, and the cushion beneath her began to shake.

Will murder *that demon.*

"Not this again," Torin muttered. A second later, she was floating—how? why?—but still the shaking continued.

The sound of clattering dishes registered. Thumping logs.

Oh, yes, she thought coldly. *Disease will suffer for all he's done…*.

Torin cursed, and she went tumbling. She…rolled down a hill? Grass and dirt filled her mouth. Dizziness struck her.

CHAPTER TWELVE

TORIN REELED. Keeley had survived another illness, and as quickly as she'd sickened, she had recovered. Within an hour of destroying the cabin, in fact, she was steady on her feet, totally racer ready, with no lingering side effects.

The first time, he'd understood. Others had recovered, too, even if they'd become carriers. But this second time...

How had she survived? He'd asked for her opinion, and her answer had been the usual, "Hello. Red Queen. Super powerful."

Maybe. Probably.

Would she survive a third? A fourth?

Considering the bargain they'd made, she might be willing to risk it. But he wasn't. Not anymore.

Heard that before.

Yeah, but I mean it this time.

Motions clipped, he led her through the forest. He remained on the lookout for vengeful giants. Dust from the ruined cabin trailed them. Keeley stayed behind him, quiet, and the silence unnerved him.

"Do you hate me?" he asked.

"Hate you? Why would I hate you?"

"Do you seriously have to ask?"

"Obviously. Because I did."

"The demon," he said on a sigh. "The vomiting."

"Um, perhaps you're forgetting *I* touched *you*."

No. He hadn't forgotten—would never forget. Her touch had proven just how base his need for her could become, how consuming...how, when he finally got his hands on her, nothing mattered but pleasure.

"Let's not talk about that." He searched for someplace safe to make camp, and when he thought he picked up the sound of footsteps he backtracked, checking for prints he never found.

Desire must be rotting his brain.

And, damn, the hot and sticky air had to be baking his insides. The weather had gone from autumn, to winter, to just plain hell, but he didn't think it had anything to do with Keeley. Her mood did not match the million-degree temperature.

"I'm eighty-sixing my shirt. Don't come within ten feet of me until I put it back on." He wrenched the material over his head, then draped it around his neck to catch the sweat trickling down his temples. "I mean it."

Keeley raked her gaze over his naked torso, and damn if it didn't feel like a caress. "You suck *so* bad," she grumbled. Maybe her mood *did* match. "I'm overheated, too, you know. I think my internal organs have become some kind of stew." She ripped the sleeves from her shirt and threw them at him.

Her sleeveless state made him think about the way she'd studied her arms and legs when she'd first woken up. Whatever she'd seen—or hadn't seen—had relaxed her. When he'd asked her why she'd done it, she'd said, "Like I'm really going to give you any ideas."

What the hell was that supposed to mean?

"Stupid double standards," she said. "If I were to remove *my* top to cool off, I'd be a tease, just begging for ravishment."

"Cool your jets, princess. I'd never make you beg." *But isn't that exactly what I've done?*

"Are you saying you'd just give it to me for free?" she asked.

"I'm not saying anything." If this kept up, they would end up where they'd started. In trouble. "But why risk insect bites? Let's find you a coat. Maybe a fur one."

"As if any insect would dare come near me."

"Still. Can't hurt to be careful." He dug inside the backpack. "I know we've got an extra top in here somewhere."

"Try to make me wear it and I'll tie you down, cut you open and let the animals use your organs as snack packs!"

"Everyone's got to eat." He pulled his empty hands out of the pack. "Unfortunately, we're out of clean clothes."

"Why don't I peel the skin from your body? *You* can be my coat."

"Smart. You'll stay warm during the next snowfall."

She stomped her foot. "My inability to rile you is maddening."

"I'll yell at you if it'll make you feel better." Hell, it might make *him* feel better, too.

She perked up, saying, "That would be extremely helpful, thank you."

He thought for a moment, shouted, "How dare you bare your arms in public! You're damn right it makes you a tease. It gives a man ideas. Makes him think you're good at carrying heavy boxes—which just happens to be *his* job! It's humiliating is what it is."

She laughed, and her breasts jiggled. Breasts he'd held in his hands. Her nipples were hard, probably aching, needing to be pinched and sucked.

Turn away! Now!

He didn't. Couldn't.

Keeley's laughter died, and quiet settled over them.

"Torin," she whispered.

"No," he said, and when she licked her lips, he forced himself to say it again. "No."

A twig snapped, signaling an end to their solitude.

Thank God. Torin palmed one of the blades he'd managed to dig from the cabin's rubble.

"Hide behind that rock." He scanned the forest, trying to ferret out any clue about their unwelcome guest. Or guests. Human, animal, or giant? Or a combination of all three?

Keeley glanced at the rock in question and scowled. "The Red Queen does not hide."

"She does when she's not wearing gloves. Don't forget, you're a carrier. Besides, you've been ill. You need to conserve your energy. And what if your emotions get the better of you? It'll probably be best if we don't destroy the entire realm while we're still in it."

Her scowl darkened.

Since the ground wasn't vibrating in time with the incoming footsteps, he doubted the visitor was a giant. As long as the creature meant Keeley no harm, it would walk away. One wrong move, in word or deed, however, and that would change.

Keeley sighed and trudged toward the safety zone. "Fine. Whatever. I'm in too good a mood to argue."

Really? "This is a good mood?" The sun wasn't exactly shining brightly.

She tripped over a vine—no, not a vine. A booby trap. Very much like the one Torin had rigged in the other realm. The ensuing *click* and *whoosh* gave it away. As she landed on her knees, a spear shot from a hole in a tree. Destination: her heart.

"No!" Torin dove in her direction.

She caught the weapon by the hilt before it could sink inside her chest—or his.

He rolled at impact and popped to his feet, his relief short-lived. Two humans burst from the foliage. His mind shot out facts like bullets. Males. Primitive. Each wore a loincloth and held one of those man-made spears. Probably the humans the giants like to hunt.

The one on the right spotted Keeley and lifted his spear, preparing to throw it.

Enemy.

Once again, Torin didn't waste time with negotiations. He simply tossed his blade; it sliced through the male's throat, blood spurting out as he tumbled to his knees, then to his face, his weapon useless.

The other man—*let's call him Tarzan*—scowled and lifted his own spear.

Torin palmed another blade. "I wouldn't if I were you."

"Oh, goody." Keeley jumped up and clapped, a ray of sunshine suddenly spotlighting her. "Two sexy warriors battling to the death. This is so much better than the spider fight. You've got my stamp of approval, Torin. Carry on."

Tarzan's dark eyes widened with a little shock and a lot of hatred. "You," he gasped out. "We'd heard you were back, but I thought the rumors were unfounded, that you would never dare return."

"Me?" She looked behind her before tapping her chest. "I think you have the wrong girl."

"As if you could be forgotten. You nearly destroyed my entire village, ripping out all of our sacred trees by the root—in a single blink—and pummeling the entire clan with them."

"Did I? Well, I'm sure I had good reason." She tapped her chin, thoughtful. "But I'm having trouble locating the memory. Perhaps this is another casualty of the Time Out box."

Torin kept his attention on Tarzan and his blade at the ready.

"Oh, I know!" Keeley said. "Your people habitually throw children into pits of fire as a sacrifice to your gods." Her eyes narrowed as the tree beside her shot out of the ground and hovered in the air. "I have a big problem with that."

"And I have a problem with you." Tarzan raced toward her, a lethal missile. Midway, she batted the tree at him. He was ready for the attack and ducked, going under the trunk—and then he just kept coming.

Torin tossed the knife, nailing the guy in the chest—no, the back. The warrior moved faster than expected... and slammed into Keeley, knocking her down, pinning her to the ground and wrapping his hands around her neck, skin-to-skin.

A dark haze fell over Torin, a savage roar bursting from deep in his throat. He threw himself at the guy, ripping him away from Keeley. They hit the ground and rolled, Tarzan taking the brunt of impact. The moment they stopped moving, Torin sat up and whaled. The guy's nose broke. His lip shredded, and his teeth popped out. His jaw snapped out of place.

"You don't touch the queen *ever*."

Tarzan's eyes closed, the rest of him going lax. His head lolled to the side.

Torin did not let up. The Red Queen was his. His alone. No one else's hands would ever make contact with her. He would die first.

"Enough," Keeley called. "Alive, he'll make an excellent lab experiment. It's the reason I didn't flash him away before he attacked."

To find out just what kind of disease she would spread? Smart.

Torin glared down at Tarzan. "Congratulations. I've decided to spare you—so that I can watch you suffer." He straightened, his gaze flicking to Keeley. She remained on the ground, and concern propelled him to her side.

"What's wrong, princess?"

She braced her weight on her elbows, hanks of bright red hair framing overbright cheeks. Bruises already marred the elegant line of her throat. After nibbling on her bottom lip, she said, "I might have twisted my ankle."

"Let me see." He gently lifted the hem of her sweats. Slight swelling, minor redness. Rage bombarded him. He made to stand up and return to Tarzan— *Will rip out his throat...with my teeth*. But Keeley wrapped her fingers around his wrist, stopping him.

"You have blood on your face," she said, a soft, girly inflection to her tone...one that made his chest constrict painfully.

"Not mine." He wanted to replace the memory of being choked with a memory of pleasure. That he couldn't...another bomb of rage detonated. "Let's get out of here before more guys with spears show up." He used vines to tie Tarzan to him, planning to drag the warrior behind him, then lifted Keeley in his arms, careful not to expose any of his skin.

She snuggled against him, happy, a ray of sunlight staying locked on them as he trudged forward. "Torin… you know how I said I twisted my ankle? Well, I did. But I also healed."

"Want me to put you down?"

"The opposite. I want you to hold me closer." She started nibbling on her bottom lip again. "Maybe I shouldn't admit this, but what we did in the cabin has only made my craving for you worse."

Strong currents of lust overtook him. "Don't talk like that."

"Don't tell the truth?"

"You only make things harder for me."

"That's the point!" she said. "We both want a happy ending. But maybe I also want it a little more in between…."

Resist.

Heading north, he came across multiple booby traps. He figured what was left of Tarzan's village was that way and switched direction. After another hour of hiking, he came across a deserted cave.

He eased Keeley atop a boulder, and though he hated to do it, released her. When she stared at his lips and licked her own, he forced himself to move away from her.

As roughly as possible, he tied the still-unconscious Tarzan to a rocky wall. "I need to secure the perimeter."

"You'll be careful."

"I always am." *Except with you.* And that had to change. Before it was too late.

Torin worked like a madman, turning branches into spears, setting vines as trip wires, digging pits and hiding them with foliage. At some point, every bit of heat was sucked out of the air, leaving a thin layer of ice. The end of his nose frosted over, and his lungs burned. He finished up and washed his gloves in a nearby river. The water iced, too, and he cursed.

He raced back to the cave before he was cryogenically frozen. First thing he noticed when he stepped inside: Tarzan was still unconscious. Second: Keeley had created a curtain from twigs and leaves and hung it from the roof of the cave, creating two compartments. Tarzan's side, and hers. A warm fire crackled on hers... close to where she leaned against the rocky wall, her knees raised and spread.

She was naked—*ready* for him.

"I wanted to welcome you back properly," she said with a slow, almost shy grin. Light and shadows twined over her, as if she'd come to life from a painting. "Also wanted to tempt you...have I?"

Torin stopped breathing. *Walk away. No,* run *away.* But already he could scent her...all that cinnamon now laced with vanilla...and already he was too close to her, couldn't even remember closing the distance. But he had, and suddenly, she was within reach and he was dropping to his knees.

"We'll be careful this time" she said. "All I need is a chance to prove there's a way."

"Yes. A chance." He trembled as he gripped her knees—electric, even with the gloves—and forced her to part farther...

Never seen anything more beautiful. He brushed a fingertip through the moist heat she offered. *Want this all to myself. Want her.*

He must have spoken the words aloud, because she moaned, arched her back, and said, "I'm yours."

"I'll take care of what's mine." *Will maintain absolute control.*

He wasn't sure what miracle had convinced her to do this, to make her so impatient to have him despite everything he'd done to her, but he would be forever grateful. Or eternally sorry.

Time would tell.

But he wouldn't be leaving. Wouldn't be stopping early. Not again.

He rolled her nipples between his fingers, then pinched them gently, wishing he could suck one, then the other. He resisted the urge—*must resist*—and returned his attention to her core. *Can't stay away.* He parted her, found the spot that would make her beg, and pressed.

"Torin," she cried. "Yes!"

He pressed harder. He'd never gone this far with a woman, but with Keeley, he wanted to go further.

"Inside me," she beseeched.

He slid a finger in nice and deep and marveled. "You're so wet for me."

"Getting wetter," she rasped.

In. Out. He worked her, savoring every sensation. The tightness of her. The slick glide. *Knew it would feel good. But this?* Exquisite.

At first, he moved slowly, always savoring. But soon, that wasn't enough for either of them and he picked up speed. Her tightness never eased up, only intensified, her inner walls clenching on him, trying to hold him inside. His erection throbbed in time with his motions, demanding the same kind of attention. He bit the side of his tongue, tasted blood—and inserted a second finger.

A gasp of delight escaped her.

The harder he worked her, the more she seemed to like it. *Never been so pleased.* She even raised her hips to meet his thrusts, and it was the sweetest agony. The clenching intensified. In and out. In and out. He quickened his pace. Thrusting and thrusting, faster and faster, using more and more force with every upward glide until she could only rock back and forth.

"My queen likes this." He was awed, humbled.

"Yes! Oh, yes," she moaned, squeezing her breasts. "But I want harder. Faster."

"Don't want to hurt you."

"Harder!"

So commanding. Unable to deny her, he gave her harder. The sounds she made after that… Purrs straight from the back of her throat, as if she couldn't quite believe this was happening. More gasps. Crude noises that electrified the air.

"Going to give you even more. Take it…I know you can." He fed her a third finger, and that's all it took. She climaxed instantly, crying his name, drawing a moan from *him*. He continued thrusting his fingers inside her as she quivered, until she could stand it no more and slumped to the floor, spent.

Driven past all sense, he tore at the waist of his pants and used her desire to lubricate his shaft. He pumped up and down with a violence that shouldn't have surprised him. She made to sit up—to do what to him, he didn't know. Couldn't dare risk finding out. He would have let her do it, whatever it was, no matter how dangerous. He pushed her down and rose above her, more and more mindless with every second that passed. He braced a hand at her temple, the other one stroking... stroking.

"One day, I want you in my mouth," she said, and ran her bottom lip through her teeth. "I want to take you all the way to the back of my throat and swallow you. You remember how I like to swallow, right?"

What she described...he could never give it to her, but oh, he could imagine it. Those red lips around him, riding him. Hot, wet suction. An intense burn began at the base of his length. He tightened his grip.

Yes...yes...about to shatter. The burn rose all the way to the tip, and he roared so loud the sound echoed off the wall. His seed jetted onto her belly. The pleasure... something so sublime it might just—

On her belly.

The words struck him. As did realization. As did horror. He reared back. It wasn't skin-to-skin contact, but it *was* contact. Possibly even more dangerous.

He returned to her and hurriedly tried to clean her up before he pushed to shaky legs, adjusted his clothing. Any vestiges of pleasure vanished.

"Torin?" she said, unsure. How perfect she looked. Hair mussed, skin flushed with satisfaction. Any other man would have gathered her close and held her for hours, simply basking in all that delicious femininity.

But while he'd satisfied her in a way he'd never satisfied another, and she'd liked it, maybe even loved it, he might have infected her. Again.

"When I get back," he croaked, "you will be dressed.

You will stay on one side of the cave, and I will stay on the other. We won't talk to each other. We won't even look at each other. If you get sick, we'll deal with it. Until then…" He strode from the cave.

KEELEY WASN'T SURE…couldn't process…*too much.*

The pleasure had been—was!—overwhelming. An hour later, she had yet to calm. Might not ever calm. And Torin, her sweet Torin turned snarling beast, had yet to return.

Avoiding me?

Where was he?

And where had he learned *that?* Using only his fingers, he'd gotten her off and then some, sating her utterly.

Now he expects me to avoid looking at him? Avoid talking to him? Ripping the moon from the sky would have been easier. She craved him more than ever.

She should have been able to logically decide how to proceed. How to deal with her growing feelings for a man who would leave her the moment he learned of her bond with him—a bond that had grown stronger with his every decadent touch. Instead, she waffled.

I have to tell him.

I don't want to tell him.

Omission is as bad as a lie.

Omission is a kindness.

For the rest of his life, she would be invested in him. In his future. Unless he committed a betrayal so fierce the bond withered, like Hades had done, she would want what was best for him, even at the cost of her own life.

Her emotions would always respond to his, his welfare far more important than her own.

She laughed without humor. *He will never be so invested in me.* He feared the effects of his demon far too much.

She had to find the Morning Star. And fast.

In the meantime, she would have to be proactive. She would do everything in her power to change Torin's mind about the bond. She would win his heart. *Then* she would tell him.

Flawless plan—if she didn't dig too far below its surface. But if anyone could succeed, it was her. She was a fighter. And that's what fighters did. They engaged in battles, and they won. She would make him want her—*all* of her—with the same intensity she wanted him. Easy.

Maybe easy.

Okay, probably hard. But she was up for the challenge! The moment Torin got rid of the primitive, she would strike.

CHAPTER THIRTEEN

ONE DAY PASSED.

Two.

Three.

Four. For the most part, Tarzan healed from his physical injuries, which wasn't a surprise. But what was? The guy never sickened. Didn't so much as sniffle. Didn't gag even once.

Torin reeled with the intoxicating knowledge that Keeley wasn't a carrier of the demon's illness. Of *any* of his illnesses.

More than that, Torin's seed hadn't sickened *her*.

He wasn't sure what to think about that. Did he dare bask in excitement? Or should he hold on to his fear?

Could he touch her again? Skin-to-skin, without consequences?

No need to ponder: it was still too risky. But he couldn't stop thinking about what he'd done to her, the erotic interlude on constant replay. He'd had his fingers inside her. And she'd liked it. *Liked* was probably too mild a word. She would have killed him if he'd removed a single digit before she was good and ready.

He grinned at the thought. Ever since her orgasm, twin suns had continued to shine outside the cave. It had blown his mind when he'd first spotted them. A beautiful bouquet of red, pink and purple wildflowers had even bloomed for a solid mile.

Her astounding reaction would hold no sway with his decision to remain hands-off. *I'm made of tougher stuff.*

But that tougher stuff blackened his mood as he prepared Keeley's breakfast. The usual twigs, leaves and mushrooms. She sat cross-legged on a pallet of soft foliage, her bright red hair hanging down her back in glossy waves. A normal man could have fisted the strands and angled her head however he wished, claiming a hard, bruising kiss.

Torin placed the food beside her with more force than he'd intended. She ignored it, just as she'd ignored everything else. Including him. She'd taken his words to heart, refusing to look at him or even speak to him.

Miss her, even though she's right here.

He'd hoped to make things easier for them both. "Eat. When you're finished," he said, worried about her lack of nourishment and rest, "we'll kill Tarzan and move on." A change of scenery might improve her mood.

"What? Really? I'm finished!" She practically leaped to her feet. A second later, Tarzan vanished. "I flashed him into his village—without his skin."

That easily. Sometimes Torin forgot just how powerful she was.

"Now we can go." She blazed from the cave, leaving the breakfast behind.

Why was she in such a big hurry? Frowning, he dumped the morsels into a clean rag. He took off after her, and because his strides were longer, faster, he soon passed her, shoving the bundle into her hand.

"Eat," he repeated. "For real."

"Sure, sure." As they trekked through the forest, she dropped the pieces on the ground.

"Stop that."

"Stop what?"

"You know what."

She folded the rag, saying, "Do I?"

Something he'd learned. When she hoped to avoid a lie but didn't want to tell the truth, she responded with questions. "Why do you never eat or sleep?" he asked.

She glared at him as if he'd just accused her of murdering kittens. "Do you really think I or anyone else could go without food or rest?"

"You could. You have. Why?"

She opened her mouth—

"Don't answer me with a question."

Her eyes narrowed. "Fine. I don't eat because the food could be poisoned. I don't sleep because I don't want to deal with nightmares and vulnerabilities. But who cares about any of that? Let's talk about what happened between us while I was naked."

The stifling heat began to get to him—in more ways than one—and he pulled at the collar of his shirt. "I would never poison you."

"Fun times were had by us both," she continued. "I'm willing to schedule a repeat, despite your abysmal finish." The statement emerged hesitantly, dripping with the vulnerabilities she claimed to despise.

His chest ached.

He hated that stupid ache.

Well, enough! Time to put an end to this. To *all* of this. "Why do you still want me?" Apparently, *not* enough. "Haven't I proven I can't ever give you want you need? Not for long, and never entirely."

"Those are excellent questions," she said, unable to meet his gaze.

Her response angered him. Killed him just a little, too.

What? He'd expected her to tell him he *could* give her everything she needed?

"Whatever my reasons, we can still enjoy each other for a time," she said, hopeful. "Can't we?"

Until someone better came along? His anger magnified, an unholy fire in his veins.

Conversation is optional. Just have to find the edge of the realm and open the door to the next, all while keeping my damn hands off her.

Impossible. He knew the tightness of her sheath, and had to experience it again. Experience *her*. She had become a sickness in his blood. He gave a razor-sharp laugh at the irony. Like the demon, she had no cure.

Can't live this way. Just might snap.

For Cameo and Viola. For Baden. For the box. Hold on, keep it together.

"I agreed to pay for your help," he said. "And I will. But I'll give you nothing more."

OUCH. BECAUSE OF the bond, Torin's attitude cut at Keeley when before it had merely challenged her. And because no other race bonded quite like hers, he would never know how much he hurt her unless she told him—which she wouldn't.

Guilt wasn't what she wanted from him. He felt enough of it already.

"If you don't want to talk about sex…" she began.

He inhaled sharply. Tone guttural, he said, "I don't."

"Then how about we discuss your soon-to-be new favorite subject? Me!" *Might have lost the first skirmish, but I'll still win the war. His heart is as good as mine.*

"I'm listening," he said.

"I've been married once. At sixteen, my parents forced me to wed the king of the Curators. The union lasted four miserable years, and I made sure there were no babies. He was a terrible father to his other children."

"Dude. I feel like an idiot. I knew you'd been given to a king, but not that you'd married him. Your title should have been my first clue."

"Well, Detective Torin, it was just a few months after the king died that I became engaged to Hades, the worst deceiver ever to walk the earth. It was the biggest mistake I've ever made." *Started negatively. End positively.* "My favorite color is rainbow, and I firmly believe raisins are nature's sweetest candy. I don't care what the haters say! I know everything about everything, and the only time I've ever been wrong is the time I thought I was wrong."

His lips might have quirked at the corners. "The fiancée of Hades. I should be used to it, but I'm still having trouble wrapping my head around the idea. What was it like?"

"Exciting. At first. He was magnetic."

"And homicidal."

"Yes, but at the time that was part of his charm. He taught me how to protect myself."

"The lesson cost you, though."

What did he mean? *Too afraid to ask.*

Grinning wryly, he said, "So...what would you say is your greatest flaw?"

"Why? Is this a job interview?"

"Could be."

For what position? "Well, my greatest flaw is probably that I'm far too unselfish...in bed."

He choked on a laugh. When he calmed he said, "You were locked away for centuries, right?"

"Right."

"Then how are you so...modern?"

"Easy. I once had a seer in my employ. She possessed the delightful ability to allow others inside her head to watch the future unfold, and I did. Often."

"Fun, but not exactly helpful. You knew the future, and yet you ended up in prison."

"True. I suspect she willfully withheld that aspect of my life. What better way to escape my sinister clutches?" But enough about her. "What about you? Give me the down-and-dirty deets."

Wrong choice of words. Or maybe the right ones. They both shuddered.

She shuddered with remembered—and still-throbbing—desire.

Why did he?

"If you want answers," he said, "you've got to eat. I mean it."

Oh, very well. He'd been honest every step of their journey. He'd said he wouldn't poison her, and she believed him. She made a big production of eating a single morsel, exaggerating every motion.

"More."

Fine! She grabbed a handful and stuffed everything inside her mouth. There was so much she could barely chew.

His eyes twinkled merrily, giving him a boyish, even roguish, appearance. "I've never been married," he said after she'd swallowed.

When he said no more, she rolled her eyes. "Wow. Slow down. I'm not sure I can handle all this new information."

"My greatest flaw is my total lack of flaws. Do you know what a burden it is, being perfect all the time?"

She fluffed her hair. "Yes, actually, I do."

He smiled and nudged her with his shoulder. Then, realizing what he'd done, he frowned and cleared his throat. "What do you want to know about me?"

She hated his upset over the spontaneous touch but really liked that he'd done it. Talk about sweet progress. "Why do you have a butterfly tattoo?"

One of his brows winged up. "Thought you knew everything about everything."

"I knew about the Lords of the Underworld before— well, before. My spies told me different reports about the tattoo."

"Spies? How cloak-and-dagger."

"I learned from the best. Hades," she added, in case he hadn't put the pieces together. She motioned to his waist. "The meaning."

"Different things to different people. I got it the day of the demon-possession."

"So…it's a mark of evil."

"For me, yes."

"Well, if you ask me," she said, "a butterfly is a weird symbol for it."

"I don't think it's a symbol. I think it's a reminder that evil can hide beneath even the prettiest of facades."

"Do you need the reminder often?"

"Only every time I look in the mirror."

She snorted. "Did you just *compliment* your pretty facade? Your ego must really need some stroking."

"*Something* needs stroking all right," he muttered, his heated gaze raking over her, making her shiver.

Need a brilliant, sexy response. "Oh, yeah?"

Good one, Your Majesty.

He stiffened and jerked his attention away from her. "As for random facts about me. My porn name is Dr. Miles Long. I would rather eat the Nephilim I captured than raisins. Sorry, Keys, but raisins are the result of nature taking a shit."

Ha! "*My* porn name is Ivanna Longone. And if you aren't careful, I will raise up an army of raisins and *we* will eat *you*."

"That might actually be fun. For me." His grin returned, lighting his entire face. "I'm good with computers, can hack into anything, and over the centuries I have killed more people than I can count. At one time," he admitted hesitantly, "I lived for it. Loved it."

"You still love it." She remembered how expertly he'd handled the spiders. "But only on the battlefield."

"And when it comes to the protection of my friends."

A familiar jealousy surged, stronger than before. To be on the receiving end of that protection…not just for a time or two, but always, her future as important to him as his own…would there ever be anything sweeter?

"Do they feel the same about you?" she asked.

"Yes."

"That must be nice."

"Better than."

"Is there a chance they would like me?" Gah! The neediness practically dripping from her tone was humiliating.

She would have snatched back the words, but he

flicked a glance at her, his expression troubled, even pained. "Princess, they are going to go bat-crap crazy for you."

THEY TRAVELED THROUGH three more realms, and Keeley began to suspect they were being followed. She said nothing to Torin. There was no reason to send him on a rampage until she had proof. And he *would* rampage. His mood had darkened more with every day that had passed. He'd even resorted to doing what he'd promised in the cave: never looking at her and never talking to her.

The first realm had been a land of total sensory deprivation. Darkness and silence. Getting through it had been painful, both physically and mentally. The second had been nothing more than a mountain of ice they'd had to climb, and since Torin had refused to cuddle, the cold had been just as bad as the darkness. The one they were in currently boasted multiple fields of ambrosia and poppy—narcotics for immortals—and at every turn they had to dodge immortal drug lords determined to protect their stash.

Torin's protective streak had returned at least, a nice change to his disregard and silence.

She liked to think he used the quiet to battle the intensity of his feelings for her as well as his desperate need to claim her and that, in the end, his desire would win. But the fantasy only carried her so far, and a light mist began to dog their every step.

This morning, he'd wandered off to hunt breakfast. For himself. Only himself. He'd made that very clear. He no longer fixed her meals or made her pallets, hoping she would stop trying to seduce him.

Well, it was working!

A twig snapped. A warrior she'd never before seen strode into camp, his head high, his shoulders back. *May not have seen him, but I know him.* He was one of the prisoners from the Realm of Wailing Tears. His lollipop scent proclaimed his identity before he ever spoke a word.

"Galen," she said with a smile of greeting.

He was as tall as Torin and almost as muscled. He had pale, curling hair and eyes as blue as a morning sky. Such an angelic appearance. His wings had been removed and were in the process of growing back, small nubbins covered in soft white down stretching over his shoulders.

A memory prodded her. After the Unspoken Ones had taken over the Realm of Wailing Tears, they'd done everything in their power to get to Galen. The thought of losing him had irritated Keeley; she'd come to like his arrogance and vigor. So she'd taunted the Unspoken Ones through the bars of her cell until one had marched over with every intention of silencing her. Only, *she* had silenced *the creature,* using a shiv to open him up from nose to navel, guts spilling everywhere.

That's right. That's why she'd killed her first Unspoken One, garnering the wrath of the brother.

"How'd you get here?" she asked. She knew a little about his history. Best friends with Torin and the other Lords…until he revealed their plan to steal and open Pandora's box to Zeus.

When all the warriors were cast to earth, a long bloody war erupted between Galen and the Lords. One still going strong.

Well, he might be Torin's enemy, but he isn't mine. Take that, warrior!

"Been shadowing you," Galen admitted. "And I'm not the only one. There are three demon-possessed crazies out for your blood. Torin's, too. But they didn't make it through the last doorway. You're welcome."

"You stopped them?"

"Violently. Couldn't let them near my girl."

She beamed at him. "That's so sweet. Thank you."

He nodded in acknowledgement.

"Hungry?" She offered up a handful of dried poppy seeds. The hard work required to steal them should have made them taste sweeter, but Torin's lack of attention had left a bitter coat on her tongue.

Galen shook his head. "I don't have long. Torin caught my tracks and is hot on my trail. I just wanted to say thank you for distracting the Unspoken Ones when they came to my cell."

"My pleasure. Honestly." Why couldn't she be attracted to *him?* He was beautiful, fierce and a bad boy to the max.

But he wasn't Torin. Stubborn, disdainful, *poisonous* Torin.

"By the way," he said. "Whatever you're doing to the warrior, keep it up. I've never seen him so riled."

Please. "He's not riled. He's as calm and cold as, well, something that's calm and cold."

"No. He watches you. A storm is brewing inside that boy, and one day, it will break free. I have a feeling you'll both be happier for it."

The light mist finally stopped, the sun shining.

"You want him happy?" she asked.

"I never said *that,*" he huffed.

Another twig snapped.

"Go," she said, shooing with her hands. But Galen

didn't move fast enough, and she had to flash him a few yards away as Torin burst into their camp. Such an act might have seemed like a betrayal to Torin, and she knew he would not like it. But it wasn't a betrayal—it was a safety precaution. No fight meant no injuries.

No injuries meant no picking sides.

"Someone was here," he said, his voice lashing like a whip. He looked left, right. "Did he threaten you? Attack you?"

There's a chance this man has been watching me.

A chance a storm is brewing inside of him.

Satisfaction filled her. Ignoring his questions, she said, "Where's your breakfast?"

Silent, he searched the camp perimeter for the culprit, and as he did so, the sun glowed a thousand times more brightly.

"Let's go," he said. "The edge of the realm is only an hour away."

Found it already? Without her?

Panic budded, only to fade. He could have left her behind, but hadn't. Galen had to be right.

The satisfaction intensified as she popped to her feet and motioned Torin forward. "I'm ready."

Scowling, he took the lead. They made it to the edge of the realm an hour later, just as predicted, and because she had kept a lock on Galen, she was able to ensure he wasn't far behind.

And, okay, yeah, that wasn't exactly a safety precaution. But she liked Galen and owed him for taking care of those demon-possessed crazies. Surely Torin would understand. One day. After he'd thrown a massive man-fit.

He looked over his shoulder and frowned at her. Why? What was he thinking?

She opened the doorway and, after he unlocked it, stepped through. She stayed close to his heels.

Honk!

A busy interaction of cars suddenly surrounded them, a vehicle swerving to avoid hitting them, then swerving again to avoid a crash with another vehicle. It ended up smashing into a pole.

The realm of the humans. Torin's realm, she realized, where his friends waited.

Dread quickly replaced her satisfaction. Everything was about to change. All too soon, Torin would meet up with the other Lords. Men and women he loved. Keeley would do as she'd promised, finding the missing girls, the spirit, and the box. Torin would do as he'd promised, pleasuring her, and then they would part ways. He would no longer need her.

But I'll still need him.

Foolish thoughts, steeped in fear of failure. *Only setting myself up to quit.*

Never! Her fight for his heart wasn't over yet. *There's time.*

More honking horns. Torin yanked her to a sidewalk, away from the traffic. Someone bumped into her. A female. The look she gave Keeley, as if Keeley had just been scraped off the bottom of her shoe, only to shift her attention to Torin and gasp, caused a droplet of anger to splash through Keeley.

"I am royalty," she snapped as the ground shook.

Firm fingers shifted through her hair, and she whipped around to face Torin.

"Yes," he said. "You certainly are."

He hadn't noticed the female; he only had eyes for Keeley—and he was touching her, willingly, happily.

"The strands are like honey," he said, his awe unmistakable.

Her heart tangoed with her ribs. The color of her hair had changed again, the tresses now a glistening golden-blond. "Summer," she replied, breathless, knowing her eyes glittered a pure baby blue.

"Gorgeous."

"Really?" Smudged by dirt, wearing a tattered T-shirt and sweatpants, without shoes, she had to be disgustingly haggard. Or worse—average. The human woman had certainly seemed to think so.

"Really. I—" He stiffened, glared at his gloved hand as if it were a toddler who'd disobeyed its daddy, and dropped it. "We're on my turf, princess. I'll have rules for you."

Rules? "You're kidding, right? I obey no one but myself, and even that's iffy." Someone else bumped into her. A male this time.

Torin scowled and pushed him. "Apologize or die."

"S-sorry, ma'am. So sorry." The guy scampered away.

"Ma'am?" she shouted, hoping to mask the inner melting Torin's fierce reaction had caused. "Am I wearing mom jeans? I don't think so!"

Torin gave his palm another hard glare. Then, scowl returning, he twined his fingers with Keeley's and tugged her down the sidewalk. Shock! *He's holding my hand now. We're actually holding hands. Like, our fingers are woven together and everything.*

"The rules," Torin said. "You don't look at other men. You don't talk to them. You don't lust after them."

Done. Done. Done. *Shouldn't appear too eager.* "Why?"

"I don't want to deal with another plague."

And a plague would break out because…he would put his hands on anyone she desired…would *hurt* them?

He's jealous. What a promising start. "It will be as you say."

"Damn right it will."

Smiling would have been an inappropriate response, yes? "So where are we going?"

"Somewhere I can charge my cell phone and call my friend Lucien. He'll be able to flash me home."

A flicker of panic… "What about me?"

"You shouldn't have any trouble tracking us."

…doused by shattering relief. "Of course I won't. I'm the Red Queen."

"Yeah, yeah. Super powerful. You will be on your best behavior."

"Aren't I always?"

"I'm serious, Keys."

"Yes, you're seriously insulting me, and you might want to reconsider."

"You will not harm my friends."

"I vowed I wouldn't."

"I know, but—"

"Do not finish that sentence," she snapped. "I might decide your tasks aren't worth my valuable time."

A pause. A snapped statement of his own: "I'm sorry."

"You don't sound sorry."

He sighed, the anger seeming to drain from him. "I am. I really am."

Too easy. It would have been better if he'd fought her on this. At least a little. Because with those five words, he'd just made it clear her abilities were what he wanted most from her, perhaps the only reason he tolerated her.

Win his heart? Did she really stand a chance?

"Just...no matter how this goes down," he said, "please don't destroy my home."

Did he have *any* faith in her? The ground shook. "Do you *want* me to leave you?"

"No." He whirled on her, eyes glittering with menace. "Princess, I'm trying to protect you from a war with my friends. That's all."

No, he was trying to save himself from having to pick sides.

Like I did?

Hardly the same! "I thought you said they'd go crazy for me."

He ran a hand through his hair. "They will. They should. But..."

But. Always but.

"Forget the Lords. I want more than protection from you." Once, she had welcomed his willingness to act as her shield, had even viewed it as a sign of his affection. Today? She saw it for what it might actually be. A way to safeguard his investment.

He softened, but only slightly. "Believe me. I know. You've made that abundantly clear."

Oh, no, he didn't. "Did you just reprimand me for doing what you secretly wanted but didn't have the courage to ask for? If so, I will gut you."

His shoulders drooped with defeat. "It wasn't a reprimand. It's the reason I've had a hard-on for four damn days."

Oh.

Oh!

Oh? Seriously? That's all I've got?

"Contrary to what you might think," he continued, the

menace returning, "I don't enjoy making you sick and wondering whether or not you're going to pull through."

"Do you think I enjoy burning up with fever, coughing up my lungs and vomiting out my insides?" Her anger returned just as swiftly, racing to a higher level. Once again, the ground began to shake. *Calm. Steady. Innocents around.* "Unlike you, I consider the chance to be with you worth the price."

"No, you consider your pleasure more important than my guilt."

Harsh words.

But also fair. Because they were true. She'd never thought in those terms before—her wants versus his emotions. But maybe she should have.

She tried to tell herself: *at least he cares about my well-being.* But it wasn't much of a consolation prize.

"Fine," she said. "You can't handle it. Noted. Our deal is off."

"Now hold on," he barked.

"I'll still help you," she spat, and his relief was palpable. Cared for her well-being? Please. The truth was suddenly abundantly clear. To him she was—and would always be—a workhorse. Nothing more. "You'll owe me favors. Nonsexual. To be named at a later date."

His inhalations came faster, shallower. "Fine," he snapped.

"Fine," she snapped back. "Now go call your friend before I forget that we're partners and lose my temper."

"We wouldn't want that, would we?" A sneer in his tone. "Princess has to get her way or everyone suffers."

Before she'd complained about his calm in the face of her temper. How foolish. "You know I struggle with control issues. Temper is my default."

"What I know is that you use your emotions as an excuse. You *could* control yourself, you simply choose not to. And how the hell can you stand there and chastise me for calling you out about your temper when it's currently reaching dangerous levels?"

Stupid men with excellent points were a nuisance. "Well, I also choose not to be around you a second longer. How about that?"

Before she did something she couldn't undo, she flashed to an underground home she'd procured secretly after moving in with Hades. Every girl needed a sanctuary. *And I need one now more than ever.* Despite everything Torin had said about still wanting to work with her, the entire argument had felt like a brush-off, and she had lived through one too many of those already.

CHAPTER FOURTEEN

CAMEO CURSED, punched a wall, kicked a nightstand, overturned a dresser, tossed the drawers across the room...but, no, her temper didn't lessen. She and Lazarus had fought their way free of the alligator-zombie hybrids—or whatever they were—and made it to a doorway without sustaining any injuries, only to end up in a suckier dimension. Or realm. Whatever!

It was a place where the buying and selling of sex slaves was an expected way of life.

They were surrounded by an army of gun-toting warriors two steps in and knocked out before a battle could be waged. While unconscious, they were disarmed, bathed, dressed in the most ridiculous clothing—or lack of clothing—and locked here...a lavish bedroom with furnishings so fine there was no way they had been crafted by human hands.

Lavish and lovely, yes, but a prison all the same. Unfortunately, the door was impenetrable and there were no windows.

Lazarus reclined on the bed as though he were a sultan awaiting the attentions of his favorite concubine. He was dressed like a sultan, too. Shirtless, though a dark velvet robe was draped over the wide expanse of his shoulders. His pants were skintight and white, with diamonds sewn into the seams.

A bowl of fruit was perched next to him. He popped a grape into his mouth and grinned silkily at her. "Why can't you simply enjoy our newest situation, sunshine?"

How she loathed when he used that stupid nickname. He grew more condescending every day they spent together. "Our captors are going to put us on the auction block. Do you not understand that?"

In went another grape. "Are you afraid no one will want you? You do have that tragic voice, after all."

He just had to go there, didn't he? He always had to go there. Why? It wasn't like she needed a reminder.

"We'll be separated," she pointed out.

Bored, he stretched his arms over his head. He looked lazy. Languid. Sexual. "And?"

"And I need you. You're my only ticket home." He knew how to find the doorways between realms; she didn't. He could see every monster in every world, his eyes opened to a spiritual plane she just couldn't perceive. And when he applied himself, he could fight his way free of any situation; she wasn't always so lucky.

Right now he was invaluable to her.

"Here's the thing, sunshine." He set the bowl of fruit on the only nightstand she hadn't damaged. "*I* don't need *you*." His dark gaze slid down the length of her with calculated purpose. "Not yet anyway."

She stiffened, saying, "What are you implying?"

He arched a brow, amused. Always freaking amused. "What do you *think* I'm implying?"

"If I don't have sex with you, you'll be more than happy to be separated from me."

"Oh, good. I thought I'd confused you."

She closed the distance and swung at him, but he ducked.

A soft, husky chuckle escaped him. "Were your other men so bad you refuse to give any others a chance?"

"I'll give someone a chance—but I have to like him first."

He shrugged. "Your loss."

"Why do you even want this? *You* don't like *me,*" she said.

He thought for a moment, gave another shrug. "Maybe I like that you're available."

Oh, the romance. Her voice as dry as dirt, she said, "How am I not throwing myself at you right this very second?"

"It's a definite mystery."

Argh! He had an answer for everything. "Here's the thing, *darkpit.* If you allow yourself to be sold without protest, I'm sure other women will be available to you. Maybe even a few men, too." She smirked at him. "Have fun with that."

The threat didn't faze him. "Exactly my point. And while I'm fine with that turn of events, we both know you are not. I'll survive. You won't."

She was not helpless! No matter what she'd thought a moment ago. "You've seen me fight. You know I'm good."

"Yes, but you're not good *enough,*" he replied easily. "Those men we encountered? They are assassins. Clearly trained by the best of the best. So, here are my terms. Strip, climb into this bed and give yourself to me, and I won't allow you to be sold to anyone."

A shiver danced through her. The thought of kissing him…touching him…*being* with him delighted her body in the most primal way. He was strength, and he was beauty. He was power in its purest form, and she would love nothing more than to have a taste. And, deep down, no matter how desperately she tried to deny it, she did want him. She wanted to be held, and comforted, and yes, pleasured. An attempt made, at least. It had been so long....

But she raised her chin and said derisively, "So, basically, you want me to prostitute myself."

Finally, a reaction other than amusement. His eyes narrowed to tiny slits. "Are you saying you feel no desire for me?"

She could have lied. She desperately wanted to lie. It was difficult for her to trust the opposite sex.

As soon as Alexander had learned about the demon inside her, he'd turned her over to her enemy.

The terrible things they'd done to her...

And yet still she hadn't blamed Alex for his actions. She'd blamed fear. When she escaped, she went to him, thinking he would love her again if only she explained her situation. He merely lured her into another trap.

As she fought her way free, the people he worked for, the Hunters, had been willing to kill him to get to her.

Come with us willingly or watch him die.

She'd watched him die.

Lazarus isn't Alex. He knew about the demon. And if she was evil, he was evil times ten. What a pair they made.

Besides, she wasn't a coward, too afraid of the consequences to speak her mind. "No," she admitted, "that's not what I'm saying. But force is force. Also, unlike thirty-eight percent of the population, I refuse to be with a man who thinks of me only as a convenience."

"That's a pretty specific number."

"I like statistics." She tended to spout them whenever her nerves kicked up. Torin used to tease her about it.

Oh, Torin. I miss you so much.

He would never have treated her this way.

Lazarus sat up and crooked his finger at her. "Come here."

Her heart skipped a treacherous beat. Gulping, she said, "Why?"

"So suspicious." He tsked. "Are you afraid of what I'll do—or of what I'll make you feel?"

"I'm not afraid of anything." She pressed her tongue to the roof of her mouth and, though she dragged her feet, put herself between his thighs. Goose bumps broke out over her skin. He looked at her, dark hair falling over his forehead, brushing against his lashes. His eyes were as black as night, and she couldn't distinguish pupil from iris, but then, it didn't matter. Both glittered with a heat that burned her to the bone.

He flattened his palms on her waist, and she gasped.

"So pretty," he praised, gaze raking over her.

She wore a pink bra made of lace and a matching pair of panties, allowing him to watch as her nipples beaded. "So sensitive."

She gulped, fought a shiver. "What are you doing?"

His grip tightened. "Your availability is only one of the reasons I want you. Ask me about the others." A harsh command.

One she refused to obey. She shook her head. She didn't want to know.

He told her anyway. "Since the moment I opened my eyes and found myself trapped in a realm with you, I've wanted to replace your sadness with pleasure. And, Cameo?" he asked huskily. "I'm going to do it."

He picked her up and twisted, tossing her on top of the mattress. His muscled weight pinned her before she finished bouncing, and she gasped again.

"I won't buy your help," she forced herself to say.

For once, his eyes were bleak, without any hint of amusement or disdain. "Maybe I'm trying to buy yours."

"But you said you didn't need—"

His lips smashed into hers, his tongue thrusting deep, cutting off her words, the sweetness of his taste invading her senses.

I feel...good. And it was good. *So good. Good, good, good.* The word echoed through her mind. *Never felt this good.*

All the reasons she should resist him ceased to matter. He was using her...fine, she would use him, too. He would probably cast her aside seconds after they finished. *Not if I cast him away first.* He didn't respect her.

"Oh, I respect you," he said, and something about the response bothered her, but caught up in pleasure as she was, she couldn't quite puzzle it out. He ripped the pins out of her hair. "Never met a woman quite like you. Have to have you. Will die if I don't. And I like you more with every second that passes...value the exquisite feel of you."

Resistance fishtailed as he dove back down for another smoldering kiss, harder this time, harsher. She loved it, loved that pleasure stripped away his calm facade and left him babbling, even as his words continued to prick sharply at the back of her mind.

Should be bothered by what he said rather than enraptured.

But why? Actually, who cared? He ripped her bra in the center, the material gaping open. Then his hands were on her breasts, kneading the aching flesh, grazing his thumbs across her throbbing nipples.

More and more misery seeped out of her and it… was…glorious.

"You like this. Will like my mouth even more." He replaced his thumbs with his mouth, his tongue flicking, creating a dizzying friction. Then he began to suck, hard, causing her back to arch up off the bed, pleasure to shoot through her, and his name to part her lips.

"Going to take you hard and fast this time," he said, giving her panties the same treatment her bra had received. He sat up long enough to cast his robe aside and tear away his pants. Leaving him naked. Gloriously, amazingly naked. "Second time will be slow and sweet."

She shivered. Having spent her life with warriors, she was used to men who had been honed on the battlefield, but Lazarus was something else entirely.

He fisted his iron-hard erection as she studied him. "This is for you. All for you. Never forget." His knees caged her thighs, keeping her legs locked tightly together as he once again raked his gaze over her.

Unlike before, when he'd looked her up and down with such calculated purpose, the action made her quiver and ache. He radiated savage intensity, hiding nothing, as if he'd lost his humanity and found the brutal animal lurking inside. As if he would kill to have her. As if he truly couldn't live without sinking inside her.

"Let me show you what's for you," she said softly.

"Yes." He slid his palms under her knees and spread her legs outside his own. He stared at her, his eyes glowing hotly. "Prettier." Slowly he leaned down, every second without his weight agony. But then, finally, he was on top of her, and she was winding her legs around his waist, ready, so ready.

As he positioned himself for penetration, she thought she heard a knock at the door. "Lazarus," she said on a moan, trying to warn him. But all she could do was plead for more. "Please. It's so good."

Sweat trickled down his temple. "Whoever it is will go away." But a second passed and then another, and he didn't enter her. He waited, and the knocking grew louder, coming faster, until Lazarus jerked upright and cursed. "What!"

The interlude gave her a chance to think. "Our captors," she gasped, her desire draining as she realized a fight was about to go down. They were about to burst into the room and drag her away to the auction block. Well, there was no way she would allow anyone to sell her. She would rather die.

The door swung open, and two armed guards marched inside.

A scowling Lazarus threw a blanket over her, covering her nakedness. She clutched the material to her chest and scrambled for her clothing.

"Your Great and Awesome Highness," one of the guards said.

Both men bowed.

Wait. Cameo stilled, her forehead furrowing with confusion.

Lazarus was as stiff as a board, silent. "You have two seconds, and then you die."

Both paled.

One said, "I know you told us not to interrupt, but you have a guest. A minion who says the Red Queen is in play. We know you've been searching for her, sire."

She puzzled over the Red Queen until realization slammed into her, making her gasp. But the realization had nothing to do with the royal. Lazarus was... he was...

Looking at her with something akin to regret. He waved the men away.

They obeyed. Because they were his men.

His.

He wasn't a prisoner, after all.

He stood and tugged on his pants. Then he looked at her again, and this time the humor was back. "Welcome to my kingdom, sunshine."

BADEN HELD PANDORA up by the neck, her legs dangling above the floor and kicking at him. He merely tightened his hold, choking her so forcefully her eyes bugged and her lips turned blue. He did this calmly. Had his emotions been involved, his hair would have already caught fire. It was an ability he'd had since before his possession, and one he'd kept after. He wasn't sure why when none of the other Lords reacted to dark emotion that way,

Pandora had dared to sneak up on him while he slept and plant a dagger in his heart. And his stomach. And his thigh. A quick *jab, jab, jab* job.

Had they lived in another realm, the action would have killed him. Again. But they didn't. They lived here, separate from other dead souls, not good enough for any level of the heavens but not yet ready for hell.

He'd experienced the pain of the cuts but not the ultimate consequence. He'd healed—and then he'd gone after her.

"Do you have anything to say to me?" he asked, just

as calm. She would apologize, or she would continue to suffer.

When she tried to nod, he loosened his hold.

"Knew you'd…react…this way," she gasped. "Hoped you…would. Planned for it."

He frowned—and then he released her. A sword sliced through his back and came out of his chest. He looked down, confused, before his knees gave out. Pandora thumped to the ground, her pained gasp blending with his.

Instinctively, he threw himself in front of her, protecting her from whichever enemy lurked behind him. It was either Cronus or Rhea, and judging by the scent of lilies in the air, he was guessing Rhea. Pandora was his to hurt—no one else's.

Only, Pandora kicked him away and, with Rhea's help, lumbered to her feet.

The former queen of the Titans grinned down at him, as smug as could be. She was a beautiful woman, with hair as black as Pandora's and skin as creamy white. But while the ex-queen had blue eyes, Pandora's were as dark as her evil heart.

The two were working together, were they? A sense of betrayal hit him.

Maybe Pandora sensed it. She spat, "What did you expect? You're planning to leave me behind when you're rescued."

"No," Rhea said, sounding assured. "He's not leaving either of us behind. And do you want to know why, Baden?"

Glaring at her, he gripped the sword by the blade, the metal cutting all the way to bone. Drops of energy dripped out rather than blood as he yanked the weapon out of his chest, the hilt dragging through him, breaking his ribs and emerging with bits of his just-healed heart.

He stayed on the ground, panting but silent.

Irritated by his nonchalance, Rhea planted her hands on her hips. "I'll tell you why. Because you know the Red Queen will use the Morning Star for her own gain. She won't give you a second thought. Or, if she does, she'll make you pay for her aid. And what do you have to give her? Nothing."

"I won't be paying." Torin would, and everyone knew it.

"You've watched the mists same as we have. You know she and Torin have parted, and she may not be willing to help him any longer. May strike out on her own. We can only rely on ourselves to find the Morning Star, and we have to do it before she does. You can strike out on your own, yes, but against such a powerful being, you'll have a better chance of success if someone is watching your back. Someone like me. But I won't help you until I have your vow to grant me whatever I desire when the Star is in your possession."

"Hey! That's not what we agreed," Pandora shouted at the queen.

Rhea flicked her hair over her shoulder, ignoring her, and said to Baden, "Until then." She strode away.

CHAPTER FIFTEEN

THE HOME KEELEY remembered leaving behind was not the home she actually returned to find. She should be in the middle of a primitive cave—albeit palatial—filled with the most beautiful sediment and all of her treasures. This was a modern-day marvel with none of her furniture, jewels or gowns. The new pieces looked to have come from a sultan's harem.

How had this happened?

There was a hot spring complete with a showering waterfall in back. Plush couches, colorful carpets throughout. A coffee table carved from beautiful rosewood and surrounded by beaded pillows. A wardrobe made from the crystal that had once graced the ceiling, bursting with an array of scanty clothing. Hip-hugging jeans. Halter tops. Microminis.

Whoever was responsible had not left any sign of his—or her—identity. And though the changes were nice, they infuriated her. Her sanctuary had been invaded without her permission.

The roof above her rattled. The walls beside her and the floor beneath her, too.

Princess has to get her way or everyone suffers.

You choose not to control it.

Torin's words haunted her. She breathed in…out… forced her mind to focus on positive things. She could

GENA SHOWALTER 239

take a long, steamy shower. She could dress to kill. Then she could return to Torin and make him hard for *another* four days. And no matter how long he begged, she wouldn't touch him! She would deny him as he seemed to enjoy denying her.

Just like that, the rattling ceased.

Maybe she could control the reaction, after all.

Keeley puttered through the entire cave, searching for security issues—finding none. That meant her benefactor could flash, which narrowed the list of zero suspects to…zero. She had no friends, no family.

Perhaps a foe?

But why would a foe help her?

Ponder it later. She showered as imagined, using her favorite soaps and oils, each fragranced with wildflowers and almonds. Though she would have welcomed a nap, her first in ages, her mystery provider had nixed the possibility. She couldn't take the chance someone would sneak up on her while she was helpless.

She dressed in a baby-blue top to match her eyes, the straps held together by—she was just guessing here—a wish, as well as a pair of short shorts, then completed the outfit with diamond-crusted cowgirl boots. Not bad. A little fun, a lot sexy.

I hope you choke on your desire for me, Torin!

"I'm glad you're here. And looking so good."

That voice…like taking a baseball bat to the head.

Slowly she turned to face the unwelcome intruder. Hades. Of course. Because that was the cherry topping on her melting sundae of a day.

He was every bit as beautiful as she recalled—no, more so. He seemed taller, more muscular. Dark and sleek. Wearing a black suit paired with a crisp white shirt and a red tie, he was an object of class and sophistication, as if he'd never known a moment of pain or suffering.

Maybe he hadn't.

But he would. Soon.

The urge to strike was immediate and strong, but she resisted. In war, there were times for battle and times for planning. Yes, she knew the final outcome she desired, but the road to get there needed work. There was no room for error with this man. Especially since she could feel the heat of multiple brimstone scars pulsing off him.

"Why did you redecorate my home?" she demanded.

"To make it prettier when you returned."

Like he'd ever expected her to return. "It was fine how it was. I want my gowns."

His smile was slow to come, but sunlight-bright when it reached full wattage. "There's my Keeleycael. The woman who used to ask me to fetch her ice cream, only to yell at me for allowing her to eat it."

A girl had to watch her caloric intake— Realization struck. "I'm not your Keeleycael," she snarled.

"Are you sure? This sounds like nagging."

"I'm not a nag. I'm a motivational speaker. But I can guess why you did what you did. You used my place as a love shack. Admit it."

"I have no need of more love shacks, pet. I have them scattered all over the world."

"I am not your pet." The urge to strike him intensified. "But how brave of you," she sneered. "Deciding to come to me yourself for once, rather than sending your minions."

He waved away the implied insult and unveiled the lazy smile that had once melted her heart—and her panties. "You are exquisite, pet. Not a day has gone by that

I haven't thought of you…missed you…craved you in my arms."

How dare he! As calmly as she was able, she said, "Not a day has gone by that I haven't thought of you, too—on the floor, your chest split open, your internal organs forming a burning circle around you."

Smile taking on a sardonic edge, he said, "Is that what it would take to win you back?"

Win her back? As if! "You lied to me, poisoned me, tricked me and ensured my imprisonment. We're past the point of second chances."

"I never poisoned you," he said with a frown.

"Then why was I always in a fog?" The answer seemed to download straight into her brain. The bond… his darkness. She'd fed from *him* on a daily basis; he'd known nothing about the fog.

Fine. One crime to strike from his ledger.

The bond with Torin did not cause any kind of fogginess—only an increase in arousal.

"Never mind," she said. "It doesn't matter. I'm older. Wiser. There is nothing you could do to change my terrible opinion of you." Besides, he didn't even want her. Not really. *I'm worth a barrel of whiskey to him.*

Like Torin, he only wanted something from her.

"Keeleycael—"

"No!" she shouted. "Don't call me that." *I'm not that foolish girl anymore.* Forcing her tone to calm once again, she said, "Is this a continuation of your plan to weaken me? To keep me from becoming more powerful than you?"

He walked through the space, tracing his fingertip over the countertop in the kitchen—

Her stomach gave an embarrassing grumble. "Because it's already too late."

—and lifting one of the knickknacks he'd given her. Mental note: *trash it.*

"What I did to you was a mistake," he said.

A mistake. A pretty word for the horrors she'd endured. "How sad for you."

"One I'll never make again."

"Because soon you'll be too busy being dead."

He sighed.

"By the way. You should give your minions a raise. All their taunting, spitting and most recently, attempting to kill me? Gold-star effort. Really."

"Taunting? Spitting...kill? Keeleycael—Keeley, you have my word I knew nothing of such treatment. I sent the minions with tools to aid your escape."

"Sure. That makes *tons* of sense. You could have aided me personally, and yet I don't recall your visit to the prison. Also, your word means nothing."

"I could not give Cronus a chance to imprison me."

"Oh, dear. You're right. But would you call that selfish of you? Or just plain cold?"

His voice was laced with menace as he added, "The minions failed to obey me, and they will be punished."

Liar! And suddenly, she couldn't bear to be around another male so determined to use her. "Leave."

One second he was across the way, the next he was in front of her, toying with the ends of her hair. He oozed seduction...carnality.

She wanted only to claw out his eyes.

"It only took a few years away from you to realize the depths of my mistake," he said.

"A few years," she replied dryly. "My appeal is *that* potent? How special for me."

"I spent time with other women, of course, but none could compare to you. I want you, more powerful than I am or not."

"Oh, I am. I'm definitely more powerful than you."

His eyes narrowed. "We would make an undefeatable team."

And there it was. The real reason he wanted her. He might as well have thrown back his head and given the evil overlord laugh. *Mwahaha.*

"I don't believe death is too good for my enemies," she said.

"See? We think alike."

"*You* are my enemy. I hate you."

"Very well. You need time, space," he said. "I get it. But soon I'm coming after you, pet. You *will* be mine again."

The arrogance! The audacity! "Sorry, but I already have a man." One she didn't like at the moment, but he was still hers. "Actually, no. I'm not sorry. He makes me laugh. He barely touches me and I go off like a rocket."

Rage detonated in Hades's dark eyes. "Who is it?"

That rage—another pretty lie meant to win her heart, to make her think he cared so she would fall for him and he could more easily hurt her. "That's none of your business. But, Hades?" she said.

"Yes, pet," he replied, and he did not sound happy.

She flashed a dagger into her hand and sank the blade deep into his stomach. She couldn't use her power against him because of those stupid scars, but she *could* use a weapon. He hissed in a breath as warm blood coated her hand. Screw waiting. Screw planning. She couldn't resist making a strike.

She expected him to erupt.

He merely smiled again—and pressed a hard kiss against her lips. "Your gowns will be returned by end of day tomorrow. Until next time, pet." He vanished.

TORIN SWEPT HIS arm over the nightstand, knocking off the lamp. Where the hell was Keeley?

Since her disappearance, he'd gone to an internet café, worked a little computer magic, visited a bank and cashed out some funds. He'd rented a posh hotel room, charged his phone. Called Lucien—left a message when it rolled straight to voice mail.

All of that in two hours.

Keeley had been gone six.

He knew she would have no problem finding him. Some flashers—*don't I wish*—could do more than go to a specific location; they could go to a specific person, someone they had some kind of a connection with. And if "some" could do it, the super powerful Red Queen could do it. She just had to *want* to find him.

Disease laughed, delighted by her continued absence.

Torin tossed a lamp across the room, the porcelain base shattering. The moment he saw her, he was going to spank her. Hard. Blistering. And he wouldn't give her any salve afterward!

If she didn't return soon, he would—

What?

Hunt her down and drag her back, that's what. They might have fought, but they definitely weren't finished. If she needed to be reminded of just who he was—

pitiless, merciless warrior—he would remind her. And he wouldn't be gentle about it.

"Keeley," he shouted. "We aren't operating on Keeley Standard Time here. We're operating on Torin Central. Return!"

When there was no response, he pushed over the nightstand itself. The drawers spilled onto the floor, cracking.

"Well, well, Charming. Who's the spoiled princess now?"

She appeared in front of him, displaying more tanned skin than she concealed, her hair falling around her face in lush, golden waves. Her eyes glittered with remnants of her anger. Her lips were slightly swollen and pinker than usual.

"Temper much?" she quipped.

His relief was palpable. She hadn't forgotten him! But the relief was quickly replaced by concern. "Are you all right? Did someone hit you?"

She blinked with confusion. "No. Why?"

"Your lips are swollen."

She rubbed them, color heating her cheeks. "Someone didn't hit me, but someone sure did hit *on* me."

Hit on her. As in *kissed* her.

Already on edge, Torin. Utterly. Erupted.

He forgot everything he'd planned to do and say and got in Keeley's face, snarling, "Who was it?"

Her eyes widened. "Hades. Why?"

"You dare ask why? You belong to me! We agreed. You do not kiss other men, Keeley. Ever. Have you forgotten my rules?"

Her jaw dropped, and she gasped out a few unintelligible words as if she couldn't quite figure out what to say to him.

He stood in place, breathing too quickly, too heavily, his throat and lungs burning. He reached for her, but as so many times before, fisted his hands and dropped them just before contact. *This is crazy. I'm crazy. I have to leave.*

"Are you...thinking about touching me?" she asked, her eyes widening again.

No, *she* had to leave. He could not be in public right now. "Go shopping. Buy yourself something pretty. My treat." He basically tossed his credit card at her. He should be calm by the time she finished. "Come back in an hour. Maybe two. Actually, we'll reconvene tomorrow."

"You are," she said. "You're thinking... Even craving me. You don't like the thought of another man's hands on me, and you want to replace the memory with *your* hands."

That. Yes. Hades would die, and Torin...Torin would touch this woman and never stop.

He gnashed his molars. "Last chance, Keeley. I suggest you take it and leave." Soon. His control was almost completely shredded.

"No way. You're the big bad warrior, yet I've had to come on to you time and time again. I've had to battle within myself—worth the price or not worth it. Well, it's your turn."

"There is no damn way you just suggested I haven't done the same. I've battled."

"When have you *ever* caved without prompting from me? You've resisted me so easily, always walking away. Sure, you've snarled while you've done the walking, but still you left me behind. So, tell me. When did you ever—"

"So *easily?*" he roared. Had she just said *so easily?* She had no clue about the intensity of his need—but he would teach her better.

Torin cupped her by the nape, yanked her close and smashed his mouth against hers. The kiss was a brutal assault meant to silence her, to dominate and possess. He held her still, making her take it, take everything. But the moment she softened against him, *welcomed* him inside her mouth, the darkness churning inside him switched gears. From the need to punish and master to the need to seduce and please.

This was Keeley. His princess. She deserved his best.

He gentled the pressure, rolling his tongue inside her mouth, learning her all over again, tasting her. Summer berries and melted honey. *So sweet. And mine. All mine.* He framed her cheeks, angled her head and rolled his tongue just a little deeper. This time, she met him with a roll of her own.

That was his undoing.

He deepened the kiss. He sucked and he bit. She did the same, her fingers tangling in his hair, tugging as she angled him the way *she* wanted him. Heady, knowing she craved him as fiercely as he craved her. Sultry. Perfect, and oh, damn, he was becoming drunk on her, the need to strip her and take everything escalating.

Strung as taut as a bow.

He anchored his hands on her hips and lifted her. She wound her legs around him, clinging to him. Blood on fire, he walked toward the bed, put a knee on the mattress and leaned, pressing her down—pinning her on her back.

"Yes," she gasped, arching up, rubbing against him. Feminine softness against all of his throbbing hardness.

"Tell me if I hurt you."

"Can't hurt me. You know I like it hard."

My woman is everything I've ever dreamed. Torin ripped off his gloves, then ripped off her shirt. No bra. Good. He kneaded her breasts, then ran his thumbs over the distended crests. His bare thumbs. As before, her flesh reminded him of silk. Her heat teased him. He'd had this only once before, but it had been enough to addict him. Forever.

Have to taste. He licked his way down, flicked his tongue over a stiffened peak, then did the same to the other. Until both were red, swollen and moist. Her moans came one after the other, the sounds music to his ears.

Her head thrashed from side to side, the sight of her uncontrolled passion nearly pushing him over the edge. "Torin."

He twined locks of her hair around his hand until he reached her scalp. Then he fisted, pulling slightly, forcing her to still, his will to overcome hers; her moans became groans of the sweetest surrender. With his other hand, he traced a burning path between her legs. He was trembling as he slid his fingers under her panties.

He thrust deep…and grunted his approval. The heat and the honey, the tight clasp, without any kind of barrier. He closed his eyes as ecstasy swept him away.

"Princess is wet." He surged up to feed her another kiss—and another finger.

She undulated her hips, sending him even deeper inside. "Torin. I need…" She was breathless, panting. "Mmm, harder. Give me harder."

He would give her anything she desired, everything

she needed. He pressed the heel of his palm against her swollen little bud, and she shattered, arching up, raking her nails down his back, crying out, spasms overtaking her. It was a beautiful sight, raw and carnal, one that almost sent him over the edge. Almost. He was stubborn, wanted *her* to finish him.

When she sagged against the mattress, he withdrew his fingers—only to lick them clean as she watched. His erection pulsed with every stroke of his tongue.

"Delicious," he rasped.

Eyes luminous, she flattened a hand on his pec and pushed him to his back. She rose above him. "My bad boy deserves a prize."

Yes. Please!

Straddling his waist, she unfastened his pants. Unzipped. The appendage that had been giving him so much trouble lately sprang free. Moisture beaded at the tip.

What would she use? Her hands…or her mouth?

His hips lifted of their own accord. "Do it."

She lowered her head, golden hair falling over his waist like a curtain. He tensed as her hot, hungry mouth gloved him, the pleasure almost pulling him from his skin.

"Please, princess." He'd beg if necessary. He tangled his hand in her hair—to pull her off or push her deeper, he wasn't sure. "Don't stop. I want it. *Need* it." Had never had it before. Had always dreamed…always hoped, a temptation almost as strong as Keeley herself.

She took him all the way to the back of her throat. Yes, yes, that was more… Was better than anything he'd ever… And…*can't think*. He arched his hips instinctively, again going all the way back to her throat. Over and over she sucked him up and down, moving faster and faster. His blood, already on fire, was only growing hotter. His body was aching and agonized, a live wire of sensation. Everything proved to be too much… not enough…

"Keeley, please."

My darling girl. She didn't let up. She cupped his sac while flicking her tongue over his tip on her next upward glide. And that was all it took. With a single moment of rational thought, he managed to pull out of her mouth and turn away, pouring his climax onto the bed.

When finally he was emptied, he plopped beside her, his heart galloping out of control. Sweat covered every inch of him. He couldn't quite catch his breath. "That was…" Everything. "Thank you."

Must have been the wrong words because her features lost their dreamy softness. A dark blanket fell over her baby blues, hiding her emotions.

"Sure," she said stiffly, rising from the bed to dress in the tattered remains of her clothing. "Whatever."

CHAPTER SIXTEEN

THANK YOU.

After everything Keeley had risked, all she might be forced to endure, *those* were Torin's first words to her?

Not…*Being with you is worth anything, princess.*

Or…*You are a necessary part of my life, Keys. Don't ever leave me.*

But, nooo. She got *Thank you.*

Like I'm a waitress and I just delivered his order.

She safety-pinned the straps of her shirt together. In his haste, Torin had ripped the material. And in her stubbornness, she hadn't packed any of the clothes Hades had provided for her. She'd have to walk around looking like a slutty hobo. Not exactly a testament to her royalty.

Perhaps I'm overreacting. A wee bit emotional. Simply looking for a reason to fight…a way to guard my—

No! *I refuse to turn this on me.*

Torin sat up, pulled on his gloves and his shirt, and then righted his pants. The shirt was new. It read, "Lucien Came Knockin, But I Was Still Rockin." His hair was sexily mussed and his cheeks still flushed with satisfaction. His eyes were bright, his lips as swollen as hers. He looked every inch the sated male—beautiful, wanton, wicked—and her chest ached, the bond between them crackling with tension.

She hated that he couldn't feel it.

Time to tell him.

No, not yet. But soon.

He watched her for a long while before breaking the silence that had settled between them. "Did I hurt you?"

"In what way?"

He thought before replying. "Physically."

"No." She adored the rough strength he wielded. Why was that so hard for him to believe?

"Emotionally?"

Yes! "I don't want to talk about it." Her feelings were too raw. She'd given him access to her body—maybe even her heart. There. She'd admitted it. *Went to battle for his, but might have just given up mine.* There was no other explanation for the wild effect he had on her, clouding her common sense, driving her to recklessness time and time again.

Thank you.

She'd never thought she would despise those words.

He's new to this, fighting it—with good reason. Maybe he doesn't know what to say or how to act.

Maybe she was making excuses for him.

Bottom line: she was tired of being Miss Right Now. Available, but discardable. Willing, but merely convenient. If Torin could have had his pick of women without having to worry about sickness, would he have chosen Keeley?

After their argument…after this? She didn't think so. *What's so wrong with me that no man can value me? Worth less than a barrel of whiskey.*

So. Yeah. She was done. She would stay with Torin, but she would no longer attempt to win his affections. Would never again throw herself at him. Would never again allow him to grab her and kiss her and bring her to orgasm. That part of their relationship was over.

He rested his elbows on his thighs and leaned forward. "Are you feeling sick already?"

Her stomach twisted at the reminder of what might come. "No."

What have I done?

"Keeley," he said. Sighing, he stood.

No way she'd endure another brush-off. "Hey, no need to try to sell me water when I'm already in the pool. I agree. We're never doing that again."

He frowned and took a step toward her. "That's not—"

"No!" She scrambled away. If he neared her, she might fall into his arms and beg. The way she'd begged Hades.

Never again!

"Keeley—"

An unfamiliar male flashed into the center of the room, silencing him.

Bristling with hostility, she faced off with the newcomer. He had shaggy black hair that framed a face tragically scarred by sword and fire, she would guess. His eyes were mismatched, one blue, one brown. He wore a black tuxedo T-shirt and ripped jeans.

Overall, he had a rugged quality she couldn't help but admire.

That didn't mean she would spare him.

"You popped in on the wrong girl, Scarface," she said, flashing a semiautomatic into her hand. A bullet to the head wouldn't kill him, but it would teach him a lesson. A lesson his damaged brain would probably forget. Oh, well.

All around her, the room shook.

Torin rushed in front of her, spreading his arms wide and saying, "Calm down, princess. This guy isn't an enemy. He's Lucien, my friend."

The name echoed in her mind until she made a connection. Lucien, Lord of the Underworld. Keeper of Death. A by-the-rule-book immortal with a fierce temper—one that might actually rival her own.

When Galen had told her about his personal experience with each of the warriors, she'd been most interested in meeting this one. But no longer. Lucien had just ushered in the change she'd feared. Torin was no longer hers, and hers alone. If he'd ever been hers at all.

"Fine. I won't slay him." She flashed the gun to the nightstand as the shaking stopped. "See? I remembered my vow like a good little girl."

Torin offered her a half smile—of reassurance? or apology?—before turning to face his friend.

Lucien locked eyes with him and grinned, his joy unmistakable. "It's you. You're really here."

"I am." Torin's voice held the same note of joy.

Keeley suddenly felt like a voyeur.

With their long, powerful legs, they quickly ate up the space between them. Torin reached out, intending to take the other man's hand, but Lucien caught himself first and stopped, remaining just out of reach. Pivoting to give both Lucien and Keeley his profile, Torin dropped his arm to his side.

He closed his eyes for a moment, breathed deeply. "Sorry," he muttered. When next he focused, he was pale but determined. "I need to retrain myself."

Meaning, he blamed Keeley for his lack of restraint. *Must hide my pain.*

"I'm sorry I missed your call," Lucien said. "Ashamed to admit I was helping Anya hide a corpse."

Anya? *Know that name…* From Galen? Or one of her spies?

Torin snickered. "You definitely got the short end of the stick in the bom-chicka-wah-wah department."

"Speaking of bom chicka wah wah…" Lucien's pointed gaze landed on her, and his head tilted to the side. Curiosity radiated from him.

"Lucien," Torin said, suddenly edgy. "This is Keeley."

Lucien nodded a greeting at her. "Nice to meet you."

"I don't doubt that." But, oh! Why did they have to do the meet-and-greet now? She wasn't at her best. And she needed to be at her best. If Torin's friends didn't like her, they wouldn't tell him he'd found a keeper. They might even tell him to get rid of her.

Things are over between us, remember?

True. But it was always nice to be accepted.

"She's going to help us find Cameo, Viola and Baden, and then destroy Pandora's box," Torin said, not mentioning the Morning Star. Not wanting to get his friend's hopes up?

He can't even do me the courtesy of introducing me as his friend. Or even as his former pleasure-buddy. Search and rescue is all I am to him.

Dance, little monkey, dance.

Irritation sprouted a head and a tail and slithered around her neck, nearly choking her.

Lucien couldn't hide his disbelief as he asked, "And just how are you going to do all this?"

"Is this an interrogation?" A strange sizzle in her blood had her shifting from one foot to the other. "And who is Anya?" She marched to the desk and sat, then kicked up her feet, quite aware she was flashing panty. Let Torin see what he would never get again.

He flew across the distance and draped a blanket over her lap, effectively covering her from waist to toe.

The action of a jealous lover.

A lie.

Lucien watched the exchange and frowned.

The sizzle drove Keeley back to her feet, the blanket falling and pooling at her feet. "You boys enjoy your re-union." Her gaze sought Torin before skittering away. He was stiff, angry. Why? *Doesn't matter.* "I'll meet you...wherever later."

His hand shot out, his fingers becoming a shackle around her wrist.

Lucien made a strangled sound and reached for her. To rip her away from Torin?

She held up her hand, releasing a stream of power to root the warrior in place. Or rather, she tried to release. Torin's scars stopped her.

He glanced at his friend, and for a moment, his expression was all kinds of tortured. "This is between Keeley and me."

"Torin," Lucien said. "Let her go."

"Don't talk to him like that," she snapped. *Taking up for him? After everything?*

Only this once. Because...because she pitied him. How many times had his friends done something just like this to protect someone from him?

She could guess: countless.

Had to tear him up inside, being seen as such a ter-ror by the people who loved him.

He focused on her, and if eyes were the windows to

the soul, his now teemed with menace. "You're staying here. What if you get sick?"

She gulped. Yeah. There was that. The only thing worse than being sick would be being sick alone.

Torin released her to rub the spot above his heart. A sure sign of his guilt.

Never should have pushed him to be with me.

He cleared his throat, then said to Lucien, "How are the others?" removing the attention from Keeley.

"I didn't tell anyone you'd called," the scarred warrior admitted. "Not yet. First I wanted to make sure it was really you."

"Understandable."

"You've been gone so long. So much has happened since your disappearance." Lucien massaged the back of his neck.

"So long? I've only been gone a few weeks," Torin said.

"No. A few months."

"Time passes differently in different realms," Keeley explained.

"Well, hell," Torin said.

"A Phoenix warrior killed William's daughter, White," Lucien said. "She exploded into thousands of tiny bugs and they are sweeping through the world, infecting people with evil. Needless to say, crime is on the rise."

Torin popped his jaw. "What else have I missed?"

"Kane married Josephina, the queen of the Fae, and she's pregnant."

Kane...keeper of Disaster.

Josephina...didn't ring a bell. Last Keeley had heard, a male blowhard ruled the Fae.

"Kane is going to be a dad? Talk about surreal." Torin frowned "How will he not kill his child? Last time I saw the man, plaster was falling on his head and a lightbulb was shorting out. And that was a good day."

"He is no longer possessed," Lucien announced.

Torin gave a slow, disbelieving shake of his head. "He actually survived the removal of the demon?"

Lucien nodded. "He did."

"How?"

"Josephina. She pulled the fiend out of his body and healed his damaged spirit with love, which is, apparently, something of a spiritual medicine."

Torin's gaze flipped to Keeley.

Wondering if she could do the same for him?

Only if you fall for me, Charming.

Or when she found the Morning Star.

"What else?" Torin asked his friend.

"Taliyah took over our fortress in the Realm of Blood and Shadow; according to a bargain she made with Kane, we have to stay away. Atlas and Nike, the Titan and Greek god and goddess of strength, moved to town. Cameo and Viola are still missing, and no one has heard even a whisper of gossip regarding their whereabouts. Anya is still planning our wedding. Like Kane and Josephina, Gideon and Scarlet are expecting their first kid. Amun and Haidee are discussing opening a halfway house for wayward teens. Gilly is planning a party to celebrate her step into adulthood and when William isn't on a violent rampage about his daughter's death, he's watching Gilly with such intense hunger everyone else wants to pluck out his eyes, then their own."

The updates seemed to hit Torin like bullets, one after the other.

A few of the names Keeley had recognized. William, the brutal, savage immortal of mysterious origins was one of Hades's adopted sons. He had lived in the underworld during the time Keeley and Hades had dated. He'd been an unrepentant rogue, seducing his way through the female population. The *married* population. He'd cared for nothing but pleasure—his own—and his sense of humor had been as dark as a black hole. He'd laughed every time he'd killed an enemy and had chuckled every time he'd stabbed a friend.

Keeley had always liked him, but had never thought one woman would be able to hold his attention. Especially not a human. She'd heard this Gilly was an emotionally fragile teenage girl whom Danika, the keeper of Pain's wife, had befriended.

Emotionally fragile…young…single. Not even close to being William's type.

"Well? Why are we just standing here?" she asked. "Let's go see everyone."

Torin did a double take and stumbled away from her, paling.

"What?" She glanced down at herself—and gasped. Boils had popped up all over her exposed flesh.

CHAPTER SEVENTEEN

TORIN HAD ONCE thought he'd plumbed the deepest depths of his guilt, that he'd treated it like a lover, stoking and satisfying its darkest desires. He had been wrong.

This was guilt.

I might just be the dumbest kid in class. Apparently I have to have every lesson pounded into my head with a hammer.

Do not touch a woman skin-to-skin—the path to a regret-free life was as plain and simple as that. But time and time again he'd failed the test.

Now all he could do was care for Keeley's every need. And yet, like the other times before, it in no way made up for what he'd allowed to happen.

Idiot!

He knew exactly how he'd gotten to this point. He'd been enraged with Hades, jealous that the male had kissed her, and the emotions had rammed through his defenses in a matter of seconds. Hardly an excuse. Definitely not good enough. But then, *nothing* would have been.

The need to put his mark on Keeley had consumed him. He'd wanted to brand her as surely as a ward. Had wanted to bind her to him in the basest way so that others knew who, exactly, she belonged to. He'd wanted her to crave him above all others. And maybe she had.

But it certainly hadn't lasted. Her regret had come even before the illness.

We're never doing that again.

The words haunted him.

He applied the herbal salves Lucien brought to Keeley's raw, oozing skin and poured medicine down her throat, then made sure she soaked in oatmeal baths. She remained in a constant state of delirium. Today he'd entered a new level of hell when she had begun thrashing atop the bed, leaving smears of blood on the sheets.

"Help me understand," Lucien said, pacing on the other side of the room. "You've touched her before? And then, after she healed, you touched her again, willingly, knowing this would happen? That her life would be forever ruined?"

Disease laughed inside his head.

Nothing but a rabid dog, remember? His time is coming.

But the guilt took Torin deeper and deeper down the pit of despair. "She isn't a carrier. She suffers, and she heals. But she isn't a carrier."

"Torin—"

"I love you, my man, but my relationship with Keeley is not your business."

"It is," Lucien insisted. "I know you. Have known you for centuries. Have watched you spiral every time you've touched someone and had to watch them—and others—die."

"She's not going to die!" He slammed his fist into the mattress.

It bounced, and Keeley moaned.

"Sorry, princess." He smoothed a gloved hand

through her hair, careful not to snag on the tangles. "I'm so sorry."

Her lids parted, revealing eyes dull and feverish, staring blindly. "When will they grow back? I need them to grow back."

"What, princess? What do you need to grow back?" It shredded him, seeing her like this. In the past, she had refused to sleep in his presence because it would have made her vulnerable. Now? She was as vulnerable as a newborn babe.

Because of me.

He would never forgive himself.

"My hands. I need my hands." Tears cascaded down her cheeks.

I made her cry.

"You've got your hands, princess. I promise."

"Have to remove my feet next. Have to escape the shackles. My hands," she ended, curling onto her side and sobbing.

His gaze jerked up to Lucien, but he quickly looked away; didn't want to see the reflection of horror in his friend's eyes. Keeley had been bound inside that prison and had somehow found the strength to remove her hands, and then her feet, to free herself.

But she'd still been trapped.

The heart *he'd* regrown wept inside his chest. Sickness churned in his stomach. He had to let her go, didn't he. No more staying with her, "protecting" her. No more playing with temptation—playing with her.

Lives were at stake, yes. Cameo's. Viola's. Baden's. Everyone he loved, really. But on the other side of the coin, *Keeley's* life was at stake.

If he had to flip that coin, she would win. No question. No fifty-fifty odds.

It was a huge revelation, but one he couldn't allow himself to probe too deeply. Or why even the *thought* of losing her made him feel as though he were sinking deeper into an ocean of acid and the only thing waiting at the bottom was death. Because honestly? His feelings didn't matter. He had to do what was best for her. For once. Her past was filled with pain and regret. He couldn't fill her future with the same.

He pressed against the coolness of the wall, his knees threatening to buckle. Gaze burning, he focused on Lucien. "Go home. Call me every day. I'll let you know when she's well. Then…I'll leave her here." He'd more than proven he couldn't be trusted around her. She looked at him and he wanted her. She asked for his touch…his kiss…and he gave it to her. Hell, she didn't even have to ask—if she neared him, he was going to reach for her.

He forgot the consequences. Or they ceased to matter. Or both. It was selfish of him, and it was cruel.

No more.

He would be cold, and he would be methodical. But he *would* end things. "I'll make sure she doesn't follow me."

There had always been a countdown for his relationship with Keeley. It had finally zeroed out. He just had to deal.

Lucien frowned at him. "We need her. Cameo—"

"I don't care!" he snarled. He'd made the mistake of explaining the extent of Keeley's power, and his friend was hell-bent on using her. "We'll find another way."

Silence.

Torin slid down the wall. He would never again witness her change colors. Never again watch her morph from Sugar Plum Fairy to Summer Fling Barbie. Never again talk to her or laugh with her. Never again hold her.

I want to hold her.

What if they found the Morning Star the very day she healed? What if they failed to find it? What if they found it in twenty years?

What if he could find it on his own and then return to her as a healthy, whole man?

No more what-ifs. Their association had to end. Today.

He looked at this decision from every angle, found no flaws. Her life was more important than his happiness, and that's all there was to it.

One day she might even thank him for this.

"Torin," Lucien said, his gentleness far more than Torin deserved.

He held up his hand. "Don't. Just…call. I'll see you when she's healed."

At first, Lucien gave no reaction. Then, he nodded reluctantly. "Until then."

KEELEY SENSED THE tension in the room before she ever opened her eyes. She jolted upright, ready to do battle. The fact that no one loomed over her, about to attack her, astonished her.

Out of habit, she checked her arms and legs to make sure no one had warded her while she'd been sleeping.

Where am I? What's going on?

Torin! He'd pulled a chair to the side of the bed. His white-blond hair stuck out in spikes, as if he'd plowed his fingers through the strands again and again. Grim lines branched from his eyes—eyes as hard as granite, watching her intently. He wore a T-shirt that read "'She's

Perfect for You. Go for It,' said Alcohol" and a new pair of black leather pants.

He met her gaze and released a long—relieved?—breath. Color returned to his pale complexion, and a weight seemed to lift from his shoulders. He sat up straighter.

He started to reach for her but stopped himself. "You survived," he said with a gruffness she'd never heard from him. "Again."

I did?

Yes. That's right. She'd been terribly, terribly sick.

"I'm not sure how," he added.

Her immense power was a factor, for sure, but there had to be more to it than that. Like…him. Torin. Streams of strength had pulsed along the bond, and they'd buoyed her.

Tell him.

Not yet.

He removed his gloves and draped them across his thighs. On both of his hands were rings. Almost every finger had one, in fact. Most were silver bands. A few boasted large blue stones. He even wore three different necklaces, each with a different pendant.

"Why so blinged up?" she asked.

"Lucien brought my things."

This was the real Torin, then. *I like. A lot.*

Delicious shivers stole through her. "So…what's got you so upset?"

"You were sick for eight days. Your heart stopped twice. I performed CPR." His bitter laugh hollowed her out. "I'm getting good at it. Only broke one of your ribs."

Dangerous subject. Proceed with caution. "Well, as you can see, I'm okay."

"That's good." He cast his attention to the window just beyond the bed. "Our relationship has always been about choices, Keeley. Fight or forgive. Touch or not touch. Stay together, risking everything, or split up. Our relationship will *always* be about choices."

"I—"

"I'm not done."

Though her heart pounded, she remained quiet.

"It's not fair to you," he said. "You shouldn't have to mortgage your health to be with me…which is why I'm ending our association."

He wanted to…part from her? "No." She shook her head.

"It's happening whether you're on board or not. Your Majesty."

So businesslike, so cold. As if their future happiness wasn't at stake.

Maybe his wasn't. But hers was. "Don't do this, Torin," she said.

"Like I told you, it's happening. Effective immediately," he announced, white-knuckling the edge of his chair. "You don't know what torture it was to go so long without the thing I craved most…and when finally I got it, I had to watch the person I care for suffer because of it."

He cares for me.

He cares!

"We're done," he said. "We have to be done."

"You're just going to give up? Throw me away as if I'm no more important than garbage? After everything we've shared?"

"You're not garbage," he bellowed, and she knew she'd offended him. "You're…" The look he cast her held a possessiveness, a *savagery,* he'd never before displayed. But he shook his head and his features blanked. "This is for the best."

"Whose best? Not mine."

"Definitely yours." Then, "I will find my friends without you. Rescue Baden's spirit without you. Locate the box without you," he added, as if she needed clarification. "I'll owe you no favors."

"What about the Morning Star?" *He can't do this. I can't let him.*

"If—when—I have it, well…" He waved his arm through the air, a gesture of impatience.

Well, what?

"Until then, you will put me in your Time Out box," he said. "Consider it a parting gift."

Forget him? Perhaps forever? He couldn't… *There was no way...how could...*

Lightbulb!

He more than cared about her, she realized. Her well-being mattered to him even more than finding his friends and the box.

Warm rays of sunshine engulfed her soul, and in moments even streamed through the room's windows.

The reason he'd taken off his gloves suddenly became clear. He couldn't trust himself with her. He thought that, without the leather barrier in place, he wouldn't fall victim to temptation and put his hands on her.

"Do you understand?" he demanded.

Can't dance. Can't sing. "Yes," she said, unable to stop her grin. "I do."

Reminding her of a bear whose cage had just been rattled, he snapped, "Are you sure?"

"Totally."

"You don't look like you do."

"What do I look like?"

"Heaven," he said and scowled. "Hell. It doesn't matter." He fished a phone from his pocket, dialed. "I'm ready."

Lucien appeared a few seconds later. Torin stood, walked to his friend.

"Go along, boys." She made a shooing motion. "I'll join you shortly."

Torin rounded on her. "You said you understood we were parting ways."

"That's not what I said—nor what I understood."

"Then what?"

You're mine, and I'm yours. We're going to be together. She'd done it. She'd won his heart, just as she'd intended. Not fully, not yet, but close.

For now, that was good enough.

"I'll tell you later," she said with a pointed glance to Lucien. "When we're alone."

"Keeley," Torin gritted.

"Charming," she sang. "Trust me. You don't want me revealing my thoughts to your friend." *Might not like hearing them yourself. I'm important to you. Irreplaceable.*

Necessary.

Lucien laughed. "You remind me of Anya."

She threw her legs over the side of the bed. Torin had dressed her in a ratty T-shirt that said "Only One of These Statements is True ßà Gideon Never Lies." The hem reached midthigh at least. "You never told me. Who's Anya?"

"My…" His mismatched eyes crinkled at the corners.

"I'm not sure how to explain my relationship with her. She's my girl. My angel."

"She's no angel." Torin glared at Keeley. "Until she's compared to someone else I know."

Keeley fluffed her hair. "Compliments will get you everywhere."

His eyes slitted farther. "Anya is a crazy person who has spent the whole of her relationship with Lucien planning a wedding that's never going to happen. She's his non-fiancée fiancée. But it doesn't matter. You're not meeting her. You're staying here."

She blew him a kiss. "See you soon."

"See you never."

"So…five minutes? Or would you prefer ten?"

"Never." He was scowling when he flashed away with Lucien.

What an amazing day!

She rushed into the bathroom, brushed her teeth and hair, then studied the clean T-shirt and sweatpants Torin had left for her. *Not this time.*

She flashed to her cave and discovered Hades had indeed returned her gowns. Keeley selected the one with chain-mail sleeves with a corset comprised of rolled leather and horse-mane, cinching in her waist. Black leather pants hugged her legs, a full-length train flaring at her hips and flowing all the way to the floor.

She plaited the top portion of her hair, allowing the rest to fall in golden waves before anchoring her crown of spiked steel and diamonds in place.

Head high, she flashed to Torin—and found herself inside a fortress.

The foyer walls were made of shiny white marble broken up by tiny rivers of gold. Hanging throughout were beautiful candelabras interspersed with portraits of—surely—the Lords and their women. Glistening chandeliers hovered overhead, and the black onyx floor speckled with diamond flecks gleamed below. It was an exquisite space. The kind she'd always wanted for herself. Opulent, but homey. Luxurious, but welcoming.

Torin stood beside Lucien, scowling at a portrait of a soldier dressed in black with his arm draped around a female wearing a gown of fine velvet and lace, a feathered headdress framing her delicate face.

Not nearly as nice as mine.

"Hello, Torin," Keeley said.

He pelted her with a glare, then raked his gaze over her once, twice, a third time, his pupils expanding more and more…his attention lingering in all the right places.

She spun slowly, letting him look his fill from every angle. "You showed me the real you. Now I am showing you the real me."

"You are… There are no words…" He stepped closer, but his friend Lucien put a hand on his shoulder, stopping him.

Keeley swallowed her irritation. "Don't you dare try to kick me out. I'm staying," she said. "End of."

Torin had pretended to study the portrait of Kane and Josephina while roars of denial threatened to break free—*just abandoned Keeley, soon I may not even be remembered by her.*

Have to get over it. I'm a man, not a baby without a paci.

When Keeley had flashed to his other side, he'd smelled the honey-dipped-berries scent before he'd turned to her…and experienced a punch of lust so strong he was surprised he remained on his feet.

Look at her. So damn gorgeous in her gown.

Disease gave a low, guttural growl, reminding Torin of his crimes.

"You have to leave, Keeley. I mean it."

"Meaning it doesn't change anything," she said.

"If you stay, I'll bring you nothing but grief and pain."

"Don't be so melodramatic. You've already brought me more than grief and pain."

"You mean cholera? Smallpox?"

Her gaze shifted to Lucien for a split second, and she raised her chin. "Pleasure."

Another punch of lust. He *had* given her pleasure, sating her in a way he'd never sated another. She had not left his bed disappointed.

"True," he grumbled.

As if they weren't discussing the life and death of their relationship, she motioned to a portrait of two people he didn't recognize. A dark-haired male and a female with a short crop of hair so black it appeared to be blue. "That's Atlas and Nike. I met him when he was a raging he-slut. Never met her, but according to my spies, she's meaner than…what's the meanest thing in the world?"

"You?" Torin said helpfully.

She nodded. "Meaner than me."

He sighed. He'd expected his comment to anger her, for her to storm off.

She really was staying put, despite his warning.

He should not have welcomed the strong tide of relief washing through him.

"Atlas and Nike found us a few weeks ago," Lucien

said. "Anya knew Nike, and the two have been hanging out. Hence the reason I had to hide a corpse again today."

Missed so much.

Laughter reverberated from the kitchen, and Torin's heart squeezed in his chest. Music drifted from the sitting room, accompanied by the pitter-patter of little feet running down.

"Incoming," Lucien said.

The footsteps increased in volume and speed, and all too soon a little boy and girl came into view. They stopped and stared at him.

"Someone brought toddlers into the fortress?" Torin asked.

"I ain't no toddler," the boy snapped.

"Sure, sure." Torin held up his palms in a gesture of surrender.

"You remember Urban and Ever, I'm sure," Lucien said. "They've, uh, grown."

No way. Just no way. "I've only been gone a few months." When he'd left, Urban and Ever had been infants.

"Maddox and Ashlyn made the mistake of asking Anya to babysit," Lucien said. "My darling female placed the children in the Cage of Compulsion and commanded them to grow up a little."

"Dude." Anyone trapped in the Cage had to obey its owner, no matter what was commanded. Anya was the current owner. "How bad a meltdown did Maddox have?"

"Him? Not too bad. Ashlyn, on the other hand…" Lucien shuddered.

Urban had the same thick black hair and serious violet eyes Torin remembered. Ever had the same curling honey-blond hair and twinkling brown eyes. And though the two looked like normal kids, dressed in dirt-smudged T-shirts and shorts, they exuded an unnatural energy that pricked at Torin's skin.

"Hello," he said. "I'm your Uncle Torin."

"No." Urban crossed his arms over his chest. "You're trespassing."

Ouch.

"That's a big word for such a little boy," Keeley said, and her tone was pure *gaga goo-goo*. "You're so cute, I'm going to allow you to call me Aunt Queen Dr. Keeley. You may express your thanks."

"Doctor?" Torin asked her.

"I have a PhD in etiquette, sarcasm and fun ways to commit murder."

Ice actually crystalized over Urban's skin as he glanced from Torin to Keeley, then back again. "I'm not calling you anything, lady. I don't like you."

Prickles of flame blazed over Ever. "Yeah. You're strangers, and strangers are the enemy. We get to hurt the enemy."

"Children," a voice admonished. "Who are you challenging this time?" Maddox, keeper of Violence, descended the staircase, his expression as soft as freaking clouds. Then his gaze landed on Torin, and he stopped abruptly. "Torin?"

He nodded, his chest constricting. "The one and only."

"But, Daaaddyyy." Ever pouted with a skill she must have been born with—too expert for one so young. "We never get to hurt no one, and William promised we'd get a chance to do serious damage very soon as long as we didn't tell Momma. Well, it's finally very soon and we won't tell Momma. Honest."

Maddox pushed out a weary breath and muttered, "I'm going to flay William alive."

"Torin!" a familiar voice called. "You're here!" Footsteps pounded, and then Anya, minor goddess of Anarchy, came flying around the corner, practically leaping over the kids…only to skid to a halt when her gaze landed on Keeley. She seemed to choke on her own tongue as she backed up. "The Red Queen! No, no, no. Lucien! You said, and I quote, Torin is with a smokin' blonde. Why not mention the fact that she's my sworn enemy?"

"Who, me?" Keeley tapped her chest.

Clearly another casualty of the Time Out box.

"As if you could forget. My friend called you Smurfette," Anya said, anchoring her hands on her hips. "You forced her to kneel before you and cut off her own flesh. Oh, and call herself Bloody Mary."

"Well, then, she got off lightly," Keeley said, chin high. "I'll hear your thanks."

"*Then* a few years later you forced Zeus to give you everything inside the royal treasury. A tax, you said, because you hadn't killed everyone he loved—only half of them."

"That, I remember. He'd just attacked my fiancé."

"Yes, the king of darkness!"

Maddox moved in front of the kids, acting as their shield.

"So she's really the enemy?" Ever asked excitedly.

"Yes," Anya shouted at the same time Torin snapped, "No!"

Anya continued, "We need to get the kids out of the

fortress before she eats their hearts for dinner and their spinal cords for dessert!"

"Hey!" Keeley scowled at her. "Only eight times have I eaten the organs I've removed, and it was only to make a point."

Torin pinched the bridge of his nose.

"No one threatens my organs!" Ever stretched out a hand, a ball of fire forming just above her palm.

The little girl tossed the flames with all her might. Torin stepped in front of Keeley. *No one, not even a child, is allowed to hurt my woman.* His princess simply reached around him and snatched the thing before it could so much as singe him.

Not my woman. Can't think like that.

"A game of catch? Sure. I'm willing." Keeley stepped beside him and tossed the crackling flames back to the little girl, who caught it with an expression of utter shock.

Urban stretched out his hand, a ball of ice forming just above *his* palm. He tossed it, and Keeley caught it with the same ease as before.

Only, this one melted in her grip before she could lob off a return. "Oops. My bad. I'm summer today, not winter."

"Who," Maddox began darkly, "is the Red Queen?"

"I am." Keeley executed a flawless curtsey. "I know, I know. You're honored to make my acquaintance, and you can hardly contain your excitement, but do your best to remain calm. I find bouts of fawning adoration embarrassing—for others."

Maddox blinked.

Torin tried not to smile.

More footsteps resounded. Then the golden Ashlyn,

blue-haired Gideon and a noticeably pregnant Scarlet raced around a corner. From different areas of the house, others came running, as well. The silent Amun and loving Haidee. The dark Reyes and his blonde bombshell, Danika. Determined Sabin and his spunky Gwen. Cocky Strider and his redheaded terror, Kaia. The newly tattooed Aeron, his lovely wife, Olivia, and their kinda sorta adopted adult daughter, Legion.

The last time Torin had seen Legion—a former demon turned real girl, à la Pinocchio—she'd been a wreck, having just been rescued from captivity and torture. The time he'd been away must have been good to her. The roses had returned to her cheeks and the sparkle to her dark eyes.

Lucien moved to Anya's side, spoke a few quiet words. As he did, Paris and Sienna materialized.

The reunion lacked only Kane, Cameo and Viola.

Differing emotions were cast Torin's way. Elation, confusion, surprise, and of course, Anya's uneasiness. That uneasiness began to annoy him. Keeley should have been welcomed, no matter what, the way he had welcomed every other new addition to the family.

"Good to have you back, my friend," said Sabin, the keeper of the demon of Doubts.

"Who's the babe?" asked Strider, the keeper of Defeat. "She's—humph."

Kaia elbowed him in the stomach.

Though a thousand things had changed in the short time of separation, this had not, and it relaxed Torin. He wanted so badly to close the distance and hug each of his friends. But not a single one of them would welcome his touch, even a protected one. Keeley was the only person who'd ever been willing to risk all for his sake.

He reached out and flattened his gloved hand on her lower back—couldn't stop himself. A show of support, gratefulness, and yes, desire.

She flicked him a confused glance.

He shrugged. He didn't know what to say.

"What's going on?" Aeron demanded. "What's this about a Red Queen?"

"I'm going to roundhouse kick her in the face!" Anya piped up. "Or watch someone else do it. Anyone? Anyone?"

"Enough!" *Or I won't be responsible for my actions.* Though Keeley maintained a neutral, even bored expression, a soft rain began to patter against the windows. She was hurting. "She has a name, and you will use it. She will be treated with respect *at all times.* Anyone who offends her will answer to me—and I promise you, the questions will hurt."

"Well, I already like her," Kaia said. "Anyone who makes Anya pee her pants in fear has to be totes amazeballs."

"I haven't peed!" Anya paused and added glumly, "More than a little."

"Torin," Lucien said, an edge to his tone. "If Keeley has done the things Anya mentioned—"

"Oh, I have," Keeley interjected, unrepentant. "Those, and more. And worse."

"Then she can't stay here. The children…"

"Please. Do you truly believe I'd want to stay in such a hovel?" Keeley walked to the nearest window and peered out. "Ask me if I've ever heard anything so ridiculous."

His heart ached for her. *So defensive.* Rejected by her parents. Rejected by Hades for a barrel of whiskey. She craved acceptance. And Torin got that. Probably better than she would have liked. Because of Disease, he'd been left behind for every battle, every celebration. He was a part of his friends' lives, but it was a part set aside, to be looked at but never handled, if that made any sense.

Rage ignited. "I go where she goes. No exceptions."

Her gasp echoed in the sudden quiet of the room. Less than an hour ago, he'd tried to get rid of her; but here he was, pledging to stay by her side. She might wonder at his reasoning, and he had no real answer for her.

Sabin and Lucien shared a long, silent communication before stepping forward.

"Stay," Sabin said with a nod.

"We just got you back," Aeron said. "We can't lose you now."

"Then no one threatens Keeley." Torin pinned Anya with a glare. "I mean it."

"Fine," the goddess huffed. "I'll make sure you never hear what I have to say."

Oh, really? "You may have witnessed the Red Queen's temper in action, but did Lucien tell you she is capable of so much more? She can find Cameo and Viola. She can bring Baden home." He paused, making sure he had everyone's undivided attention. "She can find Pandora's box." Also the Morning Star. But he once again kept that bit of news to himself. He planned to do a little research first. "However, I won't ask her to do any of those things if one unkind word is said. In my hearing or not."

Silence descended, amazement almost palpable.

Boom! The entire foundation of the fortress rocked. Dust fell from the rafters.

Boom! Boom!

He focused on Keeley. Temper issues? But she was

paying him and his friends zero attention, just staring outside.

"What's going on?" Ashlyn asked with a tremor. She secured her daughter on her hip and tugged her son to her side.

Keeley pressed her hand to the window and said, "I think…we're under attack."

CHAPTER EIGHTEEN

SPARKS OF ANGER razed Keeley's chest. Being the Red Queen came with only one disadvantage. Enemies. She made them everywhere she traveled, and often, as with the minions, they followed her.

Today's challengers? The Unspoken Ones.

They thought to threaten her new life.

They had to die.

The rain stopped, and thunder boomed just as loudly as the bombs.

She sent wisps of her power to curl around the Unspoken Ones, ready to flash them away…and follow with a hacksaw…only to realize they'd scarred themselves with brimstone. The wisps withered into nothing.

Who had told them?

Not difficult to surmise. The three demon-possessed crazies.

They'll get theirs. Later.

Time to mastermind a plan to pulverize the Unspoken Ones. She couldn't destroy the beasts the way she so desperately wanted—make them explode. And not just because of the scars. There would be other casualties. Probably a *lot* of other casualties. All of Torin's friends would explode, too, and the fortress would collapse.

Of course, she could flash everyone away before the big event, saving them all at once—except for Torin.

But Lucien could take care of him. However, that still left her with a problem: the fortress.

Don't destroy it, Torin had once said. He'd even added a please.

Now she understood why. If she brought the place crumbling down, his friends would *never* like her.

Want them to like me.

Boom!

The entire fortress shook, dust plumping the air. The Unspoken Ones had just destroyed the tall iron gate surrounding the fortress, and in turn removed some of the booby traps Galen had told her were set along its perimeter.

"Why don't they just flash inside?" she asked. They'd lost the element of surprise.

"They aren't my biggest fans," the female named Sienna said. "I took measures against them."

So, this was the new queen of the Titans. The one who'd usurped Cronus.

Not the hulking she-beast I expected.

"Are the Unspoken Ones strangers, Daddy?" Ever asked as sweet as candy.

"Yes, sweetheart."

"So I can hurt them?"

"Yes," the warrior said, his tone as hard as steel. "You can hurt them bad."

"Oh, goody!" Ever grinned and hugged her brother.

Urban's expression remained stoic even as he hugged her back.

"Actually, no," Keeley announced. "She can't." She faced the warriors as one of the rafters in the center cracked.

"Sorry, your great and powerful majesty of whatever,

but you don't get a vote in this. The big boys are going to field this one," the one named Strider said. "We're going to do things our way. The right way."

"There's right, and there's better." She blinked, flashing the children, the females and Strider to a distant location.

The rest of the warriors slid straight into a panic.

"What did you do with them?" the father of the twins roared. "Where are they?"

"Sure," Keeley said. "Blame the new girl. But okay, fine, your assumption happens to be true. And you should be rejoicing! They're safe. I'll return them after the battle." She rubbed her hands together. "Now, then. Let's get started, shall we?"

Boom!

"Torin," one of the dark-haired males demanded.

"They aren't being harmed," Torin said. "You have my word. They're safe, and they *will* be returned."

He trusts me. More of those delicious rays of sunshine found her.

She checked a wristwatch she wasn't wearing and said, "The Unspoken Ones will breach the walls soonish." She flashed in the arsenal from a bunker her spies had once told her about. Guns. Rifles. Grenades. Flamethrowers. Swords. "Take your pick, boys, with my compliments."

"I can flash you to your bedroom, Torin," Lucien said. "We won't let the creatures get to you."

Excuse me? They expected the fierce and mighty Torin to ride pine? Thought to bench their best player? Did they *want* to lose?

"He's not suffering with menstrual cramps, so stop treating him that way," she announced. Then, to Torin, she commanded, "Don't even think about tapping out. Pick a weapon."

After a moment's hesitation, he said, "Ma'am, yes, ma'am," selected two swords and a rifle and pulled his hood over his face. "And no, I don't think you're wearing mom jeans. Any jeans you wear automatically become babe jeans."

There goes a piece of my heart.

"Why can't you flash the Unspoken Ones away?" Lucien asked her. "Like you did the women and children."

Torin might… No, surely he wouldn't…. But if he *did* tattle about the brimstone, it was going to hurt. *Picking their safety over mine.* But until then, she wouldn't say a word. "I have my reasons."

A scowling Sienna materialized beside Paris. "Everyone's on a beach," she announced. She glared at Keeley. "Don't ever do that again."

Won't roll my eyes. "Or what? You'll make me regret it? Please. You can do nothing. You're hemorrhaging power, darling, and have been for a good while, it seems." Probably the reason *she* couldn't flash the Unspoken Ones away. "Don't bother trying to deny it. I can feel it seeping out of you."

Sienna's olive skin became a sickly chalk white.

"What's she talking about, baby?" Paris asked.

"It's jumping ship," Keeley continued, "and I know why. It's not yours, it's Cronus's. Meaning it hasn't bonded to you. You'll have to fix that if you hope to survive."

"Is that a threat?" Paris pointed a semiautomatic at Keeley's chest. "Because I don't react well to threats to my girl."

Torin stepped in front of Keeley and batted the gun away. "There's no time for this. And I shouldn't have to issue another warning, but I will. Don't threaten *my* girl, or I will put a bullet in your head."

I'm his. Torin's. "And while you're recovering," Keeley said, "we'll shave off all your hair."

Paris backed up, horrified, and patted his multi-colored locks.

Feeling magnanimous, Keeley added, "I'll allow you to question me about your female once the Unspoken Ones are dead. If you apologize to Torin for threatening his girl." *Me. That's me.*

"Respectfully question," Torin added.

Paris gave a stiff nod. "I'm...sorry."

Keeley flattened her palm on Torin's back. He tensed at first but soon relaxed. Then he whirled around, his gaze hotly intense.

"Stay safe," he commanded.

For you? Always. "Ditto." *Want to kiss him.*

Can't kiss him. Not now. But later...it might just be worth the risk.

The warriors ran off in different directions, some going upstairs, some down, all taking their places at windows and firing at the enemy. Too little, too late. The front door burst open, shards of wood and metal shooting through the foyer like missiles, slamming into several living targets.

A female rushed inside the foyer. And, oh. Oh, wow. Ugly had a new poster child. Rather than a nose and mouth, she had a beak. Like a rabid bird. She wore a leather shirt, but Keeley wasn't sure why the creature had bothered to pull it on. The material that should have covered the crests of her breasts had been cut out. Her nipples were pierced with diamonds. A leather skirt wrapped around her muscular waist and thighs.

The Unspoken One turned left, then right, studying her new surroundings. Small horns protruded from her spine, clear liquid leaking from the tips. Poison?

The warriors who'd stayed in the living room opened fire on her, but the bullets had no effect. She even caught the rocket-propelled grenade, crushing it in her hand as it detonated. As white-hot air and sharp debris blasted throughout the room. Keeley flashed every warrior but Torin into another part of the fortress, out of harm's way.

Stupid brimstone! How was she supposed to safeguard him at a moment's notice?

He dropped to the floor, then popped to his feet relatively unharmed.

A loud scuffle upstairs. Definitely violent. Should she interfere?

In a lightning-fast move, the female Unspoken One reached behind her back, ripped off one of her own horns and tossed it at Keeley. Torin slammed into her side, knocking her out of the way. The horn soared over both their shoulders.

My hero!

But Keeley's anger returned—and in greater force. Beak Face had almost hurt her man.

The fortress shook so intensely dust rose from the foundation.

As Keeley wrangled with her anger, Beak Face flashed to her, grabbed her by the shoulders and pitched her across the room. Not to kill her, but to get her out of the way. She picked Torin up by the neck, not understanding what the action would cost her, and grinned over at

Keeley, all *watch me, watch what I will do to the one you defend.*

Shaking, shaking. Thunder.

Keeley pushed to her feet and strode forward, summoning two daggers along the way. *Going to* gut *her!*

"Torin," she said.

He let the Unspoken One hold the bulk of his weight as he wrapped his legs around her waist. They toppled over, and he absorbed the impact even while reaching up, breaking her wrist and loosening her hold. He punched the heel of his palm into her beak. With a screech, she scrambled away from him. Blood poured down her face.

His victory did nothing to dampen Keeley's emotions. They were already engaged, her power seething, desperate for release.

"Keeley," Torin shouted over the noise.

"Keep her occupied," she instructed, then flashed to the horn. *Mine. My prize.* She grabbed it and flashed to a remote, unoccupied island in the South Atlantic.

Power exploded from her in a familiar burst, lifting her off her feet, rocking the entire island. A volcano crumbled, lava having nowhere to go but...everywhere. Large cracks appeared in the ground, a web of destruction. She inhaled smoke and coughed.

When she quieted, the worst of her rage poured into the wreckage, she returned to the fortress. *If something bad happened while I was gone...*

Torin and the Unspoken One were not where she'd left them. She flashed upstairs. Another fiend claimed her attention. He had a chest covered in scars and legs covered by carmine fur. Dark menace radiated from him as he roared and batted at Lucien, who swung a sword at him before flashing behind and swinging the sword from a different angle.

Meanwhile, Sabin sprayed the Unspoken One with a flamethrower as Gideon pelted him with ammo from an automatic rifle.

"My turn!" Keeley shouted. *Going to enjoy this.*

To her surprise, Torin's friends paused midbattle, giving her the opening she needed.

She flashed to the creature's shoulders and wrapped her legs around his neck. As he reached up to grab her and throw her off—*good luck, sucker*—she slammed the poisoned horn she still held into his eye. He bellowed in pain, his muscles seizing. He toppled over, remaining on the floor, unmoving.

Keeley crawled out from under him, stood, and spit on him. "Finish him off. Remove his head and heart and then burn the pieces." No need to take chances.

One down. Three to go.

She flashed throughout the house, finding the remaining three beasts in a bedroom, working together. The two males were so tall and wide they were like living mountains. One was bald, with shadows seeping from his skull. Shadows that were thick and black and putrid. The other had blades rather than hair. Small but sharp, they spiked from his scalp, each glistening with blood.

One of Torin's friends lay still and quiet on the floor. Aeron, the heavily tattooed one.

Keeley didn't allow herself to study him too closely. Not yet. Her emotions…

The walls of the fortress began to shake all over again. *Calm. Steady.*

Torin stood in front of his friend, sword-fighting Beak Face. Keeley paused for a moment, snared by the sight.

What a hauntingly macabre picture they made. The beaked villain whose motions were as fluid as water, and the angelic hero whose every movement was calculated and methodical.

The female flashed behind him, but he'd expected the action and turned, meeting her with the tip of his sword. Before he could deliver a deathblow, she vanished, appearing at his left. Keeley flashed to her, intending a sneak attack just as another of Torin's friends slid across the room on his knees, knocking both the Unspoken One and Keeley off their feet.

"Sorry, sorry," he rushed out.

"No worries," Keeley replied.

Torin raised his sword to stab Beak Face, only to pause when he caught sight of Keeley.

The pause cost him. Beak Face seized on the opportunity to kick him in the stomach, sending him propelling backward, through a wall and into another room.

The shaking of the walls intensified.

Keeley flashed Torin's sword into her own hand and then flashed, flashed, flashed, going from one place to another so that the Unspoken One could never get a lock on her. And when finally the creature was simply swinging in circles, batting at air, Keeley appeared a mere whisper away from her and stabbed her in the neck, then yanked the blade down…down…until it had split Beak Face's stomach and pelvis in two and come out between her thighs. Blood spurted as the female howled with agony and dropped.

Keeley grinned. "Enjoy that? I did."

The demon-possessed warrior who'd knocked Keeley down was close enough to the fallen Unspoken One to remove her head.

Two down. Two to go.

Torin returned and looked Keeley over. "You okay?"

"Better than."

"Gideon is in danger," someone called from downstairs.

Keeley flashed away and had no trouble guessing which one was Gideon. The blue-haired warrior was halfway up the steps and flat on his back. The Unspoken One with the shadows seeping from his head had an arm raised, claws elongated and at the ready.

"No!" She flashed Gideon to the other side of the fortress just as the grinning Unspoken One flashed *to her,* swinging his arm down...down...*his plan all along.*

His acid-tipped claws ripped through her jugular, cutting off her scream of agony before it even had a chance to form. Torin's shout of denial rang in her ears as she thumped to the floor.

Never burned...quite so...badly. Thoughts, breaking apart.

Though her vision hazed with spots of black, she witnessed Torin's approach to the grinning Unspoken One—only to lose sight of the pair as the shadows from the Unspoken One's scalp wound around them. No. No! But the shadows thinned as quickly as they'd thickened, revealing Torin with a beating heart in his palm.

As the Unspoken One toppled to his knees, gasping in pain, Torin stuffed the heart into his mouth. Her warrior drew back his sword and struck. The creature's head thumped to the floor and rolled away. The rest of him flopped forward, and tumbled down the stairs.

"Princess," Torin said, crouching beside her. His hands cupped her cheeks. He hissed in a breath. "Sorry. Sorry. Left blood on your face."

Don't care about that, she tried to say, but struggled to move her mouth. Black swallowed the rest of her vision. All around her, battle noises registered. Grunts. Metal slashing across bone. Cracks. Curses. Another thump. Then something soft was once again smoothing over her face.

"Stay with me." Torin's masculine scent enveloped her. "Aeron is alive. Everyone survived. I expect the same from you. Do you hear me?"

Blood gurgled from the corners of her mouth. Great! How unattractive was *that?*

"Bond with me," he continued. "Do it. Take my strength. Anything you need." The rustle of clothing.

He wants my bond?

Joy...

Torin must have ripped off his shirt because the next thing she knew, he was pressing soft cotton into the wound in her neck. "You've got nothing to do but get better. And you will. I've been here. I've had my throat slit and pulled through. You will, too. You're stronger than anyone I know. You *will* heal. That's an order, princess."

CHAPTER NINETEEN

TORIN WATCHED KEELEY, who lay on his bed. Still, so still. He'd slept in this room for hundreds of years, dreaming of a day a woman could rest beside him. But this was as far from a dream as possible—this was a nightmare.

The sheets were soaked in her blood. His Sugar Plum Fairy was dying.

"No. No! I refuse to lose you. Do you hear me?" He shouted the words to the unconscious Keeley.

She had touched him, again and again, willing to face the consequences—*this* would not be how she died.

She will never *die.*

I need her too badly.

The day Torin had gone to the prison with Mari, Danika had given him a portrait. As the All-seeing Eye, Danika often saw glimpses of the future, and so far, she had never been wrong. In this particular portrait, Torin had been reclining in a dark leather chair, a glass of something in one hand, a cigar in the other. He'd been surrounded by people, enjoying life. His, theirs. The smile on his face suggested he was sublimely happy, with no worries or unsatisfied needs.

If that was to be his future, Keeley had to survive. It was as simple as that.

He applied pressure to her wounds…and she stopped

bleeding. But as he watched, her chest stilled, no longer rising and falling.

No longer breathing.

He pounded on her sternum, one minute ticking into two…three… The wound in her neck reopened. Blood she desperately needed poured out.

He reared back, shouting, "Come on, Keys! Heal!"

The ensuing silence cut at him.

"Please! Do you have any idea how important you are to me?"

Again, silence.

But…she couldn't know. He'd never told her.

With a bellow that sprang from the deepest depths of his soul, he punched a hole in the wall, welcoming the sharp pain in his knuckles. He never should have allowed Keeley to stay here. He should have found the strength to walk away from her a second time. For good.

His weakness had cost him. Had cost her. Just not the way he'd envisioned.

"Keeley! Are you listening to me?" He toppled the dresser, the drawers spilling across the floor. He kicked over a nightstand and stomped on the remains. "You're in my bed. You said I could boss you around there. I've told you what to do, so do it!"

But she didn't.

Every inhalation a burn in his chest, he ripped a light fixture from the wall and tossed it across the room, adding a new hole to his collection.

He cared for this woman. Cared so damn much. Seeing her like this, so helpless against a wound he hadn't caused but hadn't protected her from…something broke inside him. The last shreds of his humanity, perhaps.

He fell to his knees. He felt like an animal, starved and desperate. Utterly wild. Inconsolable.

"Calm down," Lucien said, appearing beside him.

Calm down? "Why don't you shut the hell—"

His door swung open before he could finish insulting his friend, and Danika rushed inside his room, carrying a jar of...dirt?

"Sienna brought me back," she said, stopping at the side of the bed to dump the—yes, dirt. The scent of it filled the air as the grains covered Keeley's injury.

Torin was on his feet and at Danika's side before she could finish, getting in her face, almost brushing his nose against hers. Realizing how close he was, he backed off an inch. "You better have a good reason for doing that." Or else.

Danika's eyes went wide with sudden fear.

"She does," a voice said from the doorway. It belonged to her man, Reyes. "She had a vision, and it showed her how to help your girl." The keeper of Pain stood with his arms crossed over his middle, eyeing Torin with expectation. "Step away from Danika, or we will have a problem, my friend."

Can't even challenge my friends without putting their lives at risk.

Grinding his teeth, he straightened and stepped away.

Danika breathed a sigh of relief and continued on. "I'm going to lean down and make sure the dirt gets inside the cut, okay?"

"Why?" he barked.

She flinched at his vehemence, saying, "Do you know the saying *just rub some dirt on it?* Apparently, that came from her species. The Curators. Keeley is bonded to the earth and its seasons, which means she's bonded to its elements. They help her."

That...made sense, he realized. He shouldered Danika out of the way without actually touching her and crouched at Keeley's side. He gently worked the dirt into her wound. For the first time since he'd watched her fall under the Unspoken One's attack, he began to hope.

"Torin," Danika said. "Are you sure you should be doing that? You're—"

"I'm gloved," he snarled. He would not put Keeley at risk, not again. He just...he *had* to touch her in some way.

"I know, but..." Danika licked her lips as he pinned her with a glare. "Never mind."

The next few minutes of stilted silence were sheer torture. He waited, but Keeley's condition never improved. He rubbed the dirt harder, even manipulating the tears in her skin to let the dirt penetrate deep. Something burned the back of his eyes.

"I don't understand," Danika said. "This was supposed to work."

Torin got up, swiped the jar from Danika's hands and filled it with water. If one element would help, two would surely help more. He gently poured the water onto her wound.

She remained quiet, still. Too still.

Hope died; it was a swift, brutal slaying.

Disease gave an all too familiar and hated laugh.

Screaming denial after denial inside his head, Torin pressed his forehead against the mattress. He'd lost her— No. No. But he had. He'd lost his beautiful Sugar Plum Fairy. No! Monsters should die, not angels. It wasn't fair.

When had life—or death—ever been fair?

This was the end. The price of evil…darkness. Not hers, but theirs. The Unspoken Ones. Bad things happened because creatures like them had free will.

Now, there were no more seconds left on Keeley's clock.

How am I supposed to go on?

"Torin?" Danika said.

"Get out." Keeley wouldn't have wanted anyone to see her this way. "In a few seconds, I'm not going to be responsible for my actions."

"But—"

"Now!" Tears dripped from his chin, pooled in the liquid that had yet to absorb in her wound.

The numbness was going to leave him— Who was he kidding? It had left him long ago. He was going to tear through this room, this fortress, and then the entire world. No one would be safe from his wrath.

"Wait. I think she's breathing," Danika insisted.

His head snapped up. Keeley's eyes were still closed, but she was— Yes! She was breathing, her chest rising… falling…rising again.

She was alive!

"Keeley, sweetheart."

Her head lolled toward him as she moaned.

"I'm here, princess. I'm here. I'm not going to let anyone hurt you ever again." *Not even me.*

KEELEY STRETCHED AND blinked to full wakefulness. When her surroundings registered, she frowned and eased to a sitting position. She was in an unfamiliar bedroom, and there were holes all over the walls. Every piece of furniture—not including the bed—was toppled over and in shambles.

Interesting decorating choices.

Sunlight streamed through the large bay window, casting bright rays over the king-sized monstrosity she occupied...alone. There was an indention on the other side, making her think someone had spent the night with her. Torin?

The thought thrilled her. But where was he?

A voice drifted from the shadows, answering her unspoken question. "He's with his friends. They want to question you when you awaken, but he's refusing."

A voice she recognized. Smiling, she said, "Galen."

"None other."

Her gaze moved through the room a second time until she'd rooted out his location. He sat in a corner amid broken pieces of wood. Strong and stalwart, his wings several inches longer. "You risked a lot, coming here."

He nodded as he rose. He approached her. "That I did."

"To harm Torin?" As much as she liked the warrior, her acquaintanceship with him was beginning to bother her. Torin was her man, and he'd supported her, choosing her well-being over that of his friends. What kind of girlfriend would she be if she consorted with his enemy?

"No. Torin has nothing to do with it." Galen sat beside her, his thigh brushing against hers. "Or even revenge."

Interesting. *I'm still touch-deprived, surely. The nearness should affect me despite my lack of attraction to him.* But there was no tingle. No quiver.

Had Torin ruined her for all others?

"You no longer hate him?" she asked.

"Oh, I hate him." He grinned coldly. "I'll always hate him. He was once one of my closest friends, if not *the* closest. But he didn't trust me, still believes I'm the one who revealed our plan to steal Pandora's box to Zeus."

"Didn't you?"

"Of course. But did you not hear me? *He should have trusted me.*"

She rolled her eyes. "So you, the guilty party, got angry at the innocent party for daring to react to a betrayal with hurt and anger. Typical."

Unashamed, he nodded. "That about sums it up, yes."

"And you, the guilty party, hold a grudge."

His grin returned, but this time, there was a hint of warmth to it. "I like that you get me."

Another eye roll. "Why are you here? And if you tell me you're crushing on me and want a go at me, I will seriously gut you. I belong to Torin. He said so." And he better not have changed his mind. There would be hell to pay!

"That's good, because you aren't my type."

Hey! "You don't like spunky girls with temper issues?"

He playfully flicked the end of her nose. "You aren't Legion, so, no." He thought for a minute, frowned. "I suppose I should call her Honey. That's what the Lords are calling her. Apparently, she reinvented herself. Part of her recovery."

Bits and pieces of their past conversations drifted through Keeley's mind, and she sighed. "This Legion slash Honey chick." An enemy who'd given him her virginity—and then tried to kill him. Not just teasingly, but truly poisoning him. Then she'd run away from him. He'd gone after her, intending to mete out revenge, only to be slowed down by the war with the Lords. During that time, Legion—Honey—had somehow ended up in hell, where she was tortured mercilessly. "You're here to steal her away?"

He shrugged. "I don't know. Maybe. First, I just want to talk to her."

"Well, do me a solid and don't. Not yet. These people just got Torin back and just met me. Not to mention the battle with the Unspoken Ones. They're a bit overwhelmed, I'm sure, and won't react well to another disturbance." Plus, she didn't really want to explain her association with Galen right now. She and Torin were finally making progress. No reason to screw that up.

"I won't hurt her," Galen said. "She's been hurt enough. And no one else will ever know I'm here, you have my word. But I need your help. There's some kind of block on her room and I can't get inside."

It was one thing to help lead him to safety, but quite another to allow him to roam freely through Torin's home. "Give me some time. Soon Torin will owe me a few favors, and I'll be able to set up a Lords of the Underworld approved meeting with you and Honey."

Galen narrowed his eyes, shadows making the blue appear black. "Slight problem with your plan. I don't want to wait."

She patted the top of his head. "Poor brain-damaged male. Did you think I was giving you a choice?"

He opened his mouth to respond, but she held up a finger in a demand for silence. Her ears were twitching… Footsteps, she realized! Someone was approaching the bedroom door.

"Later," she said, and flashed Galen to the other side of the world. She could have flashed him to another realm, trapping him, but she did have some scruples. They were tarnished, but they were there.

Maybe.

She hurriedly finger-combed her hair and smoothed the newest T-shirt Torin had dressed her in—"Reyes is the Biggest Pain"—preparing for her next visitor. Which she really hoped was her Charming. They had a few things to discuss. Galen, yes. But also about their relationship. Things had changed. They both knew it. Soon the harder decisions would have to be made.

What was he willing to do to make this thing between them work?

What did they want from each other?

How should they proceed?

She was excited about the possible answers, but also leery. As feared, he could have changed his mind—again.

Well, she would show him!

Keeley flashed the broken furniture away and replaced every piece with something of her own. *I'm moving in, and that's that.*

Try to get rid of me, Charming. I dare you.

CHAPTER TWENTY

TORIN POUNDED UP the staircase, his every nerve scraped raw. Too many of his friends trailed behind him, and he wondered why the hell he'd been so eager to return to their midst.

"I just want to talk to her," Sabin said. "I'll be nice, I swear."

Maybe he would. But Sabin's version of *nice* meant leaving his opponent alive—on the brink of death, but alive. The guy didn't yet realize Keeley's *nice* made his seem like a day at the spa.

"Forget it."

"Let me thank her for saving Gideon," Scarlet said.

"Later."

"Let me talk to her about finding Cameo and Viola," Aeron said. "I know we couldn't speak to her while she was healing, but she's better. Right?"

"Right. But *I'll* talk to her about it."

"What about Sienna's power?" Paris asked. "Keeley promised answers."

"And she'll give them. Just not today. So what happened to Taliyah?" he asked, changing the subject before anyone else could protest. "Anyone find out why she wanted the fortress we had in the Realm of Blood and Shadows?"

Taliyah was Gwen and Kaia's older sister and, quite

frankly, colder than ice. He was pretty sure he'd gotten frostbite just by having a conversation with her. Which was why she was the only woman on earth he'd ever requested William "do that melting thing" to.

She was also the only woman on earth William had ever refused to touch.

"We still don't know," Strider replied. "Taliyah needed it sooner than expected, and we can't get to her. She won't even come to us."

By her choice?

"What of William? Does he know of my return?" Torin was astounded by just how badly he missed the guy.

Strider shook his head. "Not yet, but don't worry. He'll show up sooner rather than later. He doesn't leave Gilly and her birthday-party planning for long."

"Dear diary," Anya muttered. "It's been three hours since I killed someone. Needless to say, life sucks. My gorgeous fiancé refuses to let me kill the most loathsome creature ever. Won't even let me give her a few superficial stab wounds. I'm thinking about breaking up with him."

"I wouldn't recommend it," Reyes replied. "He may not ask for your hand in marriage a second time."

She gasped with outrage. "Lucien. Tell him!"

"I'd ask again," Lucien told him.

Okay, so maybe it was kind of great to be back amid the weirdness.

"Anyway," Anya said. "Torin, do you remember those kids we saved from Galen and his crew a while back? The ones with the supernatural abilities? Well, even after we found them new homes, I kept in touch, watched over them. I'm awesome like that. And they're doing well,

by the way. Except for one. He ran away. I need you to tell the Red Queen to find him."

"I'll *ask* her." A small smile played at Torin's mouth as he reached the door to his bedroom. "Okay, everyone. This is where we part ways." Amid boos and hisses, he shouldered his way inside. Holding a tray piled high with breakfast, he kicked the door closed.

He lost the smile as he computed the condition of his room. What. The. Hell? There were piles of gold and jewelry in every corner. So much he wasn't sure how the floor could possibly withstand the weight. There were potted plants hanging from the ceiling. A wealth of female clothing spilled from his closet. Gowns like the one Keeley had worn during the fight, looking like a pornstar version of an evil queen, totally rocking his world. There was an animal-print chaise longue with a blanket of black velvet draped over the edge. A table made of cobalt porcelain and brass flowers. A large oval mirror with cherubs dancing around the sides. And taped over his many computer screens were reminders to maim or kill certain people.

"Surprise!" she said. "I've saved you the trouble of having to ask me to move in. You're welcome."

His Sugar Plum Fairy reclined in the center of the bed, the covers plumped around her. Excitement glowed in her baby blues. Golden hair tumbled all the way to the mattress.

Like every time before, he was struck by the sudden urge to get to her, take her, his blood flashing white-hot.

He gave himself a pep talk. *My will is like iron. I'm strong enough to resist temptation—even Hurricane Keeley temptation.*

"Are you sure living together is wise?" He placed

the tray on the new nightstand, a wooden piece with the phrase "One-Night Stand" etched into the top, then eased beside her.

"We'll find a way," she said.

They had better find it fast. "How are you feeling?"

"One hundred percent."

"But...?"

She studied his face, inhaled deeply, held it...then stood and sauntered into the bathroom, not bothering to close the door behind her. She fiddled with the knobs in the shower, figured everything out, and soon water was spewing from the spout. She undressed, nearly killing him, and stepped inside, then washed with Torin's favorite products, the scent of sandalwood softly coating the air.

The glass separating the tub from the rest of the room did not fog, allowing him to watch her nipples harden... her belly quiver. Thinking of him? Wishing his hands were on her? His body pressed behind hers?

Strung as tight as a bow.

In a trance, he made his way into the bathroom and perched on the lid of the toilet. His erection was as hard as a steel pipe but had to be ignored. "But," he insisted.

"I can guess what you're going to do next, and I don't like it."

"And that is?"

"Something cruel to try to get rid of me."

"I'm not."

She continued as if he hadn't spoken. "I'm more than the most powerful immortal on earth, you know. I'm a person. With feelings and everything! I'm worth more than a barrel of whiskey."

"You're worth more than *anything*," he said quietly.

"I have a heart and it's quite capable of being br— Wait. What?" she asked.

The only fantasy he would ever have stepped out of the shower, droplets of water slicking down her delectable form. *Don't stare.* He stared, his blood burning hotter and hotter. Oh, to lick every droplet away.

"I don't want to part with you." He stood and, ignoring the tug to go to her, to touch and to please, moved into the room, creating distance. "But I can't keep hurting you. Living in the same room will increase our chances of contact."

"When we were careful, you didn't hurt me."

"What if I'm not careful next time?"

"What if sucks. It's my life, my decision."

"The guilt…"

She raised her chin. "Screw the guilt. You can do that for me…can't you?"

Her uncertainty cut through his heart like a knife. "It's a miracle you've survived my touches in the past. Very few manage such a feat even once, but you've done it three times. What will happen the fourth time? The fifth? One day, if things keep speeding down the same track, you're not going to recover. I would rather die than let that happen, Keys."

Her lips parted as she struggled to form a reply.

Why not tell her the rest? Just put it all out there? "You are special to me. I care for you. You could have murdered me time and again. You didn't. You should have feared me. You never have. You should hate me. You can't seem to manage it. You should avoid me, yet you only ever draw me closer. I want the best for you. But the best isn't me."

"Oh, Torin." Slowly she walked toward him, her motions as fluid as the water still dripping from her. "You *are* the best."

He backed away from her. His legs hit the edge of the bed, and he fell onto the mattress, bounced. She just kept coming until she was standing right in front of him. Naked. So gloriously naked.

"You are special to me," she said. "I've told you that. But what you don't know is that I care for you, too, and I want the best for you. And Torin? *I* am the best. You've seen me fight, yes? And the extent of my power? I could do more, show you more, if not for the brimstone. You would be so impressed."

Her desperation to make him believe her claims was another knife in the heart.

He wanted to promise to remove the brimstone immediately. But that would have been a lie. Forget the need to have a weapon against her. It no longer had anything to do with that. As wild as her temper could be, someone had to be able to negate her abilities at a moment's notice. And since he couldn't tolerate the thought of anyone else putting their hands on her, the burden fell to him.

"I want so badly to belong to you," she continued. "Not just in word but in deed. I ache for you, all the time."

"Keys—" Could she hear *his* desperation?

"No. Princess is still talking. You told me to bond with you, and I did. But, Torin, I have to admit the truth. I did it before you told me. And I'm not sorry! Not anymore. I didn't mean for it to happen and tried to stop it, but you, my sweet warrior, are irresistible. You don't have to worry, though. I'm not a parasite. I don't just take, I give. Have you realized you're stronger already, and so am I?

One day I'll stop getting sick. Surely. The demon will run out of diseases. I'll outlast him. Just you wait and see."

A thousand emotions battered through him. At the forefront? Arousal. They were bonded. Him and her. Connected in a way he'd never imagined possible—not for him.

Running a few steps behind the arousal were hope, fear, elation. Possessiveness—*she's truly mine.* And dread. Then even more arousal.

So much arousal…

She was begging him for a chance to be together. Begging with the hooded, heavy look of her eyes. With the softness of her voice. With the tremors sweeping through her lovely little figure. His Sugar Plum Fairy shouldn't have to beg for anything.

I'm undone.

And she…she was raw seduction, carnality made flesh. And what exquisite flesh it was, dusted with rose and so deliciously damp. He'd told himself he was strong, but he was actually weak. With her, he'd always been weak.

"What if—"

"What if we enjoy ourselves and nothing bad happens?" she finished for him.

Not what he'd planned to say, but the words were accompanied by a hope he'd never quite been able to vanquish. What if she was right?

"If we do this," he said, "we do it without skin-to-skin contact. Agree." Not a question, but a demand, and one he'd unintentionally uttered with all the ragged need locked inside him.

"No. If the only way to become fully immune to your demon is to endure each of his illnesses, then I have to—"

"No," he interjected. "Not after everything you've been through. There will be no more illnesses for you. And, Keys? I wasn't looking to have a conversation about this. Agree."

She licked her lips. Waiting for her to nod, even reluctantly, proved to be one of the greatest tortures of his life.

But when she did it, he wasted no time. He picked her up, and settled her atop his lap. She gasped at the moment of contact. He hissed, electrified, and twisted to press her against the mattress. Her lush breasts swayed, and her nipples, as pink as raspberries, mesmerized him.

She rolled her hips upward, seeking him, as much of him as she could get. The sight of her...the smell of her... the best of summer—freshly bloomed flowers, cottonwood and the musk of arousal—mixed with the darker notes of his scent. The sounds she made...moans and groans and sweet little purrs.

He couldn't get enough. *Trapped in a desert most of my life, finally found an oasis.* "The things I want to do to you..."

Her morning-sky gaze beseeched him. "Do them." A demand as ragged as his own. "All of them."

He curled his fingers under her knees, and she sucked in a breath. Like before, he could feel the heat of her skin through the fabric of the gloves as he placed her legs outside his hips, opening her up to his perusal. Pretty, pink and wet with a honey meant for him. Only for him. So badly he wanted to taste her, and cursed his demon.

Laughter sounded in the back of his mind.

Maybe there was a way. He just had to think. But his mind and body cared about only one thing: getting inside her.

He let his hands wander up...up, and brush her between her legs, stroking her, teasing her. Her gasp was a caress to his ears. He continued his upward slide…finally cupping her breasts, her nipples beading right before his eyes. *Luscious.*

The laughter stopped.

Or maybe as focused as he was on the woman spread out for his pleasure, he just couldn't hear it anymore.

As he stroked the pad of his thumbs over each rosy crest, she arched up and down, chasing sensation, as if his teasing was already too much for her. Unwilling to relinquish his hold on her, he crawled all the way onto the bed and worked his thighs under her ass, drawing her closer, pressing her most intimate need against the fly of his pants, where his erection strained for freedom. Rotating his hips again and again allowed him to move against her, with her, tormenting them both.

"Torin," she rasped. "I'm so close already."

Want her closer. He lifted up, holding her legs against his sides so that only her head and shoulders remained on the mattress, he increased the intensity and speed of his circling thrusts. Pressure built at the base of his spine, such glorious pressure.

"Wish I was inside you," he croaked. He'd never experienced a rush quite like this one, but knew instinctively the next step would far surpass it.

"Yes." She gave a wild shiver. "Yes. Inside me. Please."

It was the first time he'd heard the word *please* from her lips, not issued as a threat or a taunt, and oh, it affected him. His control bucked against the reins. *Can't. Won't.* But he thrust. And thrust. And thrust against her. Hard. Harder. So hard her head banged against the bed's headboard.

She put her weight on her elbows and lifted her hips even higher. The friction...the bliss...

Somehow she managed to take over, riding him up and down. Even harder. Even faster. *Control, nearly gone.*

Lips pulled tight over his teeth, he released her legs and gripped her hips to help her more easily glide. Their gazes met. Did his eyes gleam as wildly as hers?

"Kiss," she said.

Yes. Her mouth was lush and wet, imploring his own. "No."

"Please," she said again.

He knew she'd reached the point where nothing mattered but the next wave of pleasure. The future had ceased to exist for her.

"No," he said again. He watched as she sucked in her bottom lip, ran her teeth over it, and he very nearly spilled. "Don't... We can't... We decided." This would have to be enough.

"Can. Must. Forgive me," she said, sitting up.

He leaned back, preventing her breasts from smashing into his chest, her lips from meeting his. But deep down he willed her to keep coming, and she did—and then it happened. Her breasts...her lips...

A scream of denial blended with a groan of surrender. It was done. Contact had been made. Hating himself, his weakness, he pushed his tongue past her teeth and claimed her with a kiss hot enough to brand. Her sweet taste carried a hint of grapes just plucked from the vine, and the contrast, sweet versus wicked, attacked what remained of his control...until he had none left.

He tangled his hands in her hair and tugged, slanting her the way he'd wanted her. He took her mouth deep, rough, an endless sense of possession in the kiss, as if he sought to steal her soul. *Mine. All mine.* He would own every inch of her. Now. Always.

He thrust his erection between the apex of her legs, wishing he could thrust *inside* her. And he would have if he'd had a condom. But he'd never needed one before and didn't keep them around. *Can't risk pregnancy.*

He thrust again, harder, so damn hard, and if she'd been human, he probably would have broken her in half. As it was, she cried out incoherently with sublime, rapturous pleasure. Still. He gentled his motions.

"What are you doing? No." She bit down on his lip until he tasted blood.

The action sent him into a maddened frenzy of lust, and he thrust, thrust, thrust again. On the final slide, she convulsed against him, shouting, "Yes!"

My woman is climaxing. Loving what I'm doing to her.

The knowledge broke him. Pleasure roared through him, parting his lips, his hoarse bellow echoing through the room. His muscles locked down on bone, squeezing as he plunged against her again and again before coming in his freaking pants…coming…and coming…until he had nothing left to give and collapsed.

"Don't be mad," she rushed out. "Please, don't be mad. I couldn't help myself."

And he couldn't blame her. He'd wanted this, too.

He was panting and couldn't quite catch his breath, his heart running some kind of race inside his chest. "Can't quite manage a good mad right now." That would come later, he was sure, when he would curse them both. "Would it be wrong to pound my chest like a gorilla?"

"Wrong? No. Entertaining? Yes."

He kissed her brow. "I need to clean up."

She clung to him. "But I don't want you to go."

Determined to have an afterglow? *What my princess desires...* He got comfortable beside her, despite the humiliating condition of his pants, saying, "Tell me about the bond."

She traced her fingers over his chest. "I'm really, really not a parasite."

"I know you're not a parasite, princess." He'd thought it would make him weaker, deplete him, but she was right; he actually felt stronger. Fiercer. "What triggers the bond?"

Slowly she relaxed against him, their bodies practically fusing. "Many things. Continued close proximity. Need. Love. Even hate."

His mind snagged on the word *love.* Did he want her to love him?

He didn't know. Love complicated things.

But one thing was clear: he wanted her in his life forever. If there came a day when his touch wouldn't sicken her, both of their worlds would change. She would be his. Utterly. Completely. No reservations, nothing held back. His chest constricted with longing. If not, they would just have to deal.

He was a bad, bad man. She deserved better, just like he'd told her, but she wasn't going to get it.

"Go," she whispered, giving him a little push. "Get cleaned up."

He'd gone stiff, and he knew she'd mistaken the reason. But he padded into the bathroom anyway, thinking he needed a moment to process everything that had happened. He washed up, changed his gloves and pants... and then crawled back into bed with her without actually processing. There was no need, he decided. They were together. They would make it work.

He rolled to his side, keeping her locked in his arms. "I don't know what thoughts were rolling through your mind a moment ago, but I'm right where I want to be." Enjoying her while he could. "With you."

She placed a kiss just above his heart, then nipped at his nipple, drawing a hiss from him. "Do you want to hear one of my secrets?" she asked.

"More than anything. But tell me while you bite me."

Nibble, nibble. "Sometimes, when the loneliness of cell life got to be too much, I would imagine I was dating a nice, normal man who never made me angry." Nibble.

"That's not what you got," he said, and twisted to his back, placing her on top of him.

Her hair spilled around him, creating a curtain. Only the two of them existed. "I know. I've since realized I like being challenged. Gives me a chance to be…me."

"Good, because I happen to like you." Liked being with her, too. She might be his greatest torment, but she was also his greatest source of joy. She amused him, challenged him, played with him. Let him be the kid he'd never had a chance to be.

"Do you like what I do to you?" she asked with a throaty purr.

"You know I do."

"Good," she said, mimicking him, nibbling, nibbling away, "because I'm about to do a lot more…."

CHAPTER TWENTY-ONE

A FACT OF Baden's afterlife: alliances were a pendulum that swung one way then the other. A man had to keep his head on a swivel or a so-called friend could nail him in the back.

First Baden had been alone. Then he had ventured to Pandora's side. Then Pandora had decided to sign up for Team Rhea, opposite of him. And now...now Baden had agreed to work with Cronus, a male he despised.

Soon after the girls had turned on Baden, he'd recruited the former king to his side. And, considering Baden had an in with Torin, and thereby the Red Queen, Cronus had been more than happy with the pairing.

As they worked alongside each other, Baden tried not to remember how many times Cronus had threatened his friends—and when threatening hadn't been enough, moved on to *torturing* his friends.

What had the Red Queen once called the bastard? A Nephilim, descended from fallen angels. Baden had watched this Nephilim defeat the Greek rulers who'd once defeated him, and claim ownership of the lower level of the skies, then watched him lose his head to a demon-possessed girl.

And now he's my only ally.

Wasn't afterlife grand?

"We should have servants for this," Cronus grumbled as he shoveled another scoop of dirt aside.

Sweat rolled down Baden's back as the pain he'd been dealing with all day amplified. *Worth it.* "Well, we don't. Deal with it."

"Deal with it? You deal with it! I was born to give orders, not obey them. For that matter, I was born to lead, not to do manual labor."

"Your station doesn't matter after death, so shut up and shovel faster," Baden commanded, anchoring a thick tree limb in the hole Cronus had created.

They'd been at this for hours…maybe days. Time wasn't really time here. The past and future had long since collided with the present.

One by one, they'd sharpened countless limbs into spears, wrapped each one with a portion of the blood vine Baden had died eight times procuring, and placed the weapons around the perimeter of the vision-fog.

He shuddered with the memory of his deaths. The blood vines grew along the farthest edge of the realm, protected by poisonous foliage no one in their right mind would ever dare approach. He and Pandora had made the mistake only once, and it had been accidental. The pain the poison had caused…like nothing he'd ever experienced, in this life or the other. And it had lasted. A steady throb that had tormented for years.

Going back had been stupid—and wise. He'd had to endure another poisoning…was *still* enduring it.

Worth it, he reminded himself.

He had a plan. He—

The increase of the pain caused the sweat to begin pouring and his muscles to squeeze on bone, even breaking some. His lungs constricted, cutting off his airways.

His vision blackened. But just as quickly as the throb had begun, it faded.

Another one would come, and soon.

"Hurry," he snapped. They were almost done, but almost wasn't good enough.

"You hurry," Cronus snapped back.

"The girls will be here any moment." Early this morning, he'd managed to push them both into a pit. But they'd get out soon enough. They always did. And then they'd come here. They'd want to know where Baden was so that they could exact revenge. "And since you're a piss-poor fighter, I need all the help I can get."

Cronus shook a spear at him. "Speak to me like that again and you'll lose your tongue."

"Oh, no. Not that. Anything but that." Baden rolled his eyes. "You do know I'd just grow another one, right? And that's assuming you'd manage to overpower me. Which you wouldn't. While you were locked away in prison, I watched the world's greatest warriors live and die. I learned from their mistakes. Then, after you escaped, I watched you. I know your strengths and weaknesses better than you do."

"I have no weaknesses," the former king snapped, moving out of the way so Baden could place the second-to-last spear in one of the holes.

Baden shoved the weapon into Cronus's chest cavity instead. The male gaped at him, mouth opening and closing as he tried to speak. Screw alliances. He would do this on his own.

"Do you know where you went wrong?" Baden asked casually. He placed the other end of the spear into the ground, lifting Cronus off his feet and leaving him to dangle. "You allowed yourself to be distracted."

"I could say the same about you."

The voice had come from behind him. And the speaker had been unaware of the fact that Baden had been reaching for another spear the whole time he'd taunted Cronus. Baden twisted and hurled the pole at the woman, cutting her off midsentence.

He had not been distracted for a single second.

Impact tossed her back...back...until the spear embedded in a tree trunk, pinning her in place.

Like Cronus, Rhea had trouble articulating her shock.

Baden was grinning coldly as Pandora moved out of the shadows to stand beside the former queen.

"Impressive," she said.

He knew the compliment was genuine and inclined his head in response. Tried not to let his chest puff with pride.

"I still have to hurt you for doing it," she added.

"Of course. You may try. I expected no less."

Stride steady, sure, she approached him. Daggers she'd carved from rocks and tree limbs were clutched in both of her hands. "You aren't the same person I knew in the skies. The one beloved by his friends. You've changed. Do you think they'll like the man you've become?"

It was a question he'd asked himself every day since the Red Queen had been found.

He liked to think they would. As hard, harsh and jaded as he'd become, so had they. But he'd once been the peacemaker. The one everyone went to for help with a problem.

A twig snapped, and he blinked to attention. His eyes narrowed. Pandora was closer than she should have been and he realized she'd done to him what he'd done to Cronus—distracted him.

He withdrew one of his handmade daggers and sliced into his own palm. Blood welled—blood he then dripped over each of the vines. They came to instant life, rising like snakes—or vampires—who'd just encountered prey.

Pandora ground to a halt, her eyes widening.

"Bring her to me," he commanded.

The vines, drunk on his blood, became an extension of his arms shooting forward. Pandora turned on her heel to run, but the vines caught her after she'd taken only three steps. They wound around her ankles and yanked. She performed a comical little face-plant, then clawed at the ground as she was dragged backward, toward Baden.

When she was within his reach, the vines released her and curled around his arms to await his next order. This. This was why the poisoning had been worth it. He planted his booted foot into the small of Pandora's back. He opened his mouth to gloat but went quiet when he spotted a black fog rolling in from the forest. It was the blackest fog he'd ever seen. There was no way it was natural. It couldn't be.

Bodies seemed to writhe inside it.

Screams echoed.

"What is that?" Pandora gasped. She wasn't fighting him, he realized. She was still on the ground, watching the fog as he was.

Should they run? Or should they fight it?

Could they fight it?

Throb, throb, throb. When that pain faded, he realized his next move had been decided for him. It was too late to run. He had to fight.

Except, as the fog reached him…enveloped him…it

gripped him as surely as a thousand fists, choking him, holding him immobile…dragging him away.

LIKE A PETULANT CHILD, Cameo shoved her plate of delicious food to the floor.

At the head of the table, Lazarus set down his fork and arched a brow at her. "Not hungry, sunshine?"

"Not for food," she barked. She wanted vengeance.

He dabbed the corners of his mouth with his napkin before placing it beside the fork. "For what I can give you, then. Such a naughty girl. I approve."

"For your blood!" She jumped to her feet, planted her palms on the tabletop, and leaned toward him. "You lied to me. You let me think I was going to be sold as a sex slave. You tricked me into crawling into bed with you."

He tsked. "Don't pretend you didn't enjoy yourself."

She scooped up a handful of what looked to be mashed potatoes and threw it at him. The white glop splattered over his chest, a few specks even making it up to his face.

"Why am I here? How am I here?" she demanded.

He didn't bother cleaning himself up, just left the mess in place. "Once upon a time, half of my spirit was ripped out of my body and sucked inside the Paring Rod. Whoever wielded the Rod controlled me. As you know, that was Juliette. Then Strider beheaded me, and the other half of my spirit, as well as my body, was also sucked into the Rod. The two halves of my spirit were able to weave back together and return to my body, healing it. No, decapitation doesn't mean the end, not for a creature like me. I was spit into this realm, and though I was stronger than ever, I was still unable to travel outside a certain grid of realms. So I picked my favorite one and took over. All of that to tell you…I've named this place the Realm of Lazarus."

"Original," she said, while inside, her mind whirled. So that's part of what the Rod did? Opened a doorway between one realm and another. "How did you find me? What about all the other realms we traveled through?"

"I sense every time a new soul uses the Rod and enters my grid, and I go hunting. When I saw you, I remembered you. A friend of Strider's, the male who killed me."

"So you sought revenge?" Bastard!

He shook his dark head. "Why would I? He freed me from Juliette's hold. She owned the Paring Rod and used it against me. I owe him a debt of gratitude."

Okay. Wait. "I don't understand." Her tone softened. "Why trick me, then? Why not bring me straight here?"

His expression turned infinitely tender—and she didn't understand that, either. "Because you were not sent here. You were sent elsewhere, to the inside of the painting you were holding when you touched the Rod. To get to you, I had to leave here. To return, I had to go through other realms. And trick you? Darling, you must not know how entertaining you are."

No one had ever accused her of *that* before. "Where's Viola? She used the Rod right before me."

"I found her the same way I found you, but I let her go. She wasn't nearly as interesting."

Interesting? Me? Concentrate! "So you don't know where she ended up?"

"No. Not here, if that's what you're asking. I don't have her hidden in one of the rooms, there to service me every time the desire strikes me. I have plenty of others for that task."

Thrums of jealousy.

Which she snubbed. No reason to be jealous—he wouldn't be having any of those women ever again because he wouldn't be living much longer. She was going to kill him!

She gave the warrior her back, as if she couldn't bear the sight of him a moment longer, while stealthily palming a knife. She kept the blade pressed against her forearm. Ready. "If this is the way you repay your debts…"

"You're alive, aren't you?" There was the slightest bit of irritation in his tone.

Finally. A display of honest emotion.

"Yes. And I'm going to leave," she said.

"No," he said softly, menacingly. "You aren't. You're staying."

"Why?"

Silence.

Such oppressive silence.

"Try to stop me and I'll fight you," she said just as softly, just as menacingly.

"You're only whetting my appetite, sunshine."

Liar! He wasn't attracted to her. He couldn't be. She was an amusement, like he'd said, but nothing more.

Well, she was about to be a mistake!

She swung around. He stood, the motion lightning-fast. Before she could make a move, he grabbed her by the shoulders and yanked her against him. His erection ground against the apex of her thighs.

Any woman would do, she thought, even as heat invaded her veins.

"I want you, and you want me. Let's put ourselves out of our misery," he said, dark gaze fierce.

"How about I put myself out of mine?" She jerked her arm up and thrust the blade deep into his neck.

A pained gasp left him, but his hold on her never wavered. "Well played, sunshine. Well played."

With the weapon still embedded in his neck, he picked her up and placed her on the table, uncaring about the food or the dishes. He forcibly spread her legs and moved between them, his gaze never leaving hers. The heat in her veins intensified, and she shivered.

He planted his hands beside her thighs and leaned toward her, his nose brushing against hers. "Here's how the rest of this game is going to be played," he said, only to look past her and frown.

When he said nothing more, she licked her lips. "Tell me." *I'm excited?* Oh, what a foolish, foolish girl.

He didn't tell her anything. He straightened, though his head tilted to the side. "Something's wrong."

The last word had barely left his mouth when she heard someone scream.

Lazarus jerked the knife out of his neck, the wound healing instantly, just as the doors to the kitchen burst open and a black fog rolled into the room.

"What the hell is that?" she asked, jumping to her feet. The screaming intensified, but she wasn't sure whether it came from his people, or the fog. Or both.

"I don't know." Lazarus pulled her behind him, acting as a shield.

The action baffled her...delighted her. The first time anything like it had ever happened. She latched on to his wrist and tugged him toward the back door, which led to the living room.

The fog pursued them...and quickly reached them.

Suddenly Cameo was surrounded, unable to see...and

only able to hear more of those screams. She couldn't breathe, couldn't even move.

"Lazarus," she tried to cry. And then her mind went blank.

CHAPTER TWENTY-TWO

DON'T GET SICK, *don't get sick. Please, please, don't get sick.*

The mantra played through Keeley's mind, a broken record as Torin rose from the bed. She knew he feared what was to come. Knew he expected her to fall prey to his demon's infection. Deep down, she did, too.

Behind his back, she snatched a lamp from the nightstand, squeezed until the base shattered and flashed away the pieces before they could fall. He looked back at her, and she blinked innocently.

If she *did* sicken, she would have a terrible time convincing him to stay with her. He might be calm but there was no doubt in her mind he'd reached the end of his tolerance.

"I wish I could tell you I'm sorry," she said, "but I'm not. I like what we do to each other."

"I like it, too, but I should be man enough to deny us both."

"Can you really blame yourself? I'm irresistible."

He offered no reply.

She quietly dressed in a clean gown made entirely from strips of black leather. Though an hour had passed since he'd last had his fingers inside her, tremors of satisfaction still lingered. The sweet scent of freshly bloomed flowers wasn't helping. Her potted plants had sprouted the moment she'd climaxed and served as a constant reminder of what Torin had done to her…and what she had done to him, how he'd looked and he'd felt and he'd tasted. How he'd blissed her out without even making love to her.

What would happen when finally he got inside her?

"I don't know whether I should thank you or curse you," he said.

Don't think I'd mind a thank-you this time. "Maybe both?" she offered helpfully.

"How are you feeling?"

"Fine. Honest."

A knock at the door. "Yo, Tor Tor," Strider called. "Your girl has a visitor. Also, someone sent her prezzies."

"Prezzies?" A buzz of happiness. "For me? But no one knows I'm here."

Torin frowned. "Who's the visitor?" he called.

"William…and all three of his boys."

"William's here?" She squealed, clapping with abandon.

Torin gave her the stink eye. "You know him?"

He made it sound like a horrible crime. "I do?" She pursed her lips. What she'd meant as a statement had emerged as a question.

"*How* do you know him?"

"Hades."

"I see." He inclined his head as if he'd just made a decision. "We'll be right down," he informed Strider. Without taking his gaze from her, he asked in a more tempered tone, "How close were you two?"

Is my Charming…jealous? "We were friends, nothing more."

"The William I know doesn't make friends with women. He draws them into his lair and the next morning they wake up in his bed, thoroughly seduced." He stalked to the door and opened it, motioning for her to exit. "Let's go have a chat about his intentions toward you."

She remained in place. "If I get sick—"

His curse assaulted her ears and she flinched.

"If I get sick," she repeated, "I'll heal. I have every time before. It won't have to damage the good thing we've got going."

"Good thing?" he spat, incredulous. "Keeley, you might be the worst thing that's ever happened to me. You've made me care, and there's a very good chance I'll kill you for it." He walked away without a backward glance.

Tears welled up with surprising force, stinging as a sudden rain pattered against the window. He was worried. She knew that. And he was drowning in guilt. She knew that, too. A million times he'd asked how he could continue to do this to her, but maybe the real question was: How could she continue to do this to him?

Every couple has problems. They work through them. We're stronger than most.

Head high, she strolled into the hallway where an array of boxes was stacked against the walls. Each made from something different. Ebony. Ivory. Marble. Gold. Silver. Jade. The prezzies?

Hands trembling, she opened the one on top—and found a minion's black heart nestled inside a bed of red velvet. Also a note. From Hades.

As I said. Never again. See you soon. Yours, H

One of the best presents ever, sure, but anger flourished like the flowers in the pots, sprouting thorns rather than petals, and the fortress shook. Deep breath in… out…she crumpled up the note and let it float to the floor. Another deep breath in…out…

The shaking stopped.

Torin returned. "Is that a heart?" He bent down, picked up the paper and stiffened as he read. "Never again *what?*"

Keeley flashed a large barrel of whiskey into the hall, removed the lid, and began dumping the hearts—boxes, too—inside.

"What are you doing?" Torin asked.

"Can't you guess?" Regifting.

"What's *he* doing?"

"Trying to romance me." An impossible task.

As still as the most skilled of predators, Torin said, "He's just begging for a war, isn't he?"

With her, yes. But she didn't like the thought of Torin facing off with Hades.

"He's the one who gave me this body, you know. The previous owner was Persephone, a child of Zeus, but she had died, her spirit moving on. Hades preserved her body because he liked the look of it. And because of my ability to bond, I was the perfect candidate to take it over, but then I became more than he could handle, so he used it to destroy me." She laughed without humor. "And he thinks I'll give him another go?" Whiskey splashed over her arms, wet her gown. In went another heart. "There are only so many mistakes one person can forgive, and he reached his limit long ago."

She had to flash in two more barrels to get rid of all the boxes.

When she finished, she flashed in a Polaroid camera, took a selfie with her middle finger extended, and attached the picture to one of the barrel lids. "Return to sender," she muttered, flashing each one to the realm where Hades lived.

Swiping her hands together in a gesture of a job well done, she faced Torin. He'd gone pale, and his eyes were tormented.

"I'm not sick," she assured him.

"That's not what—" He scrubbed a hand over his face. "Never mind."

He feared something else? She sighed. *Will I ever understand him?* "William's waiting, yes?" Determined, she plowed ahead, not really knowing where she was going.

Torin stalked in front of her, changed directions, and led her into a sitting room. As she studied her new surroundings, he strode to the wet bar and poured himself a drink. Four other men, each more beautiful than the last, were positioned in front of her. She recognized William the Ever Randy, aka the Panty Melter, aka the Dark, but not the others.

William sat in a plush red chair, holding a glass of amber liquid, his black hair disheveled and his electric blues glittering. Had he just come from some married woman's bed?

Probably. Despite the centuries that had passed since she'd last seen him, he hadn't changed. *Sex walking. Or sitting.*

The other males stood behind him, flanking his chair. One was bald. One was a blond, and one was a brunette. All were warriors. Clearly. Their bodies had been chiseled on the battlefield, and in their eyes swirled horrors no person should ever have to see.

Several of the Lords and their women were also present. They were scattered throughout the room.

"Keeleycael," William acknowledged, his voice smooth and rich. Even more decadent than before. His wicked gaze traveled over her, stripping away her clothing, she was sure. He was a born seducer, simply couldn't help himself. "You're looking quite luscious this afternoon."

"As I do every afternoon, evening and morning." Confidence was as much a weapon as a sword. Not that she needed a weapon against William, but a girl had to keep her arsenal freshly polished.

"Liking her more and more," the redheaded Harpy named Kaia said.

Her man, Strider, dragged her away, muttering, "Told you one word would get you evicted."

"But bay-bee…" Their voices faded.

"It's been a long time," William continued. "I was quite sorry to hear what Hades had done to you… especially since I hadn't had the opportunity to sample you yet."

Torin moved to her side, his hand on the hilt of a dagger.

"Yes," she said dryly. "That was my one regret."

William offered her the barest hint of a smile, a display of teeth she'd watched rip through countless enemy throats. "I'd carry you to my room right this second, give you a new reason to live, but you'd become a clinger, just like everyone else, and I'm currently a little too busy to deal."

"Has nothing to do with the fact that your good buddy Torin is already imagining your head on a pike?" she quipped.

His smile grew wider. "Darling, he's giving me a come-hither look. I get them everywhere I go."

She rolled her eyes. "So who are the brutes behind you?"

"I'd make you play the guessing game, but their beauty always give away their origins. They are my children."

The "children" in question remained stoic, glaring at her as if she were next on the chopping block. "Wow. None of my spies picked up that bit of intel."

"I'd be happy to describe how these miscreants were conceived, and in great detail," William said. "I'm pretty sure your brain would be bleeding by the time I finished and you'd want to pluck out your eyes, but I'm willing to risk it if you are. Just say the word."

"The word."

"This one time, at band camp, I—"

Someone threw a handful of popcorn at him.

"Boo! Hiss!" Anya called. "I've already heard this one. Spoiler alert: the only way you can get two piccolo players to screw you in perfect harmony is to shoot one."

Keeley didn't like having the female at her back, but other than stiffening, she gave no other indication it bothered her. "Why are you here, William? Why did you summon me?"

He hitched his thumb over his shoulder, indicating all three males. "My strapping young lads request the honor of your services. A Phoenix soldier killed their sister." His voice tightened, the muscles in his jaw clenching. "The culprit has been dealt with appropriately. Of course. But her clan claims my boys went too far—" he used air quotes for the last two words "—with their vengeance and retaliate on a daily basis. My boys are winning this war, naturally, but the continuous skirmishes are…annoying me. Your particular skills would be the perfect blood-icing on the cake we will make from their organs."

She'd participated in many wars, and not once had her team lost. The constant victories used to amuse Hades. And she supposed that was one reason he'd begun to fear her power; he'd had to wonder what would happen if ever she'd turned on him.

He'd acted accordingly—and that alone had brought his fears to life.

"I'll consider it," she said, and Torin stiffened. "And if, ultimately, I agree, your strapping young lads will have to pledge their eternal loyalty to me. I'll soon be jump-starting a new kingdom, and I'm on the lookout for a royal guard."

Her announcement received several different reactions. Alarm from Torin. Amusement from William. Affront from each of his children.

"Those are my terms," she said with a shrug. "Take them or leave them."

"Does anyone want to hear *my* opinion?" Anya called.

"I would rather swallow a battery," Keeley muttered and flashed the girl into a cage at the zoo. Or rather, she tried to. Anya remained in place, smug.

Well, well. She'd scarred herself with brimstone.

Keeley glared at Torin. He'd shared her weakness with his friends already, choosing their safety over hers. And the only time he could have done it was while Keeley had been writhing in bed, recovering from an injury that would have killed Gideon, whom she'd maybe kinda sorta saved.

And yeah, okay, there was a slight chance the other

Lords had known about Curators as Torin had, but she doubted that was the case. Especially when he lifted his chin, his teeth gnashing together, his look total *what did you expect?*

The fortress began to shake. Deep breath in….out. She had been working at this relationship, giving it everything she had, trusting him, risking her life for him, and yet he had been working at handicapping her.

How much more will I tolerate?

Keeley tore her gaze from Torin. *Deal with him later.* Always later. The story of her life.

"So…why the huge crowd?" asked a voice Keeley couldn't place.

William set his drink aside and stood. No longer the picture of relaxed depravity, he morphed into a bona fide pillager—ready to spring and attack…to devour.

Keeley had never, ever, witnessed such a response from him.

A delicate-looking girl stepped through the Lords and ladies, her glossy dark hair and flawless olive skin a lovely combination. She had sensual eyes of the deepest, richest brown, and they were framed by lashes so long and thick they created a spiky fan around her lids. But as gorgeous as she was, she was young and human. Far too young and far too human for a male of William's fierce appetites.

This had to be the infamous Gilly.

Her birthday approached, Keeley remembered. Poor darling. Did she have any idea William was set to pounce? Just waiting for time on the clock to run out?

The girl waved at Keeley, an aura of sweetness and light enveloping her. "I'm Gillian. Everyone here calls me Gilly, even though I've begged them not to. You must be the Red Queen I've heard so much about."

"You may call me Dr. Keeley." *We are going to be fast friends, and I am going to teach you how to torment William of the Dark for years to come.*

"Do I not deserve a greeting, poppet?" William purred.

Gilly—Gillian—turned with a grace rivaling a ballet dancer and placed her hands on her hips. "Are you the person who burned all of my party decorations to ash?"

"I am." And he didn't sound sorry about it.

"Then no. You don't deserve a greeting."

Keeley crossed her arms over her chest, annoyed on the girl's behalf. "You burned her decorations to ash?" A little human who'd had no way to stop him.

His eyes narrowed on her. "She doesn't need a party. I have a surprise for her."

Yes, and Keeley would bet the surprise was in his pants. "Your surprise isn't what she wants, Willy, or she wouldn't have bought the decorations."

William raised his chin, flickers of red appearing in his eyes. "You getting angry, Majesty? Go ahead. Try to harm me. See what happens."

Oh, she knew what would happen. Nothing. Like Torin and Anya, he had brimstone scars.

Too bad for him she had a weapon unaffected by those scars. Information.

She flashed a brilliant smile at Torin. "Guess what? You wanted to know who stole Pandora's box after it was opened. Well, I'm ready to tell you."

Torin took a step closer to her.

A strange, high-pitched ringing suddenly filled her

ears. In seconds, massive amounts of strength seeped from her pores, her knees threatening to collapse.

Don't understand what's happening.

Something warm and thick dripped from her nose, and after she wiped, she saw streaks of crimson on her fingers.

"You should go to your room and rest," William said. "Clearly you're unwell."

Have to tell Torin... "William..." she said, forcing herself to go on. "William is the one who...stole dimOuniak...he is...your betrayer."

Her entire world went dark.

CHAPTER TWENTY-THREE

TORIN MASSAGED THE back of his neck.

Eleven days. Long enough to get over his rage with William, who'd admitted his crime. The warrior had watched the Lords and waited. He'd stolen Pandora's box seconds after it was opened, but before he'd gotten very far, Lucifer had stolen it from him.

Willy had seen no reason to tell them what he'd done, he'd claimed, because—get this—he just hadn't wanted to tell them. He wasn't sorry he'd done it, was just sorry he'd been found out. Typical.

According to William, Lucifer couldn't touch the Morning Star. His darkness would be crushed by the light, and he would face the ultimate defeat. Which was why he'd never wanted *anyone* to have it.

Something to be dealt with later.

There was nothing more important than Keeley. And eleven days also happened to be the length of her newest illness. Blood had continuously leaked from her nose, and even her eyes and ears. Torin hadn't known what was wrong until the back of her skull had basically exploded, revealing the tumor growing out of her brain.

The gruesome sight had nearly done Torin in…*my Sugar Plum Fairy in pieces*. It had been the worst moment in a life *filled* with worst moments.

Yesterday the bleeding had finally stopped and this morning her skull had healed. She was going to live.

"She'll wake up soon," he said to Lucien. They were alone in the warrior's bedroom suite, sitting across from each other. This was the first time Torin had felt comfortable enough to leave her side.

"That's good. Why do you look so miserable?"

"I have to give her the *let's just be friends* speech for what seems the thousandth time—and mean it." If they continued along their current path, she would grow to hate him the same way she hated Hades.

Hades had done too much to forgive, she'd said. Torin couldn't allow himself to reach that point.

Actually, he might have reached it already. Not because of the demon, but because he'd told his friends about the brimstone. They would have remembered on their own, but they'd freaked about the vastness of her power and what it meant for their families, and well, he'd hoped to assuage them before they could ask him to choose between them and Keeley.

But wasn't that exactly what he'd done? *She* certainly thought so.

"I can't believe I'm going to say this, but…would continuing to date her be such a bad thing?" Lucien asked. "I've never seen you so content."

Content…angry…frustrated. With Keeley, he felt more than usual. "Bad? Try terrible. I'm no good for her."

"I think she would disagree."

Which was the biggest part of the problem. "I can't keep doing this to her." He pulled at his hair, welcomed the sting. "I've tried to leave her. You saw. I failed. I think I wanted to fail. Hell, I know I did."

Lucien rubbed his scarred jaw with two fingers. "I have a theory about all of this. I think you *can* touch the Red Queen without consequences."

"Screw your theory," Torin muttered. "I've already proven it wrong."

"Can...one day," Lucien amended. "If she bonds with—"

"She *is* bonded to me."

"Let me finish. If she bonds with you...and many others. As a Curator, the more bonds she has, the stronger she'll be."

Others? Probably not a good sign that he wanted to cold-bloodedly murder anyone who ended up tethered to her. *My woman. Mine alone.* But for her—he would deal. There was only one problem. "What if, through the bond, she passes on the demon's sicknesses? She would be strong enough to combat them, but others might not be."

Lucien sighed. "Yes. There is that."

Cursing, Torin swiped his hand over the side table, sweeping an ice-filled glass to the floor. Life shouldn't be this way. Shouldn't be so hard. No matter what decision he made—stay, take off, touch, don't touch, try for something, just be friends—it was a bad one.

"I've got to do this," he said. "She means too much to me."

Lucien gave him a pitying smile. "She doesn't strike me as the type to allow a man to make decisions for her."

"Don't care. I'll be firm."

"You were firm last time, too."

"You are such a pain. I'm leaving before I donkey punch you in the face."

Lucien blinked innocently. "Was it something I said?"

Scowling, Torin stood and moved to the door. As he

reached for the knob, the door flung open and Anya rushed inside the room, almost crashing into him.

She stopped abruptly, jerked her hands behind her back and peered up at him. At least, he thought she was peering at him. She wore a hat, and the shadows cast by the brim obscured her eyes.

"On your way out?" she asked. "Good—I mean, boo, I'm super bummed. So sad we won't get to chat. Did you ask the Red Queen about the boy? Well, goodbye." She stepped aside, motioning to the hall with her chin. "Time for Lucy to give Annie some alone time."

This did not bode well—for Lucien. *My Sugar Plum Fairy would—*

Stop!

"What did you do, Anya?" Lucien demanded, coming up to Torin's side.

She shifted from one foot to the other. "Don't make me say it in front of Torin. Please, baby!"

"Say it," Lucien insisted. "Now."

"What's going on?" Torin asked.

"Well…there *might* be a slight problem with the she-devil in your room," she admitted.

What! Demon red shimmered before his eyes. "Did you harm her?"

"What? Sweet lil me?" She shook her head, all innocence. "But I may or may not have done some research and come across a bit of info that said hacking off all of her hair would severely weaken her. Then I may or may not have snuck in your bedroom with a pair of scissors and taken these." She lifted her arms and clutched in both of her hands were thick hanks of golden hair. "By the way, I may or may not know for a fact that the rumors are definitely *not* true."

Going. To. Kill. Her.

"The Red Queen may or may not have woken up mid style job," Anya continued blithely, "and may or may not have taken the scissors away from me and given me a new style of my own."

With a clipped slash of his arm, Lucien knocked off her hat. The ultrafashionable Anya sported uneven bangs and layers that hung sloppily around her face. "You may or may not look ridiculous. And adorable," he added with a grumble.

"*Not* adorable," Torin roared. It had taken weeks to convince Keeley to rest in his vicinity. Weeks to prove she was safe with him, that she could trust him to protect her from others while she was vulnerable. All his efforts had been ruined in a blink.

Anya ignored him, saying to Lucien, "We'll have to postpone the wedding until my hair grows back."

"Why am I not surprised?" the warrior replied.

"If you don't spank her, I will. And I won't wear gloves." Torin left the room before harsher words were spoken and friendships were ruined.

"Yo, Tor Tor," Strider called, running to catch up to him in the hall, then keeping pace beside him. "Kaia's been pestering me—I mean, asking sweetly. She wants you to set up a playdate with Keeley. A girl's night out with murder, mayhem and crap like that."

"I'll talk to her," he said, rounding the corner.

"You're a lifesaver," Strider replied. "But, uh, do it soon. Kaia's pestering—I mean, asking sweetly—can get painful."

Torin reached his room. He fortified his resolve—*I made a decision, and I'm sticking to it*—before he entered. Keeley stood at the edge of the bed, hands folded neatly in front of her. Waiting for him?

Hell, she was gorgeous. Her hair had indeed gotten a major trim, the waves stopping just below her shoulders. Still long enough to fist. Like Anya, she had bangs. Only she'd swooped hers to the side. Made her look younger… like a doll who'd gotten a trim at Salon Toddler.

Adorable was right.

She wore a new gown. One of scarlet silk that clung to her magnificent curves and formed a ruffled pool around her feet. Elegant—except for the deep vee between her breasts, showcasing her cleavage. *That* was straight-up hot.

He stepped back, increasing the distance between them. But it didn't help. The desire to put his hands on her was always with him, riding him, but now it utterly consumed him. *Resist!*

But…she was well and in front of him, and a bed was behind her. How easy it would be to toss her to the mattress and pin her with his weight.

"We have to break up," he bellowed. Damn it. He cleared his throat, added softly, "We'll remain friends, of course."

Her eyes narrowed to tiny slits. "Don't *let's be friends* me. I invented that speech."

"Keeley—"

"No! I knew you would try something like this. I knew it!" At least the fortress wasn't trembling. "Well, I refuse your offer of friendship *and* your breakup. We're staying together, and that's final."

The demon mewled with disappointment.

"You can't refuse a breakup," Torin thundered.

"I beg to differ. I just did."

He had zero experience to draw on and no idea how to respond to her. He went with honesty. "Breaking up is for the best, princess."

"You thought leaving me was for the best, too, but it wasn't long before you were holding me in your arms as if you couldn't bear to let me go. And do you know why you did that? *Because you couldn't freaking bear to let me go!*"

"A mistake." He scrubbed a hand down his face. "Obviously."

"You don't believe that."

"I do. I really, really do."

The color drained from her cheeks. "No. No!" She stomped her foot, the hem of the dress rippling. "You can't keep doing this to me, warrior. You're either in this relationship or you're not. I'll give you one more chance."

Do it, say it. "I don't need another chance. I ended things. You're the one still fighting it."

She drew in a heavy breath and squared her shoulders. "You're right. It's over then. We're over." No emotion from her, in word or deed. "You'll stay in here, and I'll move out."

Where's my relief? "There's a room next door to this one."

"I'll be moving into a house of my own. In town."

"Now hold on just a minute." He wanted her here so that he would always know where she was and who she was with. So he could pop in and check on her anytime he wished—and shut the front door in the face of any male stupid enough to visit her.

She arched a brow at him, haughty, disdainful, every inch the queen. "Regretting your decision already, Torin?

Well, too bad. It's too late." She walked to the closet, saying, "This time *I've* decided."

How did she strip away his resolve with so few words? "You're acting like I'm doing this simply to hurt you. Why can't you see I'm picking your life over my happiness? That I will *always* pick your life."

It was the truth, and the realization nearly drilled him into the carpet. He would pick her over anyone and anything—always. Keeley was it for him. The one he'd waited centuries to possess, not really knowing that's what he was doing but seeing it now. There would be no one else for him. And even though Keeley would be better off if he took the "no one" route, he couldn't do it— not again. Picking her life over his happiness destroyed *her* happiness, and that he couldn't, wouldn't do. Ever.

She'd been rejected all of her life. First by her parents. Then by her husband. Then by Hades. A barrel of whiskey? Torin would have paid the ultimate price: his life.

There were still a thousand reasons they should break up, and only one to stay together. But that one reason triumphed all others: *she's mine. I love her.*

I do. I love her.

He could not reject her again.

He'd made a mistake. One he would rectify.

He moved in front of her and clasped her hands. Peering down at her, earnest and fighting desperation, he said, "I'm sorry I tried to break up with you. I'm sorry I told the others about the brimstone. I'm sorry for every time I made you sick. But if you can forgive me, and I'm begging you to forgive me, if you give me that chance you just promised me, and I'm begging you to give me that chance, I will stay and do my best to make you glad you did. Not because you can find my lost friends, or the box, but because *I'm* lost without you."

At first she gave no reaction.

"Please, Keeley."

Tears welled in her eyes, trickled down her cheeks.

His chest clenched as he wiped them away with a trembling finger. "Don't do that, princess. I want to make you happy, not sad."

"I am happy," she said. "You broke me, but then you put me back together."

A dangerous admission, revealing just how much power he had over her. But then, she *owned* him. All that he had was hers. "I know I'm a project in need of major work," he said.

"Yes, but I like you anyway."

"And you're willing?"

"I am."

Thank God. He drew her against his chest, let her feel the riotous beat of his heart. "Do you forgive me?"

She released a shuddering breath. "Yes. I do. But don't hurt me again, Torin. Please."

Another *please*.

He squeezed her tighter. He knew she'd meant *don't hurt me...emotionally,* but he was who he was and part of him heard *don't hurt me...physically.*

The only honest reply he could give her? "Your heart is safe with me."

Now *she* squeezed *him* tighter. "Tell me a secret, then. Something no one else knows. Prove you're serious about this. About me. Like for like, after all. You told your friends a secret about me."

A secret... His friends had seen him at his best and at his worst and knew everything about him...except one thing. Something that made shame and guilt, as reliable of companions as Disease, prick at him. Telling Keeley wasn't wise. But denying her when he was forced to deny her so much already wasn't even an option.

He locked one arm around her neck, his shirt and the large collar of her dress protecting her skin, then wrapped the other around her waist. It was an intractable hold. She'd have to hear him out fully before he'd let her get away. Not that he would ever let her get away. It was decided. They were in this thing, right or wrong.

"There was a girl," he said.

She stiffened against him.

He fought a grin. *Wants me to herself—same way I want her.* "I did the whole candy-and-flowers thing with her."

"*I* like candy and flowers," she admitted softly.

Candy and flowers, coming up.

"Although," she said, her fingers drumming against his chest. "You gave me the zoo and the chess pieces, and those are *way* better gifts."

Technically she'd stolen the chess pieces. But that was his bad, not hers. He should have handed them over right away. *Let her always see the best in me.* "Everyone thinks I went after her because of my attraction to her. I sometimes convince *myself* of that. Makes it easier to deal with the fact that I touched her skin-to-skin, and a few days later, a plague killed thousands."

She rubbed her hand over his racing heart. "But the truth is…"

"I did it because I was angry. Every day I watched my brothers touch anyone and everyone they wanted. *Fight* anyone and everyone they wanted. Always I was left behind. This particular day, they'd just come home from a battle with the Hunters—do you know who they are?"

A tremor moved through her. "Yes. An army of humans once led by Rhea and Galen, your enemies."

"Exactly. My friends were covered in blood and high on victory. I was resentful. And there she was, standing outside the window of my hut. This beautiful girl. Mid-twenties. Widowed. A full life ahead of her. She wanted me. I knew it every time I dared go into town and our paths crossed. And that night I thought, *why not?* I deserved something good in my life and so did she—and to her, I was something good."

Keeley kissed where her hand had rubbed. "You do deserve good. You are good."

She might not think so when she heard the rest. "I was going to sleep with her. Planned on it. Thought to send her out with a bang. Make her come, then kill her before the disease could spread. Yeah. I'm a real winner."

"So you have a few flaws," she said. "Everyone does."

"But my history with women is poor," he continued. "Before the demon possession, I was too rough with them. Could never get past second base. And this time, soon after putting my hands on this girl's face, I regretted what I'd done, what I was going to do, and I left her. Left her to die. And she did. All of her family joined her."

He waited, tense and impatient, for Keeley's verdict.

"Say something," he croaked.

"What you did was terrible, yes. There's no getting around that. But we've all done something terrible, warrior. Who am I to cast stones? And you have lived with the guilt every day since, haven't you?"

A statement, not a question, but he replied anyway. "Yes."

"Don't you think you've done enough penitence, then?" she asked. "You went centuries without touching anyone else, all while carrying the guilt and sorrow and anguish. You aren't the man you used to be."

So not the words or reaction he'd expected from her. But then, this was Keeley. His sweetest surprise. "Maybe," was all he could bring himself to say. "Why don't you get some sleep. Nothing bad will happen this time, you have my word."

"I'm not tired."

"We've got a big day tomorrow."

"Why? What's going on?"

"We find my friends."

"Hooray," she said. "But I'm still not tired."

She had to be, considering Anya had interrupted her much-needed rest. "Tired or not, I want you to sleep. We're a couple, yes?" He didn't give her a chance to deny it, but picked her up and threw her on the bed. "We do crap together."

"Crap? Really? That's how you phrase it?"

"Like sleep."

"I'd rather organize our closet," she said. "Or steam-clean the floors."

"Too bad. You once told me you'd obey me in bed. Well, you're in bed."

"Fine. I'll sleep," she grumbled, "but I won't like it."

His grin was slow as he tightened his gloves. "Let's see if I can change your mind...."

CHAPTER TWENTY-FOUR

SIGN ME UP for another nap ASAP. Keeley had become a fan for life. Sleeping with Torin's scent in her nose, his heat cocooning her and his arms wrapped around her... there was nothing better.

Well, except for making out with him.

She woke up refreshed and revitalized, ready to conquer the world...and realized the need for Torin was an ache without end. If Hades had been a flame, Torin was a fire. The more he gave her, the more she wanted. And now that they'd decided to make a go of things for real...*I gots to have* all *of him.*

Torin, however, did not wake up refreshed and revitalized, aching for her, and didn't seem to want *any* part of her. He cleaned up and dressed, emotionally distant, her sweet lover of the night replaced by someone cold as ice who liked to snap orders at her.

Get dressed. Hurry.

No. No more gowns. Wear sweatpants.

Eat your breakfast. And by the way, I need you to use the artifacts to search for one more person. A boy.

Did he regret his decision to stay with her?

No, no, of course not. She was an amazing catch.

An amazing catch with secrets.

Her stomach twisted into a thousand painful knots. *We've started fresh. I have to tell him about Galen. And*

I will, just as soon as the right moment arrives. But as the next few minutes passed, all of their moments consisted of longing glances paired with narrowed glances, and gloved caresses paired with muttered curses, then small talk, and it was hard to fit "By the way, I really like your greatest enemy and want to invite him to the family Christmas party" between "Tell me what's wrong" and "What do you mean, nothing's wrong?"

I trust him. If he says he's fine, he's fine. His attitude, and whatever drove it, had nothing to do with their blooming romance.

"Let's go," he said.

Keeley had to run down the hall to keep up with him. The time to find his friends had arrived at last. And maybe *that* was the problem, she thought. Did he think she would screw this up?

He barked orders at some of the warriors. Do this. Do that. His tone was far harsher with them than it had ever been with her, and she took a strange kind of comfort from that.

Tension was tempered by hope as both the males and females did as they were told.

Paris appeared at her side and kept pace beside her. "When can we schedule that chat?"

"Soonish," Keeley said.

"Great. I'll take that to mean the moment you finish the search and rescue." He branched away.

As she passed Anya, the woman ran a finger across her neck.

Death threat? Keeley yawned.

Torin backtracked to glare at the goddess. "Never again." Fury smoldered beneath the surface of his skin. Always Keeley had feared her own temper, but maybe she would have been better served fearing his. Just then, he looked capable of the worst kind of violence.

What would he do?

Perhaps a better question: what *wouldn't* he do?

Was it bad that she shivered in anticipation?

"She's mine," he snarled, "and I will kill to protect every hair on her head. Understand?"

A bolt of awareness. A zing of joy.

"She could be lying to you about needing the artifacts, you know," Anya said, crossing her arms. "Just trying to steal them from us."

"She's not." He looked to Keeley, his eyes blazing with a fierce, carnal hunger he wasn't allowing his body to project. "I trust her. More than that, I put her first. In *all* things."

A shiver more intense than the last. "Thank you," Keeley said softly, her heart seeming to beat for him and him alone. She turned to the goddess. "And thank *you* for the much-needed trim. As you can see, I've never looked better."

"I do give a good haircut." Anya stiffened as Lucien materialized at her side. "Oh, and because I've been told to do this or else…the Cage of Compulsion is yours. *Majesty.* I pass my ownership to you."

"I'll consider it a gift for honoring you with my presence." As Torin pulled her away, she whispered, "Can I hurt her just a little?"

"Please don't. For some reason, Lucien likes her." He rounded a corner, stopped in front of an open door, and motioned for Keeley to pass him.

She flounced inside the room, purposely brushing her shoulder against his chest. He sucked in a breath.

Play with fire. Always get burned.

Play with Torin. Always get results.

The room was midsized and bare except for a rusty cage large enough to hold a crouching adult, a glass case containing the Paring Rod, and Reyes and Danika. Keeley walked around the cage, tracing a fingertip over the top edge. It was cold and solid, made from a metal that would never bend, no matter how much pressure was applied. Tingles shot up her arms.

She turned her attention to the Rod. It had a long, semi-thick shaft with a bulbous head made of glass, a sea of colors swirling inside, glowing brightly. Probably the world's best phallic symbol.

Reyes stepped in front of Danika before Keeley could study her, the All-seeing Eye. "My female has seen into your past. An evil like yours can never be redeemed."

"Well, you would know, wouldn't you?" she said, reminding him of his own crimes and pretending not to hurt. "By the way, I could move you aside without any real effort."

"Try," he said simply. "I've got this." He waved an arm scarred by brimstone.

"And I've got this. A pimp-slap of truth. Get out of my way or I won't find your friends."

He bent down, putting them nose to nose. Opened his mouth to blast her something fierce, most likely.

Torin moved in the warrior's path, forcing him to back away. "She's my honored guest and she's here to help us, Reyes. Remember that. She's not going to harm Danika. But I will harm *you* if you threaten her again."

"And you know I'll like it." Reyes glared at him for a tense moment before he held up his hands in surrender. "But all right. Do what needs doing."

Planned to. "Where's the Cloak of Invisibility?"

"Here." Reyes pulled a small gray square from his pocket.

Keeley claimed it, looked Danika over—small, fragile girl—and motioned to the Cage. "You must climb inside it."

The plug was pulled on the girl's composure, a tremor rocking her on her feet. "But why?"

Enough! "If you want to find your friends, you'll do what I say, when I say. Without argument."

"But…"

"That sounds like an argument." Keeley gave a sharp clap of her hands. "Do we want to do a little rescuing today or just chat? Either way, my time is money."

Danika looked to Reyes, who nodded stiffly. She walked over, but before she climbed inside, looked up at Keeley and said, "Thank you. For all you're doing to help us."

A lump grew in Keeley's throat—what was this? Emotion? Over well-deserved praise? *My delightful haughty outer shell has deteriorated* that *much?*

She slammed the door shut with more force than she'd intended, and at the ominous *clank,* Danika yelped.

"A little background for my audience," Keeley said. "I'm the owner of the Cage. While Danika is trapped inside it, no one will be able to remove her but me. Blah, blah."

"If you hurt her…" Reyes began.

"Haven't we covered this already? *I* won't." But the process sure would. Keeley returned to the case and removed the Rod.

"Careful with that," Torin said.

She gave him the universal look for *are you kidding me?*

"The last two women to touch that Rod vanished without a trace," he explained.

"That's because they didn't know how to use it properly." She carried the artifact to the Cage and fit the end over the hole in the center of the lid. "Move to the side," she commanded Danika and, after the girl had obeyed, pushed the shaft all the way to the bottom, anchoring it like a flag.

"Did you know it could do that?" Torin muttered to Reyes.

"No."

"We're obviously idiots."

If you only knew the half of it, darling. "Charming, how would you feel if I went for the Morning Star first? With it, we could save all the others in a blink."

"Yes. Do it."

"Morning Star?" Reyes asked.

She ignored him, saying, "Fit your hands around the Rod," to Danika. "And don't remove them until I've returned and given permission." She didn't have to end with *If you fail to obey me, you will leave me trapped inside another realm and angry,* because once a command was given, the occupant of the Cage was forced to do it.

Slowly the girl reached out.

"By the way," Keeley added. "This might not be the most pleasant experience—for you. My...apologies."

Danika curled her fingers around the shaft and screamed.

Reyes stepped toward her, but once again Torin moved into his path. The warrior sidestepped him, but Torin followed, remaining a constant block.

"Now," Keeley said to the girl. "Close your eyes and picture the Morning Star."

The girl closed her eyes but said, "I don't know what that is."

"Just think the words. Morning Star. Morning Star."

Several minutes ticked by in silence, nothing happening. Tensions grew. Were the artifacts broken?

"I don't understand," Keeley said. "Picture Cameo."

The second Danika complied, the top of the Rod switched on, making a mockery of its earlier glow. Bright colors shot out in every direction, filling the entire room. Definitely not broken. Just in front of the Cage, those colors sucked together, forming a picture of an exquisite dark-haired female being dragged up a flight of stairs by...humans? She didn't fight them, but then, she couldn't; she was unconscious, her head cracking against every new step and leaving a smear of blood.

"Cameo," Torin gasped.

"How do we get to her?" Reyes demanded.

Easy. "You step through the portal. You'll be transported to the midst of the very scene you see." As she spoke, she unfolded the Cloak of Invisibility until what had started as a tiny square had grown to size "circus tent."

"I'll go," Torin said.

Reyes gave a clipped shake of his head. "You can't. You can't touch her."

Her warrior spat a blistering curse. "Left behind again? No!"

"You know that's for the—"

Torin spoke over him with a harried, "What I know is that I don't like Keeley doing this. I know I pushed her into it, but I'm worried about her. I don't want her going through. I don't want anyone but me going through. If someone ends up hurt..."

Misguided, but sweet. She'd promised to rescue Cameo, so *she* would be the one to do this.

In the bag, baby. As they continued to argue, Keeley fit the Cloak over her shoulders and moved toward the portal.

Torin, somehow aware of her every move without seeming to focus on her, snapped, "What are you doing, princess? Don't you dare—"

"Be back soon!" With a flick of her wrist, she draped the material over her head and vanished from view.

"Get back here right this—"

She stepped through the portal, cutting off his tirade. Since the Cloak was the one and only ticket through, he would be unable to follow her.

He'll thank me later.

The scent of sulfur and rot immediately assaulted her nose, and she gagged. Okay. Had to be in one of the realms in the underworld, but there were too many to choose from. The one ruled by Lucifer. The one ruled by Hades. Oh, and she couldn't forget the thousands ruled by fallen angels, as well as Nephilim. At least the Cloak masked her in every way, the humans dragging Cameo unable to scent Keeley or even hear her.

As the group trudged upward, they muttered about the things they wanted to do to the girl…things their leader—whoever he was—had forbidden them to do. Dark, terrible things. An avalanche of anger dropped through Keeley.

The group reached the top of the staircase, turned a corner, and strode down a hallway. There were six closed doorways, and they chose the third one on the left. It was empty save for the shackles dangling from the ceiling. They managed to prop Cameo on her feet and clasp her wrists in the restraints. Three of them exited the room. The fourth stayed behind.

One of the others stopped in the doorway, saying, "Touch her, and he'll kill you."

"*If* he finds out. He won't find out."

"I wouldn't be so sure about that. He wanted this one for his own. It's why she's not with the others."

"I say again. He won't find out."

The door was shut, sealing the lingerer inside with Cameo. He reached out to squeeze her breast.

Going to pay dearly for that.

Keeley dropped the Cloak, flashed behind him and fit her hands around his neck. Definitely human, though great evil writhed inside him. Demon-possessed, then. How had he come to live in a realm usually reserved for evil spirits?

Doesn't matter. She punched into the base of his skull, grabbed hold of his spine, and ripped. *Like filleting a fish.* He was too surprised to fight her...and then too dead to react.

As he thumped to the floor, she brushed her hands together in another job well done. What should she do as an encore? Flash throughout the home, until she found and captured the one responsible? She could present the male—female?—to Torin as a gift.

But...no. Cameo needed medical attention, like, yesterday. She might be immortal, but she wasn't impermeable.

Oh, well. A straight-up rescue would have to suffice.

Keeley used the guard's keys to unshackle Cameo, wrapped the girl in streams of her power so that she would float behind while being covered by the Cloak. She retraced her steps to the portal Danika had left open by keeping her hands on the Rod. A second later, she had Cameo inside the room with the artifacts. A room fuller than when she'd left it. All of the Lords were there, most pacing, Anya muttering disparaging things about Keeley and her intentions.

Going be a reckoning one day, goddess.

Keeley settled Cameo on the floor and removed the Cloak, then folded and stuffed the material in her pocket. "We're here," she announced, materializing, gaining everyone's undivided attention.

"Cameo!" Torin burst out.

"She's alive. And you," she said to Danika, "you may take your hands off the Rod. You," she said to Reyes, "may open the Cage."

Torin barely spared Keeley a glance as he crouched beside the injured female; in fact, he actually nudged Keeley out of the way. The others gathered around the girl, as well, pushing Keeley farther back...soon forgetting her and the good deed she'd just done.

She got that the girl was hurt and needed tending. She just wished the group cared a little about *her* well-being. *It'll take time. That's all.* One day she would be an accepted part of the group.

Determined, she moved to the Cage and opened the door, allowing Danika to lumber out. Even she rushed to Cameo's side.

Time.

Aeron, the tattooed one, gently lifted Cameo into his arms and beat feet out of the room. The others followed him en masse.

I want to be loved like that. To belong.

Anya returned only to say, "Did you find the boy or what?"

The one Torin had mentioned? "Didn't get a chance to look."

The goddess raised her fist. "If you're lying just to get back at me…"

Maybe if Keeley learned to respect those around her rather than lashing out, they would learn to respect her in turn. Sow…reap. "Lie?" she said. "I never lie. When it's possible, I will find him."

"Fine. And…thanks. I guess." Anya drew in a deep breath before taking off.

Keeley moved into the hall where she remained, almost half an hour ticking by, not really knowing what to do or where to go. Finding the other girl, Viola, would have to wait until Danika had recharged.

Hands settled on her shoulders, spinning her around. She came face-to-face with Torin, and, as always, the sight of him sent her into a state of euphoria.

"Are you all right?" she asked.

His eyes were glassed over, lines of tension branching from the corners. "Can you help Cameo? She's worsening."

Near tears. For Cameo. Tendrils of jealousy wound through her. "I guess we'll find out. Lead the way."

CHAPTER TWENTY-FIVE

TORIN PACED, crazy worried. Cameo barely had the strength to breathe. Her heartbeat was dangerously sluggish, her reflexes unresponsive. Nothing his friends had done had helped her.

Keeley had shouldered everyone aside to look Cameo over. Strong, capable Keeley. She would save his best girl.

No, not his best girl. Not anymore. Keeley had claimed first place, knocking Cameo off the pedestal, and that wasn't ever going to change. But he'd clearly done something to upset her. And why not? He was a borderline moron most of the time.

Most of the time? Please. Try all of it. But this moron didn't like the wounds in his woman's eyes, darkening the precious baby blue to a soulful navy.

He had to make things right. And he would, just as soon as he unearthed the problem.

"Someone put a septa inside her soul," Keeley announced. "And because her soul is linked to her body, it's physically poisoning her, rendering her unable to respond to stimuli."

Questions and demands rang out.

"What's a septa?"

"How was something put into her *soul?*"

But one boomed above all the others. "Remove it.

Now." Sabin's hands were clenched at his sides, his knuckles already white.

"You really don't want to take that tone with me, warrior," Keeley replied evenly.

If anyone other than Torin heard her response, he couldn't tell, because everyone just kept talking.

"Out," he finally shouted at them all. "Now." They'd get nothing done this way.

Quiet descended.

"Out," he repeated. "Let her work. You're only distracting her."

There were protests. Of course there were protests. These alpha boys and girls were used to taking orders from no one. But in the end they filed out of the room, wanting Cameo better more than they wanted control of the situation.

He stayed put. He wasn't going to leave his woman, and the others would just have to deal.

All business, Keeley said, "Prop her up."

"You know I can't touch her."

"I see." The wounds in Keeley's eyes seemed to *bleed*. What the hell? "Princess," he said.

She stopped him with a snapped, "You won't sicken her. Your shirt and gloves will protect her."

True, but he wouldn't risk it, especially while Cameo's condition was so unstable.

Wanting this over with so that he and Keys could talk, he opened the door, and found everyone congregated in the hall, just as he'd expected. "Sabin," he called. "You're needed."

Conversations tapered to a quiet as the warrior pushed his way through the crowd. Torin allowed the brute into the room, but when he tried to shut the door, William pounded his way inside.

Fine. Whatever. "Prop Cameo up," he told Sabin.

Sabin asked no questions, just moved forward and gently situated himself behind the girl, his back pressing against the headboard.

Keeley crouched between Cameo's legs, flattened her hand against Cameo's heart. The girl jerked, but that was it, her only reaction.

"What are you doing?" Sabin asked.

"Are you always this chatty?" William leaned a shoulder against the wall. "And yes, by that I mean are you always this irritating."

Keeley ignored them both. She moved her hand up and down the girl's chest, side to side, slowly, so slowly—until Cameo's back arched, her scream of agony echoing from the walls.

Sabin snarled, "Whatever you're doing, stop."

"Trust me," William said. "Or don't. Probably don't. But you really don't want her to stop. If it'll make you feel better, pretend they're getting it on. I am."

The color leached from Keeley's cheeks, and her breath began to emerge shallowly. Whatever she was doing clearly hurt her as much as it did Cameo, and Torin did not like that. Did not like that *at all*. He was reaching for her, determined to pull her away, when she fell back, panting.

"Are you okay?" he demanded.

"Will…be…soon." Keeley opened her hand, revealing a—

What the hell was *that?*

It was the same length and width of an ink pen and as

black as the darkest night. Tendrils of inky mist curled from it.

"We don't want you having to deal with that ugly ole thing." Relish layered William's tone as he snatched up the septa, wrapped it in a handkerchief and stored it in his pocket. "Let me do you a huge favor, totally put myself out, and take care of it for you."

"Hades makes them," Keeley said, and Torin got real still real fast.

He'd seen the male only once, but that had been enough. Hades traveled within a black cloud, the screams of his victims echoing from within. When he looked at you, you felt as though you were already trapped in the deepest, hottest pits of hell. He did nothing without ensuring he would receive something in return, and it was quite clear he would betray his own mother for whatever he wanted in return.

Planned to take him out anyway. This just cinches it.

Cameo's eyelids flipped open, and she muttered, "They came...dark cloud..."

Torin crouched beside her and met her frenzied gaze. "Shhh. You're safe."

"Took me...tried to take Lazarus...failed."

He and Sabin shared a confused look. Lazarus? The warrior Strider had beheaded?

"Must...save him..." She reached for Torin.

He reared backward at the same time Sabin yanked her to the side, barely managing to prevent a connection. She sagged against the bed as if the small movement had used up what little energy she had left.

"The *they* she spoke of are most likely Hades's minions," William said.

Torin straightened. "Why would Hades want Cameo and an undead warrior?"

"We'll have to ask him," Sabin said with a cold grin. He focused on Keeley. "He's warded, right, and you can't flash to him?"

"Right," she replied stiffly.

"Can Danika open a portal directly to him?"

She frowned at him. "Yes, but opening a portal drains her. It'll be days before she's strong enough to do it. And do you really want Hades knowing what she can do? What we're trying to do?"

"Keeley's right. Forget him." Torin scrubbed a hand through his hair. "Rescuing Viola and Baden, then finding the box are our top priorities."

"Yes," she said. "Baden will be tricky, though. He's a spirit. I'm not. I can't touch him and pull him through the portal unless one of us is wearing serpentine wreaths."

"I've never heard of those, but I'll do whatever's necessary to obtain a pair." Sabin eased from the bed and moved to the door.

As he let the other warriors inside the room to check on Cameo, Torin lost sight of Keeley. "Out of my way," he said, and the crowd parted like the Red Sea…just in time for him to catch a glimpse of his woman striding into the hall.

He chased after her, catching up as he snaked around a corner. "What's going on in that sweet head of yours, princess?"

Silence.

Intolerable! But he held his tongue until she reached his bedroom door and marched inside. "Don't freeze me out," he said. "Talk to me."

"Like you wanted to talk this morning, before Cameo's

rescue?" She flipped her hair over her shoulder and met his eyes long enough to convey disdain. "Or should I bark one-word responses at you?"

He'd been an ass. Got it. "I was worried about you and didn't handle it well."

"Well, you sure did seem worried about Cameo. Seemed to handle *that* just fine."

"Listen, she and I dated for a while, but—" He paused when he heard her sharp indrawn breath.

"I asked if she was your girlfriend." Keeley shoved each word through clenched teeth. "You lied to me. Lied *after* I told you I would rather save an enemy who tells me the truth than a friend who tells me lies."

"I didn't. I said no, because she's not. Not anymore, not ever again."

"Semantics." Keeley grabbed a bag and began stuffing his clothes inside.

"Not semantics. What the hell are you doing?"

"Helping you move into another room. I've decided to keep this one, and since I'm the honored guest, I get first pick."

Disease cheered.

Shut it. "I'm not finding another room, Keys."

"You are, because *I'm* breaking up with *you.*"

"No way. We agreed to try to make this work." *The couple that slays together stays together.*

"With one caveat. You weren't to hurt me again." She tossed the bag at his feet. "In case you didn't catch my subtle hint, you have."

"And I'm sorry for it." He grabbed the bag and began unpacking. "But I'm also staying."

"Oh, really?"

A second later, the bag was full again. He gritted his teeth. She'd flashed the clothes.

"Not funny," he said.

"You want to know what's not funny? You and Cameo!"

"She's just a friend."

"Like hell. You were just fawning over her."

"I wasn't fawning, and our thing happened about a year ago."

"Even worse!"

"It didn't work out. It *never* would have worked out—because she isn't you."

Her countenance softened the slightest bit as she said, "Who broke it off? You or her?"

"Mutual?"

"You don't even *know?* Oh!" Fire flashed in her eyes. "Well, guess what? I like Galen. That's right," she said when he frowned. "I like him. A lot. He was a prisoner of Cronus's dungeon, and we talked. He traveled with us through the realms. I helped him. *Now* do you want to stay with me?"

Shock. Yes, he experienced it.

Anger. That, too.

Torin's mind whirled, questions he'd once entertained but forgotten suddenly finding answers. The male he'd released from the dungeon, the one he'd thought was familiar but had been unable to place…it had been Galen. The guy's cheeks had been hollowed, his usually pale hair dark because it was caked with dirt. His skin had been papery and white, his wings removed.

"*You* freed him," Keeley said.

"Yes, and I'll need to forgive myself for that," he snapped. *Should have left him there to rot!*

Galen had once been Torin's best friend but had become his betrayer. Then Baden's murderer. The warrior's sins were vast, and deplorable. There was no one Torin wanted to slay more. Not even Hades.

But even as shocked and angry as he was, he managed to say, "You asked if I still wanted to stay with you. The answer is yes. You could do anything and I'd still want you."

Her jaw dropped, snapped closed. "How can you say that?" she gasped out. "How can I believe you? You wouldn't touch your precious Cameo, but you're always more than happy to touch *me*."

Now hold on a sec. "You insist that I do."

"And like I said, you're more than happy to take me up on it," she shouted.

"Of course I'm more than happy," he shouted back. He expected the walls to shake, but they didn't. "I'm *compelled* to touch you. The urge is constant and more often than not irresistible. If I can get my hands on you, I'm going to do it. You're a temptation I can't resist. She isn't."

Keeley blinked at him, her shoulders seeming to turn in. She gulped and said, "Oh." Then she shook her head, her eyes narrowing. "If that's true, why did you forget about me the moment she arrived?"

Now my Sugar Plum Fairy is just being ridiculous. "Princess, I've never forgotten you. I'm always aware of you. Just because I'm looking at and talking to someone else doesn't change that. I knew you'd stayed behind when we took Cameo to her room, and I thought it was because you didn't want to deal with Anya. I planned to get Cameo settled and come back for you."

"Oh," she said again. She fell on the bed, bouncing.

So badly did he want to take her into his arms. He couldn't do it, but he could take care of her in other ways. "It's been too long since you've eaten," he said. "Stay here." He paused, adding, "Please. Please, don't leave me, and please don't put me in the Time Out box. Get comfortable. I'll be right back and I'll wear my favorite hoodie and we'll cuddle."

She gave him a dazed nod.

He hurried to the kitchen where he swiftly prepared a feast of fruits, raisins—gross!—nuts and breads. The only thing missing were bugs. He refused to hunt creepy crawlers…unless she asked. He had a feeling he would do *anything* she asked.

What is that girl doing to me?

He added candy and flowers to the tray and returned to the room, as promised. She hadn't left, hadn't moved an inch.

"Thank you," she said softly, sniffing one of the flowers.

He sat beside her. "So…Galen, huh?" he asked, smoothing a lock of hair from her brow.

She chewed a raisin, nodded. What a change in their relationship. She no longer eschewed the food he provided but trusted him enough to eat. Sweet moments like this made all the dark ones worth it.

"He's a liar, a betrayer. You know that, right?"

"Wrong. He *was*. People change."

Rarely. "If he's using you to get to us—"

She tossed a raisin at him, and he made her laugh when he acted like she'd lobbed a bomb.

"I'm likable, you know," she said. "My association with Galen has nothing to do with you."

"You *are* likable, that's for sure." And lickable. And,

clearly, his mouth needed a distraction; he tossed in a grape. The juice was sweet—but not nearly as sweet as his Keeley. "Just...be careful with him, all right? I trusted him, too, and he—"

Torin blinked. Keeley and the bedroom had vanished, a wealth of blackness suddenly surrounding him.

Confusion hit him. He blinked a second time and new surroundings appeared. One with metal bars. Lots and lots of bars. They were above him and beside him. Behind him and beneath him.

He was trapped inside a cell. It was different from the one he'd shared with Mari, smaller, and wasn't inside a dungeon. It was out in the open, in the center of mile after mile of dirt. Underground?

What. The. Hell?

KEELEY JUMPED TO her feet. "Torin?" He couldn't flash and yet he'd been with her one second, gone the next. "Torin!"

"I did not poison the girl Cameo."

At the sound of Hades's voice, black rage overwhelmed her, and the walls of the fortress shook. He had taken Torin from her—he would pay!

"It was Lucifer," he continued. "We are at war. Knowing him, he planned to come to you, tell you he'd rescue Cameo from my clutches if only you'd join him in the fight against me."

"Of course it was Lucifer," she mocked. "Always blame the other bad guy."

Hades leaned against the door, his arms crossed over his chest.

"What did you do with Torin?" she asked.

He snapped his teeth at her. "You should be nicer to me, pet. I hold his fate in my hands."

"Return him. Unharmed."

Ignoring her, he said, "I brought you a gift."

The walls shook more intensely. *Steady.* "Oh, goody," she replied dryly. "Something else for me to return to sender."

"This you'll want, I promise you."

"All I want is Torin. And if you dare tell me your gift is your penis, I will shove another dagger between your ribs."

His pearly whites flashed in an unrepentant grin. "Do you *want* my penis? Because all you have to do is ask, and I will give it to you. Over and over again."

Men! "Torin. Now."

His smile did not dim. "One day you'll change your mind about me."

Not likely. "Return Torin."

"Return the competition? Not wise. And I am a very wise man."

"Your presence here proves just how wrong that statement is. You lied to me, used me, tricked me, humiliated me, destroyed me and stole centuries of my life. I will never want you again."

"Give me a reason to free him, then."

"I just gave you six. But here are a few more. Because you owe me. Because he's done nothing to you. Because he makes me happy, and I deserve a little happiness. Just because! Take your pick."

A flicker of pain in his dark eyes—an emotion she'd never before seen from him. A trick, surely.

Can't soften.

"Keeley," he said on a sigh. He scrubbed a hand down his face. "I truly regret what I did to you."

"You think that's good enough? That it erases centuries of agony? Clears your ledger of crimes?" She flew to him and slapped him. Hard. Then, because it had felt so good, she slapped him again. "Return Torin."

Hades could have stopped her, but he didn't. He took it.

She slapped him again. "Return Torin!" Again. "I mean it."

As she raised her hand to deliver a fifth strike, Hades flashed to the table beside the bed and placed two metal armbands on top. Both were gold, the head of a snake at one end, its tail at the other. A pair of serpentine wreaths. "For you to use however you see fit."

"And what payment do you expect?"

"None."

Ha! This male had never given anything away without demanding some sort of payment.

"You have my word," he added.

"Not good enough."

"My blood oath, then." He flashed a dagger into one hand and slashed the other. As drops of crimson dripped to the floor, he said, "No payment is expected for the wreaths."

He…actually meant it. How shocking. She lifted her chin and snapped, "I won't say thank you."

He nodded, as if he'd expected no less. "How about when I give you this?"

A harried but unharmed Torin appeared in the center of the room. He spotted Hades and a dramatic change overtook him. His muscles visibly expanded, seeming to double in size as he prepared to attack.

Hades pegged him with a hard stare. "I can remove your demon and ensure you live. And I will."

Torin took a step toward him, only to stop.

Keeley could almost hear the creak of wheels rolling in his head. *Don't listen to him,* she longed to shout. *His bargains never end well—for the other party.*

Then, as she'd expected, Hades laid out the condition. "I'll do so…the moment you walk away from Keeley-cael, never to see or speak with her again." With a smug, toothy grin, the king of darkness vanished.

CHAPTER TWENTY-SIX

BASTARD.

Everything Torin had thought he'd ever wanted had just been offered to him. To be demon-free, able to touch anyone at any time, to *fight* anyone at any time, to have sex, and never have to worry. Never hurt another unless purposely. Never experience guilt or sorrow or regret over something he could not control. But of course, all he had to do was give up the woman he loved and craved more than breath. Never touch her, when finally he would be able to do so without harming her.

Not gonna happen.

He didn't have to mull it over. Keeley was his, and he wouldn't give her up. Not even for a dream.

Keeley turned away from him. "I can't believe I'm saying this, but…you can take Hades up on his offer, and you won't ever have to worry about hurting my feelings. I'll make sure he keeps his end of the bargain before I put you in the Time Out box, just like you once demanded."

"No." He would not be forgotten. Ever. He strode to her, the fire in his heart spreading through every inch of him. "I'm not letting you go. *Never* letting you go. I'm keeping you."

"No. This is what you've always wanted. What you need."

"*You* are what I need."

"No!"

Losing her. "He's evil. I don't trust him." When would Hades do the removal? In a few centuries? How would he do it? What state of *alive* would Torin be left in? Like entering the Cage of Compulsion and being commanded to separate from the demon and live—yes, he would live, but not well. He would remain in a vegetative state. At least in theory.

It wasn't worth the risk.

Nor was Hades. With the king of the damned, there were too many variables. Not that any of them mattered.

"I told you," she said. "I'll ensure he keeps his end of the bargain."

"Screw his bargain!"

"No, Torin, listen to me."

"No. *You* listen to *me*, Keys." She was determined to end things—for him. He got that. Been there, done that. As stubborn as she was, nothing he said would change her mind. She would do what she thought would make him the happiest in the long run, with or without his approval.

Can't let her.

Desperation seized him as he realized there was only one way to proceed. Words wouldn't work, but actions would. He had to prove they could have everything they'd ever wanted.

"You know what?" he said. "No more listening, no more talking. I want you. Fully. And I'll have you." He would prove how much he needed her. Would satisfy her so completely she would never wish to leave his side. "Afterward, you won't sicken."

Her eyes widened—and he knew he'd hooked her. "How?" she asked, breathless.

"I'll show you." If he screwed up and accidentally touched her skin-to-skin, she would do as she'd threatened. He knew that. *Can't screw this up.*

The pressure was on.

Bring it. "Are you willing?" he asked.

"I...I..."

Reeling her in. "You're strong—there's no one stronger. You can withstand anything. And how many times have you told me the prize is worth the consequences?"

"Countless." She pressed her lips together, shook her head. "Let's think this through first."

"Princess, Hades isn't my only option for freedom, and he's certainly not the most reliable one. You're forgetting the Morning Star."

"Not forgetting. Just not counting on it anymore. I tried to find it, and I failed."

Losing her again...

"Besides," she added, "you were willing to leave me before, even though the Morning Star was a possibility. What if I try again and again and can't find it?"

"What if you can?"

She shifted from one foot to the other. Opened her mouth, closed it.

She teeters...no better time. He pounced, picking her up by the waist and tossing her onto the bed. When she finished bouncing, he was pleased to note she remained where she was rather than scrambling off, her breaths coming quick and shallow.

He moved to the foot of the mattress. Her golden hair was splayed over the pillows, and her passion-glazed eyes remained locked with his. *Mine.* His blood rushed through him, a newly awakened river, the dam utterly shattered.

"We are doing this," he said. He withdrew a jacket from the closet, one that was thin, the material capable of repelling water, and tossed it at her. "Remove your bra, leave on your shirt, then put this on."

She licked her lips as she obeyed. "Are we going all the way?"

Softly asked, but no less powerful.

He gave a slow incline of his head. "All the way."

Slowly she lay back against the bed. Through her shirt and the part in the jacket, he could see her nipples were already hard and ready to be sucked.

"The jeans," he said. "Get rid of them. Panties, too."

She shimmied out of both and tossed the material aside.

Such long legs, stopping at the new center of his universe. Pink...damp. His heart almost stopped.

He walked away a second time—surely the most difficult task of his life.

"Torin?"

He'd thought about this. A lot. Thought he'd found a way to have everything he yearned for—everything *she* yearned for. He found a pair of cotton pants and a pair of gloves and gave them to her. Her tremors intensified as she pulled on both.

As she watched, her eyes practically crackling with flames, he opened his fly and removed some of the pressure from his throbbing erection; but he didn't discard a single piece of his clothing. And he wouldn't.

He donned a condom before crawling up the mattress. Keeley sucked in a breath. With deliberate leisure, he moved toward her. When finally he was situated between her legs, he curled his fingers around her ankles, the brilliant heat of her skin burning through the layers between them. She moaned as he traced his thumbs against the arches of her feet, then up…up…stopping when he reached her knees.

"Do you like having my hands on you?" he asked.

"More than anything," she gasped out.

He continued up…up…and when he reached the center of the cotton, he leaned forward, placed the edge of the jacket between her legs and pressed in with his tongue, her body totally protected from his. Even from his saliva. He licked over her hidden but not to be denied by him core. She writhed, arching her hips, seeking more of him, and he worked his tongue in harder, faster circles.

"Torin!" Moaning, she dug her feet into the mattress and reached out to run her gloved fingers through his hair. "Feels *amazing.*"

Men often spent their whole lives searching for a woman like her. But he had her. Him. Only him. The one without experience. The one who could harm her irrevocably. And yet she couldn't seem to get enough of him.

"Wish I had your honey dripping down my throat." He continued working his tongue against her, wetting the resistant material even as *she* wetted it. It wasn't long before he imagined he could actually taste her. So sweet, so damn good.

She moved against him, with him, and he brought his teeth into play, nipping at her…then sucking at her… then nipping again…and she quickened the speed of her arches, arching, arching against him, and then crying out his name, her voice a broken rasp as she came swift and hard.

But he wasn't finished with her.

He journeyed upward. Through the jacket, he licked

at her navel. He'd never given this particular area any thought. In his fantasies, he'd gone for chest and core— what he'd considered the good stuff—nothing else even a blip. But every inch of this woman was precious to him. A feast to be devoured.

"What do you want me to do to you?" she asked and gasped as he nipped at her nipple. "Please let me—"

"I just want you to enjoy. I've never had this before, and I want to give you all, everything." He kneaded her breasts, her soft, lush breasts, as he fit his lips over one of her nipples, sucked, then did the same to the other.

She'd opened her mouth to say something else—not that he would listen to anything other than "Yes, Torin, whatever you desire, Torin," but the words were replaced by a moan of surrender as her pleasure built to another fever pitch.

He sucked, hard, and the moan turned into a groan. She cupped the back of his neck, holding him in place. Her knees ran up and down his sides as he slinked a gloved hand down her stomach, tunneled under the waist of her pants… She stilled, though her grip tightened on him. He balanced on the edge of a razor-sharp cliff as he pressed his fingers against her moist heat.

Tremors rocked her against him. She groaned, then begged for more, harder. He rubbed in circles…up and down…circles again…until she was gasping, muttering incoherently, her legs spreading wide, wider.

"Fill me," she pleaded. "Please, fill me up."

Helpless to resist, he fed her a single finger. Her inner walls clamped on him, so wonderfully tight; he had to bite his tongue to stop himself from spilling then and there. He leaned his forehead into her sternum, his muscles flexing with a flood of intoxicating desire, his veins expanding with a new rush of blood, pumping white-hot pleasure to every inch of him. Sweat trickled down his temples, between his shoulder blades.

"So good, Torin. It's so good. It's driving me...mad... not sure I'll...survive. Who knew...this is how...I'd die? What are you...doing to me?"

Giving you all that I am. He fed her another finger, moved it in and out, slowly at first, then thrusting faster...even harder...like he wanted to do so desperately with his shaft. *Not yet.*

"Can you take another, princess?"

He didn't wait for her answer, just worked in the third.

KEELEY WAS ON fire with realization and need. Torin had chosen her above all others, above everything, and now her body ached from his fierce attention, her skin tingled underneath her clothing, and her limbs trembled. *Magnificent.*

He was magnificent.

She should have followed through and ended things, should not have pushed him to this point. And maybe she would regret it...tomorrow. With Torin stretched over her, his weight pinning her down, his heat and scent surrounding her, she was utterly consumed with pleasure. It saturated her bones, submerged her mind, tickled her every cell. She was alive with decadent sensation.

And Torin was...

Oh, yes! He was moving his fingers in and out of her, taking her to new heights, because *he* was the one doing the pleasuring. And oh, she had to make sure he received equal measure. No, *greater* measure. He was new to this, and should be—

His fingers brushed a spot inside her that had her screaming and pleading for more, her thoughts utterly consumed by him. *Reached the point of no return.*

Like the accomplished warrior he was, he settled in to take full advantage of this chink in her armor, rubbing and rubbing...*so good!*...and rubbing...

She reached between them, wanting her hand wrapped around his shaft. But he pinned her arms above her head with one hand and continued to torture her so exquisitely with the other, always moving in and out of her, in and out.

"Torin."

"You're so wet, princess."

"Yes," she panted. "I want you. Want everything. Give it to me. It's been so long, and I've never yearned for anyone the way I yearn for you."

TORIN WITHDREW HIS fingers from the hot clamp of Keeley's delicious wetness to pinch her chin and force her gaze to rest on him. Her cry of disappointment was music to his ears. Her eyes were glazed but glowing brightly, her cheeks flushed to a deep rose. Never had she been lovelier.

Soon she would belong to him in truth.

"I won't give you up," he said. "That's never going to change."

Her lashes fluttered closed as she arched up to rub her breasts against his chest. Those hard, luscious nipples created a heady friction. "Please. Please. Torin, it hurts."

"Don't want you hurting." A tremor swept through him, undoing him. Keeley would be his first lover... and his last. He would never want another the way he wanted her.

Other men might have panicked, thinking *only one,* but Torin rejoiced. He would never have to settle for a pale substitution, in memory or in deed.

"Ready for me, princess?" His steel-hard length stretched through his fly, and he made sure the latex remained in place. His blood burned hotter and his heart raced faster as he rasped, "Grab the headboard."

When she obeyed, he ripped a hole in the center of her pants and settled in between the cradle her legs provided. He positioned himself for entry, just the tip breaching her inner walls, and oh, hell, he could feel her molten heat already, the tightness of her, and had to bite his tongue against the instant torrent of rapture.

He trembled, battling through the unending waves of ecstasy, as he pushed in slowly, an inch at a time, giving her time to adjust to his girth. Giving himself time to adjust to his first taste of unadulterated euphoria.

He'd wanted this for so long. Had waited for it. Dreamed of it. Spent centuries cursing his lack of it. And here it was, being given to him by a woman who overshadowed all others.

"Torin!" She planted her feet on the mattress and lifted her hips, driving him deeper...so damn deep... until he was in her all the way to the base of the condom.

The tremors intensified. It was...he was...there were no words.

No, not true. There was one. Forever.

Will have this forever.

Will have her forever.

She was tight around him, tighter than any fist. She was scorching hot, luscious and soft. He wasn't sure how he'd lived without her, and knew he'd never be able to do so again.

"Move," she gasped out. "You have to move in me."

Yes. Oh, yes. As he drew back, felt the hot glide of friction, the sense of euphoria intensified and he couldn't breathe from it; she wrapped her legs around his waist, applied pressure, trying to force him to slide back in. But he didn't. He resisted, continuing to pull back...until he was almost all the way out of her. He hovered there for a moment, taunting the frayed edges of his control, knowing what awaited him when he surged back in, so hungry for it. Starving.

"Torin!" she cried.

Wanting *her* hunger to build, he waited just a little longer...just a second longer...before thrusting back in with all of his strength. The entire bed rocked, the headboard banging against the wall. A portrait fell, the glass shattering.

"Yes. Yes, yes, yes." She threw back her head, shouting, "Again."

Nothing could stop him.

He pulled back and once again hovered at her entrance before surging inside her. After that, a dam broke. There was no more hovering, no stopping him. He thrust, faster and faster, harder and harder, the banging against the wall constant. She was so wet, the glide easy despite the tightness of her hot, inner clasp. He chased his pleasure—no longer a want, but a necessity. *Going to shatter.*

For the first time, he would come inside her. Inside his woman. He would experience with her what he'd never experienced with another. He would know her, all of her. Have her, all of her. Would give her all that he was.

She sank her teeth into his chest, and even through his shirt he felt the sting—loved it. His woman surrounded him. She was everywhere, all at once. Her taste lingered

CHAPTER TWENTY-SEVEN

AFTER KEELEY CHANGED into clean clothes—a pair of boxer shorts and a T-shirt of Torin's that boldly proclaimed "Maddox Punched Here" with spots of fake blood splattered everywhere—she crawled back into bed, muttered, "I owe *you* a thank-you this time," and sank into a deep, peaceful sleep without any coaxing from him. He watched her, utterly awed by her. He petted the golden waves strewn over his pillow, drank in the purity of her features. Her lips were parted, moist, even swollen from where she'd bitten them, and he wanted so badly to taste them.

No one was more beautiful than his woman.

The things she'd made him feel…let him do.

Men liked to say a leopard couldn't change his spots and an old dog couldn't learn new tricks. Well, he'd just proven them wrong. She'd changed him, giving him what he'd once deemed unattainable. Not just sex, but unqualified acceptance. He was no longer Torin, but Keeley's man.

He kissed the crown of her head. He'd never thought the loss of his virginity would garner anything but relief, and yet he was utterly undone. His first time had been with the loveliest, wittiest, sexiest, smartest and most powerful chick on the planet. One who'd taught him the true meaning of pleasure, ruining him for any other. Though his hunger was vast, it came with only one craving: Keeley. Breakfast, lunch and dinner, and every snack in between.

And I can have her. Can be careful with her.

I can satiate her.

A commotion in the hall interrupted his thoughts. Banging, shaking. Voices.

Keeley murmured under her breath.

If anyone woke her up, there would be hell to pay.

He waited until she'd settled before he gently eased from the bed, righted his pants and stalked to the door. Lucien and Anya stood in the hallway, passing what looked to be a basket of fruit back and forth.

"Apologize," Lucien commanded.

"Never!" she shouted.

"Shut up!" Torin whisper-yelled.

Both focused on him.

"Not another word. Not another noise. Keeley is sleeping, and I will maim the person who wakes her up."

Anya's eyes narrowed, but instead of screaming as Torin expected, she thrust the basket at him and quietly said, "For your female friend. Because Lucien is sorry I cut her hair."

Lucien cleared his throat.

"And I'm sorry, too," she said. Only to add, "Sorry I didn't cut more. But I won't do it again. Okay? All right? So you can totally tell her I was spanked properly." Her gaze raked over him, taking in his mussed hair, and she smiled. "I see the Red Queen got a spanking, too."

Torin shut the door in their faces. Even the soft *snicker* annoyed him; Keeley would have absolute quiet, and that was that. He set the basket aside—not a fruit basket, after all. In it were sparkly hair barrettes, gilded brushes, silver combs, lace-covered rubber bands and a note that read, *My bad. *A*.

Women.

He padded to the side of the bed. The disturbance hadn't awakened Keeley, thank God.

He spent the next few hours on noise patrol. Reyes came to the door to apologize to Keeley for something he'd said, but Torin sent him away. And any thump, creak or rustle he heard sent him striding out of the room to whisper-yell at the offender. His friends gave him strange looks, and he knew they thought the time away had addled his brain, but he didn't care.

On the final return, William waited at the door for him. The male leaned against the wall, hands anchored behind his back.

"Heard you've gone a little cray-cray today." William's grin was sardonic. As usual. "Expecting all your friends to play the quiet or die game."

"Not expecting. Demanding."

"Well, I'm playing gorgeous messenger. Probably the most gorgeous messenger ever born. Don't pretend you haven't noticed."

Torin arched a brow. "Are you hitting on me, Willy?"

"You wish. Just like everyone else who ever crosses my path. You've seen my ass, right?"

"In need of ego stroking, I see."

"I don't believe in hubris. But I believe in me...and my awesomeness."

This could go on forever. "Just tell me what you came to say and get lost."

William made a face, all *I'd rather eat rocks than talk,* but still he said, "Tell your petri dish my boys will sign up as her royal guard in exchange for her services during our war with the Phoenix."

His fist was connecting with William's nose before he realized he'd even moved. Cartilage snapped. Blood poured. Willy calling Keeley a petri dish? Hell, no. It wasn't funny. Not even remotely. But it was true. Because that's exactly what Torin would make her if he wasn't always careful, wasn't it?

William smiled again, and there was blood on his teeth. "I hope you didn't break a nail with that little love tap."

Torin was about to respond when he got caught up on something else William had said. *Royal guard.* Reminded of the kingdom Keeley planned to "jump start," he cursed.

Was she planning to move away?

Not without me, she's not.

"Will *you* be part of the war?" he asked. Because it was looking like Torin would be. He'd help Keeley any way he could. Perhaps even fight again, he thought, excitement building.

"I'm in and out of it. There's a Sent One, Axel, who is determined to chat with me, and he's been following me. I'm determined *not* to chat with him, which means I can't stay in one location for long."

Sent Ones. Winged warriors who lived in the skies. Slayers of demons and somehow the allies of the Lords. "Here's an idea. Why don't you just *kill* Axel?"

"I have my reasons." William waved his hand through the air, dismissing the topic altogether. "Hades wants Keeleycael back. You know that, right?"

A muscle twitched under Torin's eye. "I know. He can suck a pair of hairy balls. She's mine."

William rolled his eyes. "Are you embarrassed? Because I'm embarrassed for you. *She's mine,*" he mocked. "It's sad how whipped you are. How *all* of you are. Why don't you warriors gently remove your tampons and pretend to be men."

Torin banged his chest like a gorilla. "Hey, stop me if you've heard this one...Gilly."

Instant mood killer. A tension so sharp and thick even Torin could feel it radiated from the man.

"I don't know what you're talking about," William said. "I'm her generous benefactor and she's my ungrateful dependent. I'm a...father figure." His voice snagged on the last two words, becoming nothing but a growl.

Torin grinned at him. "Deny, deny, deny, is that it?"

"Shut up."

"Dude, I hope I'm best man at your wedding."

KEELEY AWOKE WITH a jolt, gasping and sitting up, thousands of thoughts seeming to bombard her at once. The forerunner? *I'm in love with Torin.*

Her stomach bottomed out. She *loved* him?

Oh...crap. She did. Despite the fact that any skin-to-skin contact made her sick. Despite the fact that he'd tried to leave her more than once. She wasn't simply bonded to him, drawing from his strength. She was totally enraptured by him. Under his spell. His willing captive.

She scanned her surroundings, discovered she was still in his bedroom. He'd drawn a chair to the side of the bed. Noticing her wakefulness, he lifted a tray of food from the nightstand and placed it beside her.

There were dark circles under his eyes, and he'd pulled a knit cap over his hair. To hide the tangles she'd caused? He looked tired but sexy. Stressed but relieved.

"Did I sicken?" she asked, dread unfurling.

"No," he said.

She pushed out a sigh of relief.

"I've been running in and out to yell at my friends. Eat," he said. "Build your strength."

Still looking out for me.

Love him so much.

"Why did you yell at your friends?" she asked.

"Because they annoyed me."

"Cryptic answer." What didn't he want her to know?

"And yet accurate."

She popped a grape into her mouth, swallowed. The juice was cool and sweet, delicious.

"I wish Danika was ready to help me find the other girl." The sooner they had Viola in their midst, and then Baden, and then the mystery boy, the sooner Keeley could go hunting for the box...the Morning Star. "But she's not—is she?"

"Not yet. I spoke to Reyes just a little while ago. Danika is sleeping, and has roused only when he forced her so that he could feed her."

Well, bummer.

Keeley wrapped the sheets from neck to toe and settled into Torin's lap, twining her arms around him, careful not to brush against his skin. "I'll tell you a secret," she said. "As happy as I am about the thought of you being demon-free, I'm also afraid. What if you decide you want another woman?"

Would he want to go on the sexual bender he'd never before experienced? Would Keeley even be a passing thought?

Hate low self-esteem! Hate insecurities! Hate doubts!

His arms twined around her, too. "That would *never* happen," he assured her, and his vehemence pleased her.

"You say that now, but…"

"Say it. Mean it with every fiber of my being. I'm lost for you, Keys, and don't want to be found. Can't imagine a moment without you—don't want to. *You* are my treasure, my addiction, not touch. *You* are my sickness, and I want nothing to do with a cure."

The insecurities burned to ash.

He cleared his throat, suddenly uneasy. But his hold was tight on her as he said, "By the way. William's kids are onboard with being your personal guard."

"Really?" How wonderful!

"Where are you hoping to rule this kingdom of yours?"

"Well, right here. Obviously. I will be the Red Queen of the Lords of the Underworld and all of their mates. You may thank me," she couldn't help but add, teasing him…but also quite serious.

A slow grin peeked beyond the dark clouds that had overtaken his expression. "I don't think you've ever had a better idea."

"I know, right? But first things first." Her own grin snuck out. "I need a toothbrush and a shower, in that order. Make it happen."

He stroked a gloved finger over her cheek. "Bossing me already?"

"I'm your queen. That's what I'm *supposed* to do."

Flashing her another smile, one so bright it shone all the way into her heart, he said, "And I'm just supposed to obey? No resistance?"

"Oh, warrior. I hope you do resist." A husky edge entered her voice. Needy. "You'll earn a punishment."

"Oh, yeah? What kind of punishment?"

"You'll be forced to service me. Repeatedly."

His gaze fell to her lips, lingered. "Did you like having sex with me?"

Shivering, she said, "*Like* is too mild a word, Charming."

"Even though we had no skin-to-skin contact?"

"Even though."

"It will be enough for you?"

He wanted her, treasured her just as he'd said, and that would *always* be enough.

"Toothbrush. Shower. Then I'll prove just how *enough* it can be." Donning a regal air, she clapped her hands. "Make it happen, warrior, and the Red Queen will make you happy you did."

CHAPTER TWENTY-EIGHT

BADEN REMEMBERED THE black fog…and the hellish minions who had dragged him out of it. They'd carted him here, to some prison cell, while he was too winded to fight. He would have thought this was a spiritual realm rather than a natural one because 1) demons constantly passed by, and 2) they'd been able to touch him. But there were golden bands locked around his wrists, pulsing, pulsing, and he could touch things he shouldn't have been able to touch.

If he had to guess who was responsible for his capture, he would say Lucifer. The gossip he'd picked up from the fiends…

Lucifer, rounding up everything the Lords of the Underworld prized.

Lucifer, allying with some kind of queen of shadows, a female who had forced a powerful Sent One to wed her.

The Sent Ones would freak out when they discovered the truth. They were winged warriors tasked with killing demons, not aiding them.

And lastly Lucifer, preparing to overtake Hades's throne—to kill the man he'd once considered a father.

Baden could only guess he himself was to be a bargaining chip. Something to force the Lords to fight with Lucifer rather than against him. What Baden didn't understand, however, was the fact that Cronus and Rhea were trapped in the cell with him. The Lords would do nothing for the pair.

But more important, where was Pandora?

"This is an outrage!" Cronus shouted. "How dare I be treated this way. I am the king of the Titans."

"Not anymore," Rhea spat at him. "You're the king of nothing."

"Shut up, woman. Your opinion wasn't solicited."

She shrugged, then checked her cuticles. "Wasn't stating my opinion. Was stating fact."

The two continued to argue.

Baden wanted a dagger. Hell, even a spoon would work. He just wanted to open their throats and cut out their voice boxes.

The creak of a door sounded down the way.

Baden rushed to the bars of his cell. Two demons were striding down the walkway, headed in his direction. Both were around five foot ten and stacked with muscle. Horns protruded from their scalps, and wings extended from their backs.

He stuck out his hand to gain their attention, and two sets of glowing red eyes landed on him and narrowed.

"The girl. Pandora. Did you bring her to this realm?"

Both bared yellowed fangs and laughed gleefully.

Dread twisted Baden's stomach. He'd take that to mean yes, yes they had. And she wasn't being treated well.

The thought enraged him. He hated Pandora. Had rued the day he'd found himself stuck with her. But for centuries, she was all he'd had. His only companion. He couldn't abide the thought of her being tortured. Wouldn't stand for it.

He grabbed the demon on the right, slamming the

creature against the prison bars. The other one came to his buddy's rescue and punched Baden in the face. He held firm. Cronus and Rhea finally shut their mouths, realized the entire point of this endeavor, and rushed over to help him stealthily pat down the demons, hoping to discover the key to the cell.

Baden didn't find one.

When their majesties finally backed away, he released the creature and moved out of reach. His eye was swelling, even leaking blood into his mouth.

"You're lucky we've been summoned. Otherwise," said the one he'd grabbed, "I would teach you a lesson you would never forget."

Never heard that one before, he thought dryly.

The pair strode off.

"Tell me you found a key," Baden demanded.

"I did not." Cronus.

"Nor I." Rhea.

Baden kicked one of the bars. Pain radiated up his leg, then throbbed through the rest of him, reminding him that the poison had not lessened its hold on him, and he wasn't at his best.

Even still, there was only one way out of the cell.

The demons had to open the door. Which meant he had to challenge them.

"Hey," he shouted. *Please. Hear me.* "*You're* lucky you've been summoned. You could try to teach me all the lessons you want, but we both know I'd have you flat on your back and dead in a matter of seconds. Cowards!"

Nothing. No response.

He despaired.

Until he heard a rush of footsteps and the two demons

came back into view. Their eyes were narrowed, glowing brighter. Their fangs were bared, dripping saliva.

"Get ready," he told his companions. He couldn't trust them. Knew they'd leave him behind without a moment's thought if given the opportunity. "If you want the Lords to use the four artifacts to find and save you, you'll help me escape this cage."

Hinges squeaked as the demons entered the cell.

"Let's see what you can do," one of them said.

Yes. Let's.

CAMEO WAS PROPPED against the headboard of her bed. Her friends had been in and out of her room for several days, welcoming her home, checking on her.

Torin sat in a chair he'd pulled close, but out of reaching distance. She wanted so badly to curl up in his lap, to feel his arms wrap around her and offer comfort, but she didn't dare. Would never dare, for any reason. As miserable as her life was, touch and the connection with others was all she had. She couldn't give them up, become a carrier of disease. Not for any man, even this one.

Also, there was a stranger in her room. A beautiful blonde who leaned against the closed door, arms crossed, watching everything through intelligent eyes the color of a morning sky.

She wore a black gown with short laced sleeves that hung over her shoulders. The sculpted top conformed to her curves and plunged low in the center, the waist sheer—completely see-through. The ruffles on the skirt fell to knee level before puffing out in layers of tulle. She looked powerful and just as wicked.

There was a strange tension between Torin and the

woman. One that crackled. Made Cameo's skin itch for…
something.

No. *Someone.*

Why can't I forget Lazarus? He's a liar. A cheat.

But he's also captivating. Seductive.

Apparently I'm not just Misery. I'm Fool.

"I'd like some time alone with my friend," Cameo
told the girl. If centuries of war hadn't taught her to be
leery of strangers, the gorgeous male who'd teased her
with slavery certainly had.

Torin shook his head. "Sorry, Cam, but Keeley stays
with me. Always."

Such a proprietary tone. One she'd never before heard
him use.

Realization hit and hit hard, and Cameo gasped. "You
two are together."

He gave a stiff nod. His shoulders squared as if he
prepared himself for a blow. As if Cameo would yell at
him, tell him how wrong the relationship was.

The girl—Keeley—left her post and settled atop Torin's lap with the grace of a ballerina, exactly as Cameo
had wanted to do. He didn't push her away as he would
have done to Cameo, but did make sure his skin was
properly covered before cuddling her close.

Had Cameo been standing, shock would have drilled
her to her knees. "But…that's…"

"We're the cutest couple you've ever seen. We know.
You may continue." Keeley waved her hand, a gesture
that reeked of royalty

Cameo almost snapped, *He was my boyfriend first, female,* but somehow restrained herself. Torin and Cameo
had loved each other deeply…just not the way lovers
were supposed to love. Not like this.

"Is she immune to you?" Cameo asked, wanting so badly to be happy for him.

Hate my demon.

Torin shook his head, a familiar guilt spreading over his features. "No."

"But he still gives me the greatest pleasure womankind has ever known," Keeley said, her pride unmistakable.

Cameo's eyes widened. "You touch her skin-to-skin anyway?"

"I have." He shifted in the chair, clearly uncomfortable with the direction of the conversation. "But I've also found…other ways."

"I highly recommend those ways," Keeley said. "But I also highly recommend you don't try them with my man."

Torin reacted to the girl's increasingly rough tone surprisingly, smiling for the first time since Cameo had woken up. It was a punch to the gut. *I could have had that with him—amusement and jealousy, possessiveness and obsession—but I kept my distance.* Welcomed *the distance. And so did he.*

Now she was stuck craving the man who'd amused himself with her life and led her on and probably would have kicked her out once she'd given him what he wanted. Talk about poor life choices.

My specialty.

"Do you remember what happened to you before Keeley came to get you?" Torin asked her.

Keeley had rescued her? Great! *I can't not like her, can I?*

Cameo thought back. The fog had choked her. Demons had stepped from the mist and dragged her away.

Finally she had been able to breathe. But then she'd found herself flashed to a throne room. Fires crackled all around. Demons wandered this way and that. Screams filled the overhot air.

A beautiful man loomed over her. Pale hair, black magic eyes. Features so perfect they'd made her chest ache.

"You're going to help me with a little task," he'd said, his voice nothing more than a seductive whisper.

Even still, she'd shuddered, repulsed by him but also ensnared by him. Something about him...

Maybe the fact that Misery adored him, and had purred like a kitten inside her head.

She'd tried to scramble away from him, but a horde of demons had held her down. He'd stabbed her with something sharp and black—and left it inside her.

"Did you think you had a choice?" he'd asked and grinned coldly. "Well, you thought wrong." Then he'd looked to the demons. "Take her to her room."

They'd dragged her away.

She relayed all of this to Torin, embarrassed by her weakness and being unable to fight her way free. She was a warrior, but time and time again she'd come off as a damsel in distress. *Hate that!*

"Lucifer," Keeley said, and she sounded annoyed. "Hades told the truth. For once."

"Unless the two are working together," Torin said.

"Not likely. I don't know how much you've heard about Lucifer, but before his fall, he divided his time between heaven and the underworld. Since no man can truly serve two masters, he eventually had to make a choice: Hades or the Most High. He chose Hades, thinking he would receive greater power and a higher position."

"A mistake," Torin said.

"Exactly. Hades claimed him as a son merely to betray him, binding him to the underworld while allowing himself to roam free. And in the centuries since, they have hurt each other too much to ever become allies. Especially since neither one seems to have the capacity to forgive *anything*."

Cameo's gaze zinged between the pair. They were in sync. Feeding off of each other. And did Torin even realize that as he spoke, his hand moved up and down Keeley's arm in a gesture of adoring affection, as if he couldn't quite believe the treasure he held in his arms?

A pang razed her from throat to stomach. He'd never been able to look past his fear and his guilt to truly be with Cameo, but he'd certainly done so for Keeley.

Clearly his feelings ran deep.

Would Cameo ever have something like that?

Feeling sorry for myself.

Nothing new there.

Well, I have to stop.

"I wonder if he found Viola, too," Torin said.

"I didn't see her," Cameo said. But then, the underworld had been vast, and a lot of demons had come and gone, distracting her, and she'd been high as a kite from being denied air for so long. Oh, and she couldn't forget the blow she'd taken to the head when the demons had dragged her upstairs. She definitely could have missed the girl.

"If she's there," Keeley said, "and Lucifer has realized Cameo is gone, he will have stepped up security for this Viola person. Getting her will be more difficult."

"Doesn't matter. I'll get her." Torin peered at Keeley through narrowed eyes, radiating determination. "Are you listening to me? Do I have your full attention?"

He'd never spoken to Cameo that way. Trouble in paradise already?

"I have ears, don't I?" Keeley said, leaning more firmly against his chest.

"You do, and they're lovely," he replied. "But you need to do us both a solid and use them. This time, you will not go through the portal without me. I repeat. Will not. Do you understand?"

Keeley shivered as if he'd just relayed some sort of naughty bedtime story. "What will you do if I disobey?"

His hand stopped on the girl's hip and squeezed, the glove pulling taut. Heat radiated from him, so much and so hotly it actually stroked over Cameo, making *her* shiver. "I'll have to show you." He jumped to his feet, using Keeley as a shield—to hide an erection?

"You'll have to excuse us," he said, looking like a kid who'd just found out Santa had visited. "We have an argument to settle."

"Bye." Keeley waved at Cameo as he dragged her out of the room.

No trouble in paradise. He'd spoken so forcefully because he'd *felt* forcefully, wanting…needing. Cameo sank against her mound of pillows. Always in the back of her mind she'd wondered if she'd made a mistake parting with him. But no, she hadn't.

I was never going to be the right female for him.

Lazarus, on the other hand…

It was a good thing she'd been taken from him. She might have stayed with him otherwise, and eventually

CHAPTER TWENTY-NINE

KEELEY AND TORIN spent the day in bed, practicing skin-less sex—masters had to be dedicated to their craft—interrupted only by the occasional knock on the door. Paris and Sienna had been ready to chat, and Keeley had known it would be futile and cruel to deny them. She'd explained the essentials of bonding, how Sienna had to flip a mental switch and stop thinking of the powers she wielded as belonging to Cronus; she had to see them as hers. For instance, the body Keeley inhabited would have decayed if she hadn't claimed it as her own.

Keeley spent some time painstakingly outlining the other steps in the necessary process for Sienna to retain and even strengthen her powers, and the girl and Paris listened raptly. When they seemed to have grasped everything they had to do, Torin kicked them out. He'd had some more fun with Keeley, but it hadn't been long before Gideon and Scarlet had arrived to thank Keeley for flashing Gideon away from the Unspoken One before a deathblow could be delivered.

While the interruptions irritated Torin, they delighted Keeley. This team of immortals had finally accepted her. They craved her input and her approval. *All my dreams, finally coming true.*

The only crimp in her day was when, after another bout of naughty playtime, Torin had gone quiet, pensive.

Thinking about Hades's offer?

Fear showed up, bringing unwelcome thoughts. Was it only a matter of time before Torin decided this wasn't good enough for him—or her? She shook her head. She was Torin's treasure. That wasn't going to change. It was time she had faith in him.

Reyes knocked on their door late in the evening. Danika had recovered, he said, and was ready to use the artifacts again.

Keeley dressed in casual clothing, saying to Torin, "Maybe I should try to find the box again. With the Morning Star, we won't need a portal to get to Viola and Baden."

He thought on it a moment. "If it drains Danika, and we're unsuccessful, we'll be out another few days."

"Worth the risk," she said. Except, when they crowded into the room together, even though Danika did all the right things, a portal did not open.

Could there be some kind of mystical block on the box?

Who had the power to do such a thing? Very few immortals.

"I don't understand," Keeley said, flicking Torin an apologetic glance. "But I'm not going to worry about it." To the girl, she commanded, "Picture Viola."

Danika, who did look a bit fatigued already, closed her eyes. Light immediately burst from the tip of the Rod, filling up the room.

Torin moved to Keeley's side, banding his arm around her waist. On the walk to the room, his friends had tried to talk him out of going with her, sending someone else in his place. Someone who wouldn't cause a plague if things went bad. Like Anya or Kaia or even Strider. But

Torin had flat-out refused. Where Keeley was, he'd said, he would be. End of. Remembering made her shiver.

Doing that a lot lately—loving it.

Loving him.

Then the light dimmed, the air parting to reveal another realm, a doorway, and it became clear Viola was where Cameo had been. There was a throne room, just as the female had described. Fires raged, and demons scuffled throughout. Lucifer sat atop the throne of skulls that had once belonged to Hades, drumming his fingers against the arms, waiting for something. Someone?

Where was—

There. Keeley's stomach twisted. The girl had to be Viola, for she was just as Torin had portrayed her. Blond hair. Cinnamon-colored eyes. Bronzed skin. Perfect curves. She was chained to a wall, arms and legs spread, clothes stripped away. There was a gag in her mouth.

What crimes had been committed against her?

At least when Keeley had been imprisoned, she'd been alone.

Going to kill her tormentors before I save her. Might even make her my new best friend. Everyone needed a sidekick.

Torin's hold on Keeley tightened. "Ready?"

She nodded, unfolded the Cloak and covered them both. She could have flashed to the girl since she knew where to go…maybe. The underworld was a tricky place and could snare a flasher in a maze of tunnels. If she reached her, though, she could have flashed her right back…again maybe. What if Viola was warded? But what Keeley couldn't do was flash Torin, since he still had his own wards. He had to go through the portal opened by the Rod, which meant *she* was going through the portal. Of course, that meant they would both have to leave through the portal, too; once they stepped through, they would be bound to it, whether it remained open or not, until they once again stepped through it, severing the tie.

Together they walked through it, entering the throne room. Smoke thickened the air, darkened it. The scent of sulfur and rot stung her nostrils. Screams of pain and cackles of glee assaulted her ears.

The place was bigger than she remembered, the smoke thicker. The screams louder and more numerous with every minute that passed. Beside Viola was a female with short dark hair and the lean muscle mass of a warrior—also chained. Who was she?

Torin noticed her and stiffened. "Pandora."

Under the Cloak, no one could hear their conversation, so neither of them had to be quiet. "If Pandora is here, your boy Baden is probably nearby, too. But I didn't wear the serpentine wreaths and won't be able to touch them. We'll have to come back for them later." When security would be even tighter. Fabulous.

"No need. I have the wreaths under my hoodie," Torin said.

Resourceful man.

"But it looks like they won't be necessary," he added. "Pandora is wearing a pair of her own."

Keeley looked, and sure enough, there were metal bands wrapped around the girl's wrists, peeking out from underneath the chains. "Good. Let's get this rescue mission underway. Ease forward, your steps aligned with mine…good…good."

As they closed in on the females, Keeley studied the

two more intently, checking for injuries she might have previously missed. There were no visible wounds on either girl, but there *were* smears of soot on their stomachs and thighs to suggest they'd been manhandled.

Someone must pay. Keeley's hands fisted, and the walls of the palace began to shake.

Still perched upon his throne, Lucifer looked around, frowned.

Hello, Someone.

Torin's warm breath fanned her ear. "Did you know the human stomach has to produce a new layer of mucus every two weeks, otherwise it will digest itself? Also, I looked it up and discovered beetles taste like apples, wasps like pine nuts, and worms like fried bacon."

"You know the weirdest things," she said, and the shaking stopped. "But beetles actually taste like peanuts."

"I'll keep that in mind."

"We'll need to create a distraction if we're going to get the girls home without putting them through a battle," she said. And there was only one way to do that. "I'll take care of Lucifer. You get the girls through the portal, then come back for me." While she could flash throughout this realm, she wouldn't be able to reenter the portal and leave it without the Cloak. "Tomorrow we're going to have a serious discussion about the removal of your brimstone scars. What if I need to flash you out of harm's way when you reach me?"

"Consider them gone," he said, surprising her. "But I don't like your game plan. Don't like the thought of you doing *anything* with Lucifer."

"Torin—"

"Even still, I know how smart and powerful you are,"

he continued, "so I'll expect you to be careful. One tiny scratch, and I'll be angry."

The hits of awesome just kept coming.

"I wish I could kiss you," she said. *Later,* she thought with a shiver. A reward to them both—damn the consequences. "You be careful, too, or *I'll* be angry." Then she flashed just outside the throne room, leaving the Cloak with Torin.

Demons spotted her and rushed forward. *Sorry, boys, but I'm not sticking around for a powwow with you.* She pushed open the doors and strode inside like she used to do when Hades brought her with him to visit his "son."

Lucifer jumped to his feet, a triumphant grin lifting the corners of his mouth. "Keeleycael. How extraordinary. I'd heard you were free and hoped you would come to see me." His gaze raked over her. "But I did not expect you to look quite so…awful."

She raised her chin. So she wasn't in one of her gowns. So what. "*I* heard you had plans to ruin Hades."

He inclined his head, not even trying to deny it.

"Would you like my help?" she finished, and he laughed.

He didn't hesitate. "I would."

She let her gaze scan the room. Not even she could see Torin now that she was out from under the Cloak. What was he doing?

"Come to me," Lucifer said, waving her over. "Let's reacquaint ourselves."

So formal and polite; such a liar. "I'm impressed," she said—while remaining in place. "If you want to chat with me here, that means you've done something Hades never could; you've gotten the demons to follow you absolutely and know they'd never betray you. Never publically reveal the words they hear you speak in private."

His jaw clenched.

Direct hit. She'd just reminded him that they couldn't talk openly in front of his soldiers. That the fiends could—and most likely would—run tattling to Hades. Now when Lucifer ushered her out of the throne room, it would be because it was his idea, not hers.

"You're right," he said. "I have. But I've just realized there's no place for you to sit comfortably."

Can't smirk. "This is true."

As he closed in on her, she noticed the hard glint in his dark eyes—one he couldn't mask. *Evil! Never-ending pit of despair.*

He offered her the use of his arm.

Though she would have rather plucked out her eyes, she took it. He led her away, through a maze of elaborate hallways where demons fornicated in the vilest of ways, and into the master suite. The bedroom was a study of hedonism. Black satin, black velvet, black leather. Toys and weapons hanging on the walls. Mirrors everywhere. Candles glowing in the darkness.

Demons rushed in behind them, carrying trays of food. In minutes, a five-star dining experience was set up, a table occupying the center of the room. He'd always been big on appearances. Liked people to think he was solicitous, loved beginning interactions with gallantry, playing the role of helper or whatever he thought his target desired, and then, when the person was well and truly hooked, flipping the psycho switch. It was a game he played.

He held out her chair, and she sat.

"Aren't you so very gracious," she muttered. *Trying to lay a foundation he plans to rip out from underneath me.*

He poured her a glass of what looked to be wine but was probably blood and made her a plate, but she couldn't identify half of what was on there. As if she would take a single bite anyway.

Watching her, he leaned back in his chair. "My sources tell me you've joined the Lords of the Underworld."

There were threads of hatred in his voice, and she could guess why. He thought the Lords should follow him, allowing their demons to rule their lives. That the warriors continued to resist the evil inside them was a thorn in his cloven hoof.

"I had, yes," she admitted. Why deny it? "Did your sources also tell you that the Keeper of Disease infected me over and over again? That he abandoned me on multiple occasions?" Was that resentment in her tone?

Definitely. While she hated that she'd spoken ill of Torin, and to the enemy no less, the truth was the truth, and there was no way around it. At least it gave credence to her cover story.

She fiddled with her food, feigning interest. "Why do you care about this anyway?"

"Care?" He laughed. "I like to keep my options open, sweet. That's all."

"And you truly believe the Lords are an option?" She couldn't keep the incredulity from her tone.

He glared at her, and she mentally berated herself. She had to tread carefully and not antagonize him by dangling the carrot he could never quite reach in front of him. He was warded. If he decided he no longer needed her, she would be unable to use her power against him.

His bedroom door suddenly burst open, and a gorilla-like demon raced inside. "Three prisoners attempted to escape, my lord, but they didn't get far. They await your punishment."

Keeley stiffened. Torin, Viola and Pandora? Probably. *Mission fail!* Time for damage control.

"Where are they?" Lucifer asked, as calm as before.

"The throne room, my king."

"Bring them here."

The demon raced away without missing a beat.

Throat dry, Keeley asked, "What are you going to do with them? And why do you have two females chained next to your throne?"

His dark eyes glinted at her. "What would you like me to do? And because it pleased me to do so."

"Let them go?"

He smiled, shook his head. "You always had a soft heart. I had hoped that what Hades had done to you had hardened you."

It would have, permanently, if not for Mari…and then Torin.

"You know, the timing strikes me as odd," he said, his tone merely observational. "Does it you? You arrive, and suddenly there's an escape attempt."

"What strikes me as odd is the fact that your prisoners didn't try to escape sooner."

"Hmm," was all he said as the three prisoners were dragged in.

Keeley held back her sigh of relief. Not Torin, Viola and Pandora, after all, but a redheaded warrior—Baden, surely—as well as the spirits of Cronus and Rhea. All three wore serpentine wreaths.

Well, well. Her gaze narrowed on Cronus. The male

had imprisoned her for centuries and had played a sinister part in Mari's death. Though vengeance against his body had been stolen from her, there were plenty of things she could do to his spirit....

The walls began to shake.

Cronus must have suspected the direction of her thoughts. He struggled against his captors.

"I've changed my mind," she announced. "Definitely don't let them go. We'll play pin the dagger on the dead."

Rational thoughts peeked above the darkness of her desires, bright lights she couldn't ignore. Did Torin know Baden was here? Had anyone noticed his absconding with Viola and Pandora? She hoped he'd succeeded.

If he was caught...hurt...

I will burn this realm and everyone in it to the ground.

"Excellent idea." Lucifer dabbed the corners of his mouth with his napkin, even though he'd never taken a bite of the food.

"Where's Pandora?" Baden snarled. "What have you done with her? Tell me!" His wild gaze flicked to Keeley, moved back to Lucifer, only to return to Keeley and widen. "The Red Queen. You're here. Why are you here?"

He knew her?

Victim of the Time Out box?

"It would be my pleasure to show you exactly what I've done to your precious female." Lucifer stood. He helped Keeley to her feet, and she could think of no reason to protest the trip to the throne room. Surely Torin was gone.

But then, why hadn't an alarm sounded?

Lucifer led the way, never releasing her. First problem—if she couldn't break free of his grip, she couldn't flash anywhere else in the underworld. Those stupid wards!

No time to panic.

The doors were opened for Lucifer so that there was never a pause in his step. As they entered the room, he casually said, "Tonight, Keeleycael, you will warm my bed, and I will brand you as my concubine."

Uh, second problem. "How about…no."

"Did I lead you to believe you would have a choice in the matter? My apologies."

"Do you think you'll have the strength to force me?"

He laughed. "I recently captured two females beloved by the Lords of the Underworld. You may remember them from my throne room. The ones in chains. Yes? I planned to hurt them and blame Hades. The Lords would have gone after him, distracting him, allowing me to swoop in. If I'd known you would show up on my doorstep, I wouldn't have bothered. You will make a far better distraction."

As anger burned through her—*try to use me, the Red Queen, never!*—he stopped short. Viola and Pandora were gone. And none of the demons had noticed.

Impressive. Masterful. How had Torin managed *that?*

Lucifer leveled undiluted rage at her. "It seems I underestimated you. My own distraction. Bravo. But no matter," he said with another unveiling of his cold smile.

"What can you do about it?" she asked, then hit him so hard in the chest his sternum cracked. While he tried to draw in a breath, she punched him in the face. Jab, jab, jab. She turned, swooping low, and grabbed a smaller minion by the neck, turned again, going back the way she'd come, and swung. The creature's horns cut through

Lucifer's skin and cracked into his thigh, breaking his femur, the biggest bone in his body.

He grunted—and vanished. She turned, expecting him to materialize behind her. She flashed a dagger into her hand, ready to stab him. But he'd tricked her. He'd returned to the spot he'd vacated—with a piece of brimstone in hand. He pressed it into the top of her spinal cord, singeing hair, flesh and clothing. A scream burst from her as pain and weakness spilled through her.

"This, Keeleycael, is only the beginning of what I can—and will—do."

CHAPTER THIRTY

Torin hurried through the portal, shouting, "Keep it open." He dropped the two girls he'd had to carry out of the underworld under his arms like sacks of potatoes, and turned. He had to get to Keeley. But as he dove back through the portal, it closed, and he skidded into the Cage. "No! Open it, Danika."

She slumped against the Rod, panting, beaded in perspiration, her features pale. "Trying...can't...so sorry."

"She barely held it open as long as she did." Reyes tried to wrench the cage door from its hinges, but the metal held steady. "It's jammed. Why is it jammed?"

Because Keeley was the owner of the Cage, and it would only respond to her. Or...maybe to Torin, too, the possessor of the All-key. But if he freed Danika, would she lose control of the Rod, Keeley's commands voided?

Can't risk it.

He explained that to Reyes, panic and urgency riding him hard. "We need to get Keeley back."

"Dani is too exhausted." Reyes withdrew a dagger and picked unsuccessfully at the lock.

Torin rushed out of the room. All of his friends were congregated in the hall, waiting for the verdict. "Lucien," he shouted, and the warrior strode forward, pushing everyone out of the way. "Flash me to the underworld. You can do it without a portal."

"Yes, but *where* in the underworld? It's so vast, I can jump from one mile to another for days and not cover the entire expanse."

"Some palace of Lucifer's."

"You'll have to be more specific. He has as many palaces as there are miles."

Getting nowhere. "William," Torin shouted.

"You rang?" The warrior stepped up beside Lucien.

"Go to Hades." *Never thought I'd say those words, and not mean them as a curse or a threat.* The male could save Keeley; Torin couldn't. The very idea sickened him. But her survival was more important than his pride. "Ask him if he knows where Lucifer is and tell him I need him to get Keeley away from the guy."

Hades could take her anywhere inside the underworld, but not out of it. She'd entered through the Rod's portal, and so she had to leave through it. Flashing wouldn't work. But without the Cloak, she couldn't go through the portal. Torin would have to give the artifact to Hades—unless Torin went with him, which he would absolutely insist on doing. But at the end of the day, he had very little bargaining power here. Would do anything to keep Keeley safe. Whatever Hades wanted.

She might hate Torin for arranging this, but he would rather deal with her hatred than her torture and death.

Yes, she was strong, and could take care of herself, but Hades knew about the wards. Lucifer did, too. And as soon as Lucifer discovered his prisoners were missing, he would connect the dots and Keeley would be blamed. He would try to punish her.

William scratched his chest. "I can tell you're upset by this, and my heart bleeds for you. Probably. Also probably not. But I'm going to graciously decline and blame the necessity of the refusal on you. You should know me better. I don't do anything free of charge."

Torin grabbed him by the collar and shook him. "I wasn't asking."

William didn't bat an eye. "Is this a challenge? This feels like a challenge."

He wanted payment? Fine. "Your price?"

"Keeley must steal my book from Anya."

The book. His precious. Within its pages were prophecies detailing how to save his life…or something. The goddess had stolen it years ago and hidden it from the warrior. For "funnzies."

"Done."

"Then I shall return with Hades," William said and vanished.

"I won't give it up," Anya called. "You don't know what he's like when that thing is in his possession."

And he didn't care. Torin told her what she could do with herself, and it involved several things that weren't actually anatomically possible.

"Torin's done gone dark, y'all," Kaia muttered.

Get the mess cleared. Be ready. No telling how quickly William would return—and he had better return quickly. "Maddox, carry Viola to a bedroom. She needs medical attention. Lucien, Pandora is in there, too. Same condition as Viola. She's wearing wreaths, so anyone should be able to touch her."

A flurry of activity erupted as his orders were obeyed.

"Baden?" Sabin asked.

"Didn't see him."

William materialized, Hades at his side.

"Out," Torin snarled at the crowd, clearing the artifact room of everyone but Reyes and Danika.

William and Hades entered behind him, and William kicked the door closed.

Enough testosterone in this room to choke a rhino. "Can you save Keeley or not?" he demanded, glaring at Hades.

The dark lord glared right back at him but remained silent until his attention moved to Reyes. "Your woman is to rest for two days. At the end of the second, she is to open a portal for Keeleycael. I will be very displeased if she fails."

Reyes, already on edge by the turn of events, gripped his daggers by the blades. Blood poured on the floor. "How can she rest while she's trapped inside the cage?"

"She will have to find a way. And you," Hades said, at last deigning to speak to Torin. "You will come with me. You will return the Red Queen through the portal."

Meaning Hades couldn't go through, even with the Cloak? "What do you want in return?"

The male narrowed his eyes. "We both know I'll do this without demanding anything in return. For her. Not for you."

Hades...loved her? Truly?

Mine! My woman!

"But when we return," Hades continued, "I'm done waiting on the sidelines. I'm coming after her. And I *will* win her. I can give her what you have not."

Every dark emotion magnified, but he held his tongue. Now wasn't the time to indulge.

A second later, the walls of the room disappeared. Another world took shape around him. The stifling heat of the underworld. The screams and the smoke and the despair. Outside Lucifer's palace, the fires were more numerous, erupting everywhere for no seeming reason.

Demons of all shapes and sizes crawled over rocky walls and guarded the ginormous entrance that was shaped like a skull.

So far, no one had noticed them.

"She wouldn't be in this position if you had taken me up on my offer," Hades remarked.

Please. "We both know you would have ripped Disease out of me only to give me another demon."

Hades didn't deny it. "Erectile Dysfunction. Or Self-Mutilation. Probably both. Instead, I'll make you wish that's the way this had played out."

Two short swords suddenly appeared in Torin's hands. A gift from Hades—a stupid move on the male's part. "Not if I kill you first."

Ignoring the threat, Hades said, "The worst part is, you never even had to hurt her. You had the answer all along, you were just too wrapped up in your fear to see it."

What the hell was he talking about? The answer all along? What answer—the way to be with Keeley without making her sick?

"Tell me!" he demanded.

The only response he received? A cold smile that proclaimed *Never.*

There was no time to try to beat the answer out of him. At last the demons realized they were no longer alone and stopped what they were doing to lick their lips hungrily. Murmurs of delight erupted.

"You ready to fight your way in?" Hades asked.

And waste more time? "I'm ready for you to flash me in."

"Sorry, pup. Not going to happen. I'll flash myself, but you...you are on your own from this point on." Hades vanished in a blink.

Fine. Torin marched forward. Once, he'd lived for battles. Always he'd craved them. Today he would have one.

The demons rushed him, fangs bared. He swung his swords in a wide arc. One head, removed. Another head, removed. A clawed hand reached for him. Again he swung his sword. The hand thumped to the ground without the arm.

More and more demons raced toward him, swarming him. He remained in a constant state of motion, adrenaline surging through him. One pause and he would lose a limb of his own. The challenge energized him.

With a roar, Torin removed another head. Then another. An arm. A hand. Another head. The body parts piled up around him. Black blood spurted and splattered, burning him.

Eventually he worked his way past the double doors and entered the foyer. There were scratches all over him and a gouge in his thigh. Fire in his veins. Probably some kind of demon toxin. He didn't care.

Two demons rounded the corner, headed straight for him. Footsteps echoed behind him. Closing in... He swung the swords backward, felt the resistance of flesh and bone, and knew he'd stabbed the ones behind him. Then he swung the swords forward and removed the heads of those two. As the heads rolled away, red eyes on him...off him...on him again...he strode forward, determined to get his woman.

CHAINED TO LUCIFER'S throne. *Like we're Princess Leia and Jabba the freaking Hutt.* It was humiliating! But at least Keeley was wearing a T-shirt and sweatpants rather than a bikini.

Small consolation, though, considering her back was covered in stupid wards.

The first one had weakened her so much Lucifer hadn't even had to hold her down while he'd given her the others. Now she couldn't even flash a few inches away from the danger zone.

Lucifer would have given her more wards, covering her from head to toe just like his father had done, and would have made good on his threat to force her to warm his bed—where she would have fought with every bit of strength she still possessed—if a commotion hadn't erupted outside. He'd looked out the window, seen hundreds of his minions being slaughtered, and dragged her to the throne room to await his foe. Appearance was everything, after all.

At least to him. Torin was here! Her heart galloped with anticipation and excitement.

The only bummer? Hades was here, too.

Countless minions backed against the walls as their former king stalked to the edge of Lucifer's royal dais. "You wanted my attention." His calm sent a shudder through the minions. "You have it."

The two might have liked each other...once. But evil could not be faithful to evil. And Lucifer just happened to be as evil as they came. He had an insatiable need for more. More power. More praise. More territory. More control. Collateral damage meant nothing to him. He stole. He lied. He killed.

He enjoyed it.

He wanted his power to extend beyond the underworld. That's all this war was about. Once he'd taken down Hades, he assumed there would be no threat of competition. But he'd forgotten about the Most High. Not to mention William, who'd once ruled the other half of this realm, bound to it as tightly as Lucifer. Only, William had found a way to escape, just like Hades.

"What I want," Lucifer said, "is for you to bow to me. Do it and you may walk away with the girl."

A sardonic twist of Hades's mouth, one she was very familiar with. Lucy was about to be spanked. "You assume I'm under the mistaken impression that you can win a war against me. You assume I would not have taken precautions before ever handing over the keys to my kingdom."

Lucifer paled—because he knew it was true.

The doors burst open, and countless demon bodies and various severed parts tumbled inside. Torin climbed over the lifeless mountain, marching straight for Hades's side, his head high.

Hades couldn't mask his irritation.

Keeley swallowed a whimper of relief. Torin might be soaked in black goo, but he'd never looked more fierce. She made to stand, but Lucifer jerked at the chain wrapped around her neck, keeping her down.

"Give her to me," Torin snarled. "Now." He made to climb the stairs, his already-bloody swords at the ready, but Hades held out an arm, forcing him to remain in place.

She knew what Hades was thinking. That Lucifer would grab her and either cut her throat or flash away with her. Or both. He was right.

But then every minion supposedly serving under Lucifer's rule turned on him, baring fangs and claws—in challenge. Several even dropped from the ceiling, putting their bodies between Keeley and her captor.

"I told you," Hades said with a smugness that had to grate.

The words and the truth they proclaimed so confidently—that the allegiance of the minions had been feigned—enraged Lucifer, and he tried to slash at her anyway. But the minions took the blows for her, shielding her from receiving so much as a scratch.

Hades released Torin, who quickly scaled the stairs.

In typical grandiose fashion, Lucifer announced, "This isn't over," before flashing away. Realizing he'd lost this round, and quite badly, too.

The minions fell away from her as Torin hacked through the length of her chain, freeing her from the throne. He wrapped his arms around her and held her close, his heart galloping against her temple.

"You came back for me," she said. Not that she'd ever doubted him.

"For you? Always."

My sweet Prince Charming.

No. My king. My other half.

"As touching as this reunion is," Hades sneered, "we have other things to do."

He was right. And he'd come for her, too—which baffled her. He'd never been one to put himself out for another. Not even for payment.

Perhaps he *had* changed.

Did that mean she was ready to forget the past and start hanging out with him? No. Just that she might not make his murder as painful as she'd originally planned.

"Baden is here," she said.

Torin stiffened as Hades's long legs ate away at the space between them. The dark lord crouched in front of her, intent, saying, "Do you want this Baden returned to the Lords?"

"Yes," she said.

"Then I'll see that it's done. He'll be waiting for you at the fortress in Budapest."

It was difficult, but she did it—she said the words *Thank you.*

He inclined his head. "You will spend the next two days in this palace. As my honored guest, of course. I will see to your every need, ensure you are utterly protected, as we wait for the All-seeing Eye to open the portal for you."

Seeing no other option, she said, "Torin will stay, too."

Hades worked his jaw with irritation. "There's no need. I can return him *now.*"

"Torin will stay," she insisted. "We'll be bunking together."

"There are more than enough—"

"We'll be in the *same* room or we'll leave," Torin said. "I don't care what we have to face out there."

Hades did not look away from Keeley as he nodded stiffly.

She smiled at him. "You may show us to our accommodations."

CHAPTER THIRTY-ONE

THROUGHOUT THE PALACE minions were doing things that made Torin want to scrub his corneas with bleach. Also there were countless red, beady gazes lingering on his fly as if he'd hidden a snack pack beneath it.

Hades opened a door and waved them inside a spacious chamber. "All yours. Shout my name if you need anything, and I will appear." He spoke to Keeley and only to Keeley. But his menacing glare to Torin spoke volumes. "Shout *his* name and I'm not sure how I'll react."

Torin shut the door in his face.

Keeley hurried throughout the room, plugging peepholes and covering what had to be two-way mirrors.

"I know this is going to sound moronic coming from me," he said, "but I kind of feel like I'm food for every STD in the underworld." The place had probably seen more action than Paris's pants.

Keeley said nothing, just walked to him with steely determination and claimed one of his swords. She cleaned it in the en suite bathroom, then removed her shirt and revealed her freshly branded back.

Fury detonated within him.

"Cut them off me," she demanded.

First instinct: refusal. No way he'd hurt her.

But the scars were the equivalent of chains, leaving her vulnerable. And he knew how much she despised vulnerability. Someone had to do this and he'd be damned if he allowed anyone else to touch her.

"Lie on the bed," he instructed.

She obeyed without hesitation.

Such lovely curves. Skin like satin. Elegant spine.

He gave his temple a hard punch, punch. This wasn't sexy playtime.

Disease was strangely silent. Happy to be home?

"I'm sorry," Torin whispered and got to work.

Never once did she cry out, but that wasn't the blessing it should have been. It wasn't because her pain threshold was high. It was. Or that this barely registered. It did. It was because she'd had to do this before. For years. Decades. Centuries. That's how long she'd lived with so much pain—all alone. She knew what to expect and had steeled herself against it.

After all she'd endured, all she'd suffered, she'd still chosen Torin to be a part of her future.

I'm not worthy.

But he would be. He would make himself. He loved her with all of his heart, all that he was—every fiber of his being. He would be whatever she needed. Give her whatever she wanted.

He was trembling as he finished cutting out the ward. As carefully as possible he soaked the gaping wound in water, then bandaged it using strips of her shirt, the only thing currently available. He wished there were a potted plant or—

Head slap! She wasn't only bonded to the earth. She was also bonded to Torin.

Although, despite their bond, she had still sickened every time he touched her. But she hadn't reacted negatively to his semen when he'd come on her belly. That had to mean something. Maybe she wouldn't react negatively to his blood, either. Might actually react positively.

Could he base his actions on "might"?

Her blood trickled from the sides of the bandage.

Yes. Yes, he could.

He turned the sword on himself.

"What are you doing?" she asked weakly.

Hissing, he pressed the blade underneath the layers of his brimstone scars and sliced. He'd promised her he would remove them, and there was no better time. The bloody flesh plopped to the ground, reminding him of a piece of shaved ham. He peeled away Keeley's bandage and held his arm over her wound, letting droplets of crimson splash inside. After the entire area had been saturated, he returned the bandage and applied pressure—finally, blessedly, she passed out.

"Torin," she gasped a few hours later, pushing upright on her hands.

"I'm here, princess. I'm here." He tenderly brushed her cheek with a gloved hand. He hadn't left her side. "How are you feeling?"

"Better. You?"

"Fine, just fine. Lie flat again so I can check your wound."

She obeyed, and he gently peeled away the bandage. To his amazement, she was almost healed. Muscle and skin had already woven back together, leaving thin pink lines that would soon fade.

His blood *had* helped her without making her sick.

Or had the removal of the brimstone scars done the trick?

Hades's taunt teased the back of his mind. *Had the answer all along. Too wrapped in fear to realize it.*

The scar had weakened her. Might have weakened her immune system. Could Torin finally *touch* her without consequences?

Did he dare hope it was that simple? That easy?

There was only one way to find out....

"Thank you," she said, sitting up. "For everything." The sheet fell, revealing plump breasts and rosy nipples.

A blast of blistering desire, swift and sharp, overtook him. He gripped the coverlet to stop himself from reaching for her.

Soon...

"No," he said. "Thank *you*."

TWO DAYS LATER, just as planned, Danika opened a portal in the middle of the bedroom they shared.

Keeley, healed from her wounds, passed through beside Torin, the Cloak of Invisibility covering them both.

Something had changed. Torin's steps were lighter, his smiles coming quicker, more often. She loved it, but because he wouldn't discuss its source, she didn't trust it. No, *trust* wasn't the right word. She didn't know if it would last.

He removed the Cloak, allowing others to see them.

"Free Dani," Reyes said the moment he spotted Keeley.

She bounded over and opened the cage. Reyes scooped the weak, mussed blonde into his arms and carried her out of the room.

Torin was fast on the warrior's heels, dragging Keeley with him. There were a few people hanging out in the hallway, and they tried to get his attention.

"Dude. Baden's with Strider and they're playing *Call of Duty*. Did you know Baden was such a sore loser?"

"All we lack is that cursed box and that kid Anya wants to find. Can you believe it?"

Torin offered no reply. He hurried Keeley to their room, and in his haste slammed the door. But his expression was soft, tender.

"Finally." He kept her hand intertwined with his. "There's a chance I can touch you freely now. A chance I could be wrong. But my blood helped heal your wounds, didn't sicken you, and I've removed the brimstone scars, which were weakening you. I should have realized... didn't think. But if you're willing to risk it..."

He was asking to be with her...fully? Nothing held back? No clothes between them?

As if she needed to think about it. She cupped his cheek. He leaned into her touch, savoring the feel and heat of her. "I want you, Torin. All of you."

Relief shimmered over his features as he kissed her palm. "Strip, lie on your back and close your eyes."

WITHOUT HER BABY blues watching him, breaking him slowly, Torin expected a release from the tension building inside him, even in the minutest degree. He didn't get it. Being near her was like being plugged into an outlet. Power flowed and awareness sizzled. That was never going to change.

"I'm going to touch you the way I've always dreamed." Nothing held back.

"Mmm. Yes."

He discarded his gloves. She offered such a lovely canvas, her female form draped across his bed, he wished he could start everywhere at once. Jaw clenched as he steeled himself against the rapture, he brushed his fingertips over her forehead, down her nose. The warmth of her breath caressed his skin. It was intimate, erotic. A miracle of sensation, connection. He traced the plumpness of her lips, luxuriating in her softness. Her chin, her collar, her shoulders. *Dooown* her arms and the web between her fingers. Goose bumps appeared on her flesh and he relished the feel of them.

She reached for him, hoping to touch him in turn. He took her by the wrists and lifted her arms above her head. "Grip the headboard." If she put her hands on him, he would lose focus.

He waited until she'd complied, then traced each of her sensitive joints. There were many, and he adored them all. Adored every inch of her. With his hands... with his mouth. She seemed to dissolve in his mouth like cotton candy, and infuse with every one of his cells.

"Torin."

He cupped her breasts, watched as her nipples pearled. Such sweet little jewels. His mouth watered for them, but he ran a single fingertip down the center of her stomach and circled her navel. Her belly quivered, her breath coming in shallow pants. She hadn't removed her panties, and he traced his fingers along the damp center. Her back arched as she moaned.

Merciless, he teased her, outlining the edges of the material. Her hips rolled, trying to force him where she needed him most. But he always remained a whisper away, and "damp" soon became "soaked." He rewarded her by shifting the panties out of the way and plunging a finger deep, feeling not only her tightness and warmth, but her readiness for him, too.

She cried out, then cried out again as he pulled out.

Her eyelids flicked open, glowing with wild, reckless need. "Torin."

He let her watch as he sucked the moist finger into his mouth. Let her witness his enjoyment as he sampled her taste.

The roll of her hips became frenzied. "Don't be selfish. Give me a taste of your lips."

"Until I've finished touching all of you, I'll be as selfish as I please...and you'll like it." He traced the length of her legs, slowly, leisurely, up, then down, stopping to play at her knees and then her ankles before tapping the end of each of her toes. Her body was a treasure map, and every spot should have been marked with an X. No matter where he ventured, his every nerve ending reacted, catching fire.

"Torin." Her breathlessness thrilled him to his soul. *"Please."*

He tore off his shirt, and she purred her approval. He surged up, pressing his mouth into hers. Her tongue met his with a hard thrust, and it was fuel to an already-raging inferno. He kneaded her beautiful breasts, not even trying to temper his strength. But then, he knew how much she reveled in his fierceness.

Her teeth bit into his tongue, his lip. He pinched her nipple, hard, and she screamed, "Yes, oh, yes, yes!" while writhing against him, her softness providing the perfect cradle for his hardness.

He hissed in a breath, thinking this had to be the sweetest agony he'd ever known. The scent of her arousal permeated his senses, made his mouth water all over again.

"I've touched you and kissed you, you're right about

that," he said. "But next I will taste you the way I've dreamed."

A ragged purr. "Not sure I'll survive."

"Try." He chuckled with dark promise and licked his way down…down her curves. Starting with her breasts, sucking on those gorgeous nipples, stopping at her navel to play. "Keep your hands over your head," he commanded. "I mean it. Don't let go."

"Wouldn't dare." A tremor rocked her. Such a heady sight. "What my warrior wants, he gets."

He spread her legs, until her knees rested against the mattress—*completely defenseless to my every whim.* Or rather, he was completely defenseless to hers. Her panties were utterly drenched.

With a satisfied grunt, he ripped the material off her and bared her—bared perfection. *Made for me.* He took a good, long lick, his eyes closing as he savored the sweetness and heat.

A ragged plea for more escaped her. He obliged, could deny her nothing, even as his own desire raged. Another long lick before he tunneled his way inside, mimicking with his fingers what he would soon do with his shaft. When she was undulating wildly, muttering incoherently, her honey a drug he couldn't resist, he sucked on the tender bud of her arousal.

Her scream of satisfaction echoed off the walls.

Pain hadn't managed to draw that sound out of her, but pleasure had. He was smiling as he sucked harder. Her fingers tangled in his hair, urging him on.

"Demanding little princess." He loved it. But he still forced himself to stop.

She moaned, tried to push his head back down. "Torin! You're not done!"

"Hands." One word. One command. But she understood, and she obeyed. And the moment she was once again gripping the headboard, he set back to work, licking and sucking, even biting.

"It's good. So good."

Her thighs squeezed his temples, the pressure a testament to her mounting desire. But he knew what she was doing. Trying yet again to gain control. But he knew his girl and knew she didn't want control, not really, not here, so he forced her legs to part again, keeping her wide open. She trembled with vibrant desire and begged him to do more, to take her further, deeper, and he did...deeper into a realm where sensation prevailed.

He fed her dripping core a finger, and she climaxed, clamping down around it, screaming his name again and again. He inserted another finger, pushing in deep, drawing out the orgasm, making it last. Licking her, sucking her, still moving in and out of her...until she sagged against the mattress, panting.

He withdrew from her and sat up, watching her for several seconds, drinking in the sight of her satisfaction. His woman, satisfied. It was a heady thought and only increased his need for completion.

It was time.

"Unfasten my pants."

Eager, she sat up. Her hair was a tangled mess, her skin flushed a dusky rose. His chest constricted. *Mine, all mine.*

With trembling fingers Keeley freed his throbbing erection. And as she did so, she watched him lick her honey from his fingers once again.

"I could live on you, princess."

"Could you?" She took his hand, pulled his fingers

from his mouth—and sucked them into her own. "I could live on *us*."

The pressure, hot and wet, made him shudder with delicious need. *Need her. Have to have her.*

She protested when he pulled away from her. But still he did it, standing beside the bed, shucking his boots and kicking off his pants. He took a condom from the pocket and sheathed himself. Though he wanted to take her bare, to feel her that way, a child would never be an option. His motions were harried—if he wasn't inside her within the next few seconds, he might as well curl up and die.

At last free to touch him however she wished, she ran her hands over his shoulders, his chest...down his stomach. The glory of it was almost too much, as he'd known it would be. Too much, but also perfect. Another dream come true.

"All this strength," she praised.

"You like?" He curled his hand around his thick length and pumped once, twice through the latex, then tugged on his sac. In the past, he'd always been dissatisfied having a woman watch him, but that was because no other woman was Keeley. When she watched him, the pleasure on her face only added to what he felt.

"Like...and crave."

"Let's give it to you, then." He grabbed her by the ankles and yanked.

As she fell, she gasped with delight. Then, realizing her lower half was hanging over the side of the bed, she moaned. "So naughty."

He stepped between her legs, anchoring her ankles on his shoulders. The pressure there proved beyond sublime. The sights...more so, her nakedness on display before him. Breasts plump and perfect, nipples swollen and red. Belly quivering. Thatch of blond curls gleaming with her arousal.

"You're going to feel me in every cell of this sweet body," he promised. *And I will feel her.*

"Yes. Do it!"

He surged inside her, too shattered to give her time to adjust. He went all the way in. And oh, damn, the silk of her inner walls…the heat…the wet…every sensation heightened, and glorious, and yet almost unbearable. *Too good.* Her back arched as she cried out, already coming again. *So tight.* A vise around him, squeezing at him. He hammered inside her, hard and brutal, again and again, lost in every mind-blowing stroke, craving more of every sensation.

This was pleasure.

This was satisfaction.

This was…life.

But as she neared another peak, he pulled out of her. She didn't understand his purpose and whimpered.

He lowered her legs and flipped her to her stomach, then once again thrust inside her. As she praised him, begged him, urged him harder, faster, she reached up and gripped handfuls of the comforter. Soon her cries of yet another completion were blending with his grunts, filling the room. If ever she forgot him…no, no…this moment would be forever branded in her mind—forever imprinted on her soul.

"I'm so close, princess." He leaned over and bit the sensitive cord running from her neck to her shoulder.

She screamed, coiling around him, her inner walls milking him all over again. This time it wasn't just too much—it was more than enough. He could hold out no longer. He shattered completely, pouring into her, giving her every drop until she'd wrung him dry.

THEY LAUGHED AND cuddled for hours—and of course, made love again—and Torin's happiness only magnified until he practically burst with it.

So far there were no signs of sickness.

The second time they'd made love, she had taken the time to learn him, the way he'd learned her. She had massaged the rigidness from his shoulders before dragging her fingers along the bumps of his spine. The hard mounds of his backside had received an appreciative squeeze. She had moved in front of him and slid her hands down his chest, between their bodies, and fisted the base of his erection. She had traced her thumb over the moist slit, and when he'd groaned his approval, she had licked away the little bead.

She had given him every touch he'd ever craved, and he would never be the same.

"I'm going to make a few improvements to the fortress," she said, snuggling into his side, running her knee up his leg, "Currently we lack a throne room."

"And no home is complete without one. Just remember, as my queen your throne needs to be smaller than mine."

"Sorry, Charming, but even though I'm thrilled you finally admitted to the exalted status of my rule, you'll be sitting at my feet. We're going to have what's called a matriarchy."

"As old as you are, I'm surprised you haven't learned how to pronounce that word correctly. It's patriarchy. Say it with me. Pay-tree-arc-ee."

She twisted his nipple. "Torture. Say it with me."

His laughter boomed through the room.

"I will be *such* a benevolent overlord," she said. "I will demand only that everyone do exactly as I say, when I say. And bow whenever I enter a room. And bring me gifts at least once a day. And throw rose petals at my feet as I pass."

"That's all?"

"Probably not."

"Sounds fair to me," he said.

"You'll be captain of my guard, of course."

"And I will storm your castle at least three times a day." He rolled her to her back and gnawed playfully at her neck. "Who am I kidding? Six times a day."

She screeched with laughter and tried to wiggle away from him. "That tickles! Stop *immediately!*"

"Never! There's treasure to be plundered."

After her laughter had tapered into giggles, she grew quiet. "Torin?"

"Yes, princess?" He licked at the pulse hammering in her neck.

"Are you pleased with the honor to serve under me?"

Such a serious tone. "Me…under you? That's the way you want it?" He flipped her over, draping her over his lap. "I'm more than pleased with this honor."

She sat up to straddle him, the tips of her hair brushing his chest. "Oh, I like this."

Breathtaking. He reached up, fisted the hair at her nape. "Wait till you see what comes next."

CHAPTER THIRTY-TWO

FROM THE HIGHEST of highs to the lowest of lows.

Twenty-four hours had passed with no signs of sickness. But as Torin had discovered a few days ago, he'd been wrong. Ridding himself of the wards hadn't helped. Had merely delayed the inevitable. A wasting disease had struck Keeley, and struck hard. She slept, unable to be roused, unable to eat or drink, dying for lack of nourishment until Hades came to check on her and returned with the best immortal doctors.

Keeley was hooked to an IV and pumped full of medicines found only in other realms, but even still, her cheeks hollowed, her skin turned sallow and Torin…

Torin lost all hope.

He'd thought he'd figured everything out, thought he'd had the answer to happily ever after at long last. But he'd just been fooling himself.

Further, they couldn't find Pandora's box—he hadn't forgotten the block Keeley encountered when she'd tried…twice—which meant they couldn't find the Morning Star. He was out of options.

He and Keeley could continue on as before—his heart clenched—if she even survived this newest sickness. They could continue having sex with their clothes on, not daring to kiss, every caress measured, tentative, just in case the clothing had shifted, but that would not be enough. Would never be enough again. He'd had her. All of her. Nothing held back. That's what he wanted for the rest of eternity; that's what he needed.

What *she* needed. Whether she would admit it or not.

But neither of them could have it. And he was so damn tired of making mistakes. Of hoping, of trying, and then sitting front row for her suffering, knowing he was the one to blame. That if he'd only resisted, it wouldn't have happened.

He'd told himself he would never again reject her, never put her through such a hurt, but he'd just been fooling himself about that, too. He had to leave her, and this time, he had to make her accept it. Make them *both* accept it.

Words wouldn't be good enough. He had to do something permanent, something that couldn't be undone. Something she would despise.

He studied her, how still she was lying on the bed, taking in air only because of a machine. The quiet hum of its motor filled his ears, obscene to him. Hating himself, he squared his shoulders, lifted his chin. He knew what he had to do.

"WE NEED TO TALK," Torin said.

The expression on his face caused Keeley's stomach to churn. The man before her looked cruel, uncaring, and wasn't the lover of her dreams.

She'd just recovered from another disease. Had left her sickbed only this morning to shower and eat. This should be a time of celebration, not...whatever was to come. *I can guess.*

"All right." She gulped. "Talk." They were in their bedroom, alone. He leaned against the door, his hand on the knob, as if the desire to leave was stronger than the one to stay.

"We're over," he said.

Knew it!

"You will not change my mind, Keeley. Not this time."

His words, stated so baldly, held an air of finality, but still she shook her head. "No."

"I'm leaving and I won't be back. You won't flash me back, and you won't flash to me."

A warrior to her core, she planted her feet and prepared for battle. "You don't like that I sickened again. I get it. But we've forged something sweet and rare and precious. Don't give it up because you're afraid."

"Afraid," he echoed, then laughed without humor. "Try terrified."

"Torin—"

"I could lie and tell you that I don't love you or that I'm attracted to someone else, like Cameo, or that I intend to take Hades up on his offer. You hate lies, and liars, and your hate would make this easier. But the truth is, I'm tired of making you ill. I'm tired of being the reason you suffer."

"You…love me?"

"I do."

"Torin—"

"But it's not enough," he said, and again, the finality of his tone scared her.

"It is enough! Together we can overcome anything."

"We can't. As we've proven."

"We'll find the box," she said, desperation making her rash.

"Will we?" He shook his head. "No, I don't think so."

The moisture in her mouth dried. "You're making a mistake."

"No." His small smile held only sadness. "For the first time, I'm doing what's right. You wanted to be first in a man's life, to be a treasure worth saving. Well, you are. I told you that. But it's time I showed you, for actions are better than words. I'm going to save you—from me."

She took a step toward him. He wasn't as stoic as he appeared because he jolted back, slamming into the door. "Don't."

He's right. Don't beg. Never beg. "Please don't do this," she whispered anyway. There was no stopping the words. "We belong together. I love you. I love you so much and want forever with you. I don't care what that forever entails."

He blanched. "You don't get it, Keeley. It's already done."

"No. I refuse to believe that." Outside, rain began to pelt at the fortress walls. A boom of thunder. A fall of snow. *Responding to me.* Because her bond to Torin was in the process of breaking.

"I'm sorry." He turned the knob.

No! "If you walk out of this room, I won't take you back. I'll be done. Like you, I'm tired. I'm tired of the back and forth."

"Good," he said with a clipped nod.

The rain redoubled. The thunder grew louder, the snow more fierce. "One day you'll beg me to take you back. You'll realize what a huge mistake you made, that we could have made this work."

"I won't."

Like Hades before him, he refused to back down in

his quest to destroy her, unsatisfied until every tie with her had been severed. "Torin. Please."

He reached back and gripped the collar of his shirt, pulling the material over his head—revealing a chest covered in brimstone scars.

She would have rather been punched. She stumbled back, her knees hitting the edge of the bed. Down she sank, bouncing on the mattress. It was a betrayal of her trust in him. A symbol of everything she despised. A sign that he'd turned his back on everything they'd built.

In a snap, the bond withered to ash, leaving her wounded, hollow. The pain, oh, the pain. More than she'd ever been forced to bear.

Without his strength, the weather worsened tenfold.

"How could you do this?" she whispered.

"What's sad is that there's a better question to ask. Why didn't I do it sooner?"

Tears streamed down her face, her mouth opening and closing as she struggled to form a response.

But he wasn't done slicing her heart to bits. "Do us both a favor and finally put me in the Time Out box. It's where I belong." He opened up the door and left her—and soon, the fortress.

TORIN SAT IN the back of a darkened club that catered to immortals, throwing down his eighth ambrosia-laced whiskey. He was in a terrible mood. Had been since he'd walked away from Keeley and said goodbye to his friends…however long ago that was. A week? Four?

An eternity?

Some of the reactions played through his mind.

Strider: *Dude. Don't be a prick. Stay. We'll figure this out. You think it was easy for me to pair up with a woman who can kick my ass at any moment, ensuring the demon of Defeat makes me suffer for days? No. But I didn't puss up about it and leave her. She was worth fighting for. Isn't yours?*

Sabin: *You need to be kneed in the nuts.*

Baden: *I've missed you, just found you again, and you're going to leave? Did you exchange your heart for a block of ice while I was away?*

Lucien: *Go wherever you need to go, but I'm going to find you and I'm going to keep you updated...no, don't shake your head at me. The curiosity will drive you insane. One day you'll even thank me.*

One day.

He hated one day. One day Keeley would forget him—if she hadn't already. One day she would move on. Find another man. Take another lover.

Hate him! Whoever he was, he didn't deserve her.

Torin would kill him.

No, I can't kill him.

He just...damn it, he missed her. Everything about her. Her smile. The way her eyes glowed with her emotions. The way her hair changed color. The old-world charm mixed with modern verve. The fierceness of her. The strength she constantly displayed, even when she was vulnerable. The sweetness of her. The silly things she said. The brilliant things she said. The threats she made. The way she responded to him. The way she put him first, above all things. The lengths she went to protect him. The kingdom she wanted to build. Her temper. His ability to calm her from her temper.

She was precious. He could be himself with her, didn't have to worry about being nice, hurting feelings, causing tears. She was joy. She was peace. Had anyone else ever had such a pure heart?

Pure…and broken. *Because of me.*

He kept picturing her pale, waxen features as he'd calmly stated his intention to leave her. He'd damaged something deep inside her. Something that might never be fixed. She didn't know that he'd cut off the brimstone scars the day after he'd left her—couldn't know. He'd been too disgusted with himself to even look at them.

But too little too late.

I hurt her again, when I only ever wanted to make her happy. How could I do that?

I should be hung up by my collarbone, caned and *castrated.*

Today he'd come to a bar that catered to immortals, hoping to drown his emotions in whiskey. But all he was doing was working up a good mad. Keeley had made him believe in possibilities. She'd made him want a future with her, despite everything. How cruel of her. Especially since she should have known better!

The mad jumped straight into rage. She was older than him, wiser, too. If anyone should have been able to keep a clear head while in a relationship, it was her. But nooo. She had to go and muddle things up, make him think he could have more than what he was used to. And now he was supposed to live without it? Without her?

Damn her!

Was Hades romancing her?

Torin's fingers clenched his glass so tightly it shattered. Sharp stings, wells of blood. But he barely noticed the injuries.

A female sauntered past him and tried to trace his cheek with her fingertip. Snarling, he batted her away with a gloved hand, and not because he feared starting a plague. The world could suck it. Be with someone besides Keeley? No! Never. No one else compared to her, no one else ever would.

Have to forget her.

Someone slid into the chair next to his.

"Leave. Or suffer," he snapped.

"Have a feeling I'll suffer either way."

The familiar voice registered, and his head jolted up. Surely it wasn't—but it was.

Galen was here.

Deserve this. I really do.

"Nice shirt," Galen said.

Torin glanced down. The shirt read, "Property of William." He shrugged. He hadn't exactly cared what he'd pulled on today—or was it yesterday? Dude. He probably needed a shower.

Fingers snapped in front of his face, and he flipped his gaze back to Galen. His former friend had the same blond hair, same rugged features. White wings once again arched over wide shoulders. But the wings were smaller than Torin remembered, only just growing back.

Hatred should have bloomed in his chest but didn't. His guilt and misery took up too much room.

Galen stroked a hand through the feathers of one of the wings. "Cronus cut them off before imprisoning me."

"Poor you. What are you doing here?" Torin threw back another whiskey, welcomed the burn. "Come to kill me? Fine. Do it." Anything was better than living like this.

As if I'm actually living.

"Not here to fight with you. Was headed back to the

fortress when I caught word that you were slumming it. Had to see for myself."

Torin shrugged. Whatever. Once, this man had stood at his side for everything. Every war, every battle, nearly every moment of their downtime. Inseparable, that's what they'd been. And Torin might have been able to forgive the betrayal about the box, but not the centuries the guy had spent trying to murder him.

"You can go now."

Galen's gaze stayed on him, studying, intent. "Never seen you like this. So moody. When did you acquire a vagina?"

Going to go there. Okay. "I didn't know you were a misogynist pig. And you don't know me. Not anymore. Don't pretend you do." He picked up another glass. He had them lined up on the table.

Galen knocked the glass out of his hand.

Torin pursed his lips.

"No," Galen said. "I don't know you. But you don't know me, either."

"Don't care to learn."

"Well, you're going to. All this time, you and the others thought I did what I did out of jealousy or spite, and maybe I did, in part, but you never once considered the fact that I might have cared about Pandora, or that I thought we were making a huge mistake."

"Please. If that were true, you could have talked to us."

"I did!" Galen beat his fist against the table. "More than once. But no one would listen."

He—yeah, he remembered Galen expressing a few concerns. *Pandora is one of us, and yet we're going to hurt her? And what do we really know of this box?*

What's inside it? I've heard rumors...something dark, twisted...

"Fine. You're innocent. Of *that*. But you later took Baden's head."

"Everyone makes mistakes," Galen muttered.

One day you'll realize you've made a mistake.

Keeley's voice drifted through his mind once again.

"One day" again.

Can't deal with this. At a breaking point. "I'm going to ask once more, and if you don't answer me, I'm just going to start cutting. What are you really doing here?"

Galen was silent for a long while. Another woman walked past their table, stopping to tangle her fingers through the warrior's hair.

"Aren't you a pretty one," she said. When he scowled and pushed her away, she focused her predatory gaze on Torin. His dark expression sent her scampering.

"I want to see Legion. Honey," Galen corrected. "I can't concentrate without her. I can't think of anything but her. I can't eat, I can't sleep. Nothing matters but getting to her, talking to her, holding her, easing her hurts."

In the skies, Galen had been a major player. Never with the same woman twice. They'd been as exchangeable as socks. Now the man's despair called to Torin's own. Like to like.

"You love her," he said.

"I don't know."

"She didn't do well after the Unspoken Ones attacked the fortress, so Aeron and Olivia took her somewhere else, but I don't know where."

Galen scrubbed a hand down his face. "Thank you for telling me."

"Save your thanks." Torin signaled for another round of drinks. "This doesn't mean we're friends."

"Don't flatter yourself. You're my enemy today, and you'll be my enemy tomorrow."

"Good."

"Good."

The drinks arrived. But Galen didn't stand and walk away. Torin pushed one of the glasses in his direction. The warrior claimed it.

They pounded back the alcohol in perfect sync. Probably would have continued on for hours more, but their table was suddenly surrounded by the spiderlike minions Torin so loved. More than he could possibly count. Claws hovered all around him, just waiting to snap.

Torin gave a shooing motion with his fingers. "Leave or suffer."

"Hades would like a word with you," one of the creatures announced. "You did not take care of his female."

"His female!" Torin pounded a fist against the table, and the drinks toppled over. "She's mine!"

Galen laughed, slurring, "You're in trouble now, gentlemen."

Torin jumped to his feet, swayed. "You wanna fight me, fine. But you won't be happy with the results."

CHAPTER THIRTY-THREE

AFTER KEELEY'S INITIAL bout of sorrow—such a mild word for what she'd felt—a sense of numbness had settled over her. Which was a good thing. She hadn't destroyed anything. Although she *had* almost waterlogged the fortress with rain. But *almost* never counted.

Since Torin's abandonment, she'd had to fend off Hades at least once a day. He'd visited her wherever she happened to be, romancing her as promised, offering her gifts. Ancient artifacts, weapons, her favorite foods, stories about all the ways he'd love to pamper her. Last night she'd finally told him to stop, just stop. She'd had enough. Nothing was ever going to happen between them. He'd had his chance, and like Torin, he'd blown it.

Men sucked.

Except for all the other Lords. They hadn't turned away from her because Torin had. They brought her breakfast in bed, sat beside her while she cried, distracting her, telling her stories about their lives.

In her desperate state, she'd instinctively bonded to them. They'd helped her in ways they couldn't understand, strengthening her in ways she'd never known.

Buoyed by them, she'd been able to locate the boy Anya cared about. He'd been living on the streets of LA, using his ability to go invisible to his advantage. But he'd refused to come stay at the fortress, and Anya hadn't wanted to force him, so the goddess was watching over him as best she could.

Multiple times Keeley had tried to locate Pandora's box without success. She'd hoped against hope she could obtain the Morning Star and make Torin eat his words. But now...now she was done.

Done with all of it.

Her new life plan: make it through each day without crying.

She was packing a bag, ready to strike out on her own despite her new bonds, leaving her chess pieces and origami flowers behind. Tears burned her eyes as she stuffed one of her gowns inside with more force than necessary. Stupid Torin.

"So you're planning to leave? Just like that? I bet you weren't even going to say goodbye."

Anya. Great! *Can't ever catch a break*. Keeley didn't bother to turn around. "Isn't that what you'd prefer? William tells me I'm supposed to steal his book from you, and if I stay, I'll do it. Well, I'll probably do it, considering I never actually agreed to anything."

"How about I give you a page of the book, and we call it good?"

"Fine. Whatever. Mail it to me."

"For sure. I'll put half a page in the mail tomorrow."

"But you just said—"

"Don't worry. The post office is totally reliable. You'll get your quarter of a page no problem. So let's get back to this no goodbye thing. It's not very queenly behavior, is it?"

"I don't actually care."

"You should. You're a warrior, not a runner."

Even warriors got hurt and needed time to heal.

"You're two seconds away from a spine removal—through your mouth."

"Better." Anya flounced over and threw herself on the bed, shoving the bag to the floor. The contents Keeley had spent an hour organizing spilled out. "You love him, don't you?"

Him—like Keeley really had to guess the guy's identity. "Yes, but I'd still like to scoop out his black heart and eat it in front of him."

"I did that to a guy once," the girl said. "I recommend you sauté it in butter first. But guess what? We all want to kill our men. It's a side effect of living with an alpha."

Keeley returned the bag to the bed, bent down and gathered the clothing and weapons and artifacts.

Anya kicked the bag a second time.

Deep breath in…out. "I'm not afraid to hack off both of your legs and beat you to death with them, goddess."

"As fun as that sounds, I'm going to decline. But not for me. For you. You're going to need my legs." Anya stood. "Packing can wait. We're going out and we're doing filthy, dirty things. That'll get your mind off Torin and his leaving ways. He'll learn a lesson he'll never forget."

"I don't want to teach him a lesson." Her lie-dar buzzed. *I want to teach him. Bad.* "But okay, fine. I'm in."

"Great. You have five minutes to dress like a two-dollar whore while I gather my fave party animals. Kaia and Nike. Oh, and Viola! Forgot she's back. Be in the foyer and don't be late or we'll already be drunk and will probably forget all about you." Grinning, she flounced away.

Keeley spent a full minute reeling. Was the goddess for real?

She spent the next minute changing into a diamond-studded bra and shorts that arched above the curve of her bottom. She paired the "outfit" with six-inch stilettos. Then, because she had time to spare, she slathered glittery lotion all over her skin. But…no one was in the foyer when she flashed there, and as the seconds ticked by she had to wonder if Anya had tricked her. If this was to be the first nail in Keeley's battered self-esteem coffin.

Knives stabbing into my already-wounded chest.

But then Anya came flying down the steps with three women: Kaia, Nike and the gorgeously blonde Viola. They were dressed even more scantily than Keeley—in pasties, panties and garters.

Anya fist-pumped and shouted, "Ho team…assemble!"

It was in that moment Keeley bonded to the females.

More and more power flowed through her, more than she'd ever known. It was intoxicating and wonderful.

How am I going to live without these people?

Maddox came striding around a corner but stopped when he spotted them. His jaw dropped, his eyes glittering with mirth. "Do your men know this is happening?"

Kaia fluffed her bright red hair. "Of course. Strider picked my outfit."

"Mine's so awesome I must have sewn it with my own two hands," Viola said, and she didn't look like a woman who'd recently been tortured. She looked happy and carefree. "Sewing is one of my many talents, I'm just sure of it."

She didn't know? Huh. Maybe she had a Time Out box of her own.

They drove to a nearby club, an underground playground for naughty immortals. It was dim, the darkness broken only by the colorful flash of strobe lights. There were multiple mirrors on the walls. Black leather couches where couples made out or just straight-out had sex.

I miss Torin.

No! Won't dare go there.

As they strutted to the bar, Nike threw her arm around Keeley's shoulder and shouted over the loud, erratic pulse of music. "If you don't see a man you like, I'll pretend I'm bi-curious and we can go at it like little monkeys. Atlas wouldn't care—he'll just insist on details."

"How kind. Thank you." Strangely enough, her reply wasn't mocking. "But I'm not interested in pleasure. Just...forgetting."

If that's true, why haven't I utilized the Time Out box?

Just because, that's why!

Kaia offered her a sympathetic smile. "I've been there myself."

At the bar, Anya ordered a round of something called Legspreader, and after a toast, they each downed the contents of their glasses at the same time. It burned going down but settled in her stomach like liquid rainbows with a pot of gold at each end.

"More!" she demanded. And she was still commanding it eleven shots later. Clouds had settled in her mind, and the cold had melted from her bones. The numbness was starting to wear off, but instead of more rainbows and gold, she began to experience flickers of pain, her misery making itself known. She ignored it.

"I'm amazing," Viola shouted to the world, throwing out her arms and twirling. "Drink me in!"

Through the threads of the bond, Keeley felt the girl's extreme self-love, but underneath that... Oh, wow, Keeley had thought her own pain vast. This girl *suffered*.

"I'm made of so much awesome it's probably illegal," Keeley said with a nod. "And Torin is a bastard."

"Whooo hooo," the girls sang.

Keeley tossed back two more shots.

A group of immortal shifters came over, smiling like they'd just won the lottery. The one in the middle, the tallest, only had eyes for Keeley.

"The moon isn't full tonight, but I bet you could make me howl," he said.

"I could probably make you howl *twice,*" Viola told him.

But his gaze never left Keeley. "What about you, sweetness?"

"I could make her howl twice, too," Keeley told him. "As for you, I've sworn off men."

He spanned his hands across her waist and squeezed. "Give me a chance to change your mind."

"I could change your mind," Viola said.

"Do not touch without permission," Keeley snapped at the male. She backed away from him, thinking *too much, too fast. And wrong.* Torin had looked at her with adoration mixed with desire, as if he were memorizing every detail about her. This man wanted her, yes, but there was nothing but lust in his eyes. He would forget her the second he'd gotten what he wanted.

I will be just as miserable.

"You should totally give him permission," Kaia said, patting her on the shoulder. Pity wafted through the bond. "It's not like Torin has been flying solo."

Keeley lost the ability to breathe. "What?" He'd already moved on? Wasn't lost in his own misery, lamenting his stupidity? Wasn't missing her as desperately as she was missing him?

Anya slapped Kaia on the back of the head. "He just went to a club," she said to Keeley. "That's what Lucien told me anyway. My honey saw him yesterday morning. He also mentioned the fact that Torin is a mess. That he looks horrible and has a raging temper no one can assuage."

Torin in a club. Afraid to touch Keeley—but not others? On a bender that would make him reckless, uncaring?

The walls of *this* club began to shake.

When the shifter put his hands on her a second time, she shoved him away with a stream of power so intense it knocked him to the other side of the building.

"You are one handy chick to have around," Nike said as people were knocked out of the way and into others, toppling bodies and furniture.

Multiple fights broke out.

"You thinking what I'm thinking?" Nike asked.

"Absolutely. This is our cue to rule this school!" Kaia said, raising her fists.

Keeley stood in place as the girls launched into action. Viola busted a Fae male over the head with a chair. Anya struck a vampire in the stomach with broken glass. Kaia reached inside the fiery mouth of a Phoenix and ripped out her tongue.

On and on the violence continued, until finally the girls were the only ones left standing. Bloody and bruised, but standing. They high-fived.

"May we go?" Keeley asked.

A thousand conversations played between the girls as they made their way to the door, each new one beginning with "Did you see when I…"

Outside, cool air caressed Keeley's overheated skin.

"Majesty?" a feminine voice proclaimed.

Keeley searched the area. The golden light of the moon blended with the white light of the streetlamps, illuminating a lovely Fae female with pale hair and big blue eyes. Common traits among the race.

The girl raced forward and executed a formal bow reserved for the most revered of royalty. "The warrior Galen asked me to get a message to you. Told me you would pay handsomely."

A message? "Tell me."

Trembling, the Fae said, "Hades has captured him. Him and Torin. Locked them away."

"What?" the other girls proclaimed in unison, their good moods plummeting.

Like the club walls, the ground shook. Hades had Torin? Thought to use him against her?

No matter how badly Torin had hurt her, she did not want him tortured. The thought of him enduring a single scratch still had the power to enrage her.

"Give the girl one of the piles of gold in my room. I'll be back," she announced. She flashed directly to Hades.

He was in his bedroom, the one in the fortress he'd built inside the Realm of Blood and Shadow, not the one he'd stolen from Lucifer. The curtain was drawn around his bed, but Keeley knew he was there. He was speaking, his voice low and seductive. A female moaned with pleasure.

How nice. Keeley had been forgotten by him, too.

The walls of the palace trembled forcefully as she shouted, "Hades. We need to talk."

A feminine gasp of shock.

A male curse.

The rustle of moving bodies.

"That's enough out of you, Tally," Hades said, and then he was pushing the curtain aside and standing beside the bed. He dropped the curtain in place before she could catch a glimpse of his partner.

His hair stuck out in spikes. He was shirtless, his muscles on display. His pants were on but undone. His cheeks were flushed, his skin littered with bite marks and scratches.

He tilted his head to the side as he met Keeley's gaze.

"What's going on?" the woman—Tally—snapped, clearly irritated.

He ignored her, saying to Keeley, "I'm logging an official request that you never wear anything but that outfit ever again."

"You have Torin and Galen locked away."

He didn't try to deny it, didn't even look ashamed to have been caught. "I do. Torin's manner displeased me. Galen was just in the way."

"Release me," this Tally person demanded. "Immediately!" Chains rattled.

Hades slapped the curtain. "I said *enough*. Remember what happens when my orders are not heeded."

A mouthful of curses resounded.

"Let them go," Keeley commanded.

"No. And now that *that* discussion is over…would you like to join us?" He waved to the bed.

Hissing outrage from the woman.

"No, thanks," Keeley said. "Free Torin and Galen."

"Why should I? Torin filled your eyes with pain."

He couldn't be serious. "*That's* your excuse? You did the same!"

"Yes, but *I'm* trying to make amends."

"You want to make amends? Fine. Let Torin and Galen go."

He frowned at her. "Is this part of your motivational speaking? Or can we call this nagging?"

She waved her fist at him. "Do it."

Stubborn, he crossed his arms over the wide expanse of his chest. "Torin will only hurt you again. Physically and emotionally."

"Last chance," she said, the walls shaking harder… harder. "Release them."

"If I do," he replied, his voice even, "I feel like *you'll* owe *me.*"

She ground her teeth. He'd once feared her power, had considered it greater than his own. Perhaps it was time to prove that was actually the case. "You brought this on yourself." She struck.

TORIN WOKE UP with hundreds of tiny men using jackhammers inside his head. He pulled himself upright gingerly, rubbed his eyes. Galen sat across from him, covered in dried blood and bruises. His hair was a mess, sticking out at odd angles.

Torin's fingers snagged in a nest of tangles when he tried to comb his own.

Memories rolled through his mind…the minions… claws snapping at him, whiskey spilling all over him, nips at his arms and legs, something slamming into his head again and again. Then…darkness.

"Hades," Galen said. "Bastard locked us up."

The walls of the palace shook, and Torin frowned. Was Keeley here? With Hades?

Hell, no. He sprang up and raced to the cell door, then

flattened his hands on the lock. It clicked open instantly. *Thank you, All-key.* He ran down a long, narrow corridor.

"How the hell did you do that?" Galen asked.

"Doesn't matter. We need to find Keeley. I think she's here."

"I'm *sure* she's here. I sent one of the servants to find her."

"Idiot!" Torin shouted. "You shouldn't have—"

The wall in front of him utterly exploded, huge hunks of debris flying in every direction. Hades arrowed through the crude opening, and Torin doubted it was of his own volition. Dude rolled across the sea of broken stone, head bumping and banging along the way.

Keeley floated in behind the male, and oh, what a majestic sight she made. Her skin—so much of it bared—was as pale as a white rose and literally glowed, streams of bright light glimmering around her. A mane of light pink hair with hunks of green framed her face. She was beautiful, yes, but also *glorious.* Like a warhorse of old. And yeah, okay, if he spoke the comparison aloud she might grind his bones to powder. But appearance had nothing to do with it.

There had once been a time when men trained their horses for battle. Not just to charge into a fray, but to love it. Crave it. Those animals had felt no fear. They hadn't shied away from sword or spear or dagger but had flared their nostrils and stomped their hooves, daring the enemy to make a move—wanting him to. They hadn't cared if they lived or if they died, just as long as they had a taste of the action. *That* was Keeley.

Haven't really been living without her, just existing. Hades lumbered to his feet, blood dripping from his nose and ears. One of his eyes was swollen shut. His condition only seemed to strengthen Keeley's mettle.

"Think carefully about your next move," Hades said. "It might be your last."

"Is that supposed to make me cower?" she asked calmly. "I know you feed on fear, that it makes you stronger. Too bad for you I have none to offer."

The male glared at her.

"Even if you *could* kill me," she continued, "I wouldn't die huddled in a ball, crying. No, when I go out, I will go guns blazing…but I can't say the same about you." A bolt of lightning whipped from her palm and struck Hades in the chest, knocking him back.

The male was warded, and yet as powerful as Keeley currently was, those wards did nothing to stop her.

Torin put himself between the two, his gaze on the male now pushing back to his feet. He'd seen the guy fight. Knew he was holding back—shadows weren't flying out of him, surrounding Keeley, choking the life out of her while eating at her flesh. But that could change at any moment.

Hades glared at him, his hands fisting. "Not smart, Disease."

"I'm not letting you near her," Torin said.

"You won't be able to stop me," Hades replied.

"Bring it, then."

"Enough!" Keeley shouted. She strode forward, the light no longer quite so bright. She pierced Torin with her raging baby blues. "This has nothing to do with you. Go home."

Without her, he had no home. "I'm not leaving you."

"Not the first time I've heard those words," she snapped. "Now go."

He flinched. *Deserved that.* "Okay. How about this? I *don't want* to leave without you."

Hurt in her eyes, though she dismissed him with a wave. "I'm no longer your concern, just as you are no longer mine."

"Together or apart, you'll always be my concern."

"How sweet." Hades sneered.

"I said, enough!" She focused on the other male. "Hades, we don't suit and you know it. You'll always resent me for being stronger. You simply hate being told no."

He glared at her. "And you're too stubborn, Keeley-cael. I don't resent you. I'm proud of you. But despite your brave words about dying, you think you have all the time in the world, that the end will never come for you. Well, it can come. And one day, it will. For all of us. You need to let go of the past and grab onto the future with both hands before it's punted out of reach. I'm here. Grab on to me."

Like hell.

Hades's words were like an arrow through Torin's heart. They *didn't* have all the time in the world. The end *would* come. He had to grab hold of the future and never let go. Keeley was his future. Always had been, always would be.

Without her, he had nothing.

She'd told him "one day" would come and he'd regret what he'd done, and oh, had she been right. She just didn't know one day had come the very day he'd left her. He'd had a good thing going with her, the very best, and he'd given it up. Because of fear. Because he'd let it rule his thoughts once again, driving his actions.

See the truth at last. No more running scared.

"Grab on to *me*," Torin rushed out. "I made the mistake of letting go of you, but don't you let go of me. Please, Keys."

She faced him, mouth flailing. "Are you serious? You told me you would stay with me—lie. You told me I mattered to you—lie! Well, *I* told you I don't like liars, and I meant it."

No. No, he wasn't giving up. Not ever again. "I'm sorry I hurt you, so sorry I lied. You'll never know how sorry I am. But you *do* matter to me. I've learned what it's like to be without you, and it's awful. The worst thing I've ever experienced."

"Yes," she said, eyes narrowing. "I'm sure your time in strip clubs was just *awful*."

"It was. And I know you said you'd never take me back and unlike me, you never lie. But I'm begging you to do it. Just this once. Just for me. Even though I don't deserve it. But then, you're a better person than I am. You're sweeter and stronger and smarter. So much smarter. Please. *Please.* I am nothing without you, princess. Leaving you was the biggest mistake of my life."

She shook her head, stubborn to her core. "No."

He pressed on. "I didn't allow anyone to touch me, didn't touch anyone myself. All I could think about was you."

Still she remained firm, saying succinctly, "No."

"She doesn't want you, Disease," Hades snapped.

"All I wanted was—" Torin continued, only to stop as sharp, intense pain lanced through him.

Horror bathed Keeley's features and she screamed.

Torin looked down at his chest. A spear had sliced through his back and come out his front.

"Enjoy the poison," a familiar voice proclaimed. "Knew it wouldn't harm Hades or Keeley, but you…

you it will destroy from the inside out and they'll suffer over your loss."

Lucifer.

"Have fun," the guy said and dematerialized.

Torin's vision fogged, his knees gave out. He heard sounds of laughter...a struggle, growing distant...

Then...nothing.

CHAPTER THIRTY-FOUR

KEELEY SCREAMED SO loudly even immortal eardrums probably burst. She flashed to Torin's side. She wasn't wearing gloves, but she pressed her fingers into his neck anyway. Skin-to-skin. At first, there was nothing. No beat to meet her. But then she felt it. A soft thump.

Too soft.

His damaged heart shuddered, his blood pouring out of his wound. The spear was helping to stem some of the flow, but if it was poisoned as Lucifer had said—and judging by Torin's reaction, she was sure it was—it had to come out.

So, she jerked it out and tossed it aside.

"What can I do?"

Galen! She had forgotten he was here. "Your shirt!"

He pulled the material over his head and handed it to her. She pressed against Torin's chest.

He didn't even moan.

She looked to Hades, desperate. "What poison would Lucifer have used?"

Silent, he studied his cuticles.

"Hades, please. I'll do anything you want. Just help me heal him."

The dark lord faced her then and nodded. "It shall be just as you said. Anything I want."

A second later, both Hades and Torin dematerialized.

Keeley pushed to shaky legs, and it was a struggle because guilt pressed so heavily against her shoulders. Had it not been for her, Hades would not have locked Torin away and Lucifer wouldn't have been able to spear him. *All my fault.*

Was *this* the guilt Torin had been forced to live with during their association? No wonder he'd left her.

I have to forgive him, clear his ledger. For everything. Because I need him to forgive me, to clear my *ledger.*

She knew she could not have one without the other.

As she stood there, wondering if he would live or die, the hurt, pain, rejection, bitterness and anger she'd been harboring all this time—even in the face of his beautiful pleas—drained from her. Love for him filled her up.

"Keeley," Galen said, drawing her gaze. His expression was agonized. "What else can I do?"

"Tell the other Lords what's happened, that Torin will be returned just as soon as he's well." If he didn't recover… She cleared her throat to dislodge the lump growing there. At Galen's uneasy expression, she said, "Tell them the Red Queen sent you and that she'll be very displeased if you're harmed."

He nodded, and she flashed him to the fortress.

Then she flashed to Hades. He'd taken Torin to a laboratory of sorts. Cauldrons boiled over and steamed, shelves were littered with vials of things she couldn't identify, and overgrown shrubbery actually crawled up the walls—using legs.

Torin was strapped to a table, his mouth held open by a metal hook. Beside him, an older male with a humped back mixed different liquids together. She rushed to her warrior's side, clutched his hands in hers.

The other man glowered at her. "I'm Hey You. This be my area. Who you be? What do you here?"

"I am the Red Queen, and I go wherever I desire."

"It's true." Hades appeared at her side. "She does." He removed the hook from Torin's mouth—not a hook, after all, but a tube that had gone straight into his stomach.

Hey You limped over and, while Hades held Torin's mouth open, poured the concoction he'd created down the warrior's throat.

She watched Torin, waiting for a reaction. His skin remained pale, almost blue. His eyes closed. His form still. The wound in his chest, still open and leaking. "How long does it take to work?"

"All night," Hey You said, now limping away.

She'd lived so long, time meant little to her, but an entire night suddenly seemed like an eternity.

She glanced at Hades, who was watching her intently. "You touched him. Skin-to-skin."

"Anyone can, as long as they're immune."

"*You* are immune?"

A nod. "For a while."

"What do you mean, *for a while?*"

"I ingested his blood."

"His blood? His *infected* blood?"

Hades reached out, caressed her cheek, and because she owed him *whatever he wanted,* she had to stand there and tolerate it. But her expression must have reflected her dislike, because he frowned, dropped his hand.

"If he shares his blood with you," Hades said, "you won't sicken when he touches you. At least for a little while. Just long enough for his blood to travel through your veins. Takes about a day, maybe two, then you'll need another dose."

"But…you can't be right. He's shared his blood with me before, and still I sickened."

Frown deepening, Hades pricked the end of one of Torin's fingers and held it out to her.

She sucked the finger, and the blood, into her mouth, willing to try anything, however far-fetched. As an immortal, this type of thing wasn't foreign to her.

"When did he share his blood before this?" Hades asked. "Why?"

"The last time we were here, before I contracted the wasting sickness."

"Ah. The blood would have worked if you hadn't been weakened already by the removal of your brimstone scars."

"But my power returns with the removal of the scars."

"Power, yes, because it's of a spiritual nature. But your body had just been cut up to a large degree and drained. Even Torin has trouble fighting off the demon's illnesses when he's been physically injured."

"But…how is that possible?"

"The demon is a spirit, infecting *his* spirit. But the evil is housed inside his body. A body that created immunities. Those immunities are found in his blood and semen."

Magic semen? Torin could come inside her and save her from sickness? Or she could swallow him? "I've… well, I've tasted the latter," she admitted, her cheeks heating, "and still I sickened."

"A taste might stave off the illness for a bit but not eradicate it. You would need a full dose. One way or the other."

"But…why does his skin infect, yet the rest of his body does not?"

"You know better than most that the skin radiates whatever is in the spirit. You are a spirit inside a body that doesn't belong to you, and yet that skin changes with the seasons, just as your spirit does."

He was...right. Skin radiated the spirit, but fluids sprang from the body.

Which meant...

Finally! A way to have everything she'd ever wanted. Torin, health. A family. She only had to ingest his blood once a day. Or let him feed her the other thing...

Shivers of excitement stole through her. This was Torin's every dream come true, as well.

But reality returned, crushing her. She still owed Hades whatever he wanted—and she could guess what that was.

"You love him," the dark lord said.

"I do."

"But you'll stay with me if I so decree it."

She closed her eyes, nodded. A deal was a deal when she made it freely. "Is that your decree? That I stay with you?"

Oppressive silence.

She breathed deeply as she faced him. His chin was lifted, a pose of deep masculine pride, but his expression was blank. "Hades...please don't make me do this."

"I won't." Tone gruff, he added, "You would feel trapped, and I did that to you once already."

Hope unfurled soft wings. "Then what do you want?"

"Obviously I am at war with Lucifer."

"And?" she prompted when he went quiet.

"And you will be on my side, help me every step of the way."

It was more than she could have ever hoped. And in

that moment, she saw the truth. He did care for her. He did want to make amends with her. He was truly repentant for what he'd done.

"I forgive you." She released Torin and walked around the gurney, wrapping her arms around Hades. "Thank you."

He hugged her back, hugged her so tight, as if he didn't want to let go, but then he did it—he let go and stepped away from her. He cleared his throat. "Take your man and get out of here before I change my mind."

"I can't. He has wards."

"He doesn't."

He'd…cut the new ones off, as well? Keeley backtracked to lift the hem of Torin's shirt. Bronzed skin… scar free. Electric joy sizzled over her.

Wasting no time, she flashed Torin to his bedroom in Budapest. She ensured his comfort before flashing to Anya to tell her what had happened—and to mention she would personally murder anyone dumb enough to enter before she'd given the go-ahead.

Then she waited. And paced. And waited some more. She wondered if this was how Torin had spent his time while she'd been recovering from the demon's sicknesses and nodded. Yeah. Probably.

Finally, though, after so many hours she'd lost count, he gasped in a breath and jolted upright. Keeley rushed to his side.

"I'm here. You're okay. You're healed."

He shook his head as if he couldn't believe he was actually seeing her. "Keeley! You're here." He jerked her into his arms, holding her with every ounce of his considerable strength. "You're here." Then he pushed her back so that he could peer into her eyes. "Don't leave me.

Please don't leave me. But if you do, I will understand. I will also stalk you to the ends of the earth. In heaven or in hell. There is nowhere you can go that I won't find you. You are mine—I let you get away once, and I'm not doing it again. Ever. So, try to keep yourself from me, I dare you, and I will wage war with you."

"Whoa, warrior," she said with a laugh.

The laugh seemed to unnerve him. He eyed her warily.

"I'm not going anywhere," she said. "I was miserable without you. Hated every minute I spent apart from you. I don't want to spend the rest of eternity wishing you were with me just so I can prove a point and hurt you for hurting me."

His arms banded around her again, holding her ever tighter. So tight she lost her breath—*worth it!* "I'm sorry for everything."

"*I'm* sorry. And you don't have to worry about getting me sick. I—"

"Wasn't worried." He kissed the hem of her shirt. "Will let you endure anything for me. I'm a giver."

This. This was what she'd missed most. His teasing. Well, maybe not *most.* She'd missed her connection to him, too, and the intensity of him and the way he looked and the way he touched her.

"But seriously," she said as warm tingles tickled her chest. Growing hotter. And hotter. "As long as I ingest your blood or your—I almost hate admitting this because I know jokes are going to follow—but...your *semen* at least once a day, I'll be immune to your demon's sicknesses. All of them. Of course, that means we'll need another means of birth control, because I want you all to myself for a while, but we'll find something."

He lifted his head, gazed intently at her. "This blood and semen thing is proven?"

"Yes. I touched your face after you passed out, ingested your blood and well over twenty-four hours have passed and I haven't sickened."

His eyes widened. "Had the answer all along." He kissed her face, nipped at her lips. "Thank you. Thank you, princess. Thank you so much."

"It's Hades we owe."

"He's not the one who took me back and gave me another chance. And I'll make sure you never regret your decision," he said. "For the rest of my days I will do everything in my power to make up for my poor behavior." He released her, only to cup her cheeks. "I love you. You are my treasure, and you are worth anything. Worth everything. I would even eat raisins for you."

"You love me that much?" she asked softly.

"With all that I am, all that I will ever be."

"Good, because I love you, too." She flashed one of her favorite leather chairs into the corner of the room, then flashed Torin into it. Along with the things men liked. A glass of Scotch and a cigar.

He looked at both and laughed. "All I need is the crowd," he said.

"And you'll have one. This is your throne, and it will be moved into our new throne room as soon as it's ready." She stood a few feet away, drinking in the sight of her man.

My forever man.

"Now for your punishment. You'll give me an orgasm for every day we were apart, and maybe, just maybe, I'll call us even," she said.

A wicked smile curved his mouth. "Double that and

we've got a deal." He drained his drink and snuffed out the cigar, setting both aside. He cocked his finger at her. "And, princess? There's no better time to start."

EPILOGUE

A FEW DAYS LATER, Keeley stood in the doorway of the dining room, peering inside, trying not to be overwhelmed. This was her first family dinner. All of the Lords and their families were here.

And they *were* her family. Though she'd bonded to them, no one had gotten sick. Torin's demon wasn't part of the bond—he'd betrayed her so many times she would never have to worry about one forming—so there was nothing the fiend could do to any of them.

What's more, those bonds had given her the power to defeat Hades—he'd been putty in her hands before Torin had gotten hurt. They'd fed her strength—and in return, she would make every dream the Lords of the Underworld had come true. She *would* find and destroy Pandora's box. She *would* claim the Morning Star.

But that was a plan for another day.

Only Pandora was absent from the festivities. She'd taken off without a word soon after she'd woken up. But even William and his kids were here. Though William couldn't seem to tear his gaze away from Gillian. It was almost embarrassing.

The womanizer—former?—stroked his finger over his fork as if he were imagining stroking something else.

Okay. It was *definitely* embarrassing. There was such

intense heat in his eyes that even looking at him made her feel scorched by the sun.

"Can you believe this?" Galen asked Keeley.

He stood beside her, watching everyone with the same shock and awe she was feeling. Only Torin had forgiven him, but no one was trying to kill him so she'd consider it a win. Galen didn't seem to care about his less than enthusiastic reception, though.

"I almost can't. It's like every real hope I've ever entertained decided to come to fruition in a single day." Well, not every dream. The Morning Star was still missing. *But I'll find it. I'll never stop searching. I'll find it and use it and make these Lords as happy as they've made me.*

"Not all of mine. Not yet." His gaze returned to Honey. She was his only concern.

She'd returned this morning, but she'd refused to speak to him, refused to be alone with him; he wasn't pushing her, which was why he was still here. Plus Torin had invited him to the celebration, and though there had been some initial protests, everyone had gotten onboard when her man calmly announced, "The Red Queen desires it."

It wasn't that they were afraid of her. It was that they knew the lengths Torin would go to make her happy.

Her heart swelled with love as she watched him pass a bowl of peas to Urban, who grimaced and shuddered in revulsion, and then to Ever, who had the same reaction. Torin just laughed. He wasn't as staunch about maintaining distance anymore. Nor were his friends. It was amazing to behold.

Kane and Josephina had come to spend the evening with them, thanks to Keeley's flashing power, and they were now engaged in conversation with Gideon and Scarlet, the women trading stories about their pregnancies.

But as always, Keeley's attention returned to Torin. Earlier, she'd done a striptease for him while he'd sat in his chair. Afterward, she'd climbed into his lap and they'd made love. Then they'd taken a shower together. Their first. The first of many, she suspected. Their hands had been all over each other. She shivered, remembering how he'd whispered, "Do you need your vitamin D injection, princess? Or do you prefer to call it your medicine?"

Funny man. He was so proud of his magical semen. She had a feeling he was going to tease her about it for the rest of their lives. Something else to look forward to, she thought with a grin.

Laughter sounded. Blinking into focus, Keeley watched as Torin hooked Cameo under his arm and mashed his gloved hand into her hair, drawing the barest hint of a smile from her. Though the female had recovered physically from her time inside the Paring Rod, her mood was darker than ever, Torin had said.

Torin must have felt Keeley's gaze on him because he glanced over and winked at her.

She blew him a kiss.

He stood and closed the distance, and her gaze swept lovingly over his T-shirt. This one read, "I Tangled with the Red Queen and All I Lost Was My Heart." The best one yet.

He drew her into his embrace, saying, "Why aren't you eating? I know you don't think we'd poison you."

"As if anyone would dare. I'm just enjoying the scenery."

He kissed her temple, his lips lingering against

her skin. "Have I thanked you for giving me another chance?"

"A thousand times."

"Have I told you I'd be lost without you?"

"That, too."

"That you are everything to me?"

"Yep."

"Okay, I am a seriously good boyfriend."

A laugh burst from her. "You certainly are. And modest, too."

He released her, and she moaned at the loss. But she didn't have to go without him for long.

He dropped to one knee and took one of her hands. His emerald eyes peered up at her, earnest, intent. "I love you with all that I am. I am nothing without you and want to spend the rest of my life with you. Not just a little while. Because if home is where the heart is, then you're my home. So Keeleycael, Keeley, Keys, Red Queen, Princess, I'm hoping you will do me the honor of becoming Mrs. Torin."

He held up a ring, and her breath got caught up in her throat. The jewelry had a tiny snow globe in place of a diamond, just large enough for her to see the couple embracing inside. A tiny couple carved from wood. He'd made this. For her.

Tears streamed down her cheeks as she jumped up and down. "Yes! I will be Mrs. Torin and you will be Mr. Dr. Keeley and we will plan a wedding that will nutkick Anya and Lucien's."

"Hey!" Anya called. "You're just setting yourself up for failure."

Torin popped to his feet, and Keeley threw herself into his waiting arms. Once, she'd craved nothing more than being adored and pampered. She'd thought of settling down with a nice man and ruling her kingdom. Now she *was* adored. She *was* pampered. But she didn't have a nice man—she had a fierce warrior. Exactly what she'd needed.

"I'm going to make you happy," she vowed.

"Princess, you already do."

* * * * *

*If you like Gena Showalter's breathtaking
paranormal stories,
you'll love her new contemporary romance series,
THE ORIGINAL HEARTBREAKERS:
"THE ONE YOU WANT"
(in the anthology ALL FOR YOU)
THE CLOSER YOU COME
THE HOTTER YOU BURN
THE HARDER YOU FALL
coming soon!*

Turn the page for a sneak peek at two of the stories!

The One You Want

*Prequel novella to the Original Heartbreakers series
(featured in the anthology* All for You*)*

"Sit," Dane said, motioning to the couch. At the wet bar,
he poured himself three fingers of whiskey. When he
turned, Kenna was standing just where he'd left her, ner-
vously shifting from one foot to the other. Wasn't going
to trust him, or relax. Okay, then. He leaned against the
edge of the desk, unwillingly snared by her loveliness.
"I want to apologize for my behavior the last time you
were here."

"Okay. Wow. I kind of expected to be ice-picked."
She toyed with the top of her scarf, causing it to shift,
revealing even more of that freckled cleavage. "But an
apology? Not even a blip."

He felt he was falling into an oven. He was hot, sweat
suddenly trickling between his shoulder blades. His
heart pounded erratically, as if trying to escape his chest.
His hands itched, and damn if his slacks didn't tighten,
nearly choking the life out of his favorite appendage.

"If you can forgive me—" he began.

"Which I haven't," she interjected.

"But if you can—"

"Though I probably won't."

"Yeah, but if you can, I would—" The teasing glint

in her gorgeous green eyes shut him up. "Are you laughing at me?"

"Only a little." A smile lifted the corners of her lips, brightening her entire face. Suddenly she glowed, and he realized he wasn't just falling back into the oven, but rather, he'd already been cooked.

Stick a fork in me. I'm done. Charred all the way to the bone.

He must have radiated heat, because the air between them utterly sizzled. She lost her smile, her features dimming. He cursed. Other women must have glowed like that, surely, but as he racked his brain, he came up empty.

"Sorry," she said after clearing her throat. "I couldn't help myself. You were just so…intent. And really, there's no need for you to apologize, Mr. Michaelson."

"Dane."

"You were a kid," she continued. "You were reacting to the horror of the situation."

"You didn't react to the situation."

Her next smile was slower to come but no less bright. "That just means I've always been more intelligent than you."

Smart mouth.

Gorgeous mouth. How did it taste?

Stop. Stop!

What kind of rare creature continuously teased the big bad ruler of the Michaelson fortune? A golden unicorn at the end of a rainbow? It was new to him. But… he liked it, he realized.

Was this how she'd stolen the hearts of all her lovers?

He stiffened, hating the thought. Earlier he'd convinced himself that West was right…that Kenna was just a sweet girl caught up in the falsity of rumor. He suspected, perhaps, that he hadn't wanted to believe it, that he hadn't wanted her to be just like her mother. But here she was, charming the uncharmable, stoking fires of a jealousy he'd never before experienced.

"Do you have a kid?" The question left him before he could stop it.

Her features shuttered, hiding all emotion. "Yes."

Well, then. If one rumor was true...

Why not all of them?

"She's six," Kenna added. "But don't strain yourself doing the math. I'll just tell you. I got pregnant at sixteen and had her at seventeen."

Something about her tone bothered him. He heard affection and love, sure, but also sorrow and pain. "Is the father—"

"Uh, just hold on there, Mr. Michaelson."

"Dane." Her insistence on calling him Mr. Michaelson frustrated him.

A lot of things are frustrating me tonight.

"I'm not discussing that part of my life with you," she said.

Fair enough. The fact that he'd even broached the topic stunned him. He, one of the most private people in existence, often refused to answer the simplest of questions about himself, and he always despised those who dared to ask. Yet here he stood, grilling Kenna about the most intimate details of her life. As if he had a right to know.

He should walk away from her. He'd done what he'd come to do. He'd apologized. But he was loath to leave things so strained between them. They would be seeing each other again, after all.

Yeah. That was why. Not for any other reason. "I heard you say you're a student. What are you studying?"

Leery, as if she expected him to laugh, she softly said, "Elementary education."

Admirable. "When do you finish?"

"Two years. I hope."

"Why the late start?"

She pushed out a heavy sigh. "Look. I can see the curiosity in your eyes, have seen it many times before, so why don't you ask what you really want to ask? Am I a husband-stealing whore?"

A muscle ticked in his jaw. His gaze slid down her body, noting again how the dress hugged each of her delicious curves. She had gorgeous legs any man would kill to have wrapped around him, her feet encased in hooker heels.

"Are you?" he asked.

Her eyes narrowed, dark lashes fusing. While she had glowed with her amusement, she crackled savagely with her anger. What this girl felt, she really felt. Emotion affected her soul-deep.

"What if I am?" she said. Up went her chin. Back went her shoulders. She pasted that fake smile on her face, one that definitely didn't glow. "Would my past make me any less of a person with feelings capable of being hurt now?"

Hate myself. "No," he said. "You're not a whore. I had no right… Kenna, I—"

"Don't bother. Goodbye, Mr. Michaelson." She walked out of the library, and she never once looked back.

The Closer You Come

Book 1 of the Original Heartbreakers series

Jason—Jase—carted the petite bundle of fury into the backyard. She fought him every step of the way, but he held on as if she was a prized football and never lost his grip on her. The party guests watched with wide grins, enjoying the show. A few even followed him, curious to see how this little scene would play out.

Behind him, the firecracker he'd just slept with shouted, "Put my sister down this instant, you overgrown Neanderthal!"

If he hadn't regretted sleeping with Jessie Kay before Brook Lynn had stormed into his bedroom, he would have regretted it in that moment. He'd just moved to Strawberry Valley, and this was the first time he'd ever really put down roots. He'd decided not to shit where he ate, so to speak, and mess everything up. This was his fresh start. A clean canvas, and he'd intended to keep it that way. Not create a perfect storm of drama. But he'd had a few beers too many, and Jessie Kay had crawled into his lap, asked if she could welcome him to town properly and that had been that.

At least he'd had the presence of mind to make it clear there would be no repeat performance, no blooming relationship. Ever.

He liked his freedom.

Besides, it wasn't like women ever stuck around for long anyway. His mother sure hadn't. Countless foster moms hadn't. Hell, even his girlfriend hadn't. Daphne had taken off without ever saying goodbye.

Light from the porch lamps cast a golden glow over the swimming pool, illuminating the couple who'd decided to skinny-dip. They, like everyone else within a ten-mile radius, heard the commotion, and they scrambled into a shadowed corner.

Without a word, Jase tossed Brook Lynn Dillon into the deep end.

Jessie Kay beat at his arm, screeching, "Idiot! Her implants aren't supposed to be waterlogged. She's supposed to cover them with a special adhesive."

Please. "Implants are always better wet." He should know. He'd handled his fair share.

"They aren't in her boobs, you moron. They're in her ears!"

Well, hell. "Way to bury the lead," he muttered.

Brook Lynn came up sputtering. She swam to the edge and climbed out with her sister's help, then made sure her hair covered her ears before glaring up at him. An avenging angel.

He'd hoped the impromptu dunk would lessen her appeal, but...no. She wore a plain white T-shirt, and a pair of black slacks. Now each piece of clothing clung to her, revealing a breathtakingly slender build, breasts that were a perfect handful...nipples that were hard... and legs that were somehow a mile long.

Those traits in themselves would have been dangerous for any man's peace of mind. But when you paired that miracle body with the face of an angel—huge baby-blue eyes and heart-shaped lips no emissary from heaven should ever be allowed to have…wicked lips…an invitation to sin—it was almost overkill.

His thought at first glance? *I want.*

His thought the moment he discovered her identity? *Damn, I picked the wrong sister.*

But there was no help for it now. What was done was done.

"I'm sorry about your hearing aides—" or whatever they were "—but catfights aren't allowed in my room. You're supposed to save all disputes for the ring, during the Jell-O Fight Night Beck plans on hosting."

Brook Lynn lifted her chin, the very picture of stubborn female. Without looking away from him, she said, "Jessie Kay, get in the car."

For the first time that evening, her sister heeded her command and took off like her feet were on fire.

West and Beck came up beside him, both taking in the scene: a gorgeous woman who was soaking wet, probably chilled, standing as still as a statue, and Jase, who was fighting a freaking hard-on.

"What the hell happened?" Beck demanded, running a hand through his hair.

The action elicited a feminine whistle of appreciation somewhere in the background.

Standard reaction. Women tended to go batcrap crazy for Beck, despite the fact that he was a self-proclaimed he-slut and was always moving from one lover to the next.

"This is between him and me," Brook Lynn said, pointing to Jase.

"Your hand is bleeding." Frowning, West reached for her.

"I'm not your concern." She stepped away from him, avoiding contact, and would have toppled back into the pool if Jase hadn't caught her arm.

Such a slender bone structure, he noted, with skin as soft and smooth as silk, and as warm as melted honey. Not chilled, after all. The longer he held on, the more electric the contact proved to be, somehow cracking through the hard shell he'd spent years erecting around his emotions, until he practically vibrated with the desire to touch *all* of her...to hold on to her...

What the hell?

He released her and widened the distance between them. That hard shell wasn't just for grins and giggles. It was for survival. Emotions were a weakness that could be used against him. Desire, love, hate, hope. It didn't matter. He fought everything but lust, something as fleeting as it was forgettable. To feel anything else meant he'd placed value on something, whether for good or ill, and *that* meant the something—whatever it was— could be taken away from him.

Feel nothing. Want nothing. Need nothing.

Brook Lynn peered down at her wrist, as if she felt something she couldn't explain, before focusing on him, her eyes narrowing. "Don't touch me again," she said.

"Don't worry. I won't." To Beck and West, he said, "Get everyone inside. I'll handle her."

Lords of the Underworld
Glossary of Characters and Terms

Aeron—   Lord of the Underworld; former keeper of Wrath

Alexander—   human; past lover of Cameo

All-key—   a spiritual relic capable of freeing the possessor from any lock

All-seeing Eye—   human with the power to see into heaven and hell, past and future; Danika Ford

Amun—   Lord of the Underworld; keeper of Secrets

Anya—   (minor) goddess of Anarchy; beloved of Lucien

Ashlyn—   human female with supernatural ability; wife of Maddox

Atlas—   Titan god of strength

Axel—   a Sent One

Baden—   Lord of the Underworld; former keeper of Distrust

Black—   one of William's four shadow warrior children

Cage of
Compulsion—   artifact with the power to enslave anyone trapped inside

Cameo—   Lord of the Underworld; keeper of Misery

Cameron—   keeper of Obsession

Cloak of Invisibility—	artifact with the power to shield its wearer from prying eyes
Cronus—	former ruler of the Titans; former keeper of Greed
Danika—	human female; girlfriend of Reyes; known as the All-seeing Eye
dimOuniak—	see Pandora's Box
Ever—	daughter of Maddox and Ashlyn
Fae—	race of immortals that descends from Titans
Flashing—	transporting oneself with just a thought
Galen—	keeper of Jealousy and False Hope
Gideon—	Lord of the Underworld; keeper of Lies
Gilly—	human female
Greeks—	former rulers of Olympus
Green—	one of William's four shadow warrior children
Gwen—	Harpy; sister of Kaia, Bianka and Taliyah; consort of Sabin
Hades—	former ruler of the underworld
Haidee—	former Hunter; beloved of Amun
Hunters—	mortal enemies of the Lords of the Underworld
Josephina—	queen of the Fae; consort of Kane
Juliette—	a Harpy; considers herself consort of Lazarus
Irish—	keeper of Indifference

Kaia— part Harpy, part Phoenix; sister of Gwen, Taliyah and Bianka; consort of Strider

Kane— Lord of the Underworld; former keeper of Disaster

Keeleycael— a Curator; aka Keeley, aka Keys, aka Princess, aka the Red Queen

Lazarus— an immortal warrior; only son of Typhon and an unnamed gorgon

Legion— demon minion in a human body; adopted daughter of Aeron and Olivia; aka Honey

Lords of the Underworld— exiled immortal warriors now hosting the demons once locked inside Pandora's box

Lucien— coleader of the Lords of the Underworld; keeper of Death

Lucifer— king of the demons

Maddox— Lord of the Underworld; keeper of Violence

Mari— a human female

Morning Star— most powerful thing in the history of the world

Nephilim— offspring of mixed origins

Nike— Greek goddess of strength

Olivia— an angel; beloved of Aeron

Pandora— ticked-off warrioress with an ax to grind

Pandora's Box— aka dimOuniak; made of the

	bones from the goddess of Oppression; once housed demon high lords, now missing
Paring Rod—	artifact with ability to rend soul from body
Paris—	Lord of the Underworld; keeper of Promiscuity
Phoenix—	fire-thriving immortals descended from Greeks
Realm of Blood and Shadows—	location of the Lords of the Underworld's former fortress
Red—	one of William's four shadow warrior children
Reyes—	Lord of the Underworld; keeper of Pain
Rhea—	former keeper of Strife
Sabin—	coleader of the Lords of the Underworld; keeper of Doubt
Scarlet—	keeper of Nightmares; wife of Gideon
Sent Ones—	winged warriors; demon assassins
Sienna—	ruler of the Titans; beloved of Paris
Strider—	Lord of the Underworld; keeper of Defeat
Taliyah—	Harpy; sister of Bianka, Gwen and Kaia
Tartarus—	an underground holding cell for immortals

Titans—	Rulers of Titania; children of fallen angels and humans
Torin—	Lord of the Underworld; keeper of Disease
Unspoken Ones—	a bloodthirsty race of carnivorous creatures
Urban—	son of Maddox and Ashlyn
Viola—	minor goddess; keeper of Narcissism
White—	one of William's four shadow warrior children; deceased
William the Ever Randy—	immortal warrior of questionable origins; aka The Panty Melter
Winter—	keeper of Selfishness
Zeus—	king of the Greeks

PASSION. POWER.
SURRENDER

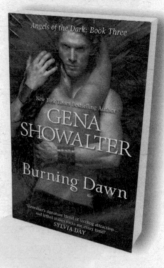

Angels of the Dark: Book Three

New York Times Bestselling Author

GENA
SHOWALTER

Burning Dawn

"Showalter's signature blend of sizzling attraction...
and lethal stakes sucks me every time!"
SYLVIA DAY

Thane is the most dangerous assassin in the skies.
He lives by a single code: no mercy. But no battle
could have prepared him for the slave he rescues
from his enemy's clutches—a beauty who
stokes the fires of his darkest desires.

For Elin Vale, her attraction to the exquisite
warrior who freed her challenges her every
boundary. But Thane's unwavering
determination to protect her means she
must face her greatest fears…

HARLEQUIN MIRA®
www.mirabooks.co.uk

HIS NAME IS KOLDO...

...he is scarred, powerful and he lives only for vengeance, determined to punish the angel who viciously removed his wings. But if he yields to the forces of hatred, he will be kicked from the heavens.

Nicola Lane is his last hope. Born with a defective heart, this fragile human shows surprising strength as demons stalk her every move. Though Koldo fights duty and destiny, his toughest battle will be the one for Nicola's life—even if he has to sacrifice his own...

WE'LL EITHER DESTROY THEM FOR GOOD, OR THEY'LL DESTROY US

Alice 'Ali' Bell thinks the worst is behind her.
She's ready to take the next step with boyfriend
Cole Holland, the leader of the zombie slayers…
until Anima Industries, the agency controlling the
zombies, launches a sneak attack, killing four of her
friends. It's then she realises that humans can be
more dangerous than monsters…and the
worst has only begun.

www.miraink.co.uk

SHE'S FOUGHT DEATH AND WON. BUT HOW CAN SHE FIGHT HER FEARS?

Avry knows hardship and trouble. She fought the plague and survived. But now her heart-mate, Kerrick, is missing and Avry fears he's gone forever.

But there's a more immediate threat. The cannibalistic Skeleton King plots to claim the Fifteen Realms for his own. Avry's healing powers are needed now more than ever.

Torn between love and loyalty, Avry must choose her path carefully. For the future of her world depends on her decision…

Step into Nora's world…
Original Sinners: The Red Years